STRATHGALLANT

by

Laura Black

Hamish Hamilton London

First published in Great Britain 1981
by Hamish Hamilton Ltd
Garden House 57–59 Long Acre London WC2E 9JZ

Copyright © 1981 by Laura Black

British Library Cataloguing in Publication Data

Black, Laura
    Strathgallant.
    I. Title
    823′.914[F]   PR6052.L2

    ISBN 0–241–10442–4

ISBN 0 241 10442 4

Photoset, printed and bound
in Great Britain by
REDWOOD BURN LIMITED
Trowbridge & Esher

1

We rode up the bank of the Ellarich Water, from its tumul-
tuous junction with our big River Gallant; we rode high and
high up Glen Ellarich between the tall hills where never a tree
could grow or a cow could graze. We rode, without reason or
excuse, to the croft of old John Doig and Eppie his wife. My horse
and my dog and I all wanted exercise. If the groom did not, why
then (so I thought in my blithe childish arrogance) he was in the
wrong trade. It was not, in any case, *my* choice that I had to take
him with me.

The season was early May. I had heard that this was already a
time of summer in the South of England: but I had not seen the
South of England, or even any part of Scotland except these
Central Highlands, since I was a baby, and brought orphaned
to Strathgallant. Whatever strange things happened in the
Southlands, here we were still shaking off winter. There was
snow yet on the tops; melting, it filled the burns that rushed
down the hillsides into the Ellarich Water, talking and laughing
among the rocks and hags, so that all the rivers were in spate,
and their waters almost freezing. Small clouds hurried by in a
buffeting wind, their shadows marching like flexible armies over
the shoulders of the hills. The birds which had spent the winter
in clamorous flocks had separated now into pairs, nesting and
breeding. The land had woken up and yawned, and stretched
and changed its clothes.

I thought this time was queen of the year: but, as a matter of
fact, I thought the same of August and March and all other
seasons, each in its turn; I thought each week, each day, 'Of
course, I remember now, *this* is the very best!'

I wanted the time to stand still, so that I could be seventeen for

1

ever, free now from governess and books, free also from the tight-lacing and social duties of the daunting future, the tinkle of teacups and the terror of ballrooms. And all at the same moment, I wanted time to rush by, so that I would immediately be grown up, and meet hundreds of fascinating people, and wear silken gowns with enormous crinolines, and dance with beautiful gentlemen of ancient family. That was a contradiction in me, and it was one of dozens. I loved my solitude; I longed for company. I liked being a girl; I wished I was a man. I was thankful that I was not in the way to inherit Strathgallant Castle; I could not bear the thought of anyone else living there.

I wanted to be in a flock, like the plovers in winter. I wanted to be alone, like the old millpond swan whose mate had died. I wanted to be one of a pair, nesting and breeding.

I rode my little Arab stallion Mameluke, that day in the Ellarich Glen. He was as sure-footed as a goat on the rocks and screes, and he had the limitless stamina of his breed, to carry me up the steep ground. To be sure, I did not weigh heavy. Behind me thumped the doleful Alasdair Lawson, a groom who seemed always to be acting a part in a Jacobean tragedy: but nobody knew why: for he was well fed and well married. He rode a big cobby horse, which slowed our progress. But there was a rule, an iron rule, that I might not ride out into the hills alone. It maddened me, this law of my tyrannical adoptive grandmother: but in a little sane part of my mind I knew it was a good law.

Sometimes ahead of me, sometimes behind Alasdair, trotted my deerhound Benjie Craufurd, named for a pantry-boy who had been my ally years before. When Benjie ran ahead, he stopped and turned constantly, as though to be sure that I was following, that he was on the right road, as though to hurry us. He was a big dog. I once heard a shepherd's wife terrify her child into obedience by threatening to throw it to Benjie Craufurd. Benjie would have wagged his tail and licked the child, so that it would have needed drying with a bath-towel. He was the gentlest living creature I ever knew – gentler than my pet rabbits, which had been known to bite the hand that fed them.

John and Eppie Doig gave me oatcakes and honey, and Alasdair Lawson a dram, and the horses handfuls of oats. They were prosperous, that pair, because their son was managing a grocer's shop in Halifax, Nova Scotia, and he sent them money once a quarter. In that year of 1863 they were the only crofters I ever knew who were prosperous.

I gave the Doigs news of her Ladyship the Countess, and of her daughter-in-law the Viscountess, and of her companion Miss Carmichael, and of her ward myself.

'The Countess has a new Bath-chair,' I said. 'She says it is easier for Miss Carmichael to push, but Miss Carmichael has not yet mastered the trick of steering it, and so she bumps into things, including people and dogs. The Viscountess has another packing-case of books from Edinburgh, in French and German, and some music by a man called Liszt. She was playing it yesterday.'

'Bonny music, Miss Pairdita?'

(Perdita is a name all too well suited, perhaps, to Highland speech. Eppie Doig made the first syllable last about eight seconds.)

'I expect we shall grow to like the music,' I said, 'when we understand it better . . .'

I told them I was to be presented later in the year at Holyrood, and then I would be Out and in Society.

'An' ye'll be the bonniest lassie in a' Embro,' said John Doig politely.

'Probably the smallest,' I said, thinking of the tall, raw-boned maidens I had seen at neighbourhood shooting-parties.

'There's mony a braw drammie tae a sma' bottle,' said John. It was a proverb I had not heard before; I thought he made it up on the spur of the moment.

None of my news was news to the Doigs. They were not isolated. They saw the castle servants in the kirk and at the market. They knew everything about all of us already. But with the punctilious courtesy of such folk, they felt obliged to ask about us, so I was obliged to answer.

I could not give them news of anybody else, because I did not know anybody else. At least, I had not seen anybody else since October, when the last guest shot the last stag, and went away back to civilization.

About noon, I saw that Alasdair Lawson was looking restive. He would not be offered another dram, in spite of the wealth of

3

the Halifax grocer. His gloom became so marked that it was almost painful. I thought he was not at all matching the politeness of the Doigs.

I said that we would not go the direct road home, back the way we had come, but a longer way; we would go up the hillside, over a saddle between the tops, and down the glen of a burn called Allt Feadalge. So we would pass the croft of Jaikie McKechnie, who made excellent trout-flies out of grouse-feathers and darning-wool.

It seemed to me that John and Eppie Doig exchanged a glance, when I mentioned Jaikie McKechnie.

In his smooth, polite voice John said, 'Ye'll be unco' late tae your dunner, Miss Dita, if ye gang yon lang road. Yon wee horse wull be fashed, an' the bit doggie forbye.'

Eppie backed him up immediately. She said the Countess would be worried if I was late for luncheon, and Alasdair's wife would be worried if he was late for his meal, and Jaikie McKechnie was away, she thought, and the croft empty, and our detour purposeless.

It was enough. I scented a mystery. Not a very big mystery, perhaps, but it made me curious. The Doigs wanted to keep me away from the McKechnies. So to the McKechnies I would most positively go.

Curiosity was an element in my character of which there had been criticism. Especially, perhaps, when I took to pieces the bracket-clock in the smoking-room, to see how it worked – or when I persuaded Benjie Craufurd (the pantry-boy, not the dog) to lower me down the well in the walled garden, in a bucket on the end of a rope, to see where the water came from. I came to no harm from that piece of scientific enquiry (though it was horribly cold thirty feet down in the well), but the bracket-clock never did recover.

Another aspect of my character, also from time to time criticised, was a great unwillingness to be pushed. They called it perversity. I daresay they were right. But whenever anybody tried to make me do something, of which I did not see the need or merit, the effect was that I pushed in the opposite direction. More by token, if somebody tried to make me *not* do something, of which I *did* see the need or merit, why then I could not rest

4

until I had done it. Which was the reason I climbed the chimneys, when I was nine years old, and they had to send for the steeplejack, all the way from Lochgrannomhead – and the reason for some other episodes, which resulted in my eating my supper standing up...

I did not think they were so very evil, my curiosity about the McKechnies or my perversity in insisting upon seeing them. Perhaps it was a little bit evil to want to punish poor Alasdair Lawson for being rude to the Doigs.

We walked our horses up the first and steepest part of the climb. When the ground flattened, Alasdair helped me to mount. (To mount unaided into a sidesaddle, without a step or a mounting-block, is perfectly easy if you are light and active, but it is considered indelicate, once one is almost grown up, owing to exhibiting the trousers worn under the habit-skirt. To my mind those trousers removed any risk of indelicacy, but the Strathgallant rules on the subject were perfectly rigid.)

As I wrapped my legs round the pommels of the side-saddle, I glanced back and down the hill. The Doigs were standing outside their croft, looking after us. Eppie Doig had a hand to her mouth...

The McKechnies were not away. Smoke rose from their roof. There was movement about the croft. People were there.

When we rode up, a stranger came out of the croft to greet us. It was a girl only a little older than myself, barefooted, with her skirt kilted up over a bright petticoat. She had black hair tied up behind, cheeks like apples, and a shy smile. She was great with child. I thought her time must be very near. She curtseyed, which was awkward for her, in that condition.

Morag McKechnie came out of the croft after the girl, smiling and bobbing. There was something not quite easy in her smile, and she was trying not to look about her over the hillside.

Any crofter that I ever met or heard of would have asked me into the croft, even if I had been a total stranger. I was not a stranger. I had known the McKechnies all my life. They did not ask me in.

Morag McKechnie presented to me her son's wife Flora. I knew that her son Dougal had married a girl from the West a

5

year before. We had sent them gifts, including money. I knew too that Dougal had been caught poaching in September – he was gripped with two big red cock-salmon taken out of the Captain's Pool on the Gallant. (These red fish, having spawned, are not dainty eating, but they do very well for pickling in a brine-tub.) Dougal was given a year in the gaol, because it was *not* his first offence. Doing immodest calculations in my head, I reckoned the baby was conceived just before Dougal's arrest. What a shame that the child should be born when the father had still six months of his sentence to serve. What a shame that the respectable McKechnies should have a scapegrace son, and this shy apple-cheeked girl a gaolbird husband.

I did not, myself, know Dougal McKechnie. As a child I had seen him, then growing into manhood, said to be wild, said to choose friends among bad characters. He had been seldom at his parents' croft, preferring a sprightlier life with more company. Well, he had company where they held him now, though his life might not be over-sprightly.

Still the folk did not ask me into the croft.

Jaikie McKechnie came out into the sunshine, bringing a handful of his grouse-feather trout-flies. They were whipped onto hairs from a grey horse's tail. He said he had walked all the way to Glendraco, to Lord Draco's stables, to find a Connemara pony with a tail the right colour and quality and length. I was going to buy a dozen flies from him, as I had often done before – grouse-and-purple, grouse-and-green, grouse-and-claret – but he insisted I take them as a gift. This was out of all order. This was all wrong, and embarrassing. There was much labour in those delicate little flies, and he had bought the hooks. They were very poor folk. But I could not insist on paying, without giving deathless offence.

Alasdair Lawson was anxious to be away. Indeed, if we left at once we should be late home.

I called for Benjie, but something was interesting him in a patch of heather a hundred yards from the croft.

'He'll hae fund the whuff o' a hare, mebbe,' said Jaikie McKechnie uneasily.

It was likely. The big blue Highland hares were very common on some of the hills. Benjie was wagging his tail. He would do so, if he found an interesting scent. I called to him. He was reluctant. Something moved. It was red. It was not a hare but a fox. Well, there were foxes on the hill too. Surely Benjie would attack the fox? Chase it? Would any dog not? Benjie barked and wagged his tail. He had made friends with the fox. I supposed it was possible – not for any other dog in the world, perhaps, but for my gentle and sentimental old Benjie.

Though it was a new friendship for Benjie, and one that gave him evident and exquisite pleasure, I called him away at last, thanked Jaikie McKechnie for the trout-flies, and started home.

I puzzled as we rode about the crofter family who would not have me in their croft. I had been made welcome there, times without number; I had been given refreshment, and paid a few pennies for trout-flies. They were pleased to entertain folk from the castle: and they would not have turned away a tinker. There was something within the croft they did not want me to see. Smuggled goods, a poached deer, a stolen calf. Something of the kind. Well, I would not have informed on them. I thought they should have known that. I was hurt that they did not trust me. Then I thought that, for them, I was a member of the enemy, though they might like me for myself. I was of the ranks of the Procurator Fiscal, the Inspector of Police, the Countess who owned the land. They were wise, perhaps, to hide from me whatever they had that was so guilty.

Still it was a little hurtful, and still it was puzzling. They were God-fearing, law-abiding people, for all their cateran son. Flora the daughter-in-law was shy and sweet. I could not imagine that they were thieves, or receivers of stolen goods. If Dougal the son were out of prison, some villainy of his might be exposed in the croft, past their hiding from Alasdair Lawson and myself. But he was fast in the Lochgrannomhead Gaol, and no possible solution to the puzzle.

Alasdair did not remark on the McKechnies' lack of hospitality. He did not remark on anything. He never did. He was cut of different cloth from mine. I would have exploded if I did not remark on almost everything, to anyone who was by. Well, I was indiscreet, and I talked too much (it was another thing that had come in for criticism), and it was often a nuisance for myself as well as for other people. But I thought it was

7

a fault on the right side.

Being very late for luncheon was a fault on the wrong side. It would have been better to have been far too early, even though that gave an impression of greed. (My appetite was yet something else which had occasioned adverse comment. They said they could not understand – indeed I could not understand either – how I remained such a midget when I ate so much.)

I had to change my clothes, before I presented myself at the table. War might sweep down Strathgallant, plague decimate the villages, all the birds of the air go mad and peck our eyes out – but still one could not appear for luncheon in a riding-habit.

I jumped off Mameluke's back in the stable-yard, and gave the reins to Alasdair.

I said, 'I am so sorry I have made you late. You must say that it was my fault.'

'Ay, Miss,' said Alasdair tragically. 'Dinna grieve yersel'.'

He was grieving himself, though. He had still to unsaddle and wisp and water the horses, and put them out into a paddock, before he went to his ham and eggs. I was conscience stricken. But I was horribly late. There was no time to mend matters. I gobbled a kind of farewell, and ran away.

I ran out of the stable-yard, and up the carriage-drive to what had once been a wooden drawbridge, and over the yawning ditch which had once been a moat, and under the great arch where once had hung a portcullis, and across the outer court-yard and the inner courtyard, and through the side door into the smaller hall, and up the side stairs, and along the picture-hung passages carpeted in tartan, and all the way to my bright little room.

I needed Mary Cochran my maid, if I was to change quickly. She was not there. She was eating boiled mutton and pease-pudding in the Servants' Hall, for it was a rule of the castle – a rule of the Countess – that servants were treated with considera-tion, and on no account kept waiting for their meals. Only the Countess herself broke this rule. She broke it almost daily. She took the view that, since she had made the rule, she was entitled to break it.

I changed as quickly as I could. I struggled out of habit,

blouse, boots and trousers. I wanted to wear a cotton morning-gown, but I could not unaided do up the buttons at the back. I put on instead a skirt with a kind of nautical jacket. It was a childish garment. I did not exactly choose the jacket. It came to hand. There was no time to be choosey. I looked at myself pessimistically in the full-length glass.

I could not linger to do so. But I did linger to do so. It was a thing I had caught myself at, increasingly, over the previous few months. It was vanity, but it was not pure vanity. It was another puzzlement. When I stared at myself in the glass, I did not quite know the person who stared back. It was not the person who had looked at me from looking-glasses even a brief year before.

It was a very small female, only a fraction over five feet tall, very slim in the waist and hips, and small-boned as to ribs and shoulders, with narrow wrists and ankles, and child-sized hands and feet, and a small face.

Sometimes the face looked to me like that of a young child, soft and unformed. Sometimes it looked to me like that of a grown woman, with a high-bridged nose and a strong chin and heavy straight eyebrows. When my face looked most like a child's, I felt most like a woman. When my face looked most like a woman's, I felt most like a child. The outside never matched the inside. It was confusing.

The figure at least was adult. It had not been so for very long, but it was so now. The ridiculous nautical jacket I had pushed myself into gave abundant evidence of the maturity of my body. That was a relief. Being so slim and small, I had wondered if I should ever acquire the contours of a grown-up lady.

My cheeks were as red as Flora McKechnie's, from the buffeting wind and from running upstairs. There was nothing I could do about that.

My hair, black and curly, was like a demented mop. There was very little I could do about that.

My eyes, which are grey, looked solemn. This was another constant surprise. My whole face looked solemn. I could not imagine why. This solemn young female with an adult figure was not what I had grown used to, all the years of my childhood.

For a long moment – for far too long a moment – I stared at myself. I was wondering if I should ever grow to feel like the person I saw. I did not do so at all. I felt like a guilty child. I *was* a guilty child. It was almost a quarter to two o'clock when I finally trotted into the breakfast parlour where, when we were alone, we always had luncheon.

The breakfast parlour was, so I had been told, very old-fashioned in furniture and decoration. So was the whole of the rest of the castle. (I could not judge for myself. I could not compare our interior with other interiors. I had seen no others.) It had been painted and papered and curtained and carpeted and furnished, almost throughout, in the days of the Regency, when the old Countess was a young Countess. Nothing had since been changed. She disliked change.

The round Regency table was set for four. Three ladies sat at it: one of eighty, one of sixty-five, and one of fifty.

The oldest, in the middle of the three, was Selina Countess of Strathgallant, widow of Hubert the 4th Earl. He had himself lived to a great age and died, it was said, of a broken heart. I remembered him with the greatest respect and affection, although in my childhood he had frightened me. I think he was not fierce at all, but he looked fierce. He was like my deerhound Benjie Craufurd. He was morally strict, with himself as with others. In this he was unlike his wife and widow, who was also extremely strict, but only with others.

The Countess sat to the table in her new Bath-chair, which had recently been delivered from Germany. She criticised it bitterly, but she would not hear a word against it from anybody else. She wore a shawl about her shoulders, and her red wig on her head. I saw that it was her second-best red wig, the one that looked as though moth had got into it. She was eating a custard-pudding, and drinking white wine, which she poured into her glass from a capacious jug. She drank wine with every meal, including breakfast. She said it was necessary to her health.

The face below the moth-eaten wig did not seem to me to have changed at all, since first I saw it leaning over my cradle. When I was a child, it made me think of something made by a man's hand – a great artist's hand. It did not seem to be flesh, skin, like my face or any of the other faces that I knew. It seemed to be made of paper, of crumpled, infinitely wrinkled white tissue-paper. But this dead-white crumpled paper had been fashioned

10

into the face of an eagle. She had a nose like the great Duke of Wellington's, and a chin very like her nose. Her eyes were the colour of amber. They were half hidden by heavy, crumpled lids, but – when she had the right spectacles by – they missed nothing. She had dozens of pairs of spectacles, and several lorgnettes; and sometimes she wore a monocle. The spectacles and lorgnettes and monocle were all for different purposes. The ones she particularly needed could never be found. It was never her fault that they were lost.

'Miserable chit,' she said when I came into the breakfast parlour. 'What a damned impudent time to be asking for your nuncheon.'

Her body might be frail, and her eyes faulty, and her skin like crumpled tissuepaper; but her voice was as strong as a trumpet. When she shouted for Miss Violet Carmichael, or for the butler or her maid or a groom, the birds flew out of the elm-trees in the park.

I never heard of anybody else who said 'nuncheon' instead of 'luncheon'. I had thought it a strange mistake, until I read the novels of Jane Austen. Then I understood that it was a word of 1810. She changed her language as little as her wallpaper. 'Damned' was also unusual among ladies. They had not been mealy-mouthed, when she was young.

'I am very sorry, Great-Aunt Selina,' I said. 'We came by way of Jaikie McKechnie's. For trout-flies, you know. Benjie Craufurd made friends with a fox.'

'Stuff,' said Great-Aunt Selina, who was not my great-aunt, or any relation at all. 'No dog ever made friends with a fox.'

'My uncle the Reverend Oscar Carmichael,' said Miss Violet Carmichael in a voice like a piccolo with a sore throat, 'brought up an orphaned fox-cub as a pet. And he used to play with the dogs! He did indeed!'

'Your uncle did?'

'The fox-cub did. It was the sweetest sight.'

'Devilish namby-pamby lap-dogs they must have been. Took their character from their master, I dare say. Proper dogs would have torn the fox-cub to pieces.'

At this extremely offensive and gratuitous remark, Miss Violet Carmichael bent her head over her custard-pudding, and ate a spoonful with a suffering air.

She too was to my eyes unchanged in seventeen years. She must have looked sixty-five when she was less than fifty; she had grown to be the age she had always looked. She was thin, and felt the cold, and always wore black. On her hands, even in the summer, were always woollen mittens, which she knitted herself, because even in the summer she suffered from chilblains. She had a little sharp nose and pale blue eyes and grey hair which was always coming out of its pins. Her father had been an unsuccessful doctor in Perth. She had been at Strathgallant for thirty years, first as governess to the Countess's daughter the Lady Isobel, then as companion to the Countess. She was not my governess. By the time I was of an age to be educated, the Countess needed all Miss Violet Carmichael's time and energy. It must have been dire necessity, that kept the poor lady there. It could not have been choice. Nobody would choose a life of such slavery and insult.

'Jaikie McKechnie,' said my Aunt Marianne (who was not my aunt). 'There was something about him. Something happened to him. I remember the talk.'

It was typical of Aunt Marianne that she should have forgotten a shocking and recent local event. She was not much involved in the life of the castle or of the countryside.

'My thoughts are flowers, and my flowers are thoughts,' she used to say. I did not then know what she meant; I do not now know.

Aunt Marianne was the Viscountess Kilmaha. Her husband had been Nicholas Viscount Kilmaha, son and heir of the Earl and Countess of Strathgallant. I remembered him as a cheery, sporting, popular man. He used to take a house in Leicestershire every winter for the foxhunting, which he adored. He adored it too much. He broke his neck, when his horse came down on a slippery road. But for that, he would have inherited the Earldom and the castle. And Aunt Marianne would have been queen of Strathgallant, and the old Countess simply a pensioner, instead of the other way about. I thought it distinctly bad luck for Aunt Marianne. She thought so, too. She assuaged her disappointment in German novels and French poetry and the music of Brahms and Liszt, and in the 'secret garden' she cultivated.

12

That was where the well was, that Benjie Craufurd the pantry-boy helped me to explore.

The trouble was, that Aunt Marianne had no money of her own. That had not mattered while her husband was alive, because he was rich and generous. It mattered now. It meant that she had only what the Countess saw fit to give her. She had nowhere else to go. She was as helpless as Violet Carmichael.

And she looked so.

I knew from two drawings and a water-colour painting that she had been very pretty when she was a young bride. It was easy to see why Lord Kilmaha had fallen in love with her. But it must have been surface prettiness, not inbuilt beauty. It did not age well. The Countess's face, though it was made of crumpled tissuepaper, was still magnificent – still an eagle. Aunt Marianne's was puffy and undistinguished. Her clothes were 'artistic'. She did not look like a Viscountess. She looked like a sad cook in fancy dress.

She had much to be sad about. She had lost more than husband and great position and great wealth. She had lost her son, too, her only child. It was the most terrible thing that could have happened, to her, to the Strathgallants, to me. He was Rupert, styled Master of Gallant. He was ten years older than I. He was my childhood idol. He was my love. He was brave and gentle and generous, and loved by high and low. He and I were to be married. This was a family joke, and not altogether a joke. He said I was as pretty as a flower and as brave as a lion and as wicked as a monkey, and that was the sort of person he liked best, and he did not want to live with anybody else for ever. He went into the army, because he wanted travel and adventure before he settled down at Strathgallant. His mother was against it – she was frightened for him – but his father warmly approved. I was frightened for him, but I warmly approved. He kissed me goodbye, looking fine in his regimentals, and said he would come home to marry me. He did not come home. He was posted to the Central India Horse, at Meerut. He was murdered on the very first day of the Indian Mutiny, in the May of 1857. I felt like a widow, at the age of twelve.

And then Lord Kilmaha the father died of a broken neck in Leicestershire. And then, after these two disasters, Lord Strathgallant the grandfather died of a broken heart in Perthshire. And they left these lonely women – my 'great-aunt' Selina the Countess, my 'aunt' Marianne the Viscountess, Miss Violet Carmichael, and me.

And I? Why was I there? It was India's doing, again. My father was Colonel George Sinclair of the Pink Hussars. When I was born, this famous regiment was stationed in England. Almost at once it was posted to India, to a station in a hot and feverish region, no place for a baby. My mother went with my father, and left me behind. This was heartbreaking, no doubt, and entirely normal. I was left in the care of my mother's dearest friend, with Lady Isobel, daughter of the Earl of Strathgallant. It was not to be for long – but it was to be for life. The ship that should have carried my parents to Bombay was caught in a tempest off Madagascar. So I, being at Strathgallant, remained at Strathgallant. I had nowhere else to go. I had not a penny of my own. I was another prisoner and pensioner, like the Viscountess Kilmaha, like Miss Violet Carmichael.

But I liked being there.

I was in a strange position in the household. I had no position, yet a sort of leading position, because I was the only one who was young. Perhaps also because of Rupert. It was *not* altogether a joke that he and I were affianced, though I was only twelve years old.

What became of Lady Isobel? Ah, what? She died almost at once after she brought me to Strathgallant. That was quite clear. Yet it was not *quite* clear. The Countess never mentioned her daughter's name, nor allowed it to be mentioned in her presence. But I had heard Aunt Marianne and Miss Violet Carmichael mention Lady Isobel. It seemed she was not dead. Somehow she was dead, but still alive. I asked, but no one would answer. I was forbidden on pain of a whipping ever to ask again. I asked again, and I was whipped. Curiosity, perversity, a rattling tongue, for the hundredth time, caused me to eat my supper standing up.

I was too old now to be whipped for being late for luncheon. But I was not too old to be deprived of luncheon. It was hard. I was ravenously hungry. I sat with my hands in my lap, and watched the others finishing their custard-pudding.

14

'Jaikie McKechnie,' said Aunt Marianne again. 'His name was in everybody's mouth a little while ago. What could it have been? A death? A disgrace? A crock of gold?'

'A damned disgrace,' said the Countess. 'His pig of a son was caught poaching my fish. They sent him to gaol. Only a year. And he was a hardened poacher. They were indulgent fools, papheads, mollycoddlers. He should have been shot or deported. As it is he escaped from the gaol. The idiots let him go. I suppose he'll be after my jewels now, or murdering us all in our beds.'

'When did he escape?' I asked.

'Two days ago. A sapskull Inspector of Police came and badgered me about it yesterday.'

'Oh,' cried Miss Violet Carmichael. 'That was what the Inspector wanted! How exciting! Why did you not tell us?'

'Because it don't concern you. It don't concern me, either, and so I told the pettifogging jack-in-office.'

'You would expect the Police gentlemen to go searching at Jaikie McKechnie's croft, rather than to come bothering you,' said Miss Carmichael.

'They did, fool. Of course they did. And drew blank. The folk hadn't seen him, or said they hadn't. I daresay they were lying. All crofters lie, all the time. People of quality lie only when necessary.'

'His wife is going to have a baby at any moment,' I said.

'Jaikie's wife?' said the Countess. 'Stuff, child. She's as old as Marianne. Dead-old. Decrepit. Far past such cantrips.'

'The son's wife,' I said. 'Dougal's wife. Flora. She found it difficult to curtsey.'

'Of course she did, if the sow's farrowing. Stupid to try. Not that you can expect sense from anybody nowadays.'

Dougal had escaped from the Lochgrannomhead Gaol. The Doigs had not wanted me to go to the McKechnies'. The Doigs would know all that went on at the McKechnies', by the magical communication of the hills. The McKechnies had not asked me into their croft. There were signs of Dougal in the croft, and nowhere in the bare little hovel to hide them.

Benjie Craufurd had made friends with a fox.

I saw a picture in my mind, a childhood memory. Dougal

15

McKechnie, leading a cow to the market. A slight young man, with a gentle smile. Red hair. A mop of fox-coloured hair.

'He may not have been at the croft when the police went there,' I said. 'But he was there this morning.'

And then I could have bitten out my tongue. For the millionth time I had said too much, too soon, without thinking.

Flora the young wife was within days of her time. That was why Dougal had escaped, to be with her, to be free when his child was born. Of course he did. Anybody would do so. It was quite right that he should escape, even though he were caught again afterwards. Flora had bright cheeks and a shy smile.

The Countess rang the bronze hand-bell that lived always in a special socket in her Bath-chair. It was needless – a footman was already in the room. But it was her instant, instinctive response to any crisis.

She said, 'It goes against the grain to do the boobies' work for them. But one must be public-spirited. You, clod, listen. Send to the stables. Prise one of those idle grooms away from his meat. Have him ride at once to the Constables in Lochgrannom-head. With this message, that the damned poacher Dougal McKechnie is hiding at his father's croft. I shall expect news during the afternoon that he has been arrested. Is that clear? Run, oaf, don't stand goggling at me like a codfish on a slab.'

Oh God, I thought, I have served those folk a dreadful turn. And Jaikie gave me a dozen exquisite trout-flies. And Flora tried to curtsey. And Dougal only wants to be with her, to help her when her time comes . . .

'In the good old days,' said the Countess, 'they would have cut off the wretch's hand. Now they put him in a comfortable gaol and feed him like a fighting-cock at our expense. The world's gone mad. And they let him go, to rob honest people. Next time, no doubt, he'll murder one of my keepers. It happens constantly. Never a day goes by without at least one murdered water-keeper.'

'I think, dear ma'am, you mean that hardly a *year* goes by without–' began Miss Violet Carmichael, with unusual daring.

'Don't tell me what I mean, old turkey-wits. I won't rest easy until I know that brute is safe behind bars again. Or killed resisting arrest. That would be best. I should have suggested that to

16

the police.'

This outrageous idea brought bleats of dismay from Miss Carmichael. I would have been very shocked myself, if I had thought the old lady meant it.

My own duty was instantly and abundantly clear. I must go at once to Jaikie McKechnie's croft to warn them. The County Police would creep up, instead of coming boldly and openly like ourselves. They would have efficient bloodhounds, to search the whole hillside, instead of one sentimental old deerhound. Dougal was as good as in gaol again, unless I warned them.

It was my duty to put the trouble right, because the trouble was all my doing. My curiosity, my perversity, my rattling un-thinking tongue. Black tragedy for those decent folk, for that shy barefooted girl.

I could do nothing, until the Countess decided to quit the table. To get up and leave before she announced that luncheon was finished – it was unthinkable. I might well be locked in my room. I should be no help to the McKechnies there. I must sit on my hands and look pleasant, and fight down my furious im-patience.

It was not easy. The Countess was savouring the last of her wine. Often she gulped it. Today she sipped it. I had an agonis-ing vision of a groom galloping down the road beside the Gallant, and into Lochgrannomhead and to the Police Station, and of the police setting forth with their dogs.

As she sipped she talked. She talked about the good old days, the days of her youth, when poachers were deported to Botany Bay, for seven full years, for taking one rabbit on a gentleman's land.

I thought she exaggerated her ferocity against poachers, for the sake of a more lively conversation. But I thought there was much reality in it. The thing was, that when she was young, the French Revolution was a recent and appalling memory. The sanctity of property became an obsession, and so they made those dreadful laws and enforced them dreadfully. Times had changed, but not Selina Countess of Strathgallant.

'And now,' she said, 'poachers swarm unpunished over the land, raping and ravishing and thieving as they like.'

'Not quite unpunished,' murmured Miss Carmichael in

protest.

'What, Carmichael? What offal are you spreading before us?'

'It was generally felt in the neighbourhood, that a year's imprisonment was a sentence of exceptional severity, for just two salmon.'

'They were my salmon,' said the Countess. 'Why in God's name are you all sitting here, wasting the best of the day? Push me to my boudoir, Carmichael, and try if you can to contrive to avoid breaking both my legs, as you did this morning.'

'I broke both . . .' gasped the poor lady.

'You have made a wonderful recovery, Great-Aunt Selina,' I said.

She laughed.

Of all the extraordinary things about her, her laugh was the most amazing. It was a young girl's, high and sweet. It was never predictable. It was impossible ever to guess what would amuse her. My pert remark might have brought down on my head a tirade in earthy Regency language. That had happened, times without number.

It was enough to keep one silent all the time, for fearing what the reaction might be, to any remark. But keeping silent was not a thing I was good at. And although I did not as a rule quite *intend* pertness, it was pertly that my words often came out, in a shape I had not meant. It made life hazardous, but prevented it from being ever dull.

I think that of all my memories of childhood and youth, the laughter of the Countess – high and sweet and unexpected – is the most vivid and the most dear. And the rage of the Countess – unpredictable, or all too readily to be predicted – is the next most vivid, and the most awesome.

On me her laugh had always the same effect. It made me laugh too. Often I was not amused at what amused her. Often I did not understand in the least what had amused her. It was her laugh that made me laugh.

I laughed at her laugh in the breakfast parlour, as always, but I felt far from laughter. I felt a desperate urgency to undo the ill I had wrought.

Miss Violet Carmichael wheeled the Countess away. I heard the latter's voice, from round the corner of the passage: 'Idiot!

Assassin! Am I to be mashed in my own house like a damned potato?'

I heard Miss Carmichael's answering, apologetic bleat.

Aunt Marianne said something I did not catch, as she often did, and went away to her books. She made many of her remarks as though she did not expect to be heard or answered. Sometimes I thought this was great humility, as though she knew that nothing she said was worth listening to; sometimes I thought it was great arrogance, as though she knew that none of us would understand her references to foreign books and strange modern music. It had the effect of separating her from other people.

I was thankful, at any rate, that she had separated herself from me. I was free.

I ran upstairs to my room, and changed back into my riding-habit. I ran the route I had run, three-quarters of an hour before, in the opposite direction, and so came to the stable-yard.

Then I stopped, struck suddenly by problems I had not considered.

Mameluke had been turned out with some other horses in a nearby paddock, for a roll and a rest. He deserved the rest, after the uphill and downhill work he had done in the morning. I could not ask of him another long, testing ride, especially as this time I must go like the wind.

But he was the only horse who was my own horse, my personal property. I could take any of the others, but only with the knowledge and permission of Hamish Ogilvy the head groom. This was a wise rule, because only Hamish knew completely what condition each horse was in, whether any tendon had filled or joint heated or saddle-patch been galled, or whether a shoe was working loose, or a tooth needed filing down before a curb-bit could be comfortable.

Well, I could ask Hamish to pick me out a horse, and a saddle that would fit the horse and myself. It would all take a long time. Too long. Hamish would be cheerful and obliging, but he would not be hurried. I had to hurry. And then I was to take a groom with me, in case of accidents. Accidents were always possible on the hills, even if one went slow and careful. I must not go slow. I had not the time for care. And the groom – what would he think of my rushing back to a place I had visited two hours before?

At two o'clock the footman had run to the stable-yard, if his dignity permitted running. At a minute past two, every man in and about the stables would have known that Dougal McKechnie was to be arrested at his father's croft by the Allt Feadalge. If I raced there – and had whispered words with Jaikie – and Dougal was *not* arrested, then it would not take a genius to realise what I had done – although it might not be quite obvious to everybody why I had done it. Hamish Ogilvy would report to the Countess . . .

All this was supremely obvious. If I had given myself time to think, I would have faced the problem already, and puzzled out a solution to it. But of course, if I had been in the way of ever giving myself time to think, the whole miserable problem would not have arisen.

I hid myself in the arch of the stable-yard, and chewed the knuckle of my glove (always an aid to thought), and I tried to make a plan.

I could take a horse from a stall. By feeling its legs and looking at its feet, I could make sure enough that it was sound for the work I wanted of it. I had spent much of my life in the stables, and I had not lacked teachers. I could pick from the tack-room a saddle and a bridle that would fit – there was a vast array of tack and harness, all beautifully kept, and I knew my way about it pretty well. I would clap the saddle to the horse's back and the bridle to his head, mount by the block, and be away before anybody was aware.

No. I could not saddle a horse and take it out of the stable without twenty pairs of ears hearing, and twenty pairs of boots thudding after me.

So I must catch a horse that was out in a paddock, and put on saddle and bridle there, and so ride quietly away over the grass.

Some of the horses were shy about being caught. They made a game of it, moving their heads away at the last moment, or turning their backs and pretending they were going to kick. I should have brought sugar, or a carrot, or an apple. I had not thought to do so. It occurred to me that no amount of thought would have helped me to find an apple, in early May. Oh God, my thoughts were a jumble, I was wasting time considering the seasons of the year when I ought to have been already riding hard for the Allt Feadalge.

I tiptoed to the door of the tack-room. It would not be locked, in the early afternoon. It was not locked. The door stood open. I saw rank upon rank of saddles of every sort and size, the leather gleaming like fresh-fallen chestnuts in the dusty sunlight from the window. I saw orderly festoons of bridles, stirrup-leathers, girths, breast-plates and martingales, and racks of irons, spurs, bits and curb-chains. I could put my hand in a second on what I needed. I glanced round behind me. The stable-yard was empty. I heard the scrape of a shod hoof on the cobbled floor of a box, and the soft whicker of a sleepy horse. I heard the drone of voices from above, from the room where the grooms ate their dinner.

I was half way through the door when I heard the chink of metal on metal, and the sound of someone whistling under his breath. Idiotically, I found myself catching and noting the lilt of the half-heard tune; it was 'Flowers of the Forest', a lament played as a slow-march by the pipes. A groom was there in the tack-room, his back towards me, at the far end of the racks of saddles. He was putting together a bridle with a double bit. I had heard the curb-bit chink against the snaffle.

I backed quickly and quietly out of the door. By no means could I pick up saddle and bridle and carry them away, without being discovered. Discovery meant arrest for Dougal McKechnie, as well as dreadful trouble for myself. Nothing was more certain.

My fine bold adventure was at an end. Through my fault – through my many, childish and disastrous faults – that red-haired ne'er-do-well with the gentle smile would be arrested, and Flora's baby born with a gaol-bird father.

All my life, the old McKechnies had been kind to me, making me welcome with the solemn pride of the crofter-folk, pressing on me little gifts they could not afford, like the trout-flies of the morning. I repaid them with misery.

Circumstances had defeated me. I did not like being defeated by circumstances. I thought I should have wits enough and boldness enough to come out victor, when circumstances and I did battle together. It did not please me to bow before luck or lot, any more than it pleased me to bow before people. I was still perverse. Pride was involved now. My motives were mixed. Though they were not all bad, they were not all good.

Very well, then. I might as well be hung for a sheep as for a lamb. I might as well break another inexorable law – made entirely for my own safety – and ride bareback with a halter.

Some of the horses which had been put out wore leather head-collars, to make them easier to catch. My new plan was to find somewhere a piece of rope, any short piece of rope, and clip or tie it, by each end, to the two sides of the head-collar, so that I had a kind of rein. I would be able to pull the horse's head this way or that, and so steer it. I might not be able to stop it. That was another problem for another time. I had more immediate problems to be solved, of which the first was finding a piece of rope, or a suitable strap, without being seen looking for it.

There were halter-ropes and leading-reins and all manner of strips and straps and strings in the tack-room. They might as well have been in Venezuela.

I never would have believed that, though I was prowling furtively round the stable-yard, and looking from bright sunlight into dark stalls and loose-boxes, anything so ordinary could have been so elusive. I could have taken a hundred buckets and brooms and pitchforks, caps and coats, and even a full set of harness for a carriage-and-pair, which was being mended in an empty stable. I left that harness and returned to it, and left it and returned to it, frightened all the time of being seen, sure that there must be some part of it that would serve as a rein, oddly reluctant to steal from the beautiful complexities of a pair-harness a strap of buckled leather for a different purpose, well aware that such an inconsiderate theft would land me in worse trouble with the Countess and the coachman and Hamish Ogilvy and everybody else who loomed large in my life . . .

And all the time I had uneasy visions of a squadron of the County Police marching to the croft by the Allt Feadalge.

I found at long last a piece of string. It was not really what I wanted, but it was the only thing that I found. I ran – using a sort of stealthy lope, not easy in a habit-skirt – to the paddocks, and saw a tubby roan pony in a leather head-collar, among some taller horses. I would have preferred a bigger animal, but there was no means by which I could mount unaided a sixteen-hand horse, in a riding-habit, without a mounting-block.

The pony was called Mustardseed. I had named him so myself, for no reason whatsoever. As a child I had ridden him bareback, and fallen off him, and broken my arm, which was the reason for the law about bareback riding.

I caught him in a cheating way, which I was ashamed of. I went up to Mustardseed with my hand outstretched and my fist clenched, as though I held a lump of sugar in my palm. He nuzzled my hand, trusting me to be honest with him, trusting that if I offered him something, I had something to offer. With my other hand I caught hold of his head-collar. I opened my fist, to show him that there was nothing in my hand. He sniffed sadly at my palm, with a betrayed expression.

It was odd that the only real feeling of guilt I had about the entire exploit, was cheating Mustardseed in that cynical way.

I tied my piece of string to the head-collar, each side of Mustardseed's head. The length was about right. I thought it would do. I walked him to the gate of the paddock. Some carriage-horses followed, because well-treated horses love people and company and activity, and they did not want to miss the fun. I struggled to get Mustardseed out of the gate, without making any noise and without letting the other horses out. I did not make much noise, but I let three horses out before I could get the gate closed again. This was a disaster. They might, all three, follow me up the hill. Without the eyes and intelligence of a rider, they might step in rabbit-holes and break their legs. I might tie Mustardseed to the fence with my piece of string, and possibly contrive to push the horses back into the field, though that would be awkward, as the gate opened outwards. Mustardseed would want to go back into the field. He would break the string, and bolt back to the company of his friends. I would never catch him again, because he knew I had no sugar in my fist.

Dear Lord, and the police probably half way to the Allt Feadalge by now.

I scrambled onto Mustardseed's back, and arranged myself as though I had a side-saddle. I thought I could ride so, on such a broad and sofa-like creature.

Well, at a walk, and without the other horses, I could have. But to go at a walk all the way I had to go would take until moonrise.

23

With a rather perilous kick I urged Mustardseed into a trot. I had forgotten that his trot was so bouncy. I could not rise to the trot, without a stirrup. I joggled and jiggled between his withers and his quarters, until I thought my teeth would fall out, though I clung to his mane as well as to my string. The string was an uncomfortable rein, cutting my fingers through my gloves.

The three loose horses cheerfully followed us. I thought the hoof-beats of the four of us would waken the ancient warriors in the castle burial-ground. I took a hand from Mustardseed's mane and flapped it at the too-friendly horses. I said, 'Go home!' in a sort of desperate whisper. They thought it was a game, and pressed closer. I needed a whip, any kind of stick or wand. I had not thought of that, when I was among hedgerows and trees. Now I was out of the park and the home-farm, and away from the banks of the Gallant, already climbing the empty hillside. A tendril of old heather was the best the hill provided by way of a whip.

I thought I heard shouts far below and behind me. I glanced back. I was looking down onto the castle, the great grey place where I lived, my prison and palace. The staid carriage-horses, liberated on the great flank of the hill for the first time in their lives, sniffed the sweet hill wind and began to prance and buck like yearlings. Desperately I tried to shoo them away, to hit them on their gentle noses, to make them feel unwelcome. At the same time I was hurrying onwards and upwards, in a race against misery for the McKechnies. It was all too much for my piece of string. It broke. I clawed at Mustardseed's mane. A horse bumped him from behind, in friendliness. He stumbled. The sky and the hilltops swung. Suddenly I was on the ground, winded, with horses pounding away from me, my left leg doubled under me, and a shocking pain in my ankle.

'So,' said the terrible old tyrant that I called Great-Aunt Selina, 'your way of returning the kindness you have been shown for seventeen years, is to risk the necks of four lovely and trusting beasts. I am not angry because you risked your own neck. I am not interested in your neck, beyond a desire to see you hanged by it. I am not so very angry because of the value of the horses you put at risk. I am very, very angry because of the fright-

24

ful agony any one of those horses might have suffered, and because you knew about that risk and that agony. If you were ignorant or stupid, excuses might be found for you. You are worse than stupid. You are spoiled, arrogant, wilful, cruel and vicious. I have not yet decided on your punishment. I have not yet decided whether you are still a resident of this house. By your reckless defiance of my wishes, by your utter lack of consideration of trusting fellow-creatures better and kinder than yourself, you have forfeited any claims upon me. I am disgusted with you. You will remain in this room until further notice. You will eat bread and water. No one will talk to you. No one wishes to talk to you. Carmichael!'

Miss Violet Carmichael scuttled into my bedroom from the passage where she had been waiting. She did not look at me, but bent to the task of steering the Bath-chair through the door.

I was left alone, in bed, with a wet bandage round my sprained ankle, ignorant of my own future, but with the sick knowledge that, through my fault, Dougal McKechnie was back in prison, and everything had been in vain.

2

For three days I stayed in my room, in bed or in the wicker-work chair or standing on my one good leg looking out of the window. The weather was glorious. The outside world cried to me to come and revel in the springtime.

The only people I saw were Mary Cochrane my maid, and a taciturn under-footman who brought me my meals. That was not arduous for him. When the Countess said bread and water, she meant bread and water. There was no butter to the bread; there was no tea or lemon-juice in the water. Mary did not speak to me. I thought she was fond of me – I thought she even loved me, so gently had she taken care of me when I needed care, so stoutly had she fought my battles for me when I needed an ally – but she did not speak to me during my disgrace. Her affection for me was less than her terror of the Countess.

On the evening of the third day I heard a familiar squeak and shuffle in the passage. My door was unlocked and thrown open. In swam the Bath-chair on its efficient German wheels. In sailed Great-Aunt Selina, crowned by her second-best red wig. In struggled Miss Violet Carmichael, her face tense with the effort of avoiding the door-post and the bed-leg and the wickerwork chair where I sat.

I rose and curtseyed to the chariot that drew up in front of me. Miss Carmichael snuffled and withdrew, closing the door very softly behind her.

'Sit down, child. You should not rest weight on a sprained ankle.'

I sat down obediently. Indeed I was thankful to do so. I could not tell from the Countess's voice whether she was still very angry, or only rather angry.

26

She said, 'I think I was not altogether honest with you three days ago, child. I was beside myself with rage. I did what you have so often done, and regretted it as you have so often had cause to do. I spoke intemperately and without thinking.'

She paused and gazed at me, from those amber-coloured eyes in their enveloping pouches. She gazed through gold-rimmed spectacles, of which the wiry arms were thrust into the moth-eaten curls of her red wig. It seemed she had found the right spectacles for gazing at adopted granddaughters, or false great-nieces.

'A mother beats her child,' she went on, 'when the child runs in front of a carriage, or walks along the top of a wall. It is an expression not of anger but of concern. The mother is terrified, for the child's sake. I admit a beating is a curious way of expressing love, but so mothers do. You must have seen it.'

I nodded. I had often seen it. I understood.

'So mothers do,' she repeated. 'And so old women do to the children they have made into their – their granddaughters.'

'Oh,' I said, feeling the beginnings of a great joy.

'I said, I think, that I had no interest in your neck, except that I should like to wring it.'

'You said you wanted me to be hanged by it, ma'am, until I was dead.'

'You are splitting hairs, Perdita. You're as bad as poor Marianne, drawing fine distinctions between one bestial foreign writer and another, as though there was the least difference between any two snail-eating scribblers. I wonder why everybody always calls her "poor" Marianne?'

'She is poor,' I said. 'She is penniless, like me.'

'She lives here. She is my daughter-in-law. She is the Viscountess Kilmaha. She has a consequence to which she was in no way born. She is grudged nothing. She can indulge her curious tastes to her heart's content. Many rich people would envy her, and rightly. That is not what I came here to discuss. I do not know why you introduce these digressions. I suppose it is in order to divert me from the remarks which, at considerable inconvenience and discomfort, I have come all this way to make to you.'

Her gaze became a glare. I looked back as meekly as I could, though I was incensed at the unfairness of what she said. I could see that she wanted me to drop my eyes. I would not do so. I suppose my eyes ceased to be meek.

She gave a little hard chuckle. It was not her laugh, which I loved, but another of the noises she sometimes made, which I had no cause to love. I was not sure that the joy I had begun to feel had, after all, any place in my bedroom.

'You and I are too much alike, child,' she said, surprising me very much. 'This is one of the largest inhabited dwellings in the British Isles, and it is barely big enough for both of us.'

I chuckled, too. I suppose it was a kind of nervous giggle. I had not thought the Countess rated me so high.

'I *was* angry,' she went on, 'because of the risk the horses were put to. But my greatest anger was not anger at all. It was terror for you, and relief that you suffered no more than a damaged ankle. You are a damned, thoughtless, inconsiderate, spoiled and selfish minx. How dare you subject me to such an agony of worry?'

I opened my mouth to answer her question, although I did not at all know what to say. It seemed to me that she required an answer. But she raised a hand like a claw to silence me.

'The question was rhetorical. I am not in the least concerned, at this moment, in the puerile and inadequate reasons you will doubtless give me for your conduct. Later I shall be grateful for an explanation, but the rigmarole of excuses I expect from you would only distract me at this present. I am concerned to explain to you why my late Lord and I, and my late son in his turn, lavished upon you a love which we were not entitled to expect that you would deserve, and which is, I suppose, one of the few wholly unselfish emotions of my life.'

I blinked at this astonishing speech, which seemed to me to mingle brutality, affection and humility in three equal parts.

'I have decided to give you this explanation,' she said, 'in order that you will understand your place in this household, and in the hearts of this family. My hope is that this understanding will awaken in you a sense of responsibility which you seem far from feeling now. I do not ask for a sense of gratitude but for a sense of duty.'

'Duty?' I repeated stupidly. I did not know I had duties. I

thought I was a waif given shelter, a kind of charity foundling. I knew my own history. I *knew* I was no more than a waif given shelter. Of course I had a duty of gratitude, and I never ceased to perform it, except when I lost my temper. And I had a duty of obedience, which I sometimes did fail to perform . . .

'You did not ask for the role you have filled,' said the Countess slowly. 'But when you understand what is this role that you have filled, you may be inclined to try to fill it with dignity and consideration.'

'Role?' I said, just as stupidly. I did not know I had a role. I thought I was just there, because I had been left there. Meanwhile it seemed to me that my contribution to the conversation was to repeat, like an ill-taught parrot, occasional words the Countess used.

'I am obliged to talk of my daughter Isobel,' said the Countess.

'Oh. I was once whipped for doing so.'

'The reason for that is another thing you will understand. Very well. Attend to me.'

Attend! A lion might have jumped through the window, and I would not have been distracted from what was to come.

'Our daughter was the light of our eyes,' said the Countess, speaking more quietly and musingly, I think, than I had ever heard her speak. 'She was beautiful and high-spirited. She was perhaps a little over-indulged, especially by her father. I did not and do not blame him. She had delightful ways. It was a pleasure to give her things, and to fall in with her wishes. At the age of eighteen she married Sir Robert McLarty, who had inherited with his title a fine estate in Stirlingshire. She took with her a substantial dowry and some excellent jewels. Though not a man of great gaiety of manner, Sir Robert seemed to us a person of good sense and kind disposition, the sort of man who would mould and guide a somewhat wayward girl, and – in short, the match was eminently suitable, and Isobel herself was in raptures at being a bride.'

I nodded. The marriage would have been in 1838 or 1840, perhaps. Girls of noble family were not by that enlightened date compelled into arranged marriages, although they might be subject to intense pressure, as they still might, twenty and more years later . . .

'Was she in love with Sir Robert?' I asked suddenly, the answer to this question seeming to me an important aspect of the story.

'That is a fair question, child, though typically pert and girlish. I do not know that I can altogether answer it. She certainly thought she was in love with him, and she led us to believe that her feelings were deeply and sincerely engaged. We had no reason to doubt it. Sir Robert was her choice, not ours. You are not to imagine a dynastic arrangement, or an Indian bride-price of twenty cows and a silver bracelet. Well, we were surprised when, within months, she took to spending weeks at a time, alone, in Sir Robert's other house, in Edinburgh, and spending also weeks at a time here. She gave us reasons – rebuilding of parts of the house, redecoration of rooms, and so forth – which we allowed to convince us. And then she gave birth to a son.'

'I never knew that,' I said.

'How should you know? He has not been mentioned in this house since you came here. Well, she brought the babe here, and we doted on him. We thought that now, with motherhood, the – the little signs of restlessness we had seen would disappear, and our wilful darling would be wife and mother and mistress of her husband's house. The more so as, soon afterwards, she had not one babe but two. You were the other. Your parents were drowned. You had no other family that we could trace. That part of the story you know. The next part I think you do not know. Isobel came here, with her son and with yourself. We knew that she was in communication with – someone – by the penny post and by messenger. We suspected an intrigue, and prayed that we were wrong. We were not wrong. She ran away with a Frenchman, to France. She took her son. She left you. We were appalled. There was a great sensation, a great scandal, a divorce. We did not mind about the sensation, for the small can prattle all they wish about the great, without harming us. But we deeply loathed and detested and deplored the breaking up of a decent home. We did not forgive Isobel and I do not forgive her. But she left a hole in our hearts. She also left you, to fill that hole. You did so. That is why you have been loved as you have been loved, and that is why I was so angry, three days ago.'

I pondered this in silence for a minute. It explained much that had puzzled me. It explained also things I had not thought about at all, such as why I was loved. When one is young, in the place one calls home, one expects to be loved. One does not look for reasons. It was curious to find that, for me, there were reasons, and reasons I could understand.

'May I ask, ma'am,' I said, 'how the story ends? Is Lady Isobel...?'

'Alive? To me she has been dead for sixteen years. Some register in an office in Paris will inform the curious, if there are any, that she recently died of grippe.'

'I am so sorry.'

'I am past sorrow, in that regard. My heart froze sixteen years ago. I have no capacity left for mourning Isobel.'

'And the Frenchman?'

'His name was Pierre Delibes. He was a diplomat, employed at the French Embassy in London. He was sent on some business to Edinburgh, and... We never saw him, of course. She wrote to us from Paris that, in Edinburgh, he had fallen passionately in love with her, and she with him. That she had not known, until then, the nature of love, but only a painted pretense of it. Fustian stuff, shameless and melodramatic excuses for unconscionable behaviour. She said that in Sir Robert McLarty's house she had found no love and no laughter. She said he was dull. My husband burned the letter. I have tried to forget it, but there are things one cannot forget. Well, she was punished. But, in her punishment, we were most grievously punished too. Our grandson, her baby, died of the enteric fever, when he was only three years old.'

'Could that — could that have been a deliberate punishment?' I asked, not liking to believe that things were managed so.

'You mean, did the good Lord visit on that sweet child a painful and fatal illness, because of the sin of his mother? I do not know. The Minister here said so, and all the Free Kirk folk believed so. Their God is a jealous and vengeful God. I do not think mine is. I am not convinced that I address prayers to a God who would take revenge on the innocent. You are making me digress again. I was telling you your own story, not entering into a theological discussion which threatens already to verge on blasphemy.'

'Yes, ma'am,' I said meekly. 'And what became of Pierre Delibes?'

'I do not know, nor wish to know.'

'And Sir Robert McLarty?'

'He died ten years ago. It emerged that we had been in a measure misled by him, and about him. Perhaps we were right that he was kind, but we were wrong that he was a man of good sense. He invested massively in the railway bubble, but he picked the wrong railways. He made unsecured loans, in the hope of high interest, of which he never recovered the principal. He built a canal, from nowhere to nowhere, believing that industry would spring up at each end. After his death, his estate was sold to pay his debts. Fortunately he had not married again. The baronetcy is extinct. It is all as though it had never been – his title and estate, his marriage, his heir . . .'

'Perhaps, then,' I said incautiously, 'Lady Isobel was better with Pierre Delibes –'

'That is an immoral and deplorable thought, that I have not permitted myself to entertain for sixteen years,' said the Countess icily. 'And I do not permit that you should entertain it now.'

I nodded. I could see that it was an immoral and deplorable thought. Even so, I considered that there might be something in it.

'Knowing what you now know,' said the Countess, 'you may perhaps think twice before adventuring on another such escapade as that which has imprisoned you here.'

'It is true, ma'am,' I said, 'that I did not realise the importance which – which chance has given me. I thought I was terribly unimportant.'

'Now you know better. Please do not be late for dinner. Carmichael!'

I hobbled next day to the stables, where I was greeted with a strange mixture of reproach and welcome.

Hamish Ogilvy himself said, 'Siccan awfu' ploy, Miss Dita, tae gang alane intil the hill wi' a haird o' nags –'

'I am sorry, Hamish,' I said. 'Truly I did not mean to lead a herd of horses with me.'

'Ah ken.'

Suddenly he grinned broadly: then, with a struggle, suppressed the grin, and began scolding me for entrusting my neck to a piece of string.

On doleful Alasdair Lawson's face I saw a broad smile for the very first time. It was not there for very long, to be sure; but, when he came out of the tack-room and saw me, the smile was there indeed, and it gave me a shock of pleasure, as though I had found a peach on a whin-bush, or come upon a bonfire in the midst of a heath on a rainy day.

To my questions they replied that none of the horses had come to any harm. To their questions I replied that my ankle would be quite mended in a day or two.

They gave me a seat on an upturned bucket. Alasdair wanted to fetch a chair, but I assured him I was content on the bucket.

All that the Countess had told me the previous evening, came back to me as I sat among those kindly folk of the stable-yard. They had known and loved and spoiled Lady Isobel. They had lost her: they, grim Free-Kirk heirs of the Covenanting Worthies, their morality as rigid as a crowbar, their God as unforgiving as that Jehovah of the parts of the Old Testament they principally read, who sent thunder-bolts to destroy any Israelite commander who failed in his duty of putting heathen babes to the sword. Their sprightly young Ladyship had betrayed them. They had set me up, as I now understood, in her place. For them as for the Countess, I now understood, a hole had been left which I had been left to fill.

Childlike, I had taken their goodwill for granted, as I had taken her love for granted. It was not to be taken for granted. It was to be earned.

I was utterly unworthy to fill the place Lady Isobel had left empty. They did not seem to think so. Perhaps that had something to do, I thought, with my being so small. Though I was grown and formed, I had the stature of a child. They were able to believe me a child, and forgive the pranks of a child.

I felt like an imposter in a dozen ways. A false princess of Strathgallant, a false child, a false Isobel.

I saw that I had a duty to Hamish Ogilvy and Alasdair

Lawson and the rest, as well as to the Countess and Marianne and Strathgallant itself, to be a worthy and proper substitute for Lady Isobel. I had a duty to be considerate and responsible, to be sane and adult and commonsensical.

I did not think I could do it, not all at once, but I saw with a certain glumness that I was bound to try. It would mean a terrible effort. It would mean making such a change in myself as I did not think I could manage. It would mean trying to become a sort of person I was not, and was not meant to be, and did not greatly like.

That was it. The paragon they wanted and deserved, considerate and responsible and commonsensical, was a prig. They wanted me to be a prig. I was bound to try to be what they wanted, now that I knew what I knew. My glumness increased. The grooms were concerned. They thought my ankle was paining me. I said that it was so. Consequently, ignoring my strenuous objections, Alasdair Lawson did fetch a chair, and he and a strapper called Euan Gilchrist carried me back into the castle.

And so, when they left me in the hall, I wept for the love they bore me. I wept because they had placed me in a niche where I did not belong, or deserve to be.

With new eyes I saw all the servants and the folk of the castle, as they welcomed me back to liberty, as they crooned over my bandaged ankle, and exclaimed with dismay at my adventure.

I had been content to be the waif they had taken in, whom they tolerated, who sometimes made them laugh, and sometimes made them beat her. As that waif, I could have gone on as I had gone on. Now I could not. I was cast in a larger role, an awesome role, a substitute Ladyship, a surrogate idol.

With new eyes, I saw all this in their eyes. I had not seen it before, because I had not known to look.

I understood why the Countess had told me the story of Lady Isobel. But I devoutly wished she had not.

If only Rupert had lived, Master of Gallant, my affianced love when I was twelve years old, who would have been Earl of Strathgallant now. If he had lived, he would have been idol and darling enough for the whole of Perthshire. My role, however close to him, would have been comfortably subordinate. So much would not have been asked of me.

I turned up for the hundredth time the last letter that Rupert wrote, that he did not finish. I had copied it out laboriously, at the age of twelve, so that I should have a copy of my own. My copy was smudged with my twelve-year-old tears.

Meerut, 10 May 1857

My dear Grandfather, I begin this letter early as I have much to write about. We have had a mutiny in this regiment, like several others, on the cartridge question. Of course you have heard in Scotland that the 19th had refused to bite the greased cartridges because they were supposed to have pig's fat on them. The 19th are disbanded. Some other regiments made a fuss about it; so an order was issued that the men were to tear the top of the cartridge off with their fingers, instead of their teeth. Our Colonel Smyth, most injudiciously, ordered a parade of the skirmishers of the regiment to show them the new way of tearing the cartridges. I say injudiciously, because there was no necessity to have the parade at all or to make any fuss of the sort just now; no other Colonel of Cavalry thought of doing such a thing, as they knew at this unsettled time their men would refuse to be the first to fire the cartridges, but that by not asking they would not give their men the chance of refusing, and that next parade season when the row had blown over they would begin to fire as a matter of course, and think nothing of it. But Colonel Smyth orders a parade at once. The night before, Captain Craigie, who knows everything that is going on in the regiment, wrote to the Adjutant to ask the Colonel to put the parade off, as he had got information that the men would refuse to fire. The men themselves also humbly petitioned the Colonel to put the parade off until this disturbance in India had gone over. He was half inclined to indulge them, but sent for the Adjutant and asked him what he advised. Fancy a Colonel asking his Adjutant! He ought to be able to make his own mind up without another man's assistance, if he is fit to command a regiment.

The Adjutant, who is always severe to the men, said it would look like being afraid of the men and said he had better abide by what he had ordered. He might have countermanded the parade without seeming to be afraid of the men and then, if they took any improper advantage of it, he might then have pulled them up sharp; but the great mistake was ordering a parade at all. Then he went on making more mistakes. At a skirmishers' parade the Colonel is never present nor any other European officer; but on this occasion he goes down and addresses the men, and tells them that they are to tear the cartridges with their fingers instead of their teeth. The men instantly think, why, these cannot be the cartridges we have fired all our lives, there must be something wrong if we are not to put them in our mouths. So they refused to fire them, as they did not want to be the first regiment who had fired, for then they would lose caste, as the other natives would not believe that they were not greased cartridges.

A day or two after, these 85 skirmishers were marched into an empty hospital and there confined. They were then tried by Court Martial and sentenced to 10 years on the roads in chains. They could not have hit upon a more severe punishment as it is much worse to them than death. They will never see their wives and families. They are degraded, and one poor old man who has been 40 years in the regiment and would have got his pension is now thrown back the whole of his service.

It is a great pity it has happened in my regiment: 'The old and steady 3rd.' And brought on us in such a useless manner. It is the first disgrace the regiment has ever had. We were paraded at 4 o'clock on foot, and marched up to the grand parade ground. I pity Colonel Smyth for he must feel it very much and of course –

He pitied Colonel Smyth! He had just written those words, when he was called away from the mess to his quarters. He was murdered. He was murdered because of the obstinate folly of Colonel Smyth. The very last words that he wrote, were in pity of Colonel Smyth.

Always he ended his letters with a message of affection for me. He did not get to that part, in his letter of 10 May.

From the letter, you can see that he had the capacity of admiration, the capacity of stern disapproval, the capacity of clear thinking, and the capacity of sympathy. That was Rupert, my love, mourned ever since by me and by the world.

And, by me, missed more sorely than ever, now that I knew what I knew.

After luncheon (or, as she called it, 'nuncheon') the Countess said to me, 'I am now in a mind to wonder why you embarked on an equestrian perforance suited only to the sawdust of a circus-ring.'

'Well,' I said, 'I had to get somewhere quickly.'

'You *had* to?'

'I felt it was my duty to go, yes.'

'In discussing duty with you yesterday evening, I had other things in mind.'

'Yes, ma'am, but there are – duties and duties.'

I thought drably of my failure in that duty. I thought of Dougal McKechnie in gaol, with a longer sentence for his escape.

The Countess gazed at me, her amber-coloured eyes missing nothing, I knew, though they gazed from a chalk-white face made of crumpled tissue-paper, though they gazed from beneath her second-best black wig, worn as a mark of respect, because an aged tenant-farmer had died.

She said, 'I once, when a little younger than you, abstracted a pony from my father's stables at Eredine, and rode helter-skelter to a croft. I thought it was my duty. I reached the croft. I did better than you, Perdita. I had more sense than you. I had a saddle.'

I found it very difficult to picture the Countess as a spirited young girl, younger than myself, riding helter-skelter. But I found it easy to picture her abstracting anything from any-where. Her ancestors had been bandits. She retained, I thought, a streak of bandit.

I asked, 'What was your duty then, Great-Aunt Selina?'

'The crofter's son had stolen a dog. Unfortunately, the dog belonged to my brother Henry. Henry discovered the loss and the name of the culprit. I went to warn the lad. It was, I collected, my duty.'

'But why?'

'Because I had told the lad to steal the dog.'

Banditry, I thought, and incitement to banditry.

'But,' I said, '*why?*'

'I had seen Henry, as I thought, cruelly whipping the dog.'

'Then it was right that it should be stolen!'

'Not altogether. Henry was not cruel, then or ever. He was correcting the dog, for worrying our father's gamecocks. Had he not been taught so, the dog would have been drowned, or sent away. This I discovered later.'

'But – did you do your duty, Great-Aunt Selina? Did you warn the crofter-boy in time?'

'No. Henry was before me.'

'And the police were before me,' I murmured. I told her the story. I was nervous of her reception of it, because of her hatred of poachers, especially if they poached her game. To be on that side was very far from the performance of my duty – my other duty – the duty I had just learned about.

When I had finished my story, which I made as brief as I could, the Countess sat in silence for a little while, looking at me, inscrutable as one of the helmeted effigies in the great hall.

At last she said, 'I have a number of comments to hang, as it were, upon your narrative. Probably I shall make them in an illogical and confusing order. First, I know you are telling me the exact truth, which is agreeable.'

'Well, yes,' I said, surprised, 'it is true, but how did you know?'

'Because, dear child, you have never in your life told a lie. At least, if you have, it was such an adroit lie that it was and remains believed.'

'"Persons of quality tell lies only when necessary,"' I quoted.

'That is an epigram, or apothegm, at once ill-expressed and of odious import. What goose dribbled such idiot stuff?'

'Well, you did, ma'am, at luncheon, the day of my – my equestrian exhibition.'

'I did? The remark does, after all, on re-examination, have a certain elegance of expression, and it contains a golden nugget of truth. One irrelevant to yourself, child. I believe you to be incapable of falsehood, even when necessary.'

'I do find the truth easier,' I admitted. 'It is just laziness, really. Invention is such an effort.'

'My second comment,' the Countess went on after a pause, 'relates to the moral obligation you felt you were under. The circumstances were not precisely as in my case. You had not poached the salmon. I *had* procured the theft. I agree that you had a duty in the matter. I require, absolutely, henceforth, two things of you.'

I looked at her nervously. I did not like the ring of an absolute requirement, to say nothing of two of the things.

'First,' said the Countess, raising a talon and pointing it at me, as though condemning me to death, 'when you see your duty as plainly as you saw it four days ago, you are to perform it. Let nothing stand in your way. If there is opposition, ride over it. If you cannot ride over it, ride round it, or wriggle under it. Of all the things I cannot abide, a damned shirker is the most verminous.'

'You mean – I did *right*?'

'No, of course not. Hear me out. How can I think clearly and connectedly, if you are forever babbling at me like a damned starling in the thatch of a steading? You did not do right. You did damned stupidly. You did everything wrong. It's no good having fine and generous motives, if you fall off your pony and break your neck.'

'I only sprained my ankle,' I objected.

'Will you be silent? I have lost the thread of my discourse again. Next time, go about things with a little more intelligence. That is my second requirement. What good are you to me with a broken neck? Especially if you break it needlessly.'

'There seemed to me a need,' I said.

'There was no need, sapskull. Dougal McKechnie may have realised that you had seen him. They may have realised that you would hear about his escape. At any rate, he was not there when the police arrived. The folk said that he had come and gone. They said that they had not harboured him, which would have been a crime. I do not know what will become of him. I think he is a man who will survive.'

'I do not know what will become of Flora,' I said.

'She is here.'

39

'*What?*'

'You told me four days ago that she was near her time. That croft is no place for such doings, even for a Highland sow to farrow.'

'Oh. That is kind of you, Great-Aunt Selina.'

'You will often have heard it said that great position carries great responsibility. It is the cant of the hacks and the politicians, the pap of public platforms and the swill of scribblers. And, as a matter of fact, it is perfectly true. What business would I have, queening it in a castle, if I did not help a crofter-lass to have her babe in safety?'

'I do not think, Great-Aunt Selina,' I said, 'I have ever heard you express such a sentiment before.'

'"Express such a sentiment,"' she mimicked me cruelly. 'What long words we are using, to be sure, now that we are a grown woman with a bust and a bottom. No, of course you have not heard me say such things before. Who would I say them to? Marianne? She would give me in reply some curdled slop from a German philosopher. Carmichael? She would bleat some moralistic twaddle from the sermons of her damned uncle the Minister. Thank God you are grown, child, so that I have someone to talk to. I forbid you to break your neck, if only for that reason. Now leave me. You have exhausted me with your prattle. I shall have a little sleep, to be fit for my tea.'

I thought that conversation was the most extraordinary I had ever taken part in.

I was pleased and proud. I was thankful about Dougal and about Flora. I was gratified that I was someone worth talking to. I did not think I was worth talking to, because I had been nowhere and I knew nothing. I would not have chosen myself for conversation, but someone like Hamish Ogilvy, who knew so very much about horses, or the head stalker Ronald Dewar, who had sailed in his youth in a wind-jammer to America.

But I was perturbed about this question of duty. It was more complicated than I had supposed. Conscience, it seemed, might require banditry, so that banditry became a duty. But at the same time I must be a paragon, or betray the obligations I had.

I thought that, when I was eighteen and out in the world, I

might understand better. But I was only just out of the school-room, and I felt very young and confused.

One immediate duty was clear, at least, and it was nothing but a pleasure to me. I asked Mary Cochrane where Flora was to be found. Flora was in the care of Mrs McQueen the housekeeer. That was good. That was the care I would have wished to entrust myself to.

In some houses, so I had been told, I would have rung a bell, to summon Mrs McQueen. That was not the Strathgallant way. Only the Countess rang bells, though she did so constantly, often several at once, so that servants ran at her from all directions, like the Jacquerie of the French Revolution. I hobbled to Mrs McQueen's sunny room, and there were Mrs McQueen, and Flora in a rocking-chair, and Morag McKechnie her mother-in-law, all drinking tea and talking at once.

I walked into a sudden silence, which was full of broad, embarrassed smiles. I realised with a shock that they had been talking about me. It is a thing you cannot be wrong about. It explained the silence and the embarrassment. I did not know how to explain the breadth of the smiles.

Morag stood and curtseyed. Flora tried to do so. But it was even more awkward for her to rise from a rocking-chair than from an ordinary chair. I put a hand on her shoulder, to keep her seated.

I talked to them for a little time, and accepted a cup of the chocolate-brown tea they drank in the housekeeper's room. I did not stay with them long, because I knew I would spoil their party, and force them to be strained and respectful.

They said they did not know where Dougal had gone. I was sure they were lying and that they were right to lie. It was far better that I did not know where Dougal bided, because I might inadvertently tell someone, as I had done so often before. I got the impression that they were happy about Dougal, that they knew he lay safe.

Doctor McPhee had already come out from Lochgrannom-head to see Flora, at the Countess's command and at her charges. He had terrified Flora. It was the manner he used, to hide his kindness.

41

As I left, Morag curtseyed again, and made a little speech in the Gaelic. I did not understand all that she said, but I understood that she was asking God's blessing on my head, and thanking me, and saying that the McKechnies were henceforth my bondmen.

I thought this was kind in her, but a little excessive. I had walked a few yards to see them, and spent a few minutes with them. It was not a great thing. The stately courtesy of the crofter-folk could be carried, I thought, a little too far.

Yet Morag McKechnie was not a fool, and certainly far too proud to curry favour among the gentry with obsequious speeches, even in the Gaelic.

Why was she so very grateful?

And then I understood what, if I had stopped to think, I should have realised from the first.

The footman the Countess had sent to the stables, to tell a groom to ride to the police, had not rested silent, after giving Hamish Ogilvy that message. Of course he had not. No one could or would. He had told the whole story to the whole stable-yard – that I had blurted out that Dougal was at his father's croft. If the stable-yard knew at two o'clock, then the whole castle knew by ten minutes past the hour.

They knew that I had ridden off with a piece of string tied to an unsaddled pony's halter. They knew in which direction. They knew why. The Countess had had to ask me, but her servants already knew.

It was that that they had been discussing, Morag and Flora and Mrs McQueen, when I came into the room. That accounted for the silence and for the smiles. That accounted for Morag's speech.

I did not want the McKechnies to feel that they must be my bondmen. I had rather they had not known. I had rather that none of them had known. I felt uneasy, in that deluge of gratitude. It was another thing to live up to, and I had too much to live up to already.

I thought I should take Benjie Craufurd for a walk. At least, he thought I should take him for a walk. I could walk a short way, not comfortably; and he could run round and round me,

42

and so get the exercise he needed.

We set off, coming out from a little side door onto the west terrace, where there were little boxwood hedges in geometrical designs. It always made me think of a Continental watering-place, although I had never seen a Continental watering-place. Those parterres and their disciplined hedges were redolent of tight boots and mineral-water, of gossip and miniature poodle-dogs, of old ladies and old jokes. It was no place for me or Benjie. But it was a good way out into the park.

It was a bad way out into the park. Miss Violet Carmichael was wheeling the Countess up and down the gravel paths, listening to a monologue. The Countess had changed into her red wig (second best) and carried a parasol. Poor Miss Carmichael could not carry a parasol while she wheeled the Bath-chair. The first hot sun of the year beat down upon her unmercifully. In the evening her sharp little nose would be red, and her mild eyes more watery than ever.

Benjie and I tried to escape, but we were trapped. I was compelled on to a wrought-iron seat, exquisitely uncomfortable, to listen to the Countess. Benjie lay in the shade of the Bath-chair, looking at me with eyes as reproachful as Hamish Ogilvy's.

'I am old and ill,' said the Countess.

I could think of no reply to this. I made none.

'Nobody knows,' she said, 'how ill I am.'

If so, I thought, it is not through lack of information.

'I have lived too long,' she said. 'I am weary. I shall not ask your indulgence for many more months.'

It was true that she was old. None of the rest was true. She was not ill, or weary. She did not ask for our indulgence, but demanded our servitude.

'Once upon a time,' she said, 'I was independent. I gloried in my independence. I asked for no help from anybody in anything.'

Another lie. She had never less than fifty servants, flying to and fro to pick up whatever she had dropped.

'Now I am a helpless passenger, at the mercy of whatever pair of hands is kind enough to propel me from one place to another.'

That at least was true. Dr McPhee said she was as healthy as a horse – he gave her the thousand potions she wanted, simply to

43

keep her amused – but her rheumatics made walking almost impossible.

'I need you here, child,' she said to me.

'I am here, Great-Aunt Selina.'

'Now, yes. But for how long?'

'For ever, I suppose. Where else am I to go?'

'That depends who you marry, nitwit.'

'Oh . . .'

It was not a new thought to me, that I should be married. I had had a strange and solitary life, but I think I was a very ordinary girl. I had read the normal novels and drawing-room poems, and heard sad music, and seen blazing sunsets. I had normal sentimental dreams, and a normal physical restlessness.

But I had not thought about the matter seriously. I did not know how to go about thinking of marriage seriously. I saw no one. I should do so, when I was presented and took my place in the glittering adult world. But that was for later. Later in the year. The whole summer away. A lifetime away.

'I do not think,' said the Countess, 'that I can manage without you, child.'

'That is quite true, Perdita dear,' said Miss Carmichael unexpectedly. 'I do not myself think her Ladyship could *possibly* manage without you.'

'But – I do nothing for you, Great-Aunt Selina,' I said.

'You do everything for me. You keep me alive and sane.'

'Miss Carmichael does everything for you!'

'She does her best, I suppose. She is a ninnyhammer. Are not you, idiot?'

'Yes, ma'am,' said Miss Carmichael, lowering her head despondently.

'When first you came here, child,' said the Countess, 'you were the daughter of my daughter's friend. You became most tragically a starveling orphan, for whom my daughter took responsibility. You then became, through her disgrace, our responsibility. And you became, through her disgrace, her successor, her substitute, our grandchild. You then became, by dint of I know not what, the future Countess of Strathgallant.'

'What?'

'You know that, better than anybody. No missish airs, child,

44

for the Lord's sake. Child as you were, our dearest Rupert adored you. It might not have turned out so, as you grew up and he grew older. But we prayed that it would, and I think it would. Do not you?'

'Yes,' I said.

'Yes.' She paused, and then said suddenly, 'Do you think you have been brought up as befits a dowerless foundling?'

'Well,' I said, 'no. I suppose I have been brought up as . . .'

'What a dead bore you are, obliging me to repeat myself. You have been brought up as mistress of Strathgallant. Think!'

I thought. I did not know what I was supposed to be thinking about, but I tried. What I found myself thinking was that Benjie Craufurd would never forgive me, for promising him a walk and then sitting on the west terrace.

'We have an estate of thirty thousand acres,' said the Countess, 'and you know every yard of it. We have a castle of one hundred rooms, and you know every inch of them. You know every tenant and crofter, every groom and gillie, every herd and his wife and bairns too. You know which farms are suited by which stock or crop, which maidservants are subject to colds in the nose in winter, and what flowers look best in the bowls in the morning-room. You can ride a horse, row a boat, catch a trout, course a hare, climb a cliff, dance a reel, and make conversation to a Provost or a greengrocer. Why should you need these arts, as a penniless foundling, or as the wife of an engineer with a position in the Argentine? Are they not supremely superorgatory? Would they not make you dissatisfied, if you lived the life to which your tragedy and your poverty condemn you?'

'Oh,' I said. 'How spoiled I have been.'

'On the contrary. You have been prodded unmercifully into knowledge. I admit that you have generally outrun the goad. You have learned no more than you needed to know, to be a worthy mistress of Strathgallant. To be the Countess of Strathgallant.'

'There is no Earl, ma'am.'

'There is no Earl, since our dear Rupert died. That dream died with him.'

'I think, ma'am,' I said awkwardly, 'more than that dream died with Rupert. I think a – a part of each of us died with him.'

45

She nodded. The red wig was like to topple. That was not funny, as it might have been at another time, because she was looking inwards, those amber-coloured eyes opaque, reliving the heartbreak of Rupert's murder at Meerut.

'With the death of my husband and my son and my grandson,' said the Countess, 'there is no male heir to Strathgallant. There is no heiress. Of our blood, there is no one.'

'Aunt Marianne –' I began.

'Pah. She is no more of our blood than yourself, than poor Carmichael here. She is what she is. I suppose that is to her credit. She does not pretend to be what she is not. But what she is, is not chatelaine of Strathgallant. The idea is ridiculous. It only has to be examined to be dismissed as grotesque. Even when my son her husband was alive, she never, I think, set foot on a farm. Eh, Carmichael? Do you remember Marianne ever so much as setting foot in the parlour of a farmhouse, to meet the wife and physic the children and accept a jar of home-made preserve?'

'I do not *believe*,' quavered Miss Carmichael, taken aback at being thus suddenly appealed to, 'that dear Lady Kilmaha went much about among the tenants. And now, of course, so immersed as she is in literary and musical preoccupations . . .'

'All very estimable in their way, I daresay,' said the Countess. 'Fit for a city. Of no relevance here. Are you likely to become immersed in literary preoccupations, child?'

'No,' I said. 'I am afraid, Great-Aunt Selina, that –'

'Stuff. It may be absolutely better, in the ultimate scheme of things, to read that gasbag philosophy, and play that bestial music, than to have a clash with your people and a fish from your pool. But I am not concerned with the ultimate scheme of things. I am concerned with the future of Strathgallant. The Good Lord has His responsibilities, concerning the universe and so forth, and I have mine. I have fulfilled them to date, to the best of my not inconsiderable abilities, by bringing up a successor to myself.'

'Oh,' I said.

'Are you surprised, child?'

'Yes, ma'am.'

'I am a little surprised myself. We brought you up as a wife for Rupert, and then things, as it were, ran away with us. After his

46

death, we went on as we were going. Well for Strathgallant that we did. The events of four days ago have clarified my mind in the matter.'

'My stealing a pony to warn a poacher. . . ?'

'Borrowing. You were not intending to sell the animal. Poacher? Yes, technically, but he only took two red fish. A year in gaol was a grossly disproportionate sentence. We have been all through that affair. Do be silent and attend. I need you here, that has become plain to me, for the weeks or months that remain to me.'

'I will stay, ma'am,' I said.

'Of course you will. You have no choice. I need you. Strathgallant needs you. You are stupid, ignorant, immature, callow, headstrong, thoughtless, obstinate and probably vicious, but you know a little about this castle and this estate. I will not have my investment wasted. I say that you shall stay here.'

'Yes, ma'am,' I said weakly.

'Your equestrienne circus-act confirmed me in my suspicion that you are not entirely selfish. It also confirmed my conviction that you are not to be allowed out alone.'

'I will take a groom next time, Great-Aunt Selina.'

'I am speaking of life, not rides up the hillside. I am speaking not of a groom but of a bridegroom.'

'That,' said Miss Violet Carmichael, 'is *most* happily expressed, dear ma'am.'

'Yes,' said the Countess, 'I was rather pleased with it myself.'

'Of course we shall all be overjoyed to see dear Perdita happily settled.'

'And soon,' said the Countess, 'before they carry me feet-first out to the burial-ground. My duty is clear in the matter, and there is very little time.'

'You are not at death's door, ma'am,' I said.

'Oh yes I am. It is not only the future of Strathgallant that exercises me, that I must see assured in the brief flicker left to me. I have a duty to you also, Perdita. I must see your future settled. I am quite clear on the point. My mind is quite made up. You must have somebody to look after you, when I am become the *table-d'hôte* of those gross worms in the burial-ground. Did you know that they are said to be the best for catching trout in a

47

spate?'

'No, ma'am,' I said, much startled.

'Only in a spate. When the water is low and clear, other worms have been found superior. So there is something about Strathgallant you do not know. How fortunate that I discovered the lacuna, in time to supply the deficiency. There we are, then, all right and tight, as we used to say in better times.'

'But,' I said uneasily, 'I do not know any gentlemen, ma'am. I mean, young gentlemen. Not even one. Not one has been here, since Rupert . . .'

'That is immaterial.'

'*Immaterial*, ma'am? I am to pick from a bran-tub?'

'I mean, dunderhead, that your lack of acquaintance can be put right. Besides, you will be guided by me.'

'You mean,' I said, 'you have chosen a husband for me?'

'Yes,' said the Countess. 'I think so. I must give the matter a little further thought. Only a little. And then you shall hear what I have decided. *En avant*, Carmichael. Earn your bread woman. Push!'

3

After dinner we sat, as we sat always, in the small drawing-room. In the great drawing-room, we would have been like lonely nomads, camped in the corner of a howling wilderness. The small drawing-room was more completely Regency in taste than, perhaps, any other room in the castle. It had striped wall-paper, pink and gold, elegant little chairs upholstered in striped brocade, small paintings in the Chinese taste, in gilt frames simulating bamboo, and nothing on which one could stretch out and be comfortable. Except for the Countess. She was quite comfortable, in her padded German Bath-chair.

Aunt Marianne sat at a little distance from the rest of us, so that she could read without our chattering disturbing her. She was dressed in a sort of Grecian robe. Perhaps it was Assyrian, or even French. It was undoubtedly artistic. It hid her dumpy figure. From its neck poked her puffy, discontented face. It was difficult to see that she had once been so very pretty. Her hair, the colour of sandy mud, was arranged artistically too. I think the arrangement should be called artistic. It was not like anybody else's hair, that I had ever seen. She was reading a book about Vienna.

'About Vienna, you know,' she said to me, although I had not enquired. '*Schöne Wien*. City of music! The walls built of dreams, the spires pointing to . . .'

Her voice trailed off, and she made a large, artistic gesture with her hand. Her hand was large, too.

'I yearn to travel,' she said, 'to tread the hallowed streets of . . .'

Vienna, I supposed.

Miss Violet Carmichael, wearing mittens, was knitting a pair

49

of mittens. I thought she would wear out the mittens she had on, by the energy of her knitting. She was knitting as though in a desperate race against time – as though, when the little gilt clock struck ten, knitting would suddenly be forever forbidden.

I was wearing a simple little dress, because I had only simple little dresses. I wanted to be a fine lady – to bare my shoulders, and put up my hair. That day would come. At least, I thought it would. Meanwhile there was very little point in dressing for company, when there was no company.

The Countess did, though, at least in part. She was wearing her white evening wig, which made no concessions to modern styles, and an ancient, formidable gown of stiff brocade. The effect was marred, or at least qualified, by the tattered tartan shawl round her shoulders (my dog Benjie Craufurd had been chewing it), and by the carpet-slippers on her feet, visible at the hem of her gown on the foot-board of the Bath-chair.

She was staring into the little coal fire which, on a May evening, was still necessary in the small drawing-room, at least for Miss Violet Carmichael. The fire made a sort of fluttering noise, and baby flames ran about amongst the lumps of sea-coal in the grate. Miss Carmichael's knitting-needles rattled like dice in a furious game of backgammon. Aunt Marianne turned her pages, and sighed for mysterious cities.

I was waiting for the Countess to speak. I knew she would speak, to me and about me. She had the expression of someone about to make an announcement.

After so many revelations, the identity of the husband chosen for me was of no particular interest. I did not intend to be chosen for. Of course I was deep in the Countess's debt, but not as deep as that. There was no debt as deep as that. When I came out, I would meet hundreds of gentlemen. From them all, I would choose the very best.

It was possible, I supposed, that the one I chose would not choose me. Then I would have a broken heart. That would be horrid, perhaps, but at the same time romantic.

The Countess said, 'You understand, child, that we are in a somewhat unusual situation. I need you, more than I would have expected. My dependance on you is disagreeable and humiliating for me, but it is a significant factor. Strathgallant

50

needs you, especially the very many people in the house and on the estate for whom I am responsible, responsibility for whom I must entrust to the right hands. For your part, we have agreed that you need a husband, a safe and settled future. You need a firm hand, a man's hand. You probably need to be beaten from time to time. I should be failing in my duty if I did not make provision for that.'

Miss Carmichael bleated in dismay. The Countess chuckled. It was the little hard chuckle which was quite unlike the high childish laugh.

No doubt, I thought, my need of regular beatings would have influenced the Countess's choice of my husband. Let her choose. I was not playing this game.

'Putting all our requirements together,' she said, 'we find that they demand a rather special solution. It is, of course, quite obvious. It is that your husband must live here, with us, with me.'

Well of course, now that she had said it, it was indeed obvious that *her* requirements demanded this solution. Mine might not. I thought that, if ever I did marry, my husband's might not.

I stared at her silently. This was not a time to start entering objections. She had been thinking deeply, and her words were the result of her thoughts. She would not care to be interrupted.

'The man who comes here as your husband, child, will be your consort and your lord. He will require to be acceptable to me and to Strathgallant. Where is he to be found? Later in this year and in the years thereafter, you will meet a great number of attractive persons, for some of whom, green chit as you are, you will doubtless imagine that you entertain a deathless passion. You might bring home here someone with whom I would not be comfortable.'

I thought this more than probable. I did not say so.

'To fling you out into the world, to catch what husband you can, smacks too much of a lottery, to my taste,' said the Countess. 'Especially as you have not so much as a brass farthing of your own.'

I nodded. This was fair. The Countess could not be expected to dower me to a man of whom she disapproved.

'In another sense, I am not prepared to wait on chance, to

51

gamble on a satisfactory outcome of your adventures in the marriage-market. I am old and ill. It amuses you all to flatter yourselves that I am quite healthy. Well, laugh while you may. I am at the mercy of that impertinent leech in the town. I may have short months only in which to settle matters. I dare not wait. I have not the right. I would be failing in my duty if I took that chance. Circumstances require not only a correct solution but also a speedy one. Attend to me now. Silence those damned needles, Carmichael! How can I think and speak when you rattle at me like a damned Spanish dancer?'

Miss Carmichael bleated and stopped knitting. There was a hissing from the grate. The clock ticked. Aunt Marianne turned a page, at the far end of the room. There was no other sound.

'A problem is,' said the Countess, 'that we see nobody. Eligible young men do not beat a path to our door, to be entertained by an antique harridan, an old sheep in woollen mittens, a twittering bluestocking, and a little Miss just out of the schoolroom. Besides, we are somewhat remote for afternoon calls. There is this also, that I do not wish to impose a husband on you.'

'Oh,' I said. 'I thought you did.'

'How dare you accuse me of so draconic and unreasonable an intention? Of course you must choose.'

'Thank you, ma'am.'

'You must choose from a selection of acceptable candidates. How are we to find those candidates, assure ourselves of their suitability for the gigantic responsibilities of this place, assure ourselves that they will not, once here, drive me into paroxysms of boredom or irritation?'

'Well, how, Great-Aunt Selina?' I asked.

'Of all the eligible young men in Scotland,' said the Countess, 'there are four, just four, about whom I am fully informed, about whose blood and upbringing I can be comfortable, to whom I can in full knowledge entrust the double responsibility of Strathgallant and yourself, Perdita. And who will not drive me insane. And who will come here when I require them to.'

She paused impressively.

The light broke. I knew which four young men she meant. I knew them, too – at least, I had known them as young schoolboys when they came to Strathgallant for their summer holidays.

'The Ramsays,' I said.

'I wish you will not leap in and snatch the words from my mouth,' said the Countess. 'Have the goodness to allow me to develop my theme in an orderly and logical manner.'

'I am somewhat affected,' I said mildly.

'Of course you are, muttonwit. We are discussing your husband. Now then. My late brother Henry Ramsay, Lord Eredine, had three sons. Henry, my eldest nephew, now Lord Eredine, a dull stick. Matthew, my second nephew, latterly General Sir Matthew Ramsay, now deceased. Another dull stick. And George Ramsay, my youngest nephew, also now deceased, and the dullest stick of all. Henry had a son, also named Henry. Matthew had a son. He is called Colin. George had twin sons, an extravagance of which his friends might have believed him incapable. All four of my great-nephews are of suitable age. None is married. All are tied to me by blood. No breath of impropriety attaches to the family of any. They were all good-looking boys.'

'That is true,' I said, remembering those long-ago summers when, under the leadership of my beloved Rupert, we all ran wild over the hills.

I remembered Harry as proud, Colin as daredevil, James the elder twin as rather solemn and bookish, Alexander his brother as very gentle. I loved them all. They were my cousins, although they were not my cousins. I was pleased at the thought of seeing them again. The idea that I was to be obliged to marry one of them was too ludicrous to contemplate.

'I have fully informed myself about the latest circumstances of all four,' said the Countess, 'as to character, reputation, ability, career, prospects and the like.'

'Oh,' I said. 'What has become of them all?'

'Harry assists his father in the management of the Eredine estates. He has, in fact, largely assumed responsibility for them. I believe they have a considerable struggle, owing to my brother's mismanagement fifty years ago.'

'Poor Harry. He was so proud.'

'He is poor. And I understand he is still proud. We turn to Colin. He followed the example of his father and of our dearest

53

Rupert, and entered the army. He is now a Captain. He commands a half-company of the Lennox Highlanders, stationed at Peshawur. He has been awarded medals for gallantry, and is said to have a brilliant future.'

'He is too far away to come here,' I said.

'Idiot, he is at home on leave, and will remain so until October.'

'Oh, good!'

'Yes, it is a fortunate chance. He has a little more than his pay, but only a little. He will be well suited in his career by a rich wife.'

'He will not find one here,' I said.

'Yes he will. Very rich. Turning to the other two, the twin sons of my late brother George. They also have their ways to make, as the sons of a youngest son. The elder, James, is pursuing a legal career. He is said to have political ambitions, and already to have attracted the favourable notice of Mr Gladstone. He is notable for diligence, and for aspiring to the very highest honours. He sounds to me as dull a stick as his father, but I daresay one should be cautious about judging.'

The day the Countess became cautious about judging would be an event, indeed. James did sound dull. I thought the heroic Colin would be more to my taste, if I allowed myself to become involved with this distasteful charade.

'His younger brother Alexander is still at the University,' the Countess went on, 'having proceeded from Edinburgh to Oxford. I would have supposed one University was more than enough, but he requires two. His mother writes that he is undecided about his future but that, in whatever he selects, he will make a great mark. I daresay she is partial. He is probably another dull stick, going to all those Universities. Well, if he marries you he won't need a career.'

I did not understand this, nor the reference to Colin coming to Strathgallant for a rich wife. The only person at Strathgallant with any money at all was the Countess. To be sure, she had a very great deal.

'My decision is this,' said the Countess. 'My four great-nephews will come here as soon as their existing commitments permit. In the case of Alexander, for example, it will presumably not be before the end of his University term. They will, of course,

54

attend the ball with which we shall celebrate your eighteenth birthday.'

'Oh,' I said, startled, and pleased by at least one thing I was hearing.

'Do you think we'd launch you with a tea-party, fluffskull? By the occasion of your nineteenth birthday, you will have wed one of the four. You will, on that day, become my heiress. Certain conditions will be attached to that arrangement, which will be enforced by trustees.'

I looked at her dumbly.

'Conditions,' she went on blandly, 'which you yourself will in any case wish to fulfil. For example, you will maintain the castle and estate of Strathgallant. You will not evict any tenant unless guilty of felony or cruelty. You will provide a home here for my daughter-in-law Marianne, for as long as she wishes it.'

I glanced across the room at Marianne. She was reading. I supposed she had shut herself off from us, and was wandering in fancy through the streets of Vienna.

'You will provide a home,' said the Countess, 'after my death, for my companion this idiot Carmichael, for as long as *she* wants it.'

'Oh! Good gracious! How kind, ma'am! What a kindly thought, indeed!' babbled Miss Carmichael, dropping her knitting in her agitation.

'Well,' I said, 'of course I would do all those things, except that I shall not do any of them.'

'What slush is this?'

'Ma'am, I am not a piece on a chess-board, to be placed on a square of your choosing.'

'You are a penniless chit to whom I am offering a great estate and a fortune.'

'And a husband. One of four.'

'Do you want more than one? Are you contemplating poly-andry? What drivel are you spraying at me?'

'I cannot undertake to fall in love with any of your candi-dates.'

'For the love of God, spare me your girlish twaddle. I have explained to you my motives. I have spelled out, in simple words, the logic of my decision. I have done you that favour. I have exhausted myself in doing it. If you cannot see the inescapable rightness of my decision – to say nothing of its generosity – then you had better go back to the schoolroom.'

'*Le coeur a ses raisons*, ma'am,' said Miss Carmichael bravely, '*que la raison ne connait pas.*'

'Don't spout Italian at me.'

'Dear Perdita's heart –'

'Devil take her heart. We are talking of duty, mine and hers. I have discovered the way to fulfil mine, the only way. I am pointing out hers. Besides, why the devil shouldn't she fall in love with one of my great-nephews? Does she think they are not good enough for her? Does she suppose herself of greater birth or accomplishment? What does she expect, the Heir to the Throne?'

'No,' I said, 'I expect only to marry the man I love, if he asks me –'

'Then fall in love, curse it to hell,' the Countess shouted, 'just make sure you do so with one of my great-nephews! Good God, the pair of you will make me ill with rage. Look what I am condemning you to – look!' She waved round at the small drawing-room. I thought she intended the gesture to include the whole estate, and the thirty thousand acres in which it was set – the fat farming land girdled by hill grazing, deer-forest, grouse-moor, and the grim granite tops, the big river and the burns, the lochs and lochans . . .

By our nervous murmurs of doubt, Miss Carmichael and I had done all that was necessary to confirm the Countess utterly in her decision.

She was right in one thing – she and I were too much alike.

I might have consented, I thought, to marry one of her great-nephews, if it had been put to me right, if I had been wooed by one of them. After all, I had loved them as children. Then, afterwards, I could be heiress to anything. Afterwards, I would be quite agreeable to becoming extremely rich. But to be commanded into wedlock, to suit the Countess's tidy schemes. . . !

'I do not want your castle,' I said. 'I will not take it.'

I saw that Aunt Marianne was at last listening. What she made of such a conversation, of which she had not attended to the first part, I could not imagine.

'You,' said the Countess to me, in a voice of absolute fury, 'are an ungrateful slut. You will do my bidding or you will . . .'

She began to choke. She clutched at her heart. Her chalk-white face darkened. Miss Carmichael wailed, and dived into her reticule for smelling-salts. Aunt Marianne rose from her chair and started forward, twittering with dismay.

The fit frightened us all nearly to death. After it, the Countess was breathing with difficulty, noisily. It was a shocking sound. Her eyes were closed. We stared at each other.

Suddenly, without opening her eyes, she said, 'Brandy.'

'Oh, dear ma'am,' said Miss Carmichael, 'I do not think Dr McPhee would advise it.'

'Thunder and turf, will you do as you're asked, lard-head?'

With each word, the old voice strengthened. By the time she arrived at the point of calling poor Miss Carmichael 'lard-head', it had reached its trumpet timbre.

Casting a piteous look at Aunt Marianne and me, Miss Car-michael took a decanter of brandy and a glass from the corner-cupboard where they were kept against the Countess's sudden need or whim. The poor lady was so distressed by the Countess's attack, that she could not hold glass and decanter steady enough to pour. I took them from her. I found to my annoyance that my own hands were shaking, after the shock of the dreadful choking fit, and the noise of that laboured breathing.

'You must consent, dear,' Miss Carmichael whispered to me. 'It is quite an improper and immoral plan of her Ladyship's – but you must pretend to consent.'

I nodded, almost spilling the brandy.

This was one occasion when – although I was not really a person of quality – I must obey the Countess's rule, and tell a necessary lie. My continued refusal would enrage the old lady, and rage bring on another attack, and we must not risk that, at her great age, and with her dangerously volatile temper.

As I handed the brandy-glass to her I said, 'Of course I will do as you wish, Great-Aunt Selina. It came as a surprise, you know, but now I am more used to the idea.'

'Of being the richest woman in Scotland? Yes, I thought that was an idea you'd get used to.'

She opened her eyes when she felt the glass in her hand. She

57

took a great swallow. It did seem to be good for her. At least, she was immediately more cheerful.

I was not. I had promised to do something which I had not the least intention of doing, just because the Countess choked. I was going to be obliged to continue to promise, in case she had another fit, and still without any intention of keeping the promise. I did not like this position. I felt that I was cheating my benefactress.

It was only later that I wondered if she had been cheating me. I wondered if she had put on her choking fit, to compel my surrender. She was quite capable of that.

The thought almost gave me a choking fit. It almost drove me also to the brandy, except that I hated the taste.

The Countess was perfectly recovered in the morning – if, indeed, there had ever been anything wrong with her. She said that she did not need Dr McPhee. Clearly, she did not. Victory had been all the tonic she required.

In high good humour she said, as Miss Carmichael pushed her about in the sunshine on the west terrace, 'One thing is, of course, crucial to the success of our plan.'

It was 'our' plan, now. Even Miss Carmichael was by implication credited with a share in it.

'Nobody, absolutely nobody, is to know that you are my heiress, Perdita. Those boys are to be asked here to meet you, to celebrate your birthday. It is to be assumed that they will fall in love with you, probably all four of them –'

'Why?' I said, as startled as at any moment during those amazing days.

'Don't fish for compliments, Miss. Apart from being such a skimpy little runt, you're a raving beauty. I was one myself, so I am in a position to speak positively in the matter.'

I glanced involuntary at Miss Carmichael. She nodded, with more decision than she usually allowed herself. 'Not quite classical regularity,' she bleated, 'but a highly personal style. And such animation! Such liveliness of expression! I can watch Perdita by the hour, ma'am. I *do* watch her by the hour.'

'I know you do, saphead,' said the Countess. 'You gape at the chit when you ought to be attending to me. Very well. These

58

bumptious boys fall in love with Perdita, believing her to be penniless. Or they resist falling in love with her, believing her penniless. Either way, we know they're honest. If *they* knew she was my heiress, *we* should never be quite certain why they wanted her.'

'I would dislike to be married for my money,' I admitted.

'Yes, of course. So, to which ever of the boys you choose, the money will come as a delightful surprise – as the icing, so to call it, on the wedding-cake.'

'What a lot of icing,' I said, looking far up at the great gaunt towers of Strathgallant, and down at the roll of the valley farmland we could see from the terrace, and across at the high hills beyond the river.

'A substantial layer of icing,' agreed the Countess. 'Enough to make a man sick. Which of the four will vomit, I wonder, from the richness of all this marzipan? Harry? Colin? James? Alexander? We ought to make a book on the contest. Six-to-four the field, eleven-to-four bar two. Which do you fancy, Carmichael? Landowner, soldier, lawyer, student? It sounds like a game with cherry-stones. Tinker, tailor, soldier, sailor, rich man, poor man, beggarman, thief. My brother Henry, when we were children, was so determined to be a rich man, that he always ate the cherry-stones that would have made him a poor man or a beggarman or a thief. Much good it did him. I convinced him once that the stones would sprout and take root inside his head, and cherry-trees would grow out of his pate. He acquired the habit thereafter of constantly feeling the top of his head, to make sure no tree was breaking through.'

'Did Lord Eredine truly believe ma'am –' began Miss Carmichael anxiously, but relieved, I thought, that the conversation had got away from the betting on my future bridegroom.

'To the end of his life,' said the Countess. 'A cotton-brain, if ever there was one. Luckily he married a clever woman, and his son married a clever woman, and Harry has thereby inherited at least normal intelligence. Enough, I hope, not to destroy this garden. I trust, Perdita, that when I am myself manuring the grass of the burial-ground, you will preserve the garden? I created it, you know. If you grub up my roses, I shall rise from my couch of clay, and clamorously haunt the scene of your desecration. You will not have an easy moment. You will feel a

59

clammy hand on your shoulder, and hear a spectral voice in your ear. It will quite turn you against the garden, and serve you right for spoiling it.'

'I will not touch the roses, Great-Aunt Selina,' I promised, glad to have the chance to tell what I knew was the truth.

She was in holiday spirits, because she had won a victory. Her conversation jumped this way and that, like a snipe in front of the guns, or a hare in front of the coursing greyhounds. She made me laugh; she even made Miss Carmichael laugh. This last was a rare sound, and resembled not the husky, bleating flute of her usual speech, but a bassoon in treacle. Though I was not in a mood to forgive the Countess, for the way she was trying to coerce me, yet I could not help enjoying her company in this sunny and sparkling strain.

One forgot the moth-eaten second-best red wig, and the chalk-white, crumpled-tissue-paper face. One was conscious of the strong trumpet voice, the all-seeing amber-coloured eyes, and the flow of talk as rapid and unexpected as a burn running between rocks on a hillside.

Oh, she was in holiday spirits that morning, was Selina Countess of Strathgallant, because she had secured my acquiescence in an obscene scheme, by having a choking fit, or pretending to have a choking fit. And she knew that she could at any moment secure confirmation of my promise, by having another choking fit, or pretending to have one. She could trade on the gratitude I owed her, and the concern she knew I felt for her in her great age and frailty, to induce me to sell myself for Strathgallant.

Well, she could not. In my mind, my fingers were crossed. Nothing hardened me more, in my disgust at her scheme for my future, than her visible glee that she had outgeneralled me.

I still enjoyed the dazzling firecracker conversation.

Flora McKechnie had her baby, at eleven o'clock that morning. All went so well and so smooth that we would not have been aware, except for the happy, excited faces of the parlourmaids. They were very sentimental about the baby, and so were we. We drank a toast to mother and child at the luncheon table, three of us in lemon-barley-water from the stillroom, the

60

Countess in white wine.

I visited Flora after luncheon. Morag McKechnie was with her, and Mrs McQueen. Dr McPhee had come, and was now gone to prescribe more tinctures and tonics to amuse the Countess. Flora was sitting up in bed in her little room by the house-keeper's room, with the baby asleep on her shoulder. She looked tired and happy.

The baby was a boy, and Flora told me she would call him Charles Edward. I remembered that she came from the West, where there was still a strong Jacobite sentiment, more than a century after the horror of Culloden. She was herself one of thousands of Floras, all named for the girl who took the Bonny Prince to Skye and to safety.

Flora asked me, nervous and blushing against her pillows, if I would stand sponsor to the babe at his baptism. I was very pleased. Mrs McQueen had been asked also, so that she and I formed a sort of committee, to look after Charles Edward, and help him through his life.

To Miss Carmichael, that afternoon after tea in the small drawing-room, the Countess dictated her letters. Miss Carmichael wrote a most elegant Italian hand, and her spelling was reliable. But she wrote slowly. The Countess became irritated and, as usual, outspoken. Miss Carmichael became flustered, and lost her concentration. Into the dictated invitations were consequently injected blasts of rage against poor Miss Carmichael, who began obediently writing 'sapskull' and 'cloth-brain' and 'tortoise', before realising that the words were not intended for the eyes of Harry Ramsay and the rest; so she had to start the letters all over again, which annoyed the Countess even more.

Letters were directed to Lord and Lady Eredine of Eredine House, by Nairn, and to the Honourable Henry Ramsay at the same address; to Captain Colin Ramsay of the Lennox Highlanders, care of the War Office in London, to whom he was obliged to make known his whereabouts, in case he were needed in an emergency; to the Honourable Mrs George Ramsay in Palmerston Place, Edinburgh, as well as to James Ramsay Esquire and Alexander Ramsay Esquire of the same address.

At the same time, the order was sent to the engraver in Loch-grannomhead, to produce the cards of invitation to my eighteenth birthday ball, and the programmes to which, in the fulness of time, little gold pencils would be attached by little gold strings.

The replies trickled back over the weeks that followed.

Lady Eredine wrote that her husband had injured his leg, while catching a salmon on the Findhorn. His condition gave not the slightest cause for alarm, but he could not travel. Much though Lady Eredine herself would have liked to revisit Strathgallant, after so long an interval, she felt that her place was by her injured husband's side.

'A pity,' said the Countess. 'I always liked that woman. I like my nephew Henry too, dull stick as he is. I suppose we shall have young Harry's reply, when the damned insolent pup sees fit to put pen to paper. People had more courtesy when I was young. Worse morals but better manners, so life was more agreeable from all points of view.'

Miss Carmichael choked with dismay.

The Honourable Mrs Ramsay replied from Edinburgh. She was enchanted to accept the Countess's invitation, and hoped to be allowed to make a considerable stay at Strathgallant, so beautiful in the summer after the stuffiness of the city, so hospitable as the Countess had always been. James her older twin son would likewise beg to be allowed to arrive shortly, as the Edinburgh courts were in recess until the autumn, and he was quite at liberty. He had been working so very hard all winter and spring, and would benefit so very much from the glorious Strathgallant air. Alexander her younger twin was equally delighted to accept his Great-Aunt's invitation, and would do so as soon as his term ended at Oxford.

'That is typical of my luck,' said the Countess. 'I would have been quite pleased to entertain Euphon Eredine. But what I get, for weeks and weeks, is Lucinda Ramsay.'

I remembered Mrs Ramsay with difficulty. She had come to Strathgallant with her sons, for those far-off golden summer holidays; but we children were not in the way of spending much time with the grown-ups, and escaped whenever we could from their constricting world. What I did remember of the Edinburgh lady was an impression of solidity, even of massiveness – a sense that she creaked when she walked, and boomed when she spoke. Of her husband George I remembered nothing. I knew, as a matter of historical fact, that he too had come to Strathgallant: but he had made no impression on my memory.

'It is odd, Great-Aunt Selina,' I said, 'that Mrs Ramsay writes on behalf of the twins. They are grown up. Could they not be trusted to write their own letters?'

'Not by Lucinda,' said the Countess. 'She bullied my poor nephew George to death, and she'll do the same to those boys, if they let her.'

'The late Mr George Ramsay was carried off by a pernicious fever,' said Miss Carmichael. 'So foggy and unhealthy as Edinburgh is! It seeps into your lungs, you know!'

'Lucinda had so weakened George by bullying, that he had no resistance to the fever,' said the Countess. 'The effect was consequently the same. What I said was effectively true.'

Even when she was in the wrong, she put herself in the right.

Captain Colin Ramsay wrote from the house of a friend in Hampshire, in the South of England, where he had gone for the mayfly fishing, and to which his invitation had been forwarded from London. He could not without great rudeness do what he wanted to do, which was to drop everything and rush immediately to Scotland, but he would come in three or four weeks' time. He looked forward avidly to seeing the Countess again, and Strathgallant again, and me again. His was the only letter that mentioned me. I remembered Colin with admiration; I now thought of him with affection.

'It is a pity both his parents are dead,' said the Countess. 'Matthew was a stick, but his wife amused me. Perhaps Colin will amuse me. It is years since anybody tried. That may, to be sure, be explained in part by the fact that I never see anybody. I have had enough, I think, of being a recluse. With my husband and my son and my grandson dead, I did not want the world to come bothering me. Now it is time for the world to come here to be bothered. You time your birthday well, Perdita. It is a comfort to find that you do something well. Your festivities coincide with my desire to re-enter society. And the mountain will come to Mahomet.'

63

'Except Harry,' I said.

Still no letter had come from Harry. I was surprised. The Countess was furious. Indeed it was very odd behaviour, very bad behaviour.

The Countess exaggerated, as usual. She had never been quite a recluse. Certain old friends came every year to catch the salmon, stalk the deer and shoot the grouse. They were not quite her contemporaries – those of the friends of her youth who were still alive were bedridden or, like herself, the prisoners of Bath-chairs. But they were old. To me they seemed immemorially old. They did not much cheer the Countess up. She did not ask them for her benefit, but for theirs. They were poor. But for her invitations, they would have had no sport. That was the basis upon which they were selected. I used to wonder why she, who did not suffer fools gladly, suffered these dull and shabby retired officers of infantry; it was Aunt Marianne who explained matters to me, in one of her rare moments of lucidity.

'So charitable as she is,' said Aunt Marianne, 'to Colonel Scott, and Major McCalmont, and Sir Malcolm Cardew. And to me!'

'And to me,' I said.

Aunt Marianne despised the Colonel and the Major and poor old Sir Malcolm, because they were not artistic or literary, and had travelled to India but not to Venice or Vienna. I did not despise them, but they did not much amuse me, or I them.

Among the castle's sporting guests there were no young men. Before Rupert's death, throngs would come of his cheerful friends, from Eton and Oxford and from the army, as well as his four cousins the young Ramsays. After his death no more were asked, as the Ramsay boys were no more asked, because they would have reminded the Countess of Rupert.

There was society within reach, in Glen Draco and Strathlar-rig, and on Loch Chinn side and Loch Grannom side. But it chanced that, in the great houses, there were no boys of my age. In the greatest houses, there were babies. The Dracos had two babies, and the Ravenburns a baby, and the Grants of Strathlar-rig a baby. They were adorable babies; I talked to them and tickled them; they were not precisely company for me. I think that, if there had been young men, they would not have been welcome at Strathgallant. They would have reminded the Countess of Rupert.

There were balls in the great houses, and in the Assembly Rooms at Lochgrannomhead, and at the Rannoch Meeting; there were races and shows and games. I was not yet of an age for such diversions. There were weddings and christenings and such. The Countess was asked to all of them, but attended none. Since she had taken to her Bath-chair, she had never once fared further from her own drawing-room than the west terrace of the castle. To get into and out of a carriage would have been exhausting and painful for her: and for Miss Carmichael, and half the castle servants. Aunt Marianne could have gone to these festivities, but she did not care to. The conversation, she said, would have been of sport and politics, like the conversation of Colonel Scott and Major McCalmont and Sir Malcolm Cardew.

So it came about that when, in the middle of June, the Honourable Mrs George Ramsay arrived at Strathgallant with her elder son, he was the very first young man of my own class that I had met – that I had shaken hands with and properly spoken to – since I was twelve years old.

The meeting might have been expected to make a notable impression on me. It did.

Mrs Ramsay I remembered as alarming. She was still alarming. She still creaked and boomed. She was a companion for Aunt Marianne. I heard them discussing the novels of George Eliot and Mr Trollope. She discussed her sons a good deal, too. For her, the sun rose and set about their shoulders. They were brave, brilliant, beautiful, universally beloved, and bound for the most glittering honours.

'All that limits my Twin Jewels,' said Mrs Ramsay to Aunt Marianne, 'is Poverty.'

She spoke as though many of her words began with capital letters.

'You are speaking relatively, Lucinda,' said Aunt Marianne, who became more coherent than when talking to anybody else. 'You do not know real poverty. Compared to me, your sons are Rothschilds.'

65

'We live very simply in Edinburgh. We do not entertain Lavishly. Friends deign to call, of course. They are kind enough to say that they find, under my roof, more of Rational and Cultured Discourse than can readily be found elsewhere in the city. Of course, my Twin Jewels are much sought after. Every hostess endeavours to secure their presence.'

I thought the hostesses were right, in a way. I saw that Mrs Ramsay herself was right, in a way. I could not judge about Alexander, but she was right about James.

He was all that his mother said. He was beautiful. He was slim, and of medium height, which was nice, as he did not top me by more than eight inches. There was the colour of health in his face, and his hair was thick and fair and gleamed like the petals of a buttercup in the June sunshine. His nose was straight. His mouth and chin were firm. His brow was high and his eyes wide-set and grey. He had a light, attractive voice.

All this I saw in the first second, when he jumped out of the carriage in the courtyard. I saw that he was active and vigorous. I saw that he was polite.

My heart gave a little girlish bounce.

I was like a child, perhaps, that is kept too carefully by an anxious mother from all dirt and danger and infection, so that, when he is one day subjected to it, he suffers the more. I had been not over-protected merely, but isolated, marooned among lonely women. No wonder I was susceptible.

I was a little frightened. Before even we met, in the seconds when I first saw him, I wanted his good opinion more than anything else in the world. It was terribly important to me. I did not see how I could earn it. He was a clever lawyer, a budding politician, a future Prime Minister. I was a half-educated country mouse. What was more daunting was, that he looked like a lawyer and a politician. It did not make him less beautiful, but more alarming. I remembered him as grave and bookish. He still seemed dreadfully solemn. In his manner as he bowed, when he shook the Countess's hand, he seemed fifty-four instead of twenty-four.

He shook hands with Aunt Marianne and with Miss Violet Carmichael. Miss Carmichael, not expecting to be noticed, was flustered and incoherent.

66

'And you remember Perdita, of course,' said the Countess.

'Yes,' said James, turning to me. 'But I would have had diffi-culty recognising her. How do you do?'

That was what he said to me: 'How do you do?' As though we had not climbed up hills and fallen into burns together as chil-dren; as though he had never pulled my hair; as though I had never put a snail down his neck.

We shook hands. His was dry and firm. He did not hold mine for a moment, as he might have done, since we had been play-mates. He did not smile, but just said, 'How do you do?'

I thought that he despised me already. I thought: he remem-bers a silly little schoolgirl, and he sees one still.

He turned away from me. Gravely he supervised the unload-ing of the bags from the carriage.

Miss Carmichael wheeled the Countess away, convoyed by Aunt Marianne and Mrs Ramsay. I stood dithering in the court-yard, hoping that James would talk to me. He did not, but fol-lowed the footmen indoors. I went dolefully for a walk with my deerhound Benjie Craufurd, who was not very intelligent, but was at least cheerful and frivolous.

Then I heard Aunt Marianne and Mrs Ramsay talking. And with reservations I agreed with what Mrs Ramsay said about her son.

At dinner James said little. Indeed, it would not have been easy for him to say much. The Countess was in full flood of elo-quence, stimulated by new faces, new listeners. She was out-rageous, even by her standards.

'You are thinking of politics, James?' she said. 'In the name of God, why?'

He opened his mouth to reply. But she sailed on, waving her fork at him to silence him.

'They are a scrubby lot,' she said. 'They tell so many lies in public that one wonders how they perform in private. They must get out of the way of telling the truth. Lord Melbourne was a gentleman, but there is bad blood in that family. Palmerston used to hunt in Berkshire. Why would a sane man do that? Glad-stone is a wind-bag, and Disraeli an upstart with a rich wife. I have not admired any politician since John Wilkes. Lord Sandwich said to him, "Sir, you will die of the pox or on the gallows!" Wilkes replied, "That depends, sir, on whether I embrace your mistress or your principles."'

There was a sharp intake of breath at this Regency coarseness from Mrs Ramsay, under whose cultured roof the word 'pox' was probably not used, a sort of moan from Aunt Marianne, a whinny of dismay from Miss Carmichael at the shameless mention of a 'mistress', and a giggle from me. I had heard the story about Lord Sandwich and John Wilkes a great many times, for it was one of the Countess's favourites, but it still made me laugh.

It did not make James Ramsay laugh. He looked gravely at the Countess, and said, 'The level of public discussion is higher now than in the days of the North Briton.'

'Stuff,' said the Countess. 'They tell just as many lies, but they're boring about it. At least Charles Fox made his lies amusing.'

'Did you know Mr Fox, ma'am?'

'He died when I was just married,' said the Countess, 'in 1807.' She thus avoided a direct answer to James's question. I concluded that she had *not* known Charles James Fox, but did not wish to admit so.

'Mr Fox died in 1806,' said James.

'Twaddle. I was there. Not at his deathbed, but walking the earth.'

James inclined his head, accepting this correction. His face said that he knew he was right. I was sure he was right.

Although he was beautiful, and deserved the adjectives his mother used about him, I thought it was boring that he should be right about something as boring as a date.

The Countess thought so too.

'I was afraid he'd turn out to be a stick, and he is one,' she said in the morning. 'He could hardly fail to be, with a father like my nephew George and a mother like Lucinda.'

'A *leetle* ponderous in manner, perhaps, for his age,' said Miss Carmichael.

'That,' said the Countess, 'is simply a verbose and flatulent way of saying what I've just said. At least Marianne keeps Lucinda out of my way. I suppose a lot of books or briefs or pamphlets keep James out of my way. Thank God for small mercies. Large ones, indeed. The only excuse for being young is to be lively and amusing. Not too lively, Perdita. You carry everything to excess. It is a fault on the right side. I never could abide moderation.'

James could. He drank lemonade with his luncheon.

After luncheon, Aunt Marianne said that she would play the piano in the music-room. Mrs Ramsay said that she would listen. Aunt Marianne was pleased – she had been hoping for an audience. This solved the problem for both of them of how to spend the afternoon.

'And what shall you do, dearest boy?' said Mrs Ramsay to James.

James said he would return to the study of documents concerning the Irish question, about which he was to give an address in Edinburgh later in the year.

'The Irish question,' said the Countess, 'is like the drip on the end of Carmichael's nose. It never goes away. It is irritating and even disgusting, but one would quite miss it if it disappeared.'

I tried not to laugh, out of pity for poor bullied Miss Carmichael. But I could not stifle a sort of small shout.

James looked at me gravely, as though concerned that I should be doing farmyard imitations in the drawing-room.

The Countess also glanced at me. She looked as though she wanted to wink.

Miss Carmichael wheeled the Countess away, to her afternoon sleep. Aunt Marianne went off to the music-room with Mrs Ramsay. I thought James would be off to his documents.

Instead, as soon as we were alone, he said, 'Did I see you walking with a dog yesterday afternoon?'

'Those,' I said, 'are the first words you have spoken to me since you said "How do you do."'

'Yes. Shall you walk again today? May I come?'

'You would prefer that to studying documents about Violet Carmichael's nose, I mean the Irish question?'

He smiled. I had not thought that he could smile. He had a good smile, a nice broad one, which showed very white teeth.

He said, 'I mentioned the documents so that my Mamma would think I was being a dutiful political apprentice. There is a time for documents and a time for walking with dogs.'

'I do believe,' I said, 'you are human, after all.'

'Of course I am, Dita. All too human.'

'Do they still call you Jamie?'

'Certainly not. It is far too boyish and frivolous for a serious fellow like me. If you do not call me Jamie, I'll pull your hair again.'

'If you do that I'll put another snail down your neck.'

He not only smiled then, but actually laughed. It was a happy laugh. There was something in it of the Countess's clear, infectious laugh.

We fetched Benjie Craufurd from the kennels, and set off in great content.

'We must avoid the windows of the music-room,' said Jamie.

'Why? Because your Mamma thinks you should be reading documents?'

'Because she thinks I should not be paying court to you.'

'Is that what you are doing?'

'Not yet, Dita. But I won't be able to restrain myself much longer. You are a miniature Madonna. Have you heard of Lady Florence Paget? She eloped with Lord Hastings, just the other day, when she was on the point of marrying Henry Chaplin. The newspapers were full of it. She is called the "pocket Venus". I have never seen her, but I cannot imagine that the name suits her as well as it suits you.'

'You are surprising me more and more,' I said.

'Well, my public performance does get tedious. I am quite serious about the law and about politics, you know, but not all the time.'

'Benjie Craufurd is quite serious about chasing hares, but not all the time. When he catches up with one he is so frightened that he runs away.'

'I don't believe it.'

'You are quite right. I made that up.'

'In some ways you haven't changed at all. In other ways you are miraculously transformed. Why did you make it up?'

'To try to make you laugh again.'

He laughed again, and I with him.

'Why must your mother not see you with me?' I asked.

'For the same reason that I have not talked to you. For the same reason that I have pretended not to look at you. That I have pretended not to be interested in you. It is your fault.'

'How can it be?'

'It is your fault for being so beautiful. If you were fat and had buck-teeth, and were cross-eyed and covered in pimples, my Mamma might think me safe. Obviously, since you are the siren of Strathgallant, I am not safe.'

I liked 'siren of Strathgallant'. I liked 'miniature Madonna' and 'pocket Venus', too.

'I am ambitious,' said Jamie, 'but I am not as ambitious for myself as my mother is for me.'

'I heard her telling Aunt Marianne that you were bound for the highest honours.'

'Yes, but not without money. And she knows you have none.'

'Good God, Jamie, would you marry for money?'

'No. The very thought makes me feel ill. I am romantic. I believe in love and in the happiness and strength that love can give. But imagine my mother if I produced a penniless bride for her inspection.'

'She could not eat you.'

'She'd try. She'd certainly eat the poor girl.'

'Cooked or raw?'

'Raw. Off the bone. On the drawing-room carpet.'

I digested this – much as, in Jamie's fancy, his ogrish mother would digest his penniless bride.

'I do not see how you can manage,' I said. 'If you – hum – fall in love with a penniless bride –'

'I do not see how we can manage either,' he said. 'But you were always very resourceful, and I expect you still are.'

'I? We?'

'Yes, dear Dita. I have waited long enough. Politeness is served, don't you think? A decent pause for conversation? Now I shall pay court to you. Respectfully at first, you know. Nothing ardent all at once.'

I was excited and flattered. I found, when I put a hand to my brow, that it was shaking.

Jamie's grey eyes were clear and good and his smile was broad and sweet. He looked at me with an expression I recognized. I

71

could not at once think where I had seen that look in other eyes.

He looked at me with Benjie Craufurd's eyes – I mean the dear adoring dog, not the adventurous pantry-boy. There was love in Jamie's eyes. My head swam with the strength of my sudden emotion. I put out a hand, involuntarily. He took it. He kissed it.

Benjie Craufurd pranced round us on the great bare hillside, thinking it foolish to be standing still.

Jamie and I walked on. He still had hold of my hand. It seemed the most natural thing in the world, that we should be walking hand in hand.

'I have met hundreds of girls in Edinburgh,' he said, 'from all over the Lothians, from all over Scotland. Some of them were beautiful and some delightful, and some even both –'

'And rich?'

'Some beautiful and delightful and very, very rich. The future my mother has designed for me could be agreeable enough. I had begun to resign myself to it. I did not think you would destroy all those tidy plans. You were such a skinny little runt as a child.'

'I am still a runt.'

'You are an excellent size and, if I can say so without crudity, of a quite excellent shape. The moment I arrived I knew that those tidy plans were in the waste-paper-basket.'

'You jumped out of the carriage.'

'And I wanted to go on jumping, like a kangaroo, over to where you were standing.'

'That would have been polite. *Can* you jump like a kangaroo?'

'I doubt it, but to be polite I will try.'

He began to proceed in a series of awkward leaps, his feet together. Benjie Craufurd was enchanted, and jumped too, barking. Jamie's hat fell off. He caught his foot in a tendril of tough old leather, and went sprawling. Benjie Craufurd leapt upon him, and lavished large wet kisses on Jamie's face.

I laughed so that I had to sit down.

Jamie was flushed with exertion. His buttercup hair was on end, and something had caught in it. The solemn young lawyer, the budding politician, was a boisterous boy clowning to amuse a girl.

It was at that moment that I thought: I am in love with him.

72

4

Of course I had read about love. It filled the hearts of young females, even those of excellent family, so that they felt stifled, powerless, agonised, elated. I had believed in all this, though with difficulty. I had not seriously discussed the matter with anybody. As a little girl, 'love' had meant for me friendship and trust and shared adventures – it was what I felt for the Ramsay boys, for Harry and Colin and Jamie and Alex, and for some of Rupert's friends. What I felt for Rupert was, perhaps, deeper, but I was only twelve years old when he was killed.

There was a kind of love which could be distinguished from my love of my playmates – the love (I supposed it was love) that I felt for the Countess, for Aunt Marianne, for Miss Violet Carmichael, who were all part of my life, the greatest part of my life, all my life. There was my grey, gentle, vanished governess. There were such as Mary Cochrane my maid, Mrs McQueen the housekeeper, Hamish Ogilvy the head groom. I loved them, indeed I did. I loved Benjie Craufurd my dog, and Mameluke my Arab pony.

But I knew from the romances, and from the agony and bitterness and joy of some of the old songs, that there was a whole countryside into which I had never set foot. It was a grown-up thing. I waited for it, throughout my girlhood, from Rupert's death until I was seventeen. I waited with a certain anxiety. Chagrin d'amour. Oh bring back my bonny to me. Christ that my love were in my arms. I am aweary, aweary. But I and my true love will never meet again. Last night the queen had four Marys. It all seemed very wretched, yet it was the major emotion of a female's life, her principal experience, the point of her existence. The romances and the songs were all at one as to that.

73

People in and about the castle must have suffered this strange disease. They showed no signs of it. Alerted by the romances, I looked for sudden pallor or deep, rosy blushes, for kindling eyes or uneven breathing. I scrutinised the younger maidservants, and the footmen and grooms. They went about their business, cheerful or gloomy according to character and mood and the weather, and showed no glimpses of glorious insanity.

The Countess must have loved. But that was fifty or sixty years before, when everything was quite different. Aunt Marianne must have loved. It was not easy to imagine. Perhaps Miss Violet Carmichael had loved. It was flatly impossible to imagine.

And now, suddenly, on the great empty hillside above Strath-gallant, it all came alive to me. I felt stifled, powerless, agonised, elated. And all at the same time I was still laughing, at Jamie fighting off the passionate attentions of Benjie Craufurd the deerhound.

I thought: Benjie is showing me that I am right.

I thought: there is no need for the others to come. There is no need for Colin or Alex even to bother to come, and it does not matter that Harry has not written. That is my love there, rolling in the heather with a dog, his face scarlet and muddy and his hair on end.

I thought that, in our childhood, Jamie had stood a little apart from the others. We were all a tribe under Rupert's leadership, but Jamie was not quite in the warpaint of the rest. He was cleverer, perhaps, and more serious. Serious! His tie was under his ear, and he was having a sort of boxing-match with Benjie Craufurd, who was barking like a maniac. Yet he was serious. He was serious, and he was an adorable clown. I had not thought such a mixture possible. I liked it very much. It was a mixture that suited me.

Jamie scrambled over the heather to where I was sitting, fighting off the affectionate onslaughts of Benjie Craufurd. He sat down beside me. He looked as though he had been pulled backwards through a whin-bush. He looked beautiful.

He said, 'I did not hop very well, but I hopped for love.'

'You hopped beautifully,' I said, with difficulty, because I was still laughing, and because I was suffocated by the first ex-

74

plosion of first love.

'I want to hop and skip and jump and dance, to your piping, for the rest of my life,' he said.

'Please sit down sometimes.'

'Yes, sometimes, but I am so excited it is difficult. I believe, at this moment, if you asked me, I could fly.'

'Yes, I think you could. I think you could do anything.'

'You are a witch,' he said. 'You are too beautiful to be real. You are lovely and funny and wicked and sweet, and you pretend to be solemn, and I could almost put you in my pocket.'

'Which pocket?'

'My breast-pocket. This one. By my heart.'

'Oh Jamie,' I said. I had stopped laughing, but on my face I could feel the breadth of my smile.

I stretched out a hand to him. Before he could take it, Benjie Craufurd had leaped. He thought the hand was for him. He thrust his nose into my hand, and snuffled lovingly, and wagged his tail.

Jamie laughed. 'This is a new variant of the eternal triangle,' he said. 'I might have known you would introduce a note of lunatic absurdity into my courtship of you.'

'Well,' I said, 'push the lunatic absurdity out of the way, and please get on with the courtship.'

'Am I to? Do you want that, dearest Dita?'

'Yes, of course I do.'

I know that this was forward and unmaidenly. I knew it at the time. I did not care at all. Jamie was good and kind, and clever and serious and ridiculous, and we had been playmates as children, and I had fallen in love with him, and he with me.

'I don't see why you say "Of course,"' said Jamie. 'There is no "Of course" about it. I am poor. I am not very big or powerful. I am considered pompous, by the best judges in Edinburgh. I cannot even jump like a kangaroo, without falling down. You deserve better, little miracle. You deserve at least a man who can hop.'

'Benjie Craufurd thinks you are a champion. He prefers you to fall down.'

'Yes, he did kiss me extensively.'

'He does go in for extensive kissing, once he starts.'

75

'I indulged the notion that he was acting as your agent.'

'That is a nice notion. Yes, Benjie Craufurd was my agent.'

'Do you kiss extensively, once you start, dear little Dita?'

'I have never started,' I said nervously, 'but I expect that, once I do ...'

'Let us see how we go,' he said, in a funny little husky voice.

He rose to his knees, and turned to face me, and put his hands on my shoulders. His face, flushed and muddy, swam towards mine. I shut my eyes. I felt his lips on my brow and on my cheek, very gentle, like affectionate mice.

I found that, without my having made any conscious movement, my arms were about his neck. His were behind my shoulders. We strained together. I felt his lips on mine, warm, dry, gentle.

I felt a sudden slobbering wetness on my cheek and ear. It took me utterly by surprise. Kissing, it seemed, contained unexpected shocks, of which the novels had not warned me. I gave a cry, of surprise and dismay, and opened my eyes: and found that Benjie Craufurd had joined us again after a brief excursion, and was following Jamie's example, by kissing me with passionate enthusiasm.

'I thought that was you,' I said to Jamie.

He gave a shout of laughter, and rolled laughing over the heather, in a wrestling match with Benjie.

'I see I must share you,' he said, as soon as he could speak. 'It is humiliating.'

'Well, I am beginning to feel jealous myself,' I said, 'since it is clear that you prefer embracing that odious dog.'

He stood up. Suddenly he was serious. He said, 'Oh Dita, my heart bursts when I look at you. I didn't think it was possible to feel so much so quickly.'

'Nor did I,' I admitted.

'I know I love you. I am already certain. It is huge and everlasting. My God, I should not be speaking so.'

'Why ever not?' I said.

'It is too soon, and I can offer you nothing.'

He put out a hand. I took it, and he helped me to my feet.

Standing close to me, he said, 'I know that I have a future. I offer it to you. It is not this. It is not Strathgallant, and never will

76

be. But such as it is, it is yours.'

'You are perfect in every respect,' I said, 'except one.'

'What am I doing wrong? I know I have a million faults – '

'No,' I said. 'Only one.'

'What is it, dearest Dita?'

'You talk too much,' I said. 'You should take a lesson from Benjie Craufurd.'

He laughed, and drew me into his arms. He had to lean down to kiss me, though he was not a big man, and though I stood on tip-toe. I felt his lips comfortably on mine. I felt the smile on his lips and on my own lips. I felt his cheek against my cheek and his arms about my waist.

Something wriggled furiously against my shins: a large, hairy, energetic body. Benjie Craufurd had joined the party again.

We walked homewards slowly, hand in hand like children, with Benjie Craufurd cavorting round us.

'I want to boast to the whole world that I have kissed you, and that I expect to do so again,' said Jamie. 'Unless I take too much for granted, dearest girl?'

'I think you can take that much for granted,' I said.

I tried to look demure, to counterbalance the shamelessness of my words. I do not think I succeeded.

'But,' he said, 'I must dissemble.'

'You are good at that.'

'Thank you. I believe that is a back-handed compliment, but I treasure any compliment from you. Yes, living with someone as – as demanding as my mother, I have had to dissemble. You must not think I am unnatural or ungrateful – '

'I do not think you unnatural, Jamie.'

He smiled, knowing well what I meant.

'But,' he said, 'it will be much harder to pretend not to be in love with you, than to pretend to be an ambitious little beaver twenty-four hours a day, when I am only one for about twenty-two hours. But you must see that it is necessary. For a time only, my dearest. We must live a sort of lie for a time.'

'Persons of quality lie only when necessary,' I said. 'I have that on Great-Aunt Selina's authority.'

'Then we may take it as accepted doctrine,' said Jamie. 'Anyway at Strathgallant. I am not a person of much quality –'

'Yes, you are,' I said. 'But I am a person of no quality at all.'

'Even my adoration of you will not allow me to allow *you* to talk such rubbish. You are fire and air and music, you are a monkey and an angel, beauty and the beast –'

'What beast?'

'A monkey.'

'Oh yes. I was fishing for a compliment, you know, not an insult.'

'But I hope you are a discreet monkey.'

'I hope so too,' I said dubiously, 'but I have never had to dissemble about anything, you know, and when one tries something one has not practised, one may be clumsy at it. Like the first time I cast a salmon-fly. I caught the fly in the back of my skirt, and when I threw forward I pulled my skirt over my head. Ronald Dewar laughed so much he fell into the river.'

'Is that true?'

'I improved the story a little,' I said with dignity, 'in order to amuse you. Jamie, we must speak to one another. I mean, it will look odd if we never do.'

'We must say good-morning and good-night, yes, and exchange remarks about the weather, and ask for the salt at luncheon, and so forth.'

'We could do without salt, perhaps. We could make that sacrifice.'

He laughed, but he said again that, because of his mother, we must hide our love for one another.

For myself, I had another secret, and that too must be kept.

It was glorious to see the love in Jamie's eyes and to hear it in his voice; it was glorious to know that he loved me in the belief that I had not a penny piece, and would have none. And it was glorious to know that, in taking a penniless bride, he would suddenly find himself richer than any Edinburgh heiress his mother approved.

I was tempted to tell him. He had declared his love for me, by word and most beautifully by deed. But I had promised the Countess that I would not tell him or anyone, and I knew she was right to make me do so. We must be at the very altar, in the face of

God and the congregation, before he knew. Only so would we – the Countess and I – be perfectly, permanently certain that my charm did not lie in bank-books.

Well, I was certain already. But the Countess had to be certain too. They were her bank-books.

'I do not see,' I said, reluctantly dissembling, as best I could, to my dear Jamie, 'how your mother is to be made to welcome me.'

'Time will help. Your adorable face, daily. Your smile and voice. You, in short. How can she help loving you?'

'Other people manage not to.'

'Who? Name a single person who knows you, who does not love you.'

'Well,' I said, 'hum, there is . . . Or there is . . .'

I pondered as we tramped downhill, just out of sight of the castle windows, choosing our route as a part of dissembling our love.

I thought about the folk in the castle and in the crofts, in the great house and the little ones and the streets and shops of Lochgrannomhead. I could not, off-hand, think of a single face which did not seem to have a tendency to smile when I appeared. There did seem to be an enormous amount of goodwill in my life. I had not thought about it; I had taken it for granted; I had assumed, I suppose, that people were affectionate to me because they were affectionate people. Jamie was putting an idea into my head that was almost indecently flattering.

However, I thought it was his privilege to flatter me. I hoped he would take full advantage of the privilege. It is nice to be praised by anyone: but it is nicest, as I now discovered, to be praised by someone whom you love.

I was not very sure he was right, though, that Mrs Ramsay would at last enfold me to the granite cliff of her bosom, even if I gave her my best smile and curtsey a thousand times a day. She might think I was touched in the head; and she might think I was trying to worm my way into her good graces.

At the moment, and until his career took wing, Jamie was financially dependent on his mother. He made that clear to me, rather shame-facedly, as a reason for our dissembling.

'It is not a very manly condition to be in, at my age,' he said.

'But the world has to know me a little, before it rushes at me with profitable briefs, and votes me into Parliament. I do not want great wealth, you know, except that I want to buy you everything your heart desires. But I must have some money, to buy freedom. If I am chained to a desk in Edinburgh, I cannot be putting the world to rights in London.'

It was ironic. In fact, at the moment of our marriage, he could snap his fingers in his mother's face: though indeed he would never do anything so horrid. But he must not know this central fact about his future. The Countess had got us all into a ridiculous toil, with her ridiculous scheme.

I had to admit to myself, however, that her scheme had worked – smoother, neater, quicker than even she could have hoped. Here was I, loved by and loving one of the four men she had picked for me.

My husband must live at Strathgallant. Could Jamie do so? I asked him, ever so casually. He said that he could, for a good part of the year, and would love to: but that he could not imagine the Countess would want another pensioner.

'And for the rest of the year, you will be putting the world to rights. Is that what you really intend, Jamie?'

'Yes,' he said seriously. 'It is difficult to say what I want to do, without sounding priggish – '

'Don't be afraid Benjie Craufurd will spread tales about you.'

'I want to free slaves in Arabia and Zanzibar. I want to stop the exploitation of Russian labourers. I want to save the Armenians from the Turks, and the Irish from each other, and children in sweat-shops from their masters . . . That is part of my programme. Will it do, to be going on with?'

I saw that he deeply meant it, that he was angry at cruelty and suffering. I felt abashed, reproved, that I had spared so little thought for all the victims he wanted to befriend. I felt elated that a man with such ideals should pick on me as the companion of his life.

With the castle and the fortune that would be mine, he could do far more for the world. He would be happy with that thought. I was happy with it.

We reached the little wood by the river, below the castle, and Jamie said that we must separate.

'My mother cannot be relied upon to spend all afternoon with Cousin Marianne,' he said. 'She may see me coming in. I can say that I needed exercise, and went for a walk. It is true. But I shall only tell that part of the truth. As a lawyer, I am trained to tell only part of the truth, you know, and as a politician I must make it quite habitual.'

'It would not be so very wicked and peculiar to go for a walk with me,' I said, 'or to have met me by chance on the hillside.'

'It would to my mother,' said Jamie. 'I haven't quite told you the whole – '

'Being a lawyer and a politician.'

'Being a lover.'

'Oh. What a nice word that is.'

'My mother warned me before we came here, that I must on no account become entangled with you.'

'Because I am a penniless waif?'

'Yes. For no other reason. She knows no other ill of you. How could she? There is none. Well, yesterday evening before dinner she came all the way to my bedroom – '

'The bachelors' wing is not very far.'

'It is for her. Her ankles pain her. That is one of the reasons she is so angry at being poor – she cannot afford a fashionable modern carriage or good horses, but she cannot pretend to enjoy walking. Oh, dearest Dita, how difficult it is to tell you things. It is not only that your beauty distracts me, but also that you interrupt.'

'It has been complained of,' I admitted.

'My mother came to my room to renew her warning. She said you were an evident minx and probably an adventuress.'

'I do not know quite what a minx is,' I said. 'I mean, I don't know how minxes are supposed to behave. But it is a nice word. Not as nice as "lover", but still nice. I do not mind being a minx. You may tell your mother so. As to being an adventuress, what adventures does she suppose I have here? Am I to beguile fortunes out of the stable-boys?'

'You mustn't be cross, darling Dita.'

'I do not like people warning people against me.'

'It made not a ha'porth of difference, to what I already felt about you.'

81

'That is nice. Being called "darling" is nice, too. You know some nice words.'

'I know many more, and I shall use them the next time we are alone together. But now I must leave you, and go back to the castle by the upper path.'

'Goodbye.'

'Goodbye, dearest and most beautiful Dita.'

He kissed me, and we clung together, until Benjie Craufurd nearly knocked us both over, barking that we were being selfish, and not paying attention to him.

Jamie strode away, his buttercup hair gleaming under his hat-brim. I had to sit down on a log, because of the trembling of my knees after his kisses.

Oh yes, I was the child that had been kept by an over-anxious mother from all dirt and infection, so that, when the infection laid its hand upon me, I was at once in a raging fever, in a delirium which rocked my brain and loosened all my joints.

It was absurdly sudden. Love at first sight for us both, a declaration within hours, kisses we should not have exchanged until weeks had gone by. It was all unseemly folly, and it was all supremely right.

There was precedent, in novels I had read. I had learned what to expect. It was as the authors said. I had not quite believed them, but now I knew that they understated the matter. I had hardly ever been unhappy in my life, except at the deaths of people I loved. Even when most severely punished for my frolics, I had not been wretched for long. But now, as I sat weak and trembling on the log, I realised that I had not known what happiness could be.

There were savage problems. Jamie thought he must get his mother's consent, and I must pretend to him to think so too. That consent did not matter but it mattered terribly.

Benjie Craufurd put a paw on my knee. There was a certain anxiety in his eyes, for I was not given to sitting a-tremble on logs. I stroked his dear old head. The head I wanted to stroke was not his. I wanted to stroke Jamie's buttercup hair. I could not think why I had not done so, a few minutes before, when I had the chance. I would put the omission right, the moment we were next alone together.

I wondered how, when the time came, the Countess would react to my choice. She thought Jamie was a stick. She would learn better. She would be amused that he pretended to be solemn and single-minded, in order to have a quiet life with his mother. I thought she would admire him, for the skill with which he hid his gaiety of spirit. I thought she would welcome him, in time, as Lord of Strathgallant and of me.

Well, even if she did not, she would keep her part of the bargain. I was sure of that. She would go through with her project to the end, exactly as she had planned it, not from honour but from obstinacy.

At tea-time we dissembled, and in the evening we continued to dissemble. I forced myself to look at Jamie with casual indifference, when politeness demanded, and to turn away as casually. I wanted to sit and gaze at him. I wanted to smile. I wanted to sing, and burst out laughing. I wanted to rush across the room to stroke his hair.

I caught him looking at me, when no one was looking at him. The dissembling became hard. I was melted by the love in his eyes, like a blob of butter in a frying-pan.

Mrs Ramsay treated me, that second evening, with lofty friendliness. She did not accept me as an equal in the household, but she did recognize my existence as a human being. She asked me in a gracious way about my horse, and about the books I read, and about my plans for life.

'I have not got to the point of making firm plans, ma'am,' I said (telling a most necessary lie, as the Countess directed).

'But you must have an Aim! You must direct your Efforts to a Goal!'

'The child is only just out of the schoolroom, Lucinda,' said the Countess. 'How the devil should she know which road to travel?'

'I have always known my road,' said Aunt Marianne unexpectedly. 'But I have never been able to travel it. The realms of gold! Salons! Bohemia! The stimulation of the finest minds! Wit, glitter, music, art . . .'

Aunt Marianne was exceptionally artistic in appearance that

evening. Mrs Ramsay was magnificent. The Countess was magnificent except for her carpet-slippers. Evening dress well suited Jamie; his hair gleamed in the candle-light as bright as in sunlight. Miss Carmichael and I were frankly dowdy. I was to have new clothes, but they were not yet made.

At ten o'clock the Countess signalled that she was to be wheeled away to bed. This meant that I too was to go to bed. I would have lingered, on the chance of a little time alone with Jamie. But I was not of an age – at least, the Countess's law said that I was not yet of an age – to choose my bed-time.

In any case, Mrs Ramsay said that she would read a few pages of her book, in company with her son; and Aunt Marianne still sat like an artistic dumpling, reading about Vienna.

I said goodnight to Jamie, calling him 'James'. He said goodnight to me, with polite indifference, calling me 'Miss Perdita'.

Jamie had to be studious with his documents in the morning. This was not pretence, to please his mother. He really did have to master the most awesome details of rents paid and unpaid, and the laws of landlord and tenant, and the conduct of agents and bailiffs. He had to master the intricacies of the Irish question. It was a large part of his life. I was a large part, but I was not the only part. I felt jealous of the Irish question. But in a sensible part of my mind I knew that it was good for Jamie, for any man, to have serious concerns, to have ambitions and ideals. I knew I could not have loved him so much, if he had had nothing to do except make love to me.

But I knew that I would always think of the Irish question as the drop on the end of Miss Carmichael's nose.

In the middle of the morning, Dr McPhee drove up in his gig from Lochgrannomhead. He had come to see Flora McKechnie, and of course he had come to see the Countess. He saw the Countess, and then Flora and the baby, and then the Countess again.

He said that Flora might at last go home, to the croft by the Allt Feadalge. He had not permitted it before, because of the uncertainty of the weather in the early summer in the hills, and because he was not quite happy about a cough that Flora sometimes had. But he was satisfied now that the weather was mended and the cough was mended, and Morag McKechnie could be trusted to look after her grandchild.

There had been, the family said, no news of the cateran Dougal. He had disappeared entirely, going far West or North or South, to places where he was not known. I did not believe it. He had not seen his babe, his firstborn. There were hundreds of crofts and steadings where he could be harboured. Even such as the respectable Doigs would give him food and a place to lie.

Charles Edward was not to be baptised in the castle chapel, as I has supposed. To the Wee Free McKechnies, our episcopalian rites would have been scandalously popish and idolatrous. So Mrs McQueen and I would go one day to the little grey kirk in the village, to make our vows on behalf of this small new soldier of Christ.

It was a terrible shame that Dougal would not be there. But the County Police would be watching, and our own keepers. But I was very sure that, when Flora and the babe were home, he would contrive to see them.

Dr McPhee's second conference with the Countess liberated Miss Carmichael. Sometimes she was required to stay when the doctor came, sometimes to go. Discussion of so high and mysterious a matter as the Countess's health had to be sometimes a large debate, sometimes an intimate whisper.

I might have gone riding or walking, when all was settled about Flora. But I thought Jamie might weary of the Irish question before luncheon, and come to look for me. So I kept myself available, on the off-chance. I sat on a wrought-iron seat on the west terrace, reading the love poems of the Cavaliers.

I could not love thee, Dear, so much,
Lov'd I not Honour more.

I adapted these lines to fit our case:

I could not love thee, Dita, so much,
Lov'd I not the Irish Question too.

Miss Carmichael joined me on the seat, fluting about the sunshine and the blossom. I was quite glad to see her. I liked her and I was sorry for her. I would have said that I loved her, but that I had just learned the meaning of 'love'. But I did not pay her any

85

attention. In my pitiless seventeen-year-old arrogance, I did not think she was a person one need pay any attention to.

I could see for myself that the sun was shining, and the espalier pear-trees which bordered the terrace were in flower.

Then, through the mists of my selfish indifference, I heard that she had introduced a new topic.

'So handsome as he is! Quite a classic cut of feature! And that Viking hair! My cousin Davina Carmichael had such hair. But of course she is a woman, which is a different thing ... And his gravity of manner quite suits him, I find! I was put off by it at first, but now ... And so clever and ambitious as he is! Sure to scale the highest peaks! As his dear mother says! Of course she is partial, but one must allow ... Do you not think him handsome, dear?'

'Who?' I asked, dissembling innocently.

'Why, James, to be sure! First in the field! If I were in your shoes, dear, I do not scruple to avow to you ...'

The idea of Miss Carmichael in my shoes distracted me for a moment from what she was saying. My shoes, because I was so undersized, were very small. Hers were like violin cases. But I deduced that she approved of Jamie.

Dissembling, always dissembling, I said, 'Do I think James handsome? I really don't know. I had not thought about it. I suppose he is quite nice looking.'

'A very Adonis! A *grave* Adonis, unmarred by the frivolity which, too often ... How romantic it is! Do not you feel so? Young Lochinvar, but riding out of the East instead of the West ... From the learned bustle of the courts of law, from the embattled arena of politics, the young Champion rides into our backwater ...'

'He came in a carriage,' I objected. 'It was necessary, you know, because his mother had so much luggage.'

'Oh, Perdita! Have you not eyes to see, nor heart to feel?'

'I expect I shall have,' I said, 'when I am older.'

'Of course there is Captain Colin Ramsay to come. We remember him as a *splendid* boy! All that was chivalrous, all that was honourable and brave! What travellers' tales we shall hear, what clash of arms, what feats of daring! And there is Alexander, too! From the cloistered seat, from the Groves of Academe,

laying down his books to sport with Amaryllis in the shade...
But James! What a wise and gentle eye! Has he not sought you out, dear? Alone as he is in the field? Did he but know...'

'He doesn't,' I said. 'He mustn't.'

'That is quite true, dear. Her Ladyship's position in the matter is most wise, most prudent! Though I cannot convince myself of the morality of her plan, one must admit that, even if there were no other than James... Mr Gladstone, you know, is said to have noticed him favourably. Already! Attorney General, I daresay! Lord Chancellor!'

From a window came the clanging of an unmistakable hand-bell.

'Oh! Dear! I am needed!' cried Miss Carmichael, and jumped to her feet, and trotted awkwardly away.

And I had agreed with every word she said.

At luncheon, with her eye, Miss Carmichael mutely be-seeched me to see how handsome Jamie was, and how beautifully he ate a mutton-chop.

I had to look away from her, and from Jamie also, or I should have burst out laughing. That was quite permissible, if the Countess made a joke, but she was in one of her sour moods. I guessed that Dr McPhee had told her that her heart, lungs, liver and so forth were all in excellent working order, and she had failed to convince him she needed him twice a day.

Jamie and I stole an hour in the afternoon. He suggested leaving Benjie Craufurd behind, or else drowning him, because he did not like having either a chaperon or a rival.

'You have no rival,' I said. 'You will never have a rival.'

'How can you be sure?'

'I do not know how I know. But I know that I know.'

'Isn't it extraordinary?'

'It is extraordinary that you should feel as you say you do, about me. But it is not at all extraordinary that I should feel as I do about you.'

'I don't deserve that you do.'

'Of course you do. Violet Carmichael says you are a grave Adonis. Of course, she has not seen your imitation of a gouty kangaroo.'

'It was meant to be a healthy kangaroo. An amorous kangaroo. Oh Dita, dearest girl, tiny Titania, midget miracle of grace and goodness and beauty, every second I spend with you I am more certain of my heart.'

I nodded. I could not speak. He kissed me, and continued gently and passionately kissing me until Benjie Craufurd could bear it no longer.

Before we parted, in the little wood below the castle, Jamie said, 'Dita, you know that I want to marry you.'

'Well, yes,' I said, surprised, 'I did not expect you to set me up as a, hum, what John Wilkes discussed with Lord Sandwich.'

'I have asked, and you have accepted.'

'I think I accepted before you asked.'

'Then it is quite clear between us? It is a secret, but we are betrothed? I am promised to you and you to me?'

'What a lawyer you are being,' I said. 'Do you want it in writing? Of course it is all arranged. Benjie Craufurd has given his consent. Now it is up to your mother.'

'That will come right. I know it will. We shall be here for weeks – '

'Yes, that is lucky.'

'And she will see not only that I cannot live without you, but that I would be foolish to try.'

'I shall be very cross if you try,' I said. 'I will set my dog on you.'

'And he will give me a bath . . I find it very difficult to hide my feelings, when you catch my eye across the table.'

'I tried to avoid it, but you were staring at me like a fish.'

'A *fish*?'

'A hake.'

'An amorous hake. Is this the language of love, Dita?'

'You called me a monkey,' I said.

'But crossed with an angel.'

'Well, you are a hake crossed with an angel. Will you play your harp with your fins?'

So we talked inconsequent nonsense, no more rational than Benjie Craufurd. We had no need to declare our love for one another. We did so by actions, which spoke louder to our hearts than words. I became bold at returning his kisses.

I stroked his hair, and he said, 'I am your faithful dog. One of your faithful dogs.'

I had to stroke the other faithful dog, because his feelings were easily hurt.

Before dinner I saw Mrs Ramsay returning from the bachelors' wing. It was a part of the castle which had once been a monastery. Indeed, the monastery was there before ever the castle grew up beside it, and the first lords of Strathgallant were the lay abbots of the monastery, which was the usual arrangement in the Celtic church. The bedrooms in the bachelors' wing were still like cells. Bachelors are expected to suffer austerity with a smile. The wing was empty, except for Jamie. Mrs Ramsay had been to talk with him again – a second private conference, among his books and boot-jacks.

Was she still warning him against me? Had she seen how he looked at me, or I at him?

For all her booming manner, I knew she was not a stupid woman. Her friends were Edinburgh lawyers and professors. She could discuss with Aunt Marianne, by the hour, intellectual matters far beyond the rest of us. She was the mother of clever sons. She could not be beaten in argument by the Countess because, though the Countess had the quicker wit, Mrs Ramsay had far more information. Too much information, which she was happy to parade.

It would not be long, I thought, before she guessed how things lay between Jamie and myself. Then what? Dismay? Hysterics? I thought not. An iron refusal to consent to such a misalliance for her ewe-lamb? Probably. A cautious welcome, a provisional approval? This was the best that could be hoped for.

'Tomorrow,' said the Countess at dinner, 'my health permitting, we shall begin serious preparations for the ball. It is so long since we gave one, that everybody has forgotten where the orchestra is to go, and where the champagne is served, and where ladies retire to pin up their hair, and how many pipers we need for the reels, and whether reversing in the waltz is permitted, and how many candles we require in the ballroom, and how many persons can be accommodated for supper, at any given moment, in the great saloon, and so forth. Since I can trust nobody's memory and nobody's good sense, I am obliged to take charge of everything myself. That is if my health permits. We will double our doses, Carmichael, of all the rubbishy tinctures that bungling sawbones sells me. I am doing this entirely for you, Perdita.'

'Thank you, Great-Aunt Selina,' I said.

'Thank me loudly and often, child, in order that I may forget that I am doing it to amuse myself. We'll show Scotland how a ball should be given. It will probably kill me, but I think I shall enjoy it. Tomorrow, Carmichael, we shall begin making lists.'

'Lists, ma'am?'

'Lists, cloth-head, of things we shall require. Pins, candles, extra men and maids, those miserable little gilt chairs that break when you graze them with a toe, Perdita's clothes, my clothes, extra forage for visiting horses . . . I daresay we shall have,' she said with relish, 'two or three hundred items by the time we are done.'

'Oh! Mercy! Ma'am!' cried Miss Carmichael faintly, foreseeing the dictation that would be asked of her.

'We,' said Mrs Ramsay, 'are at your Service in any capacity where we can assist.'

'Thank you, Lucinda,' said the Countess. 'We will see to what use we can put you. A hitching-post, perhaps? And you, James, can deploy your legal brain to arbitrate on precedence if two ladies arrive wearing the same gown. Do you want a new dress, Marianne? Order whatever you need. I am not in a mood to stint.'

Aunt Marianne thanked her, but she did not look as pleased as one might have expected. There was still discontent on her puffy face. I supposed she despised the Countess's ideas of amusement.

I did not. There had been no ball at Strathgallant in my lifetime. There had been mourning, but no merriment. Now the mourning was to be put off at last, and the frivolous glories revived. And I was the reason – at least, I was the excuse. I would be at the very centre of it all. I thought that would be very nice.

The Countess was as good as her word, and even better. I

thought it wise to keep very well clear. She was dictating more lists, and faster, than poor Miss Carmichael could cope with. I did *not* write a fine Italian hand, and my spelling was *not* reliable, but I could manage such words as 'pins' and 'candles'. To be indoors on a blowing June day seemed to suit the others, but it did not suit me.

I went fishing in a burn, for little trout. There was a rule, that if one fished in the big river, there must always be a gillie by. People had drowned – the last, according to tradition, in 1761, and he was drunk. It was not quite clear if the rule extended to the little burns and lochans. I took it that it did not.

I caught no fish. I fell in. I squelched furtively to my room to change every stitch I had on, and was late for luncheon.

For once it did not matter. The Countess was late too. She had insisted on finishing the menu of the supper for my ball, and specifying the different flavours of the ice creams to be provided, and would not be deflected in case she lost her train of thought, and omitted almond or blaeberry or brandy.

The Countess did not punish herself for being late, by forbidding herself to eat. Still less, by forbidding herself to drink. Making lists had given her a prodigious thirst, which she quenched with white Burgundy. She was in excellent spirits. She was enjoying the ball already, eight weeks before it took place.

Aunt Marianne said, 'Such a strange thing! I was talking to Mrs McQueen about ... I cannot remember what about! My mind was on other things, on the odes of Schiller ... And she mentioned that she had seen John Donaldson the fish-boy.'

'As John Donaldson has driven his cart to our door every other day for ten years,' said the Countess, 'that is one of the least strange stories I have ever heard. Are we to expect you, Marianne, to be thrown into fits of amazement when the postman arrives tomorrow morning?'

'But I have not come to the strange part!'

'Put on more sail,' said the Countess. 'Press ahead. This story threatens to exhaust me.'

'John Donaldson had been to Duninveran, before he came here.'

'Observe us all stupefied,' said the Countess. 'For ten years

91

John Donaldson has delivered his fish to Duninveran before coming here. I cannot fairly object to the arrangement, although it gives Jean Dalrymple first choice of the fish. The sequence is imposed by the logic of geography. And I think you will not find a better-turned phrase than that,' she added to Mrs Ramsay, 'in your Edinburgh salons.'

Poor Aunt Marianne was so evidently bursting to continue her story, that I said, 'Did John Donaldson see something strange at Duninveran, Aunt Marianne?'

'Yes, dear, he did! He saw . . . Who was it he saw?'

'God Almighty,' said the Countess, in a resigned voice.

Mrs Ramsay's eyebrows shot up in astonishment. So, I noticed with amusement, did Jamie's. They were not used as we were used to the Countess's regency blasphemies.

'No!' said Aunt Marianne, who had apparently misunderstood her mother-in-law's remark. 'It has come back to me. You will never guess who is staying at Duninveran for the fishing!'

'No,' agreed the Countess, 'I don't suppose we shall. Are we to have a game, Marianne? If I guess, what prize do I win? The privilege of another story? Or may I ask a riddle too? Question – what makes the gorge rise and the spirit sink? Answer – never mind the answer. I might become offensive.'

'Harry Ramsay!' said Aunt Marianne triumphantly.

The Countess stared at her blankly. We all did. I think my mouth dropped open.

Harry was staying with Sir Euan Dalrymple at Duninveran, a pleasant little house five miles downstream on the Gallant, which the Dalrymples used as a sporting lodge in the summer. It was not credible.

'The fishing at Duninveran,' said the Countess in a terrible voice, 'is not as good as ours. It never has been. The salmon run up through their pools to our water. They always have. The damned isolent young puppy has not even that excuse.'

'Mr Henry Ramsay cannot have received your letter, ma'am,' said Miss Carmichael anxiously. 'Perhaps I may have written the direction wrong . . .'

'Stuff. You addressed the letter to Eredine. Euphon Eredine got her letter. She had the grace to reply. Harry ought to be whipped.'

The Countess was seriously angry – as angry as I ever remembered seeing her – as angry as when I refused to marry one of her great-nephews.

Miss Carmichael and I exchanged worried looks. We were both terrified of another choking fit.

Aunt Marianne seemed quietly gratified at the reception of her news. She seldom commanded such attention. She was almost smiling, which was quite unusual.

'To fail to reply to your letter, ma'am,' said Mrs Ramsay impressively, 'was Remiss and Impertinent enough. But to sojourn in your immediate neighbourhood smacks of the Brazen.'

'For once I agree with you, Lucinda,' said the Countess.

So did I. It was monstrous of Harry. It could only have been meant as deliberate rudeness, defiance.

It was rude to me, too, now that I thought of it. It was a crude, cruel, conscious snub. Harry was always proud. He must have been insufferable. 'Damned insolent puppy' did well enough to describe him, though it tended on the side of kindness.

The rest of luncheon was dominated by a dissection of Harry's character, as remembered and as revealed by this outrage, in which the Countess and Mrs Ramsay outdid each other. Miss Carmichael fluted agreement. Aunt Marianne seemed somewhat amazed at the power of the bomb she had ignited. I seethed in silence, biting at an eclair as though it was Harry's leg.

Jamie made a mild effort to defend Harry. He said, 'In all fairness, Great-Aunt Selina, you should not judge until you know what brought Harry to Duninveran. There may be any kind of crisis we cannot guess at – '

'Are you speaking as a lawyer or as my guest?'

'Well, I am both – '

'You will not be the latter much longer, if you spew such insolent twaddle at me.'

Jamie flushed slightly, and fell silent. He was wise. I supposed that what he said was right, but it was silly to say it. The Countess had been first flouted and then insulted. She was in no mood for legal niceties.

After luncheon, a message was brought to me in the drawing-room by a footman. Hamish Ogilvy the head groom sent to remind me that Mameluke had not been ridden for four days, and was jumping with energy and eagerness, and if I did not ride that afternoon, Hamish would send him out under a stable-boy for a blow on the hillside.

I was very surprised. I tried to cross-examine the footman. But he was repeating exactly what Hamish had told him to say to me, and he knew no more. I thought he was as puzzled as I was.

On the face of it, the message was reasonable. I *had* neglected Mameluke, because of Jamie. Love took precedence. He *was* a horse who needed plenty of exercise, or he become so full of himself that he tried to jump out of his loose-box. But Hamish had never sent such a message before. Often, at other times, something had kept me out of the saddle for as much as a week, and then Hamish on his own authority sent off a stable-boy to ride him. All the boys jumped at the chance, becase he was a lovely ride. Why must I give permission? Because I was nearly eighteen? I could not make it out, but I could not ignore it. I could ignore Miss Carmichael and even Aunt Marianne, but I could not ignore Hamish Ogilvy.

'Please tell Hamish I will ride Mameluke this afternoon,' I said.

The footman went away, looking relieved that his strange errand was accomplished.

The Countess was wheeled away for her nap, still seething like a stock-pot. I did not think she would sleep easy, or Miss Carmichael have a restful afternoon.

Mrs Ramsay went off with Aunt Marianne to the latter's 'secret garden', to admire the artistic things Aunt Marianne had done there.

I was left alone with Jamie.

I said, 'You must ride, too.'

'Oh no.'

'The stables are full of lovely horses. We have the best horses in Perthshire, and the best head groom.'

'I am a creature of the city, Dita. When I travel I walk, or I take an omnibus, or I take a train.'

'You mean you don't ride?'

'How and where and when would I ride?'

'You rode ponies here, in the old days.'

'Never.'

'But we all did. Rupert and Colin and that detestable Harry –'

'And my brother Alex, but not I.'

'Oh.' I tried to remember. 'No, perhaps you did not. But why?'

'I preferred to feel the ground under my feet. I still do.'

'Well, we will find you a quiet horse. The kind they call a schoolmaster. You will enjoy it, Jamie, truly you will.'

'I have no boots or breeches.'

'Hamish Ogilvy has racks and racks of boots, and shelves and shelves of breeches, in every size you can imagine, to fit all the grooms who come here.'

'No, Dita. Thank you, dearest, but no. I should spoil your pleasure. I should slow you down. Also, I should look clumsy and inept. I should look at a disadvantage. I do not want to appear to you at anything less than my best.'

'Do you think I would mind?'

'Perhaps not. But I would mind.'

I was puzzled. I was hurt that he did not want to come with me. He might not look his best in the saddle, but I rather fancied that I did. I said, 'I do not love you *in spite* of your making a fool of yourself by hopping like a kangaroo and falling down. I love you *because* of that. I will not love you less because you are a beginner at riding. If you fall off, I will kiss the place and make it better. Well, of course, that may depend on where the place is . . .'

He laughed. But he would not ride. He came with me to the stables, and saw me off with Alasdair Lawson, but he would not ride.

It was only as we cantered away down the bank of the Gallant, that a little, horrid suspicion began to creep into my mind. I threw it out, and it scuttled back, like a centipede.

I thought perhaps Jamie was afraid.

We rode down the river bank at Alasdair Lawson's suggestion. He seemed anxious that we should. I did not know why. I did not care. It was a lovely way, with the company of the big river, and all the birds of the river. I was happy to be riding again, to feel the wind in my face and the confident spring of Mameluke under me.

There was a shoulder of low, grassy hill between two arms of the river; it was grazed by our blackfaced sheep so that it was near as smooth as a lawn. Here by habit Mameluke stretched into a gallop, with Alasdair thudding behind and Benjie Craufurd racing on a line of his own to the left.

We pulled up when we regained the river bank, to breathe the horses, and walked them between mossy rocks and whin-bushes. Mameluke was better for the gallop, and so was I.

'Why have we come this way, Alasdair?' I asked suddenly.

''Tis a braw raud, Miss Dita.'

'Yes, but is there another reason?'

'Ay.'

I waited, wondering what was in his mind.

He said at last that the folk at the toll-bridge of Achnacarron wanted to see me. There had not been tolls charged at the bridge for many years, but it was still called the toll-bridge, and the house by the bridge was still called the toll-house. The folk were the Erskines. I hardly knew them. They were not tenants of Strathgallant, but of the estate on which Duninveran stood. I could not imagine why they should want to see me. But I had been brought up to believe that, if any of the plain folk wanted us, we must go to them. Only so could we justify living in a castle.

And so I nodded, and we rode on towards Achnacarron, with Benjie Craufurd running before or behind, his tongue lolling almost to his toes.

Above the bridge there was a long and famous stretch of smooth water, logically called the Bridge Pool. The Countess had said that the salmon ran up through the Duninveran pools into the Strathgallant water. But by her way of it, everything belonging to Strathgallant was better than anything anywhere else, and, in fact, enough salmon lingered in the Bridge Pool to make it an angler's Mecca. I was not surprised to see a man fishing. He was on our bank, some twelve feet below the path where we rode. He stood on a shingly shelf at the lip of the water. He was casting with a long rod – sixteen feet, I judged – which looked like greenheart. I reined in as we approached, so as not to interfere with his back-cast. He cast beautifully, the line lifted high and high behind him, and then whistling powerfully forward with the whip of the rod, to land as gentle as thistle-down, the big fly almost under the far bank. The angler wore a light tweed coat, trousers or knickerbockers that looked like whipcord, wading-boots to his thighs, and a broad-brimmed hat. There was a gaff at his belt and a basket on the bank nearby.

He mended his line with a switch of his right arm, which sent a ripple all along the silk, and plopped the fly into a new place of his choosing; then he fished out his cast, until his line hung directly downstream of him. No fish came to his fly. I expected him to take a pace downstream, and cast again, and so in time cover the whole of the pool. Instead, he put his rod down, leaving the line to trail in the current close up under the bank. He turned and looked up at me, at the same time taking off his hat.

I saw that he was about Jamie's age, twenty-four or five. He was taller than Jamie, slim but with broad shoulders. His face was brown from the sun. His hair was dark. It looked stiff and unruly. I thought, at a distance, that his eyes were green. His nose was aquiline, his brows heavy, his mouth thin. I thought it was a cruel mouth. I thought it was a cruel, ill-tempered face. I recognized it. I could not at once place it, but I knew that I knew it.

He said, in a voice with a certain harshness, 'Miss Perdita Sinclair, I believe? And what is the news from the slave-market? Have you sold yourself with Strathgallant yet, or are you waiting for a higher bidder?'

Of course it was Harry Ramsay. And of course I was so angry that I nearly hit him with my whip.

97

5

I turned from him. I said, 'Alasdair, you brought me here. You tricked me.'

He shook his head with his usual air of misery. He said, 'Hamish Ogilvy said the folk o' the toll-brig waur gey anxshus tae clash wi' ye, Miss Dita.'

'Then we must go at once to see them.'

'The Erskines are away,' said Harry. 'They are staying, I believe, with Eppie Erskine's brother, near Rannoch.'

'Then you are lying,' I said to Alasdair Lawson.

He shook his head. A flush of anger joined the misery in his face. I knew that he was not lying. He had been tricked, as well as I. I apologised to him.

'We will go home,' I said. 'Benjie!'

'Since we do chance to have met,' said Harry from the brink of the water.

'We have met and now we part,' I said. 'I am not wasting a fine afternoon talking to someone who has behaved with such disgusting rudeness to an old lady.'

'A disgusting proposal merits a rude response,' he said, the harshness in his voice intensified, and his heavy dark brows closing in a frown.

'You were asked to stay. You were asked to my birthday party. You did not even answer. You have the manners of a pig.'

'You and your patroness have morals of which a pig would be ashamed. Do you want Strathgallant so badly?'

'It was not my idea – '

'But you are a complaisant accomplice. You have put yourself up for sale. Well, I am not in the market.'

'That is true indeed,' I said.

He climbed up the bank, so that he stood by Mameluke's head.

'I was revolted,' he said, 'when I understood the reason for an invitation which otherwise I would have accepted with pleasure, and with much curiosity about yourself.'

'If there were a reason for the invitation,' I said, 'you could not possibly know about it.'

'I have made it obvious to you that I do know about it,' he said impatiently. 'My father has known his aunt all his life, naturally. He saw her constantly, and knew her intimately, until she became a recluse a few years ago. Consequently he knows that she is immoral, devious and grasping, that she goes to all lengths to gratify her own wishes, that she is unwilling to trust anyone who is not a close relative. Strathgallant has no male heir. You are approaching your eighteenth birthday. You have been cozening and cajoling her for seventeen years. Suddenly she summons her four great-nephews. It is supremely obvious what she is about. And I find it degrading. I will have no part in it.'

'I will not listen to such talk about the Countess!' I screamed at him.

'Then let us discuss your own part. I flattered you, by picturing you upon the block in a slave-auction. No – you are a painted creature in grubby satin, led out by a blowsy madame into the ante-room of a bordello, there to be inspected by the clients, and taken by one of them to a creaking bed. You are playing the part of a whore, Miss Sinclair, to be paid with Strathgallant. I do not deign to be your purchaser.'

Then I did hit him with my whip. He saw the blow coming, and fended it off with his hand. The whip hit his hand. I saw at once a livid red weal across the back of his hand. It must have been very painful. I hoped it was.

I could see him controlling his temper with extreme difficulty. His face was dark with anger, and his mouth was like an iron trap. He took hold of Mameluke's bridle, so that I could not ride away.

He said, in a voice like ice on granite, 'I would not accept even Strathgallant under such conditions. I would not accept anything from that depraved old woman under any conditions. I

99

would not accept what you have shown yourself to be, though you brought the Bank of Scotland under your garters. I will not degrade myself by taking part in your squalid play. But I will send a substitute. He will present himself, at his convenience and at mine. He will surprise you.'

A substitute! This was the crowning insult. This was intolerable. I hit at him again with my whip. He caught it in his hand, pulled it from mine, and broke it across his knee. He tossed the two pieces into the great smooth breast of the river.

'You should not mind,' he said. 'Soon your commercialised body will have bought enough gold for a hundred million whips.'

In breaking my whip, he had perforce let go of my bridle. I turned Mameluke, and started away up the path.

Benjie Craufurd rushed up, from a muddy exploration of holes in the river bank. But instead of at once following me, he made an affectionate plunge at Harry Ramsay. I called him. But Harry was patting him, and he would not come.

That made me angrier even than before.

I was too angry as we rode home to think about anything except the gross and cruel things Harry Ramsay had said.

It was only as we rode into the stable yard that I realised that I had thought and said – somewhat less brutally – the same things myself.

Hamish Ogilvy swore that *he* had a message, from Achnacarron or Duninveran, that the Erskines in the toll-house wanted to see me.

I tried to imagine the conversation at Eredine, when they received the Countess's letters. Of course it was true that they had known her intimately. They had guessed the plan. They had guessed correctly. They had not, it seemed, been quite fair to the Countess – to her, the plan was moral, necessary, humane.

They had not been quite fair to me, either. I felt myself blushing furiously, when I imagined what Lord and Lady Eredine and their son had said about me.

I might have told Harry how it was, if he had not made me so angry.

There were things I regretted not asking Harry, as well as things I regretted not telling him. One should be prepared for conversations, but of course one never is. They come upon one unawares, and one suffers afterwards from what Aunt Marianne called *esprit d'escalier*. In my case, *esprit de rivage*.

I might have asked him what he was doing at Duninveran, when he could have been catching the Strathgallant salmon – when he could have stayed at Eredine and caught his father's fish.

He had, perhaps, or thought he had, some reason for staying away from Strathgallant – had been given one, it seemed, by the Eredines who had read between the lines of their invitations – but why should he be so gratuitously offensive as then to appear on a neighbour's water? Why was he bent on adding insult to insult, and injury to injury?

And I might have asked him who his 'substitute' was.

I wondered what account of the meeting to give to the Countess. I thought I would tell her only part of the truth, apply-ing Jamie's legal and political method. If I told her what Harry said about herself, and what he said his parents had said, her rage would probably bring on a choking fit.

I told her, after tea, that I had seen Harry, fishing the Bridge Pool above Achnacarron.

'Was he catching fish?' she asked, with an affectation of cas-ualness that would not have deceived Benjie Craufurd.

'Not that we saw.'

'Good. Did he attempt to justify his verminous behaviour?'

This was where I was obliged to edit my report.

I said, 'No, not really . . . He said that, hum, it was not an invi-tation he felt able to accept.'

'He tricked you into going there, into meeting him?'

'Well, yes, I think he must have.'

'Why?'

Well, why? I had not asked myself this supremely obvious question.

'As he is not coming himself,' I said, 'he is sending a

substitute.'

For once, the Countess was speechless. Indeed, it was the crowning insolence.

I could tell the Countess neither who the substitute was, nor when he was to be expected.

'You managed the conversation like a cottonpate,' she said. 'I would have expected better of you. But I have gone through life expecting people to behave, to talk, to think with some glimmer of the intelligence of the lower animals. I ought to have learned by now that the whole human race is mutton-headed. This substitute will have to talk extremely quickly even to get his name out, before he is thrown out of the house and into the river.'

'Well,' I said, 'it will be interesting to see who Harry picks as a substitute.'

'No, it will not,' said the Countess. 'I do not intend to meet, see or listen to the damned impostor. Nor shall I permit you to do so.'

For Jamie I had to edit my story even more than for the Countess. By no breath must I convey even the smallest hint that Harry guessed why he had been asked to Strathgallant: or I would be telling Jamie why *he* had been asked.

Jamie said, 'You see the merit of not riding. I was spared an unpleasant meeting.'

'I thought you liked Harry.'

'I did. I do. But I have always been a little – wary in my dealings with him.'

'As with horses.'

'Yes, if you like.

I did not quite like.

He said, 'Harry was always prickly and arrogant, quick to take offence, too quick to lash out at any imagined insult. He called it honour, but I would call it vanity and ill-temper. Have you ever seen a sea-urchin, Dita?'

'I have never even seen the sea.'

'Well, I have not seen a sea-urchin either, as they live in warm waters, but I have read about them. They are like eggs covered in spines, like tiny hedgehogs. If you tickle them with a piece of seaweed, all the spines bristle and wave, and they are sharp and venomous.'

102

'I did not tickle Harry with a piece of seaweed,' I said. 'I only tickled him with my whip.'

'Good heavens. What an extraordinary scene.'

'It does not happen every day,' I admitted. 'That is just as well, if my bill for new whips is not to become excessive.'

'It is a pity after all that I was not there.'

'To defend me?'

'To bring Harry to a sense of the – the crassness of his behaviour.'

'Speaking as a lawyer or as a politician?'

'Speaking as his cousin. But using, I suppose, whatever I have learned in the way of words.'

'Well, I used whatever I have learned in the way of whips,' I said. 'And I think it answered better.'

'But that is shocking, Dita. That is barbarous.'

'I am barbarous. I am a savage. I have never been to a city, and I have no education. I am not a glib Roman, but a Pict with a club or a Celt with a skean dhu. I am sorry. I daresay it is shocking. But next time I see Harry, I hope I have a whip again.'

'If I'm there, you won't use it.'

'You won't be there,' I said, 'if you're still frightened of horses.'

'That is not fair, Dita.'

'I know. I'm sorry. I'm sorry, Jamie. I would be terrified of half the things you do, of getting up in court and reading learned papers and addressing meetings . . .'

'I think we need each other, Dita.'

I nodded, and he kissed me. But I did not drown in the sweetness of his kisses, as I had grown used to doing. I was preoccupied. I was thinking that, the next time I met Harry, I should have with me not a riding-crop with a wooden handle, but a plaited leather whip that he could not break . . .

The Countess had for the time being completed her lists, to the manifest relief of Miss Carmichael, who had grown quite haggard with dictation. She turned her attention to moving the furniture in the public rooms.

'Is it not a *leetle* soon, ma'am?' asked Miss Carmichael.

'No, bacon-brain, it is not. I am not proposing the furniture to

103

remain moved for the next six weeks. I am proposing to consider the effect of various arrangements. You will make notes of the exact dispositions of the pieces as we try them, and of my comments thereon.'

Miss Carmichael trembled. The Countess's comments would be, as she knew better than anyone, strong stuff for the gentle lady to write.

Men were called from all over the castle, stables, coach-house, home-farm, coverts and river-banks. Aproned and in shirt-sleeves, they performed a sort of amazing cotillion, a squadron of chairs advancing one way, a regiment of little tables sweeping another, sofas and armchairs lumbering between, the Countess shouting commands and countermanding them, Miss Carmichael in despair, all in confusion.

I watched from a hiding place, a niche in the gallery which had been useful to me all my life. The country-dance of furniture was too good to miss – but I did not think I would be of any help to them.

When the furniture of the five great rooms had become inextricably mixed, all in the wrong places, in a hopeless and impractical muddle, the Countess called a halt.

She laughed. All the men laughed, with her and at themselves, and at the ridiculous ballet they had been performing. They could no more resist her laughter than I could.

She called out in her trumpet voice. 'You have all done very well and I have done very badly. Is there anybody in the world clever enough to put it back as it was?'

Cheerily, they put it all back as it had been, under the patient direction of Mrs McQueen the housekeeper.

The following day the Countess caused Aunt Marianne to draw a map of the rooms; since she was artistic she was, it seemed, the right person for this. Miss Carmichael then cut up sheets of cardboard into small pieces, and wrote on each 'chair', 'table' and the like. The Countess then spent happy hours playing a sort of lunatic chess, deploying her armies of furniture here and there until she was satisfied. She commanded that no one touch – no one so much as breathe upon – the arrangement she had made of cards on map. She told Miss Carmichael to wheel her away for a rest. The Bath-chair, as so often, took command – careered into the fragile table where the map was displayed – knocked all into confusion, so that the map flew off the table, and the cards flew about the drawing-room like snow-flakes . . .

The orchestra was engaged, the pipers recruited, the champagne ordered; and I was measured for my first grown-up ball-gown.

The dressmaker showed me pictures, cut from French journals of fashion, so that I could see how my gown would be. I goggled. My shoulders and arms would be bare. It appeared that most of my bosom would be bare. I had never seen such clothes. They were not worn at Strathgallant. Well, they had not been, in my lifetime. The dressmaker said that the pictures I saw were correct, *de rigueur*, the *dernier cri*. My skirt was to have a hoop eight feet across. The gown was to employ a very great deal of material below the waist, and practically none above it. Since I had an exquisite figure (the dressmaker's words) I was to display it to advantage. I did not want to look, said the dressmaker, like a dowd, a governess, a schoolmistress. I agreed that I did not. I did not want to catch a cold, either, and I thought I was bound to do so, even in August, in such garments.

'Champagne will prevent that,' said the Countess.

After this exciting but unnerving conference, I went for a walk with Benjie Craufurd. Jamie could not come. He was with his mother and Aunt Marianne, a prisoner of intellectual discussion. He shrugged at me, and made a little face, behind their backs. It was a funny face, and I smiled. I switched off the smile when Mrs Ramsay turned.

We walked high up the hill called Ben Salachry, which was joined by a high saddle to the next hill. It was an empty, beautiful place, full of the hill birds and the hill wind. Once there had been a good track, rideable, from the glen beyond and over the saddle, and down to the Gallant water. It was a useful short-cut to Lochgrannomhead. But there had been a landslip, four years before. They said it had been caused by ice splitting great rocks. However that might be, the effect was to interrupt the track with what was almost a precipice. I

105

could scramble up and down it on foot, but it took away the merit of that route to Lochgrannomhead.

Benjie Craufurd and I were a hundred yards from the land-slip, which still looked like a raw new scar on the hillside. The wind was coming over the saddle, and buffeting into our faces. I took off my hat, so that the wind might stream through my hair. It would be making me look, I knew, like the wild man of Borneo. It did not go with those Parisian gowns I had been inspecting. Well, I would be childish while I could. I was not like to meet anybody. The only eyes to see me would be those of ravens and rabbits.

And then, to my astonishment, I saw a horseman breast the top of the pass, where the track had been, in the middle of the saddle. It was a big man, on a big horse. I could see no more than that, because the afternoon sun was behind him. He started down the track. I screamed a warning. But the wind plucked my voice from my mouth, and flung it away, down towards the Gallant. I waved and pointed. He saw me. He stopped, and waved. I began to run forward, with Benjie Craufurd bouncing and barking round my legs. I tripped and fell, and scrambled up, and ran on.

He walked his horse forward, to a place where he could see what had happened to the track. He stopped. I could see him looking down at the precipitous slope. I stopped also, panting, my hair doubtless wilder than ever, my face scarlet. The horse-man would turn back. Of course he would. It was as well. I was not in a state to be seen by anybody.

He did not turn back. He leaned far back on his horse's quart-ers, and pushed his feet far forward by its neck; he gave his horse a slack rein, and started down the precipice. I watched in horri-fied admiration. The horse was sure-footed. He came down very slowly, sensibly, picking his way, the rider's weight placed so as least to embarrass him.

The horse's shoes rang on the rocks and crunched in the patches of scree; downwind, these small noises came clearly to my ears, and the man's voice chatting to his horse, and en-couraging it and praising it.

They were doing something I had never tried, never dared to do. They made it look safe and easy. In a moment they were

106

down, and trotting towards us.

I still could not clearly see the rider because he was silhouetted against the brilliant sky. But I could see the horse. It was tall and powerful, with a rather heavy, oblong head, massive hocks and quarters, big feet. It made me think of a cavalry charger, although I had never seen such a thing.

I saw that the rider wore a sort of shooting-coat, and a hard hat. I saw that his boots were almost unbelievably shiny – quite painfully so, in the strong sunlight. At last he was near enough so that I could see his face. It was strange to me. He was a young man, older a little than Jamie. His face was the sort of dark red-brown which a fair skin takes after much exposure to sun and weather. He wore a neat moustache. His hair was brown, and cut short. He had enormous shoulders and big, ungloved brown hands. Across his cheeks and chin was a band of pale colour, as though the sun had never reached that part. It gave his face a curious divided look, as though it had been cut off and stuck on again.

He was smiling broadly as he rode up. His teeth were very white in the brown of his face. His eyes were blue, startling against the tan.

He said, 'How are you, Dita? I thought it must be you as soon as I saw you. What fun to meet like this.'

'Colin!' I screamed.

Benjie Craufurd thought I was in agonies, and rushed up to save me, and almost knocked me over.

Colin laughed. He had a deep, gurgling laugh. I saw that he had a scar on his chin.

I said, idiotically, 'Why have you got a pale stripe down your face?'

'Chinstrap,' he said. 'The thing that keeps one's hat on.'

'Oh yes. I might have thought of that. What possessed you to ride down that precipice?'

'It's new. I don't remember it.'

'*Why*, Colin?'

'Oh, because I was sure it was you.'

'That is nice. Yes, that is a nice answer. But how could you be sure, at that distance, after all this time?'

'Easy. Size of a shrimp. Hair like seaweed in a soot-bath.

107

Coming up the hill like a stag. Who could it be except you?'

'I would have kept my hat on, if I ever expected . . .'

'I'm glad you didn't. I always liked your hair, and I still do.'

He jumped off his horse, and looped the reins over his arm. He took off his own hat. His hair was thick and soft, as I remembered, and blew about on top of his head in the wind. He was very neat in his dress. He looked like a soldier, even in his casual sporting clothes.

He put out a hand and I joyfully took it. He kissed my hand. I felt his moustache on my fingers – an experience entirely new to me.

'I know I'm not supposed to do that,' he said. 'But you're my little Dita. Grown into a big Dita. No, not a big one, but a very beautiful one. I am thankful.'

His voice was deep and musical, a big man's voice. He sounded as though he would sing well in a bass part. It was quite unlike the attractive lightness of Jamie's voice, or the odd harshness of Harry's.

He towered over me, and from his great height he smiled down at me.

'How did you get that scar?' I said. 'And where have you come from? And how have you come? Have you ridden all the way? Where is your luggage? When must you go back to India? What sort of horse is that?'

He laughed, and held up a hand, as though to ward off my questions. (It was precisely the gesture Harry had used, to ward off my whip.) So we proceeded more slowly, as he walked his horse downhill beside me, and Benjie Craufurd told us to hurry up or to go more slowly, depending on the smells he found.

'I came from Hampshire to London as soon as I could,' he said. 'Then I had to see some people at the War Office. Then I got Uffiz Khan out of the livery-stable, and put him and myself and my box on a train to Glasgow. Then I put myself on Uffiz Khan and my box on a cart to come to Lochgrannomhead, and here I am. Of course I have some luggage with me.'

He patted his pockets, and pointed to a small roll, very neat, done up in canvas and strapped to the cantle of his saddle.

'You rode all the way from Glasgow?'

'It's only sixty miles as the crow flies. Not that Uffiz Khan is a crow. I went a short distance on the first day, and a moderate distance yesterday, and I have been a short distance today.'

'Did you sleep under whin-bushes?'

'In this weather it would be no hardship, would it? No, I slept under comfortable roofs, in the houses of friends. They hardly even showed surprise. In India you get used to people arriving out of the blue, with their wardrobes in their pockets.'

'Your horse is magnificent.'

'Yes. He is a Waler, an Australian, almost thoroughbred. They're wonderful horses, better than thoroughbreds for India. I was allowed to buy him from the Remount Service and bring him home. I want to hunt him in Leicestershire, like poor Cousin Nicholas Kilmaha.'

'It was madness to come down that cliff!'

'Yes, I was terrified. I shut my eyes and clung to Uffiz Khan's mane and commended my soul to God and hoped I'd look handsome in death.'

'Please don't do it again. I prefer you alive.'

'Thank you, Dita.'

'I want to hear all your adventures and about your battles and medals and Indian princesses in the moonlight and so forth, and you still haven't told me how you got your scar, and you had better wear a chin-strap so that you don't get sunburn where your skin's pale, and how will you dress for dinner until your box comes to Lochgrannomhead?'

'For somebody who's changed as much as you have, Dita, you haven't changed at all.'

He told me about some battles he had been in, against the Pathans on the North-West Frontier. By his way of it, he had been a clown and a coward, either running away or falling down. I could not get out of him a serious account, because nothing would induce him to say anything that sounded boastful.

I remembered this about him as a schoolboy. For somebody who had changed as much as he had, he had not changed at all. He always belittled himself, and made himself out a figure of fun. It used to annoy me when I was small, that he would not take the credit he deserved.

We went first to the stables, where his reunion with Hamish Ogilvy was a joy to them both.

All the grooms and strappers and stable-boys crowded round him, and he shook a score of hands. He towered over them all. It was notable that, though by Hamish's strict rule all the grooms were neat and very clean in their dress, Colin was neater than any – spick and span after riding all the way from Glasgow with his wardrobe, as he said, in his pocket.

The big Australian horse was admired and petted, and Colin saw him into an empty loose-box with hay and water and a deep bed of straw.

'He has enjoyed the last three days,' said Colin, pulling affectionately at the long silky ears of his favourite. 'He likes Scotland. He likes the air and the hills and the hay. So do I. It's wonderful to be home after so long.'

'What is home, Colin?' I said. 'Where do you live?'

'Nowhere. When my father died, my mother sold the house and went to live with her sister in Berwickshire, also a widow. It was a happy arrangement, an excellent arrangement, by what she wrote to me. But all too brief. They are both dead. That house too was sold. I never saw it.'

'I am so sorry.'

'I could not get back. My mother's last illness was brief. She was dead before I knew that she was sick.'

'I remember your mother. She came here. She was kind to me. She seemed younger than the other grown-ups.'

'Yes. She was married young, she was widowed young, and she died still young.'

'That is horrid for you, but perhaps not for her.'

'So I tell myself, Dita, but it is not quite easy to accept. Now I must present myself to a lady who is *not* dying young.'

So there was another merry reunion, in the small drawing room, in which Colin looked like a dapper elephant amongst the gimcrack Regency furniture.

'You're too big,' said the Countess. 'It is not civilized to be a mammoth. You make the rest of us nervous. Don't make any sudden gestures, or you'll pull the whole castle down like Jericho. You make Perdita look even more like a flea than usual.'

'A beautiful flea,' said Colin. 'I envy the dog she inhabits.'

'Don't flatter the chit. She's vain enough already. Why are you skewbald? I know – the chinstrap of your helmet. I remem-

110

ber your father had the same disfigurement and the same excuse.'

Miss Violet Carmichael was thrown into a joyous flutter by Colin's arrival and by the friendliness of his greeting. She pressed him, as I had, for serious military tales, but with no better success.

Aunt Marianne seemed pleased to see Colin: but, since she repeatedly called him 'Matthew', it appeared that she was confusing him with his father. Perhaps the mark of his chinstrap was responsible, as well as her preoccupation with the odes of Schiller.

Colin and Jamie shook hands with great heartiness, each saying that he would not have known the other; but their greeting was masculine and restrained, without our gush of feminine exclamations.

Mrs Ramsay also forbore to gush. She congratulated Colin in a stately way on his promotion and his decorations. She did not speak as though she quite approved of the army. There was a suggestion in what she said that Jamie was engaged in an altogether nobler career. Even she was dwarfed beside Colin, which was a new effect.

The impact of Colin on our staid little party was startling. He seemed to be painted in higher colours – to bring into the room the brilliant heat and sunshine of India, and its immensity and variety. He radiated cheerfulness and strength.

Beside him, Jamie looked not only small, but also pallid and feeble.

In Colin's huge brown hand, a teacup looked like a thimble. But his movements were delicate. One was not afraid that he would crack or crush the eggshell china. I remembered that he had tied trout-flies as good as Jaikie McKechnie's.

Colin's box – a great oblong coffin of buffalo-hide – arrived on the carrier's cart from Lochgrannomhead. He could dress for dinner. This removed a silly worry I had, about losing his company for dinner.

As I changed my own clothes for dinner, I found myself making odious comparisons. I did not choose to make them.

111

They were manifestly unfair. They forced themselves on me.

Between intervals of rage, the Countess had for days been unusually cheerful, because of the fun of the preparations for the
ball. Colin cheered her up still more. He was *not* a stick. He was a
happy person. He was able to reply to the Countess's outrageous
sallies with an audacity that amazed me. Being a soldier and
being a giant gave him, perhaps, a sort of right to cross swords
with the old lady: but it was more than that. It was the basic,
visible, pervading happiness and benevolence of his character
that gave him licence. He was instantly privileged, because he
was what he was.

I never remembered an evening at Strathgallant with so
much unrestrained laughter.

Jamie laughed with us, but his laughter was not unrestrained.
His mother would not have liked helpless mirth. He looked at
Colin oddly, almost warily. He looked at me with eyes that
reminded me of Benjie Craufurd's, when I went out without
him.

To me, Colin was like an affectionate uncle all that evening.
Well, I had never had a real uncle, but 'Uncle' Nicholas
Kilmaha had treated me so. Colin teased me without a trace of
malice for being a pigmy, and for having hair like seaweed in a
soot-bath. He promised me that I should ride Uffiz Khan, if we
could find a side-saddle big enough to fit him. He said he would
come fishing and rabbiting with me. He would join in my games.

With Jamie, I felt that he and I were the same age. With Colin
I felt like a child. He had travelled so widely and done so much,
commanded men in battle, made life-and-death decisions,
killed and risked death. His banter did not quite conceal what he
once or twice let plainly show – that he was in his life as much a
dedicated professional as Jamie in his. He revealed, as it were by
accident, his ambition, his concern for the health and welfare of
his men, his study of tactics and of the tangled politics of North
India. Mrs Ramsay and Jamie both read serious journals
seriously; they produced – she magisterially, he deprecatingly –
awesome knowledge of Russian policies, the views of the
Viceroy, the position of Her Majesty's Government. He knew as
much as they: and he could speak to Punjabi natives in their own

112

tongue. These glimpses abashed me, as Jamie's passionate concern with cruelty and suffering abashed me. I was a child strayed prematurely into a grown-up world, and it was as a child that Colin viewed me and treated me.

Of course he was right. But it was a little galling.

I went to bed in great confusion of mind.

At the edge of my brain hung Jamie's buttercup hair, and the charming memory of his kangaroo hops over the heather and his wrestling-match with Benjie Craufurd, and the sweetness of his kisses, and his unexpected laughter – unrestrained, with me, on the hillside – and his lovely declarations of love.

But in the middle of my brain stood the gigantic figure of this new, affectionate, teasing uncle, who had ridden coolly down the precipice, and would mount me on his great bay horse.

He was old. He was nearly thirty. He was a confirmed bachelor. Of course he did not know why he had been asked to Strathgallant. He treated me as a child, because to him I was a child, with a child's ways and a child's understanding.

If I thought of him as an uncle, there was no problem, no conflict. I did not think of Jamie as an uncle, though he knew so much more than I, and had a serious life in the great world.

It came back to me, as I turned restlessly on the crumpled pillows, that Jamie was the very first young man I had ever properly met. The very next eclipsed him, and dazzled me. But, to this next, I was a child to be befriended and amused – no more.

The over-protected child had caught not one fever only, but two.

They found a large old side-saddle that fitted the great muscled back of Uffiz Khan. Colin lifted me into it as though I had been a doll. I squeaked with amazement to find myself so far above the ground. Hamish Ogilvy looked a little anxious, because I had not strength to hold such a big horse if he should take it into his mind to bolt. Colin reassured him, and mounted a raw-boned animal put usually between the shafts of a wagonette.

We set off. Even at a walk, Uffiz Khan moved with a sort of massive power that was exciting. It was not alarming, because his mouth was so responsive and his manners so good. It was not alarming, because Colin was by, and he dispersed fright just by being there, as breath disperses frost on a window-pane.

Benjie Craufurd ran between the legs of the horses, a habit of which I had never succeeded in breaking him. Uffiz Khan was untroubled. He even gave me the impression that he was amused.

I saw a figure watching us go, from the gardens below the castle. It was Jamie.

We did not go far or fast, because Uffiz Khan had had three hard days. He showed no signs of it. He surged forward under me, as I imagined the surge of the sea. It made me want to shout and sing. So I did sing, feeling that Uffiz Khan would not mind, and hoping that Colin would not mind. He did not, but joined in 'Robin Adair' and 'The Flowers of the Forest' in an enormous bass.

It was much more fun than riding with a groom like Alasdair Lawson.

Colin was indulging me, as one indulges a child.

When we were back, I said, 'Thank you for letting me ride Uffiz Khan.'

'I was watching your hands, Dita. That curb has a high port and long arms.'

'Oh dear. What did I do wrong?'

'Nothing. Women often have better hands than men, and yours are the best I have ever seen.'

'Oh. May I tell Hamish Ogilvy you said so? He will be pleased, because he taught me to ride.'

'Of course you may tell him, but there is no need. He already knows. I did not want to give you such a severe bit, which can do a horse great damage in clumsy hands. But Hamish insisted. He said that a jockey as tiny as you must have the machinery to stop a big horse, but you could be trusted to do nothing to hurt his mouth.'

I took off my hat, and shook out what Colin called my sooty-seaweed hair. My face must have shown my pleasure. Colin put a hand on my head for a moment, as one does to a dog or a nice child. At least that suggested he thought I was a nice child. Or perhaps it suggested he thought I was a dog.

It chanced that, that very afternoon, the dressmaker arrived from Perth, with her little assistant, and a hamper of dresses for me. Not my dress for the great ball, for which special hoops of watchspring steel were on order from a city in the English Midlands, but morning-gowns, afternoon-gowns, evening-gowns, walking-coats, riding-habits, hats...

Though I was not quite Out, I thought as I tried them on that I was jumping from being a bud into being a flower.

I came downstairs in an afternoon dress in a grey silk which matched my eyes, which made my waist look the size of a wrist, which I adored the moment I saw it, and which made the dressmaker purr like a cat when I pulled it over my head and her assistant buttoned me up at the back.

The silk made a starchy rustle as I walked. I thought it a sound more beautiful than music. I had never worn a silk dress before.

I found Miss Carmichael alone on the terrace, which was disappointing. I had hoped for a larger audience. But Jamie had gone for a walk alone, as I was involved with the dressmaker; Colin had gone fishing alone, for the same reason; Aunt Marianne and Mrs Ramsay were out together with their paints and easels; and the Countess was still sleeping off the exertions of the morning (engaging extra servants for the ball) or the effects of luncheon (half a bottle of red wine from the Rhône).

Miss Carmichael went into raptures over my dress.

'You will break all hearts, dear!' she cried. 'Shatter them! So exquisite as you are! A little queen!'

I had always liked her. At that moment I loved her devotedly.

'And how agreeable it is,' she went on, 'how fortunate, that we have company here fit to appreciate!'

The same thought had crossed my mind.

'I had thought,' she said, 'Mr James handsome, with that becoming gravity, and those *noble* ideas. But Captain Colin! So splendid a figure of a man! And with such infectious gaiety! Even dear Lady Kilmaha laughs! Even dear Mrs Ramsay! Immoral as I must still judge her dear Ladyship's decision, you will fare well, dear, now that the Captain is come!'

She was as fickle as I was.

'But,' I said, 'he thinks I am a child.'

'No, dear,' said Miss Carmichael after a moment. 'I do not think anyone would make that mistake.'

For a man to succeed, I suppose, he must have some streak of steel. He must have determination, even ruthlessness, or in the hurly-burly of life he would be trampled, or simply left behind by stronger and swifter men.

This was not an original thought. But it was prompted by the men I had about me.

Jamie had diligence and brains. He had the will to thrive. But I had wondered if he were not too gentle to clamber up his crowded chosen ladder.

Comparison with Colin, of course, reinforced this suspicion. For all Colin's happiness of disposition, no one could doubt the toughness of his spirit. He had already shown it. His rank and his medals showed it.

Jamie was too sweet, I thought, too vulnerable, to turn his wish into fact. Perhaps his mother had too much moulded him, so that he came from her hands soft, lacking an enamel shell or an iron backbone.

So I thought, until he came onto the terrace from the park below, returned from his walk. I was alone. Miss Carmichael had responded, with little shrieks, to the clangour of the Countess's hand-bell. I was strolling among the parterres, looking at the flowers which had just been bedded out. Jamie saw me. He stopped dead. He stared. I saw his eyes go down my new silk dress to the hem, and up again to my face.

On his face was an expression I had not seen there before. Not the gravity of his public face; not the laughter and love of his private face; but a look of passionate determination, almost of ferocity.

He said, in a voice that cut like a cleaver, 'We have made vows to one another, you and I. We shall keep them.'

I was frightened of his face and of his voice. I had never expected to be frightened of Jamie. I did not know this grim, effective man.

He said, 'I shall not give you up. No one will take you away from me. Not Colin. Not my own brother. Not any of the gilded boys who will come here for your ball. Not the Duke of Bodmin, not the Prince of Wales. I love you and I shall have you.'

This was a new Jamie indeed. He was showing the steel he had kept hidden. I was rapidly revising my opinion of him. This was no performance. This was the reality of a man who would be Prime Minister, who would be powerful in the councils of the world, who would tread on opposition like a beetle.

He said, 'I would kill to keep you.'

From anyone else, at any other time, this would have been fustian. Jamie meant it.

In a feeble effort to lighten the atmosphere, I said, 'It is just because I am wearing a new dress that you – '

He cut my words short with a savage, chopping gesture, as though my speech were a stick he wanted to burn.

He said, 'I want you. I need you. I shall have you. Nothing will stand in my way.'

'You frighten me.'

'I do not mean to frighten you. Simply to tell you how things are. You are my love and my life and my necessity. We shall go a great distance together. We shall climb great heights. That is not a hope but a fact. You can see that is is a fact. You can see that nothing will stop me. I am telling you how things are.'

I did not know what to say to this man of steel and stone. His face was sunburned. His hair was buttercup-yellow in the sun. His mouth was a thin line and his eyes were chips of ice.

Suddenly he relaxed. He smiled. He drew a curtain down, over the rooms inside himself which he had shown me.

He said, 'I remember your kisses, Dita, and your words of love. Don't you forget them.'

He nodded in a friendly way, and set off into the castle.

I was aghast. I was excited and unnerved. I did not know what to think or what to feel.

Jamie was not too lacking in steel, but too full of it. I had thought perhaps he was not the man for me – after Colin came – because he was too soft. I thought now that, perhaps, he was not the man for me because he was too hard.

But life with him would be, beyond doubt, an upward ride. Faster, for a fortune. The prospect of glittering peaks was not

117

unattractive, to a country mouse.

He might be of his mother's moulding but, if so, he had been fired in a furnace after, and left as hard as porcelain.

I thought that anyone too close to him would be bruised by that ceramic hardness. I was too small and soft for such contact.

But it was exciting to be the object of such determined passion. He said that he would kill to keep me, and I thought he meant it. It was exciting to find myself a woman a man would kill for.

I was very young. I did not know what to think or what to feel.

Jamie had spoken as he had spoken, because Colin was come. Colin had picked me up and whisked me away on horseback and on waves of laughter. Colin was a huge and handsome man, already a success in his profession. He was most evidently favoured by the Countess. He was favoured by me. He thought I was a child. I did not know where that left me.

I wore another of my new gowns that night at dinner. It was silk, in a colour the dressmaker had called 'old-rose'. She said it would suit my dark hair. They were all complimentary.

The Countess said, 'How fortunate you are to have beautiful shoulders, child. It is nice to see them. Why have you kept them hidden?'

'Because I have worn clothes of your choosing, Great-Aunt Selina.'

'An answer which combines an accuracy which I deplore with an impertinence which I can appreciate. How luckily things have turned out. No one could have guessed, when you came here as a baby, that you would turn out a beauty.'

'Perdita was a pretty baby,' said Aunt Marianne unexpectedly.

'Stuff. There is no such thing. All babies are repulsive. My son Nicholas was. Even Rupert was. Colin certainly was. Of course you have grown as well as changed, Goliath. Perdita has changed but hardly grown.'

Miss Violet Carmichael said, 'A little empress! A veritable nymph!'

Aunt Marianne said, 'Is that the new style, dear? It would not suit me, but it looks well on you.'

Colin said, 'It would not suit me, either, but it looks very well on you, Dita.'

Jamie said, temperately, so as not to betray his feelings to his mother, 'It is a charming colour.'

'It is indeed an enchanting colour,' said Mrs Ramsay, addressing me with great if stately friendliness. 'I do not remember seeing a prettier gown in any Edinburgh drawing-room.'

At dinner, I saw that Jamie's eyes were on me – on my bare shoulders and skin-tight bodice – with an obviousness which I did not think his mother could fail to see.

Colin's eyes were on me, too. I read laughter and friendship in them. I did not think I could read anything else.

After dinner, Mrs Ramsay devoted herself to me, instead of going off into a corner with Aunt Marianne. She talked, as she often did, about her sons. She said she was anxious to see them married. 'And when they are,' she said solemnly, 'shall I be one of those Mothers, of whom one sees too many, who interfere Ceaselessly?'

I thought it likely that she would.

'I will not,' she announced. 'Nothing more gravely jeopardises the Tranquility and Trust of a young Household, than that figure of merited Derision the interfering mother-in-law.'

'That is true, Lucinda,' said the Countess, 'but I am surprised to hear you say it.'

'When my Twin Jewels set up their own Establishments, ma'am, I will come gladly, but only at the Invitation of the Mistress of the house.'

'I made that rule, too, when my son married,' said the Countess. 'But I don't think I kept it, eh, Marianne?'

Aunt Marianne was not listening. She was looking at a book of engravings of Rome, and her lips moved as she read the captions.

Mrs Ramsay continued to expound to me impressively her theory of right behaviour in a mother-in-law. I agreed with all that she said, but I could not imagine why she was saying it.

Man of steel Jamie might be – potential murderer, future Prime Minister – but he could do nothing to prevent my riding with Colin in the morning.

All needlessly, the Countess urged this exercise. She had a tendresse for Colin. She hoped he would choose me, and I him. She had not said so out loud, but she had come very close to doing so.

I rode Mameluke and Colin Uffiz Khan, and Benjie Craufurd protected us with his barking from the racing shadows of the little clouds. My neat little Arab had to trot to keep up with the Waler's walk, and canter to keep up with his trot. I was wearing a new green habit, with a green hat which had a red plume. The habit was cut very tight and stylish. I felt smart and adult. Colin did not seem to notice.

We rode by the Ellarich Water, and over the hill to the Allt Feadalge. We rode by the McKechnies' croft. I jumped off, and gave my reins to Colin, and tickled Charles Edward in the cradle the Countess had given him.

Colin could not come into the croft, because he was holding the horses. He could not have stood up inside it, without lifting the turfs from the roof. He stood by the doorway, arguing with Jaikie McKechnie about the dressing of trout flies. They knew each other of old, those two, and theirs was a friendly rivalry. Jaikie deemed some of Colin's patterns to be heretical, and Colin accused Jaikie of reactionary bigotry.

There was no mention of Dougal, and I did not ask about him.

After we took our leave, Colin said, 'Do you mind if we go on our own feet for a little, Dita?'

'No, not at all, but why?'

'Because I have something to say that I cannot shout from one horse to another.'

I looked up at his face. I saw the friendliness. I saw no laughter. I saw something else.

I took off my hat, as we started walking. I liked the feeling of the sun on my head and the wind in my hair.

He said, 'I have met a thousand women of all colours, but I have never met a girl like you.'

'How I am different?' I asked, with difficulty.

'Better,' he said.

I looked away, to hide the blush and the broad, excited smile I could feel. The thought came to me, that if many more men spoke to me so, I should become swollen-headed.

'The best,' Colin said. 'The one and only. I thought I was a confirmed bachelor. Many men in my profession are. Without you I shall still be one. Always.'

He was talking in a clipped, abrupt way which was unlike him. Usually his words flowed like a burn in the sunshine. I glanced again at his kindly brown face. It was full of emotion. He was having as much difficulty speaking, as I would have had.

'I had got into – a bachelor habit of mind,' he said jerkily. 'So when I saw you first on the hillside – I thought only – what a dear girl, what a lovely little thing.'

'Child,' I croaked.

'Yes. Child. I know you better. Well, enough, after these days. No child, at dinner last night. I should wait longer. Can't do it. Must know. Is there a chance? A chance for me? Is there anybody else? Jamie?'

'I don't know,' I said.

We both stopped. The horses shifted their feet. Mameluke put his nose on my shoulder, and whistled into my ear. Benjie Craufurd lay between Uffiz Khan's great feet.

I said, as jerkily as he, 'You see – I thought myself in love – with the very first man that I ever met. He said he loved me. He does love me. But I was wrong about myself, I think. I was so new to it. It was too sudden. I was not prepared. It made me doubt myself. I do doubt myself. I do not want to be caught again, in that muddle. I must have time, Colin.'

'Time. Yes. There is time. But I am desperate to know that you are not – committed. That you do not intend . . . Is there a chance for me, Dita?'

'Of course there is a chance,' I said.

I did not know why I was so cautious. I did not know why I did not all at once accept Colin's love and joyfully return it. I had been sure that I would do so, if ever he offered it. I did not understand my own uncertainty, my pleading for time, my offering him no more than a chance.

But I spoke my heart, and that was what my heart said.

I wondered if I was frightened of Jamie. Or whether there was that in Jamie which still held part of my heart.

I wished I had had some experience – any silly, normal, girlish experience – to equip me to understand my own feelings.

'A chance,' repeated Colin softly. 'There is a chance.'

I heard the joy in his voice and saw the joy in his face.

He leaned down, far down, towards me. He kissed me on the brow. I dropped my hat. I took his free hand with mine, and put it to my cheek. I did not know that I was going to do that, until I had done it.

With his hand on my cheek, I found that I could speak more freely, which was not at all what I would have expected. I said, 'You see, you are only the second man I have ever truly met. Well, the third, counting Harry, but he does not count.'

He seemed to speak easier, too, with his hand to my cheek. He said, 'Of course it is unfair to ask you to be definite. Wrong, premature, unreal. I ask of you now, dearest girl, only what you have given me – the assurance that there is a chance.'

He lifted me onto Mameluke, and hoisted himself into Uffiz Khan's saddle. We rode homewards gently. There was a little constraint between us. He did not use words of love. I thought they did not come easy to him, as other words did. He had been – he had thought himself – a confirmed bachelor.

He said that I must meet dozens of men – hundreds of men – and compare them all, and choose the very best.

Still I puzzled myself. I could not imagine a better than Colin. The Countess, who had known her dozens and her hundreds of men, could not imagine a better for me than Colin. She had all but said so. Of course I could not say 'no' to him. I did not know why I could not say 'yes'. 'Perhaps' was the best that I could say. Although it seemed to satisfy him, it did not satisfy me.

I walked back from the stable-yard to the castle, leaving Colin in colloquy with Hamish Ogilvy about the old method of feeding beans to horses.

I saw that someone was leaning, as I thought dangerously, out of a window of the castle. I saw that it was Miss Violet Carmichael. The absurd thought jumped into my head – into the midst of the confusion of thoughts and feelings that was already there, my disgust at my ignorance of myself, at my hopeless lack of a clear sense of direction or even of desire – the absurd thought that Miss Carmichael was about to destroy herself, able to bear

122

no longer the whimsical tyranny of the Countess.

But it was me she wanted. She was looking out for me. Seeing me, she waved and beckoned with mittened hands. I could not see her face, but her manner was agitated.

I had a sudden fear for the Countess's health. I hurried in and up the stairs, to the sewing-room from which Miss Carmichael had waved.

'Perdita dear – thank goodness you are come – it is imperative that I have a private word with you!'

'Is she ill? Has she been choking again?'

'No one is ill, dear – I wish it were only that! – though I find myself half distracted – oh, I do not know how I can so much as begin to explain . . . Close the door, dear, we must be private. Oh dear! I wish that this task had been entrusted to anyone else, but, since it has been entrusted to me . . .'

I was completely mystified. I tried to calm Miss Carmichael, who did in truth seem on the verge of hysterical collapse.

With a great effort she pulled herself together.

'A letter has arrived into my hands,' she said, 'enclosing a document. Alas, the letter is manifestly true. Its truth is proved by the document, which is manifestly genuine.'

I stared at her blankly. Speculations raced through my head. This was about my own parentage, perhaps? I was not who I thought I was? Did it matter?

'I do not know how closely this concerns you,' Miss Carmichael went on, 'since of course I do not know how things stand. But from what I have seen, what we have all seen . . . Her Ladyship, and all of us . . . I suppose it may concern you very deeply, at some future date if not at this moment . . . At any rate, it is my clear but repugnant duty to make known to you what . . . In sort . . . Oh, dear Perdita! I wish I might be spared this, and I wish you might be spared it! Captain Colin Ramsay . . .'

'Yes?'

'Is married.'

6

I sat down, suddenly in one of the wickerwork chairs of the sewing-room. For the second time that morning, I dropped my hat.

'This information was given to me,' said Miss Carmichael, 'so that it should not reach her Ladyship. The effect on her would be – calamitous! I cannot show you the actual letter, dear, without a breach of confidence which I could never ... In short, you will understand that I cannot! The story seemed to be dreadfully complicated at first, but when I studied it, it turned out quite simple! An officer of Colin's regiment wrote to the late Lady Ramsay, Colin's mother, in the strictest confidence, with the news that Colin was entangled with a shop-girl, and like to be obliged to marry her. The letter was misdirected. By the time it reached Lady Ramsay, Colin *had* been forced into marriage with the girl, on the very eve of his embarkation to India! To which she did not accompany him. Through lawyers, Lady Ramsay secured a copy of the marriage-lines. Signed by a Justice of the Peace or some such, to show that the document is genuine! There is an office in London, you know, where *anybody* may secure such copies, on payment of a small fee! The marriage took place in the March of 1859, in London. A child was born! But it died! I daresay the mother was not good with it, and the air of a great city so unhealthy ... She lives in Bethnal Green. I believe it is a dreadful slum! She lives on money which Colin sends. For this reason she is content to keep quiet, and not bother him. Think what an embarrassment in his career! He was the victim of a trap, of his own good-nature and sense of honour – that the letter from his brother-officer to his mother made quite clear! And I daresay the girl was pretty ...'

124

I said drably, 'He told me he was a confirmed bachelor.'

'In a sense, dear, that is almost accurate! He is *obliged* to be a sort of bachelor!'

'The sort who makes love to girls ... And is all this true?'

'I am appalled to have to tell you, dear – that it is beyond doubt true.'

'I can understand – whoever it was – not writing to Great-Aunt Selina. It would have been cruel and dangerous. But why write to you? Why write to anybody? Why tell us?'

'The writer knew that Captain Colin was coming here. Having been told so, perhaps, by Captain Colin himself! His movements would not be a secret, a mystery! The purpose of writing to me, was so that I might privately warn any young lady – yourself, dear, or any other – of the misery ... oh dear ... of the impossibility – in short, the purpose of the letter was just such a dreadful conversation as we are having now! Is the warning needful, dear? Can I enquire as to that, without prying? Is it as well that the letter was written?'

'It is just as well,' I said.

'And you believe me?'

'Of course. I must believe you. No, I cannot believe you. How can I possibly believe you?'

Without a word, Miss Carmichael handed me a folded sheet. It was called a Certified Copy of an Entry in the Registry. It said that on the 13th of March, 1859, in the Church of St Luke, Cambric Lane, Stepney, by the Reverend Joseph Carper in the presence of named witnesses, Lieutenant Colin Ramsay, Bachelor, of the Lennox Highlanders, was married to Maudie Plimstock, Spinster, of that parish. The witnesses were John Plimstock, Albert Plimstock and Egbert Plimstock.

'Her father and brothers, one may guess,' said Miss Carmichael, 'who abetted the miserable girl in her intrigue.'

I nodded. One could almost picture the scene. Colin gigantic but powerless, like Samson shorn and blinded, a simpering girl from behind a draper's counter, and her implacable, pig-eyed, greedy, conniving relations, in vulgar waistcoats and billycock hats ...

I was sorry for Colin. I was sorry for myself. I was very shocked. I was very angry.

Had Colin planned bigamy? Would he have his wife murdered? Was he, like Jamie, prepared to kill to get me? How could he speak as he had spoken? How could he beg me for a chance, and kiss my forehead?

He could not. There must be some confusion, some lie, some misunderstanding. Colin could not serve me so. If honour and pity had forced him into that marriage, honour and pity would have prevented those words to me.

'I think, dear, we should tell no one,' said Miss Carmichael. 'No good will come of the scandal. You had to be told, but . . . Nothing is gained by Mrs Ramsay knowing, for example . . .'

I agreed. If it were all a lie, it would be dreadful to tell them. And if it were all true, it would be dreadful to tell them.

Suddenly I stook up, clutching the document. Though Miss Carmichael bleated to me to stop, reflect, consider, I ran out of the room. I ran downstairs and out of the castle, and trotted towards the stable-yard.

'Were you in London in the March of 1859?' I said.

Colin, whom I waylaid between stable-yard and castle, looked completely astonished.

'Yes,' he said. 'Part of March. What an extraordinary question. I was in London on embarkation leave. I went to Southampton on the boat-train, and boarded the P & O. That was about the 20th.'

'You had a short honeymoon, then.'

'What?'

'Did you go to Stepney?'

He continued to look amazed. He began, I thought, to look a little embarrassed.

'Yes,' he said. 'I had cause to go to that dismal place.'

'To see Maudie Plimstock?'

He was shaken. I did not suppose gunfire would shake him, but that name did.

'How in the world, Dita, did you come by . . . ?'

'A – sort of poison-pen letter, I suppose.'

'Poisonous indeed, after five years, Yes. Young men on embarkation leave in London do meet the Maudie Plimstocks of this world.'

'Just meet?'

'Flirt with. She was my first experiment in that line, and my last.'

'I can understand that she would be your last.'

'Yes. She was a vapid girl. Flirting with a pretty girl was the manly, doggish thing for a young officer. I had no talent for it.'

'Just flirting?'

'There will come a moment, Dita, when I shall tell you to mind your own business.'

'I am doing that,' I said. 'You asked me about a chance.'

'You said there was a chance.'

'There is a chance now for you to tell me.'

'What?'

'Oh Colin, you know what!'

'No, I don't know. What letter is this you mentioned? From whom? What dirty-minded slug is pushing this under your nose?'

I felt the document, his marriage-lines, crackle under my hand in the pocket of my habit-skirt.

I had had a wild theory, as I ran downstairs, that there were two men called Lieutenant Colin Ramsay, in the Lennox Highlanders, in 1859. Neither Christian name nor surname was uncommon in Scotland, and every man in the regiment was Scottish. But there could not be two such men involved with Maudie Plimstock.

By the way he told me to mind my own business, Colin was virtually admitting that he had seduced, or been seduced by, Maudie Plimstock. And then he stopped short. Like Jamie, he edited the truth.

Oh what a screaming, horrible shame. It was bad enough that this neat and friendly mammoth, this mountain of laughter, this brave and successful man, should be married to a drab from a back-street. But it was worse that he should lie to me about it. If his marriage killed everything between us, the lie spat on the grave.

The succession of emotions was too much for me. I burst into tears. Furious with myself, I tried to control them, but great ugly sobs made my shoulders heave. I turned and hurried back into the castle, sightless with tears.

I think Colin did not follow me, but stood watching me go.

Luncheon was more than I could face. My eyes were puffy and my cheeks puddled and I could not stop the tears. I sent a message, by Mary Cochrane, excusing myself.

She reported to me that it caused some consternation, because I had scarcely ever before in my life missed a meal. It had been a source of astonishment over the years, to myself as well as to the others, that I should eat so much and grow so little. That day, food would have choked me, and company destroyed me. I knew I would weep. The Countess would not have cared for that. There would have been questions. I could not have answered them. Miss Carmichael would have understood, and pitied me. Colin would have understood in part. I did not know how he would have felt.

Mary Cochrane brought me some soup, some rich chicken broth. I did not want it, but she stood over me implacably while I forced it down. I made myself do so. I knew she was right. Starvation would be no help to my puzzled and miserable heart. Besides, Mary had taken such trouble, and shown such kindness, that the least return I could make was to drink the soup.

She was going without her own meal. She said she did not want it. She did not like the mutton on the servants'-hall table that day. It was a kind lie – the sort of necessary lie that persons of quality were by Strathgallant rules allowed to tell. It was not a lie like Colin's.

I sat in my room, in the sunlight of early afternoon, exhausted by shock and by my tears.

Only Colin and Mary Cochrane had seen my tears. Only Colin and Miss Carmichael knew the cause of my misery. What would the others think? They would know only that, having ridden with Colin, I did not want luncheon. They would guess at cause and effect. That he had not made a declaration I expected, or made one I did not expect.

The Countess would want an explanation. Meals were not missed at Strathgallant. I must find another necessary lie. A headache was the best I could come up with. Aunt Marianne had them. For me it was not very good, because I had never had a

128

headache in my life.

Miss Carmichael came to comfort me, because she was the only person who understood. It was a kind thought, but it started me weeping again.

She wept also, in sorrow for my sorrow. And I thought she felt betrayed by Colin, whom she had idolised all his life.

In the late afternoon, I saw from my window Jamie crossing the park. He was on a solitary walk.

About him I knew everything. There might be in him something frightening, but there was nothing secret. For certain he was not married.

There was comfort in the certainty of Jamie's love for me, and his right to feel that love. He might be as hard as a rock, but rocks are safe because they are hard. There might be a steel girder inside him, but that was something to cling to.

I ran down, and out, and down the broad granite steps of the terrace, and over the ha-ha into the park. I ran to Jamie, and he took my hand.

He was gentle. Gentleness hid the rock, but not from me. I clutched at the rock, and felt safe from the sucking tides.

He said, 'What did Colin say or do, to take away your appetite?'

'I shall not carry tales,' I said, 'even to you.'

'Can I help in any way?'

'Just by holding my hand.'

'I shall do that for the rest of our lives.'

He talked about my hair and eyes, and face and figure, and about our future happiness. He was quite clear about that. He spoke as though Colin posed no threat to him – never had posed any threat. He was not in the least surprised that it was his hand I held, not Colin's, though Colin was by, though he was beautiful and bemedalled, though I had taken obvious pleasure in his company. It was in the order of things, that I should be Jamie's. He was the future Prime Minister.

I found it startling, this acceptance of victory as inevitable. In anybody else, it would have been amazingly complacent. But you could not use that word about Jamie's confident certainty.

It was how, that golden evening, he let the rock show through the gentleness.

For myself, I did not face the question, whether Jamie's hand was the hand I wanted to hold for the rest of my life. I felt too battered and weakened to face any large questions. But Jamie's was, for certain, the hand I wanted to hold that evening.

I had not wished to discuss Colin with Jamie. Indeed, I was very clear that I would not do so.

But I suddenly found myself intensely curious on one point – one little, unimportant point. I said, 'Jamie, how was Colin at luncheon?'

'Well, he was there. He ate luncheon.'

'Merrily?'

'No, Dita. He looked like a man under sentence of death.' Jamie glanced at me, and added lightly, 'Is he? Do you want me to carry out the sentence?'

'Not yet,' I said. 'Was my absence discussed?'

'Of course, by us all, with wonder and concern.'

'By Colin?'

'No. He did not contribute to that discussion. To any discussion, I think.'

'Was not *that* discussed? His silence, I mean?'

'Oh yes. It was animadverted upon by Great-Aunt Selina, in terms suitable to a London coffee-house in a coarser age. It aroused anxious concern in Miss Carmichael. Cousin Marianne Kilmaha did not, I think, notice it. My mother, I regret to say, was rather pleased than otherwise.'

'Filling the gap herself.'

'With somewhat different material. Oh Lord, I must guard against sounding so ungrateful and unnatural.'

'But,' I said, frowning, brooding, 'Colin ate his luncheon with a good appetite?'

'I did not notice his appetite, Dita. I was worried about yours. I still am. I wish I could help.'

'You are still helping,' I said, 'by holding my hand.'

Jamie's hand strengthened me to face the Countess at dinner, and to tell her that I had had a headache, now cured. It strengthened me to face the sympathetic grimaces and fluttering mittens of Miss Carmichael, the knowing stateliness of Mrs Ramsay, the vague commiseration of Aunt Marianne.

It almost strengthened me to face Colin. But I avoided his eye. He made no effort to speak to me directly. He was muted, almost leaden. The Countess teased him for being so dull, her eyes sparkling with curiosity. He apologised; he said that he had slept badly the night before, and was heavy with lack of sleep. Oddly, that was just how he looked.

I thought it was how I looked, too. My tears were long dry and my face recovered from its puffiness, by dint of the comfort of holding Jamie's hand; but when I examined myself in the glass just before coming downstairs, I saw dark circles under my eyes.

'If every meal is going to be like the last two,' said the Countess, 'we had better engage a jester. Cap, bells, motley. Do you suppose those oddly-dressed creatures were *funny*? Most, I believe, were deformed or half-witted. Therein lay their risibility. Would you be funnier, Colin, if you were deformed or half-witted? Or you, Lucinda? In your case, Carmichael, the question would be absurd, since you are both deformed and half-witted, and you are not funny at all. James is of normal shape and intelligence, and *he* is not funny at all. There seems no rule in the matter, nothing to guide us usefully in our choice of jester. What do you think, Perdita? Your silence is as depressing as Lucinda's conversation. It is not enough, you know, to look like a French doll. You must wind yourself up, and sing for your supper.'

'Singing would bring my headache back, Great-Aunt Selina,' I said.

I thought of singing 'Robin Adair' and 'The Flowers of the Forest', while I was riding Uffiz Khan; I thought of Colin's huge bass joining in. I felt new tears pricking at my lids, so that I bent over my plate, and became very busy impaling peas on the prongs of my fork.

I thought Colin would go away. He showed no signs of doing so. As far as he knew, I was the only one who knew about Maudie Plimstock. Miss Carmichael was surprisingly discreet about it all, and gave away nothing.

I had no dealings with Colin, beyond the barest courtesy.

131

How could I? He had said that he loved and wanted me. I was on the brink of being in love with him – at least, that was how it seemed to me, but I was horribly aware of ignorance.

I thought it would have been kinder to me if he had left, and kinder to himself. Miss Carmichael thought so too. But I said nothing to him about it, and neither of us said anything to anybody else. Whatever his reasons, he stayed.

He gave himself over to sport, which made things easier if not easy. He left early in the morning, taking a chicken-leg and a hunk of bread in his pocket, and returned late. He fished the most distant lochans. He explored the hills, in preparation for the deer-stalking. He built fences in imitation of Leicestershire oxers, and schooled Uffiz Khan over them. He recovered some of his merriment, but to my eyes it had a forced air, and he would fall silent when I came into a room.

I daily expected an examination by the Countess, since things had gone so plainly wrong with her favourite candidate. I had answers ready. Some were variants of what Colin had said to me: 'Mind your own business'; and some were variants of what I had said to him: 'Give me time'.

I was surprised she did not question me. I was sure she must be bursting with curiosity. It concerned, after all, the future of Strathgallant. I concluded that she was too clever to.

I did not know if she questioned Colin. I knew very well that she would have learned nothing from him.

What did she suppose had happened, to sour things between us? I guessed she thought Colin had besieged me too suddenly and too ardently. Being so enormous and powerful, he had frightened or disgusted me. That he stayed on at Strathgallant in the hope of repairing the damage. That he would not wish, if he loved me, to leave the field open to Jamie, or his brother, or any of the swarming rank and fashion who were coming to my birthday ball.

So the days went by awkwardly, and my consolations were the preparations for the ball, my new and lovely clothes, Benjie Craufurd, Mameluke, and Jamie.

Mameluke took me away from Jamie. He could have ridden with me. Then we could have gone without a groom, and had the hill-tops to ourselves. I urged him to ride – begged him. He

132

would not.

Still he made the calm assumption that he had won me – that we were vowed to one another. Still his certainty gave me a feeling of safety. But I had deep inner reservations. Colin had shaken my imagined devotion to Jamie so easily, that I had doubted the reality of my feelings for Colin himself. I had learned a lot, since the delirium of that first gentle love-making, which bowled me over like a skittle, and convinced me I was in love.

I did not know my heart, but I did not tell Jamie so. It struck me that I was using him for my own comfort, unfairly, cheating him. But it was not really so. He would simply not have believed my doubts. He was himself, and I had promised myself to him. He would have dismissed my reservations as a girlish attempt at modesty, after the immodesty of my first response. Or as a pathetic effort to make him more devoted, by making him jealous or anxious.

No, since his certainty was unshakable, there was no purpose in shaking it. But I still felt uneasy at letting him believe that I was eternally bound to him.

There was this about it, too – I was far from certain that I was *not* eternally bound to him.

I wondered what his brother Alexander was like.

I thought I knew, when a slim young man with dark hair climbed out of a Lochgrannomhead hackney-carriage.

It was in the little main street of the village of Auchinfort. The village was on the Strathgallant estate, and every soul was the Countess's tenant. Consequently the roofs of the houses were sound, and the street well-paved. At the end of the street was the kirk. There Mrs McQueen and I had gone, to stand sponsor at the baptism of Charles Edward McKechnie.

Flora McKechnie wore shoes and stockings, to which I thought she was not accustomed. She looked very pretty and excited.

In the kirk, in the street outside, and at the other end of the village, I saw officers of the County Police. I saw two or three of the Strathgallant water-keepers. They were watching for Dougal. I thought that, though it broke his heart, he would have

133

sense to stay away.

But for this sad gap, it was a joyful little ceremony. Flora was as proud of her babe as the goose of her golden egg, and Morag and Jaikie bewitched by their eldest grandchild. The Minister was an elderly man with a face as grim and grey as the stone of the kirk. His Calvinistic doctrine was abhorrent to us in the castle, and our near-popish ritual was to him the work of Satan: and he and the Countess esteemed one another mightily (it was said in the village that she was the only person who had ever made him laugh out loud) and he made me warmly welcome.

When our cheerful work was done, and Charles Edward was a baptised Wee Free Worthy, we came out into the sunshine, and shook hands with the village of Auchinfort.

It was then that the hackney-carriage came slowly up the road from Lochgrannomhead. The driver was leading his horse, which was lame; it was then that the pale young man climbed down into the street, and looked around with friendly interest.

He was beautifully dressed, absurdly dressed, in a silk frock coat and a tall silk hat. He looked among the villagers like a glossy thoroughbred in a herd of cows.

The driver explained, to anyone who would listen, that they were bound for the castle but the horse could go no farther.

'Boond tae the cassel, Miss Dita,' said Mrs McQueen. 'Wha'll be yon gorgious felly? Whisht, I ken! Yon'll be Muster Alex! Alexander Ramsay! An' yon'll be Oxford claes, nae doot.'

I thought Mrs McQueen must be right. I was not sure if a silk frock coat was really Oxford garb, but for all I knew it might be. The young man was as handsome as all the other Ramsays, and indeed had a look of them. Alexander and Jamie were not identical twins, and had been in boyhood quite different. It all seemed to fit.

'We can give him a lift,' I said, 'and send a horse for the hackney.'

I walked over to the newcomer, and said, 'How do you do? Are you Alexander Ramsay?'

He smiled. He had a delightful smile. His eyes were grey, like mine, like Jamie's.

He said, 'I think you must be Miss Perdita Sinclair. You were described to me, but not at all adequately.'

His voice was not quite like the voices I was used to, either the 'English' voices of the castle party, or the broad Scots of the village. It was educated, 'English', clear, fluent: but still a little different. I supposed it must be the way they spoke at Oxford.

'Would you have known me?' I asked.

'We have not met,' he said.

I looked at him blankly.

'But you are going to Strathgallant?' I said, stupidly, because I knew he was bound there.

'I hope so. I come from a Ramsay, but I have not the honour to be one. I come from Mr Henry Ramsay – from Harry. I am his substitute.'

I goggled. Harry had said that his substitute would surprise me. He did.

I said, 'The Countess is very angry with Harry. We all are. He has been very rude.'

'He thinks he has a reason, although I do not know what is the reason.'

'Yes. But the Countess said she would throw the substitute into the river.'

'I can swim. But it will *not* be good for my coat.'

'Is that an Oxford coat?' I asked. 'Oh – of course – you are not Alex. Where do you come from?'

'From France. From Paris. It is a Paris coat. If the Countess will listen to just three words from me, perhaps she will not throw me in the river.'

'They will have to be quick words,' I said dubiously. 'And very good words.'

We made room for him and his luggage in the victoria, and rattled up towards Strathgallant.

I was bursting to ask who this elegant, affable stranger was, and why he was advancing his head into the furnace of the Countess's wrath, and all about him. I had liked him on sight, and I liked him more and more. He was the third man I had met, not counting Harry, who did not count. His position was highly peculiar, he was an exotic, he was charming and attractive. But Mrs McQueen was sitting beside me, and there was a coachman in front and a groom behind, with flapping ears, and it would not have done to ask Harry's substitute why he was there. Too much

135

would be given away which was not for the servants'-hall or the stable-yard.

The Countess would be very angry, if the servants knew the whole story before she did. I thought she would be very angry, in any case.

The stranger gasped at his first sight of the castle. I understood. I had lived there all my life, but I had still never quite got used to its immensity or its beauty.

'Now I am frightened,' he said.

'It is not the castle that is frightening,' I said.

'But the dragon inside, breathing fire? Yes, Harry has told me.'

It did not matter the servants hearing this. They knew it very well for themselves.

I had left the Countess on the west terrace, dictating letters to Miss Carmichael under a great striped parasol. I thought they would still be there, and they were. No one else was to be seen.

Nervously, I led my resplendent new friend towards the parasol: towards the dragon. She looked up sharply, hearing our feet on the gravel. She looked considerably amazed, when she saw my companion. She took off the spectacles she had on, and raised instead a lorgnette. Under her basilisk eye he smiled and bowed. If he was frightened, he did not show it.

But he must have been frightened. Anybody would have been. The Countess's second-best red wig flamed like a gigantic begonia in the sunshine, and even in the shade of the parasol. She wore a silk gown, and carpet-slippers. Her amber-coloured eyes were as hard as pebbles, in that chalk-white crumpled-tissue-paper face. I was used to her, but – like Strathgallant itself – it all made for something it was impossible quite to get used to.

Bowing, the Frenchman said, '*Je viens de Paris, Madame la Comtesse, pour vous saluer.*'

'Don't jabber Italian at me. Do you always wear a hat like that in the country?'

'I have other hats, madame, but I judged this one correct for today.'

'Oh, you do speak a civilized language. I thought I was going to have to send for my daughter-in-law, to discover what the devil this is all about.'

'I speak English, madame, because I had an English mother. To be more exact, a Scottish mother, as I have recently discovered.'

'I await some indication that I should care a hoot whether your mother was a Turk or a tomato.'

The Frenchman bowed again. He *must* have been frightened, but he hardly showed it.

'I came to England after my mother's death, to discover who she had been, who I was. I had the assistance of the French Embassy in London. It became a sport, *la chasse*, to discover my lineage. It was simple. My mother was noble, which I had not at all understood, so all was written out in printed books.'

'This story,' said the Countess, 'may possibly yet amaze me by justifying its prolixity and tedium, but it shows no signs of doing so yet.'

'When I had so very easily learned, madame, the names of my Scottish – antecedents (is that a correct word? I have never used it before) a Secretary of the Embassy who is fond of the sport in Scotland said that he knew a member of that family. I met him. That was Mr Harry Ramsay, then by chance in London.'

'We do not,' said the Countess in a terrible voice, 'mention that name in this house.'

'So I understand, and so he understands. He told me further who I was, who my mother had been, who her mother had been. He was very kind to me, and patient with my ignorance. I learned about my grandmother, madame.' He drew a deep breath. 'It is you. I am Jules Delibes. I am the surviving son of your daughter, of Miladi Isobel.'

A long silence, of utter astonishment, greeted this announcement. Jules Delibes stood looking with grave friendliness at his grandmother, still hiding a terror he probably had no reason any longer to feel.

The silence was broken by Miss Carmichael, who said, in a tiny voice, 'Mercy.'

The Countess said, 'Can this be proved?'

'Of course,' said Jules Delibes.

'Yes, of course. Impudent hacks record the births, marriages and deaths of people like us. Very useful it is, too. I shall want to hear about Isobel's life in France. Latterly I regretted that we . . . So I have a grandson. I had two others, who died . . . I did not know I had a third. Son of Delibes. What of Delibes?'

'My father? Dead, madame.'

'Another orphan. I am beset with them.'

They stared at one another, the pale and ancient lady, the pale and exquisite young man. He took a nervous step towards the Bath-chair. She extended her arms, wide, towards him. He knelt by the Bath-chair, and they embraced.

I caught Miss Carmichael's astonished eye. She made a mittened gesture, which I understood. We tiptoed away together.

'A miracle!' cried Miss Carmichael, when we were out of earshot. 'A visitation from heaven!'

'Not really,' I said, having recovered from my amazement enough to think about it. 'Lady Isobel was still young when she eloped with Pierre Delibes. She was divorced. She married him. Why should they not have a child? And of course he was brought up to speak English as well as French. And of course he wanted to know who he was. And of course, as soon as he knew who Lady Isobel had been, it was easy to find out. And when he had found out, of course he came here. There is only one part of the story that I find strange.'

'I see the sense of what you say, dear, but still I find it *all* most strange.'

'The strange part is that Harry was kind. I didn't think Harry was capable of being kind to anyone.'

'That is not charitable, dear, or just. You scarcely know Mr Harry as an adult.'

'Well enough. Too well.' A thought struck me, that brought mixed feelings. 'This,' I said, 'will put an end to those plans about me.'

'Mercy, so it will!' said Miss Carmichael. Then, voicing my own thoughts, she said, 'That cuts both ways for you, dear. You are spared the *unseemly* position into which her Ladyship placed you . . .'

'But I lose Strathgallant. Well, I never wanted it, you know, on those terms.'

But as I raised my eyes, and stared at the soaring well-loved towers and battlements of the castle, basking like a hound in the

138

summer sunshine: as I looked across the broad glen of the Gallant, and at the big hills beyond, I felt a sense of most painful loss.

I, the penniless waif, had come to think of it as mine. I was well served for this greedy presumption.

The Countess had other ideas.

Jules was taken away by a footman, to be shown a bedroom and to change into more fitting clothes. With her hand-bell, the Countess summoned Miss Carmichael and me to the parasol.

She said, 'That delightful boy is my grandson. It gives me a very peculiar sensation, to have a descendant after all. But he is half French, and a bastard.'

'No!' I said.

'Yes, child. The law may recognize divorce, but the Church does not. I do not.' She made her own refusal more important than the Church's. In this instance, it was. 'Isobel lived and died the wife of that feckless ninny Sir Robert McLarty. Obviously she should not have married him, but, since she did so, she was his wife. Good God, the words of the marriage service are perfectly explicit on the point.'

'Till death us do part,' I quoted.

'That, as I take it, means what it says, and it is part of a sacrament. I repeat that this boy is a frog-eating bastard. Which does not mean I do not like him. I find I am prepared to like him very well. He is amazingly ignorant. I suppose he can be taught.'

'We must hope so, Great-Aunt Selina,' I said, 'since he will inherit –'

'Inherit, fiddlesticks. Can you imagine a silk-hatted snail-eater lord of all I survey? The idea is preposterous. He's a bastard. Are we to difference the arms with the badge of Isobel's folly? However . . . However . . .'

'Yes, ma'am?'

'I suppose the ties of blood oblige me to admit him, as it were in a probationary capacity, to the ranks of your suitors, Perdita. I will go that far for him. Is that agreeable to you? Don't answer – it makes not the smallest difference.'

'Harry sent a substitute indeed,' I said.

'Did not he? Were Harry not unforgivable, I would almost

incline to forgive him.'

Jules Delibes reappeared on the terrace in clothes even more astonishing, in their way, than his long silk coat and his tall silk hat. He was dressed exactly as though he had lived, all his life, the life of Strathgallant. He was dressed very much as Jamie and Colin were dressed. It occurred to me that he had seen them, and modelled his *ensemble* on theirs. But he had not. Neither was by. Colin was far away on some sporting expedition; Jamie was no one knew where. Jules Delibes had out of his own wit or instinct dressed for an occasion and a place utterly remote from anything he had ever known.

His garments were no less startling for being humdrum. He wore a light worsted jacket, of a kind of Lovat colour, cotton drill trousers of a pale brown, shiny brown shoes, and a soft shirt with a silk tie. He carried a straw hat, with a broad brim, own brother to that which Colin wore when he was fishing in such weather. All that was foreign about his was the pallor of his skin and the blue-black sheen of his hair, which seemed in the sunshine iridescent like a hoodie-crow's wing.

That, something in his voice, something in his bow. They were slightly foreign, too.

There was unmistakable Ramsay in his face, as I had thought when I had thought he was Alexander. Colin and Jamie, though so different in so many ways, were recognisably kinsmen; Jules Delibes, though so different from both, was recognisably their kinsman. This proved the truth of a story which was already unarguably true.

'Now you look like a gentleman on holiday, instead of a mute at a funeral,' said the Countess.

What she herself looked like it would be difficult to say, with her aquiline chalk-white face – paler even than his – and her huge, moth-eaten red wig. I thought it would be impossible to imagine two human creatures more different: but they, too, were recognisably kin.

I supposed Jules had taken after his mother. But this was only supposition. I had no idea what she had looked like. All pictures of her had been banished from Strathgallant, at the time she disgraced herself and her name.

140

'How did you know,' I blurted out, 'that those were the clothes to wear?'

He turned to me, smiling. 'They have your approval, Miss Sinclair? They are correct?'

'What an extraordinary thing to say, Perdita,' said the Countess. 'Are there no limits to your impertinent curiosity?'

'I am afraid not, ma'am,' I said.

'Nor to mine. I am glad you asked that question, because I was asking myself the same question, and wondering how best to voice it. How *did* you know, Jules, that those are exactly the clothes a gentleman wears in Scotland in hot weather?'

'I received instructions,' said Jules cheerfully, seeming unabashed at the way we were bullying him.

'Good God,' said the Countess. 'From whom?'

'From my cousin. Your great-nephew, madame. Harry Ramsay.'

'How that damned name keeps jumping up at me. Harry has been kinder to you than he has to me, boy.'

'He has been very kind to me, yes.'

'He has not been very kind to me, no. He has been a mannerless toad. We will not spoil a joyous afternoon by discussion of my least favoured topic. Now tell me about your father. *He* was my least favoured topic, but now I am anxious for information. My curiosity is as unbridled as Perdita's. He lived in Paris?'

'He continued at the Quai d'Orsay, until ill-health compelled his early retirement.'

'Retirement did not save him?'

'It would have done, I think. He was killed by a fall from his horse in the Bois.'

'Clumsy of him.'

'My mother forbade me to ride, after that accident.'

'Another one of those. We should put that right.'

'Oh yes.'

'You want to ride?'

'Very much.'

'Do you think you can? Do you think he can, Perdita? He doesn't look strong enough to walk.'

Jules laughed. It was the first time I had heard him laugh. It was a delightful laugh, somewhere between Jamie's infectious light laugh and Colin's infectious deep laugh, though quite different from either, and with something in it of the Countess's high childlike laugh.

It was another laugh to make you want to laugh. So I laughed, though really I could see nothing to laugh at.

He said, 'I do not look big and strong, but I am very sure I can climb to the top of that tree.'

He pointed at an enormous elm in the park, the nearest big tree to the terrace. I knew he could not climb it. I had tried and failed (and been beaten for trying) at a time when I believed myself tree-climbing champion of Perthshire.

'You can't possibly,' I said.

'We bet, Miss Sinclair?'

'Bet?' said the Countess, with a certain eagerness. She had brought into our age the passion for gambling of the age when she was young. Then she recollected herself. 'I forbid such suicidal folly. I do not consent to acquire a grandson, only to lose him, all between luncheon and tea. You hear me, Jules? ... All the same, what would you have bet?'

'If I won, a riding lesson from Miss Sinclair.'

'Ha. You are a quick beginner. As one has always heard of the French ... And if you lost?'

'I would not have lost,' he said, with a calm certainty that was unnervingly reminiscent of Jamie's.

Mrs Ramsay and Aunt Marianne approached us across the terrace. They had heard from Mrs McQueen that a stranger had arrived. that Harry Ramsay's insulting substitute had arrived.

'You come in a good hour, my dears,' said the Countess.

I saw in her amber eye a gleam of the purest mischief. She was about to astonish them. She liked astonishing people.

'Allow me to present you, boy,' she said, 'to two of your female connections. Since you have studied the reference-books, you will appreciate the relationships when I identify the ladies.'

'I hope so,' said Jules, dubiously, but with calm good humour.

'On the left, the smaller lady, clad as I think she imagines they appear at musical evenings in Vienna, is my daughter-in-law the Viscountess Kilmaha.'

Jules made his bow to Aunt Marianne. It was quite a foreign

142

bow again, deep, rather eighteenth century; I imagined it being taught in a Parisian dancing class.

Aunt Marianne looked at him with an expression of utter blankness.

'On the right, the larger lady,' went on the Countess cheerfully, 'is Mrs Ramsay, widow of my nephew George.'

Jules bowed, having half turned to his right. There was on his face a droll hint of baffled panic. I thought he was desperately trying to fit the Countess's nephew George into what he could visualise of the family tree of the Ramsays.

The blankness on Mrs Ramsay's face matched that on Aunt Marianne's. They looked supremely ridiculous, standing side by side in front of the Countess's Bath-chair, goggling at Jules. I did what I should not have done. I burst out laughing.

The Countess glanced at me. I could not swear that she winked. But she came very, very close to it.

She went on briskly, 'This curious little person, my dears, who keeps bobbing up and down like a mechanical doll, is a discovery I am cautiously prepared to welcome. Your nephew by marriage, Marianne. Your first cousin, once removed, by marriage, Lucinda. In a word, my grandson.'

An almost endless silence was punctuated only by a sniff from Miss Carmichael.

'Impossible,' boomed Mrs Ramsay finally.

'Not even improbable,' said the Countess. 'Isobel was only twenty-one when she ran off to France. She did not take the veil. She merely adventured on the wrong side of the blanket. This peculiar boy may be an impostor, but he says he can prove he is Isobel's son.'

'Of course he is dear Isobel's son,' said Aunt Marianne. 'One can see the likeness.'

'That, Marianne,' said the Countess, 'is the first intelligent and perceptive remark I have heard you make in twenty-five years.'

'And of course I expected Jules to come here one day,' said Aunt Marianne.

'How do you know his name, Aunt Marianne?' I asked. For it came to me that it had not been mentioned since their arrival.

She looked at me vaguely. 'But, of course, Isobel wrote to me,' she said.

'What?' shouted the Countess. 'You carried on a correspondence with the outcast?'

'Yes, ma'am,' said Aunt Marianne. 'I thought it dreadful that ... I thought we should not all ... She and I had been close ... She wanted news of the family.'

'Well, I'm damned,' said the Countess. 'Treachery, under my very nose. I daresay you did right, Marianne. So you knew Jules existed. Why did you not tell me?'

'A decree,' said Aunt Marianne, with one of her large artistic gestures. 'We were none of us to mention ...'

'I was beaten for mentioning Lady Isobel,' I said.

Jules glanced at me, startled. I smiled at him, and he smiled back.

To Jules, Aunt Marianne said, '*Je vous avoue mes sentiments les plus gentils.*'

He bowed. He looked even more startled. I guessed Aunt Marianne's French accent was a little peculiar, her dreams of foreign travel never having been realised.

'Your Grandson, ma'am,' said Mrs Ramsay, giving the word an exceptionally large capital letter. She stared at Jules as though he might either bite, or peel off his clothes and perform an immodest dance.

'I shall know better how to react, when I have recovered from my own astonishment,' said the Countess. 'That will be, I hope, by the hour of dinner, provided I am vouchsafed an hour of sleep in the meantime. Carmichael!'

She rang her brazen hand-bell. Poor Miss Carmichael, who was standing immediately by the arm of the Bath-chair, nearly jumped out of her fiddle-case shoes. She stumped round to the back of the chair, to push the Countess indoors.

'Allow me,' said Jules.

He bowed to Miss Carmichael (he really was rather like a mechanical doll) and himself took the handles of the chair.

'A grandson's privilege?' said the Countess. 'An imagined duty? A courtesy? Or are you simply trying to curry favour?'

'Simply that, *grand-mère*,' said Jules.

'Prudent of you, boy. I commend your good sense. Start as you mean to go on. Curry favour assiduously, and perhaps you will receive a reward.'

In the early evening, Jules was presented to the upper servants, in a stately ceremony which would have terrified me, if I had been Jules. But he was calm and friendly, and shook hands with them all. He greeted Mrs McQueen as an old acquaintance because they had travelled together a few miles in the victoria.

The Countess had hoped to astonish the servants, as she had astonished Mrs Ramsay. But they were not in the least astonished, because they already knew all about Jules. I did not know how, for no maids or footmen had been by when we heard the revelations on the terrace. But castles have ears and servants tongues, and I was sure that, by dinner time, all the farms and crofts and villages would know that a grandson had invaded Strathgallant.

The Countess was much angered at the absence of astonishment.

They were not amazed to learn news which they already knew; but they did look at Jules with undisguised and avid curiosity. That was natural. I had done so myself, as soon as I knew who he was. There was also – on the part not of all the servants but of some of them – a restraint, a frigidity, a stone-faced refusal to respond to his friendliness. For a moment I was shocked and surprised at this: until I remembered the Covenanting conscience, the Wee Free morality. By their way of it, Jules was the bastard of a scandalous runaway who had betrayed them all. He was the embodiment of sin and Satan. I thought this would make problems for him.

As it happened, both Colin and Jamie returned late from their separate expeditions, only just in time to change for dinner, and so did not meet their relative until we were in the dining room.

It was curious, to see the three of them together. They were poles apart, each from the other: yet they were unmistakably kinsmen. They varied in degree in all sorts of ways – they were at different points on various scales: Jamie's hair was buttercup yellow, Colin's light brown, Jules' blue-black; Colin's face was weather-beaten to mahogany (even the pale chin-strap stripe was disappearing), Jamie's had become a sort of warm brown

145

brick, from his weeks in the sun, Jules' was still ivory pale; Colin was enormous, Jamie of medium size, Jules slight and slim; Colin was exuberantly sunny and cheerful (except sometimes, when I was by), Jules smiling and pleasant, Jamie grave (except sometimes, when only I was by).

There were gaps in my knowledge, developing this thought as I watched them together in the dining room, as we awaited the Countess before taking our seats.

I knew Jamie and Colin to be serious professionals in their widely different spheres. Jules was too young to be any such thing: but where was he bound? He was probably not rich, as his father had been only a Ministry official, and his mother disinherited.

Again: Jamie was clever, Colin not intellectual but certainly able: where stood Jules?

Again: Colin was a hero, Jamie had (it was impossible to blink the fact) a streak of physical timidity: where stood Jules?

Again: Colin was a pioneer and a countryman, a man of hillsides and campfires, Jamie, scholar and student, a man of streets and houses and libraries: where stood Jules?

Of course, neither Colin nor Jamie could have guessed that Jules existed (though in logic they might, like the rest of us, have done so) and they were staggered when Aunt Marianne made them known to one another.

Under his mother's eye, Jamie greeted Jules with solemnity, shaking hands as though with a foreign ambassador, making a little speech as though to a public meeting.

There was nothing wrong with his speech. It was the fact that he made one that was wrong. I knew why he did it: but I thought Jules might be surprised.

Jules's evening clothes were better than Jamie's, and as good, to my eye, even as Colin's. I supposed London or Paris tailors were better than those of Edinburgh. If Jamie had eye enough to realise the difference, it would not make him love Jules the better.

Nor would I make him do so. Jamie glanced from Jules to me and back again, his face impassive after the necessary smile of greeting. I thought there was a set to his jaw and a grimness to his mouth. I thought I could read his thoughts: will this little

146

Frenchman presume to try to take what is mine?

Colin was boisterous in his welcome to Jules: shaking his hand, he seemed like to throw him about the dining room, as Benjie Craufurd would have thrown a rag doll from his jaws. He had Jules laughing in a moment: but his own laughter died when he caught my eye.

I wished again that Colin would go away, and wondered again why he did not.

In the first days after his arrival, Colin had been the centre of attention at the dinner table, in that it was to him that the Countess talked. (Then, of course, there was an interval of glumness.) That night, it was Jules. The fun was not uproarious. He was not a licensed buffoon, as Colin had been. Although he was master of the language, Jules was in a strange world. He was not shy, nor visibly nervous, but he was modest and self-deprecating. This allowed Mrs Ramsay a chance to speak – the dialogue of Colin and the Countess had almost silenced her – and she questioned Jules magisterially about his Aims and Ideals.

'My ambition? It is to marry a rich wife and live happily ever after,' said Jules.

For a moment Mrs Ramsay took him seriously.

At ten o'clock the Countess trumpeted to Miss Carmichael to wheel her away to bed. That made it my bed-time, also. And Jules said that, as he was tired after his journey, it was his bed-time.

We went out together from the drawing-room into the hall, in the vociferous wake of the Bath-chair.

I had been wearing about my bare shoulders a little knitted shawl of fine wool; it was dark red, a gift from Aunt Marianne, useful to me for the first time now that I was fashionably half naked. As we crossed the hall, I chanced to be carrying it in my hand.

Jules said softly, 'Miss Perdita, may I borrow your – scarf, should I call it?'

'My shawl?' I said. 'Yes, of course, but why?'

'You will see. I shall not hurt it. Please.'

'Have you a toothache? Or ear-ache? Or stomach-ache? Or a

sore throat? Or a hole in your eiderdown? What in the world can you want with a shawl?'

'It is to do,' he said, 'with a wager.'

I was up early in the morning (as I was always supposed to be, and sometimes was, and sometimes not) and I strolled out onto the terrace, my mind full of the strange events of the day before.

I thought about Jules, naturally. I thought that he was friendly, polite, gently amusing: and that he was altogether too frail and exquisite and urban for life in Scotland, for life at Strathgallant. He was not so very much bigger than myself, and was not in the way of being one half so active. Even more than Jamie, he seemed to me a creature of heated drawing-rooms, soft chairs, elegant interiors; his nearest contact with wild nature would have been with ferns in a conservatory. His smile was charming and his laughter infectious: but I agreed with the Countess: he had best not try riding.

It was a pity. He and I were of an age to be companions, without the unnerving tempests aroused by Colin and Jamie. If he seemed older than I, it was only because of the assurance of his manners and the excellence of his clothes. It was a pity that he was no companion for me, but it was so. The things I did every day would break him in half.

I felt a little impatient, a little contemptuous, that a boy of my age should be a hot-house flower, visibly incapable of all the things that Strathgallant offered.

And then I raised my eyes, to the gigantic elm tree nearest the terrace. Something fluttered, very near the topmost twigs. A great red bird. An enormous, impossible red blossom.

A knitted woollen shawl.

7

I caught him on the way to the breakfast room. He saw from my face that I had seen my shawl. He grinned. It was not a smile, it was a little boy's triumphant grin.

I whispered urgently, (for we were near the open door of the breakfast room, and I could hear the rattle of cutlery in chafing dishes) '*How*, Jules? It's impossible! I tried once. I was beaten ... *When?*'

'I have won?'

'Of course you have won.'

'Then you pay? I have my riding lesson?'

'Of course you do!'

He took my hand and kissed it. He was young to do such a thing. He did it very nicely. I wondered how many times he had done it before. Paris had a reputation. Jules bore out the reputation. At the same time, he, not I, was the champion tree climber of Perthshire.

Holding my hand, he said softly, '*Chère instructrice.*'

I looked at him suspiciously. I was not sure what he was calling me, and I was not sure what he was laughing at.

'Dear teacher,' he translated.

We were both laughing when we went together into the breakfast room.

I did not like the look in Jamie's eye. I did not see the look in Colin's eye.

A Scottish country breakfast was a series of mysteries to Jules, which he inspected with something like alarm – porridge, fishcakes, warm baps, kidneys, cutlets, all in silver dishes over spirit-lamps on the sideboard; cold meat, cold bird, devilled bones on another sideboard; toast, marmalade, a honeycomb, a

149

dozen preserves from the still-room on the table. He surveyed all this, shrugged, and turned to me helplessly.

'You must start with porridge,' I told him.

'Porridge,' he repeated nervously, digging a tentative spoon into the greyish stodge in the dish.

'With salt, not sugar,' I said. 'And when you eat it, you must stand up, with your back to the fireplace.'

He looked at me as though I was mad.

I explained, 'The reason is that otherwise your enemy might stab you, which he would easily do, because salty porridge is so delicious that you would be engrossed in eating it, and not see him creeping up behind you.'

'But I have no enemy,' wailed Jules, wanting to sit down and eat food he recognized.

Glancing at Jamie's face, I was not so sure.

Jules had brought with him riding-breeches and boots, made in London. All that was wrong with them was that they were so very new. In other ways they were exactly right. Harry Ramsay had taken him to tailor and boot-maker, and advised him in everything. Jules said again how grateful he was to Harry. I supposed the tradesmen gave Harry a commission.

Dressed for riding, Jules looked better than Jamie would have looked, because Jamie would have worn reach-me-downs from Hamish Ogilvy's store-cupboard.

A boy who could climb that elm tree would not be afraid of any horse.

As he walked to the stables, Jules told me he had climbed the tree in the dawn. He did not want to be seen, but he wanted to be able to see. The only difficulty was, that the flimsy loose stitches of the shawl kept catching in snags and twigs.

I had been as wrong about him as I had been about Jamie, and almost as wrong as I had been about Colin. I despaired of my judgement. I thought that, whatever I first felt about anyone, I must conclude that the truth was the exact opposite.

'I have been called a monkey,' I said – remembering, with a sort of pang and a sort of guilt, Jamie's first words of love to me. 'But you are a better monkey than I am.'

Jules did an imitation of a monkey, there and then in the driveway, jumping and snarling and scratching under his

150

armpit.

Alasdair Lawson, most morose of grooms, came out of the stable-yard arch at that moment, and stood staring at Jules with an expression of shocked amazement. I was already laughing. I laughed louder. Jules did not all at once see Alasdair. When he did, he recovered himself, and tried to be dignified and adult, and blushed furiously.

He was dressed up like a gentleman about to take horse-exercise. He was a funny little boy. I saw in him just the awkward, in-between mixture that I knew in myself.

I had liked Jules, before ever I knew who he was. Now that I knew *what* he was (champion tree-climber, among other things) he began to be one of my favourite people.

Of course, the world from which I chose my favourite people was still a very, very small one. But it was getting gradually bigger, in surprising ways.

I had not had a playmate since I was twelve years old.

Of course Hamish Ogilvy and all the others had known about Jules since tea-time the day before. They inspected him with curiosity but without surprise. There was in some faces a stony Wee Free disapproval.

It was there in Hamish Ogilvy's kindly old face. I remembered that he was an elder in the kirk in Auchinfort, where Charles Edward McKechnie had been baptised.

Hamish took one look at Jules, seemingly so dandified and frail, and called to Euan Gilchrist to fetch out Hannibal. Hannibal was the oldest, slowest, quietest, fattest and smallest pony in all the Strathgallant stables. He was kept for very young and very nervous children. I had had my own very first lesson on Hannibal, thirteen years before, when he was already old. I wondered if Hamish intended a deliberate insult.

I could not interfere. This was Hamish's kingdom. I could not tell him that Jules had climbed the elm tree.

Hannibal was saddled and bridled, and led out to the paddock beside the stable-yard.

Of course it was not I who was to give the Countess's grandson his first riding lesson. Whatever he felt about French fops and bastards, Hamish Ogilvy himself must do so.

He began to do so, teaching Jules how to sit and grip and hold the reins. I sat watching on the rail of the paddock. I was anxious to ride myself, but more anxious to see how Jules got on.

Jules was immediately graceful and convincing in the saddle, although, small as he was, he was ridiculously big for the little pony. He walked, stopping and starting and turning. He trotted, understanding immediately the rhythm of rising to the trot. I did not think anyone had been made to trot, so soon after first starting to ride.

Presently I said nervously to Hamish, 'I think Mr Jules would get on better with a bigger pony.'

'Ay,' said Hamish grudgingly.

And Jules was put up on a dainty Galloway, which I sometimes rode when I could not have Mameluke.

Jules himself was concentrating, working at learning, trying to understand everything that Hamish said (which cannot have been easy). He was a young boy again – not the prancing monkey of the drive-way, but a serious, ambitious little boy, deeply anxious to do well, to please his master.

And he did so.

'Yon,' said Hamish Ogilvy, 'waur a remairkable exhibee-shun. Ay canna believe Muster Jools hae no' crossit a nag in his leef.'

Dismounting stiffly, Jules was grinning from ear to ear.

We arranged that he should have another lesson, the very next morning.

'Before that,' said Jules, 'I will get your scarf back.'

'Shawl. No, don't! I don't need it. I have a dozen shawls. You must not climb that tree again, Jules.'

'Somebody will see it up there. It is red.'

'It blew there. The wind took it.'

'I do not want to seem afraid.'

'I know you are not afraid. You do not need to prove it twice. I am afraid, not you.'

'You know I am not afraid, Dita? You promise that?'

'Yes, of course I do.'

'Then I have no need to climb the tree.'

'None.'

'None. But, to tell you the truth . . .'

152

'Yes, please do that.'

'I am a little glad I need not climb again. The branches at the top are – flexible, you know.'

I said, 'Jules, you were a little afraid, but still you were going to climb the tree again, to prove that you were *not* afraid . . . Of course, that is much braver than if you were truly not afraid.'

'When you say that, almost you make me climb the tree again.'

'Please do not. It won't make me like you any better.'

He thought about this for a moment. Then he smiled.

He said, 'Will you take me fishing?'

'Yes. This afternoon. What a good idea. Have you ever been fishing?'

'I have lived in Paris all my life.'

'I was given some beautiful flies the other day, which I have not used . . .'

Jamie wanted me to go for one of those walks, with Benjie Craufurd, which had been so magical. I was not sure now what power that magic had. I was less and less sure of anything, except that I was sure I wanted to go fishing with Jules.

'He is only a boy,' I said to Jamie after luncheon. 'He has never done anything like that. He has lived in a city all his life. You must see that I have a kind of duty to – play with him, if you like.'

'Keep your games within limits, dearest Dita,' said Jamie gently. 'And remember your other duty.'

'You will not let me forget it.'

'No, I will not.'

Our fishing expedition was a ludicrous failure and a glorious success.

We went up from the Falls of Ellarich, up the Ellarich Water from the Gallant, and reached the chain of little pools where, in the right conditions, speckled trout came greedily to the fly. The conditions were not right. The water was too low and clear, the sun too high and bright, and the wind gusting in the least convenient direction.

I tried to demonstrate to Jules, and first caught my cast of flies in a tussock of heather behind, and then had a puff of wind blow all in a tangle on my head. At last I got my line out against the wind, and fished the pool down. I turned triumphantly to Jules.

There was no smile on his face. He was frowning, concentrating, learning. He had on the intent face that he had worn when he was learning to ride, five hours before.

Before he tried to cast, he examined all the tackle, and questioned me about it – the ten-foot greenheart rod, the brass winch at the butt, the undressed silk line, the casting-line of silkworm gut, the three flies from Jaikie McKechnie – tail and two droppers – whipped onto single strands from the tail of a Connemara pony.

Of course, his first cast landed in a bird's-nest at his feet, his second in a tangle behind him, and the third impaled all the flies in the worsted of his coat.

His fourth went out like an arrow.

I was so excited that I fell in. Five minutes later, he fell in.

I left a cast of Jaikie's flies on a sunken snag. Jules left a cast of flies on a weedy rock.

I cut my hand on a sliver of broken stone, so that it bled. He slipped and fell, and cut his chin so that it bled.

He lost a boot, and retrieved it full of water. I lost a boot, and retrieved it full of mud.

We did not see or touch a fish.

His pallor was lost in a first flush of sun-burn, and in a copious smearing of mud.

I never enjoyed an afternoon's fishing more.

We trudged home, squelching and exhausted.

Jules said that he now had two ambitions – to marry his rich wife and life happily ever after, and to catch a trout.

'My McLarty grandson and you played together as babies,' said the Countess to me, when we were both on our way to change for dinner. 'I suppose he loved you, if one revolting baby has the capacity to love another revolting baby. Our dearest Rupert certainly loved you, although he was a grown man and you a grubby little chit in the schoolroom. And now Jules. Are you insatiable? Are you determined to enslave all my grandsons?'

'Jules wants to learn about things,' I explained. 'I am free to help him, because I have nothing else to do.'

'That is not all Jules wants. Of course you could not see yourself, when you came back this afternoon.'

'I must have looked like a tattiebogle, ma'am. My hat fell off, and the wind got in my hair. Also I think some mud found its way to my face . . .'

'I do not know whether Jules adores you because of the mud on your face, or in spite of the mud on your face. He certainly adores you.'

'But he is a child!'

'A child of distinct maturity, in some regards. I suppose that is the effect of Paris. Indians, you know, get married when they are six years old. I am not sure what is implied by the word "marriage", in such a case. We must ask Colin. I am not suggesting that Paris is quite like India. I daresay it could be described as half way between India and ourselves. In which case, Jules should consider being married immediately. Which is what, judging by the look on his face this afternoon, he has in mind. At least, I hope marriage is what he has in mind. From what one hears of Frenchmen . . . I hear he acquitted himself creditably in the saddle this morning.'

'Yes, he did indeed, and with the fly-rod this afternoon.'

'And in the top of the elm tree.'

Miss Carmichael, wheeling the Bath-chair, bleated with dismay. Of course we spoke freely in front of her, and always had, because she was always there. This might have been a kind of compliment, or a kind of insult.

'Don't let him do that again, Perdita,' said the Countess. 'I am growing fond of the boy. Look after him.'

'I will try, Great-Aunt Selina.'

It was when I came down again for dinner, unusually early, in the 'old-rose' dress the others had been kind about, that I heard unexpected sounds from the music room. Somebody was playing the piano. I did not think it was Aunt Marianne. It was not the kind of music she played. It was a simple air, played simply but delicately (Aunt Marianne thumped). A voice rose, a pleasing light baritone. It sang in French. It was Jules. I could not understand many of the words, but I thought it was a street

155

song, a simple ballad about the pretty girls of Paris.

I crept into the music room, and waited until the song was done. I clapped. Jules spun round on the piano-stool. When he saw me, he blushed as he had blushed when Alasdair watched him being a monkey.

'That is good,' I said. 'I like that very much.'

'I thought I was alone,' he said, blushing almost painfully. 'I thought nobody was yet downstairs for dinner.'

'But why should you not want people to hear?'

'I am –' he groped for a word – 'self-conscious. Bashful, you know.'

'There is no need here. Aunt Marianne isn't bashful.'

'Ah, but she is serious. She would despise a little song of the cafés. She likes only very important and serious music. Cousin Lucinda Ramsay also. They have told me so.'

'Don't you?'

'Yes,' he said, 'I do, very much. My father loved music and taught me to love it. But I do not try to play Beethoven or to sing Schubert.'

'Why not?'

'Because one should do only what one can do.'

'But that is wrong, Jules! You should try to do what you *can't* do. Even what I can't do. Like climbing the elm tree ... You know your grandmother knows you climbed it?'

'Yes. I told her.'

'*You* told her?'

'She asked me, you know. She saw the scarf – shawl.'

'You could have said that the wind ... You could have lied.'

'Not to her. And not to you.'

Jules said he was stiff and sore the following day. Still he obediently ate his salty porridge, standing up with his back to the fireplace. He was working hard at being a Scotsman.

Colin had already left, on one of his distant expeditions. I was glad. It was more difficult to meet him in the cheerful, informal atmosphere of breakfast, than in the stiffer dressed-up evening.

Jamie looked gravely at my riding-habit. He began to talk to Jules about French politics. He knew much more about them than Jules did. Jules knew which ministers were linked by gossip

156

to actresses and dancers, and what was being performed at the Opéra, and what was expected to win the big trotting-race at Chantilly. I thought the things Jules knew were more interesting than the things Jamie knew.

It was funny to see that boy, beautifully dressed in London riding clothes, eating his porridge like an ancient laird, talking about Parisian scandals and trotting-races.

In the stable-yard there was a slightly different atmosphere. Of course, there was no longer curiosity, because they knew what Jules looked like. It seemed to me there was no longer so much shocked and granite disapproval. Hamish Ogilvy beamed when we walked in through the stable arch. All my life he had beamed at me: but the day before he had not beamed at Jules.

Three horses were already saddled and waiting in the yard – Sycamore the Galloway, my own dear Mameluke, and the cob that Hamish rode. We were to go out together. Hamish was giving another morning to Jules. The countenance he showed him was full of cautious goodwill. Jules's scandalous origins were not forgotten, but they were put in their proper place, in the background of Hamish's attitude. Jules had dissolved some of the granite – not by playing the piano and singing, not by climbing trees, not by imitating a monkey, or having a charming smile – but simply by showing an aptitude for riding.

Alasdair Lawson stood holding Sycamore and Mameluke. He looked even glummer than usual. I thought his Calvinistic conscience was not mollified so easily as Hamish Ogilvy's. Then, glancing back as we rode out of the stable yard, I saw his face. It wore an expression of the purest envy. He wanted to come with us, instead of Hamish.

Hamish let Jules canter. He said that in a week he would be galloping, and in a fortnight jumping.

It was noticeable that Jules was learning not only to understand riding, but also to understand Hamish. The Scottish speech that had been so difficult for him the day before, was becoming easy. He even used some of Hamish's own phrases back to him.

It was as well, because he asked the old man a thousand

questions, as we rode slowly home to let our horses get cool. He asked about horses and ponies, saddles and bridles, feeding and schooling; he asked how stables were best built, and what iron was used for horseshoes. He was like a sponge, soaking up everything.

When we walked back from the stable-yard to the castle, Jules questioned me as earnestly as he had questioned Hamish. He asked me about Hamish and the other grooms. He wanted to know where they lived, what families they had, how much they were paid and how much given instead of pay, what books they read and what God they worshipped, what their children were taught, and what happened to them when they were too old to work. To some of his questions, about Hamish as about horses, I had known the answers all my life. Some I had never thought even to ask.

I wondered for a moment why he wanted to become expert in the private lives of grooms. I thought there was no reason. He saw them, an unfamiliar race; he liked them; they interested him; he wanted to know all about them. He was like a child, pelting us with questions. But they were not childish questions.

After luncheon, I found myself alone with Jules and Jamie.

Jules wanted to go fishing. He asked Jamie to come too. I did not know if he wanted to ask him, but it would have been odd if he had not.

Jamie would not go fishing. He did not care for it. He did not like taking any life. He had given up all sports of that kind.

'Then you should not eat any meat or bird or fish,' I said. 'They have all all been killed.'

'That is absurd, Dita.'

'No, it is logical. Colin told me there are people in India who walk about with muslin over their faces, in case they breathe in a gnat and accidentally kill it.'

'You should not eat a potato,' said Jules. 'That has been killed.'

'They scream when they are boiled,' I said. 'Only the sound is too high to hear.'

Jamie smiled. He did not think he was illogical.

Jamie wanted to go for a walk, with me. I expected him to ask Jules. Jules expected it, too. But Jamie did not ask him.

He said, 'You have had Dita for all of yesterday and half of today, Jules. You must agree that it is my turn.'

I said, 'I am not a cake, to be shared round between you.'

To me, softly, Jamie said, 'I have not been sharing you, dearest girl. I have been lending you.'

Part of me liked this. Part of me liked being owned. Part resented it.

Jules was a child of my own age – younger than myself, though Paris had made him seem older. If he adored me as the Countess said he did, it was as a playmate and a teacher.

Feeling as he did, Jamie had perhaps a right to claim a sort of ownership. I could not forget that I had made promises to match his promises, when he was the only man I knew.

I did not want Jamie angry with me, and I did not want him angry with Jules. Jamie belonged at Strathgallant. Jules was still precarious. He was still on probation. He was still, to his grandmother, a foreigner and a bastard. Jules needed all the goodwill he could secure. I thought Jamie's goodwill was important to him. So, for this reason and for some other reasons, I told Jules he must amuse himself.

He went away forlornly. He was a little boy again, kept out of the games of bigger children.

I said to Jamie, 'He will tell the others that you and I are together.'

'Are you ashamed of that?' said Jamie, smiling.

'No, of course not, but your mother . . .'

'Is reconciled to the idea that you exist, that courtesy obliges me to pay some attention to you while I am a guest in this place.'

He did pay attention to me: he paid too much attention to me.

He sent Benjie Craufurd away to chase the plovers on the hill. Then he knelt beside me, on a hill-top, and kissed me with a sort of violence. It was exciting, and I felt a jumping of my heart and a strange new sick yearning in the pit of my stomach. His hands brushed against my breasts under the thin cotton coat I wore, and seemed to waken them to a tingling life of their own. The tingle carried to my fingertips and to secret parts of me to which such sensation was new and lovely and frightening.

Jamie was beautiful. There was no doubt of that. If he was a rock, he was most pleasantly formed and covered. Sunburn

159

suited his face, and gave a new depth and brilliance to his grey eyes. His buttercup hair was even paler and brighter for its bleaching in the sun. His face was strong and gentle and classically symmetrical. Half drowning in his kisses, dizzy with excitement, full of new and strange sensations, I forgot all doubts. I forgot all other faces and voices. I forgot myself and, to be truthful, I forgot him – I was adrift on a tide of emotion and excitement and I wanted it to go on for ever.

I wanted it to stop at once.

Not content with embracing me as I sat and he knelt, he bore me over backwards until I was lying on the springy grass, and pinned me so with the weight of his own body. That was frightening but still exciting. He kissed me more roughly, and he hurt my lip on his tooth. The pain was not truly severe, but it woke me up from the sweet and treacherous delirium of those kisses. I tried to struggle away from him. He held me fast in his arms and under his weight. I twisted my face away from his and struggled with my arms and legs. I shouted at him to let me go, when my mouth escaped from his. He was oblivious, demented. Twisting one arm free, I put my hand to the back of his head. I took a handful of his hair and pulled it with all my might.

He gave a bark of pain and astonishment. He sat up suddenly. His face was crimson, his hair wild, his tie under one ear. He was panting as though he had run a mile. He looked at me, blinking, as though I had just woken him up out of a dream of paradise.

I put my finger on my lip where he had hurt it. It came away with a little drop of blood on the fingertip. It was a very little drop. Mutely I showed it to Jamie. An expression of horror and contrition filled his face. He lowered his head into my lap, as though to hide his face from me, as though in shame, as though for comfort. I found that my fingers were stroking his hair. Somewhere in the tangles of his thick yellow hair disappeared the drop of blood on my fingertip.

'The miserable Jules,' said the Countess over the teacups, 'has been drawing on the terrace all afternoon, with a scratching of his pencil on the paper which nearly drove us demented. And now he will not show us the result.'

'You would not like it, Grandmère,' said Jules, with an

anxious expression.

'How do you know, cloth-head, until I have seen it? Do not presume to make my artistic judgements for me. Marianne does it, but fortunately I never listen to anything she says, even on the rare occasions when I can understand her. What have you done to your mouth, Perdita? Your lip appears swollen. Has a bee stung it? It rather suits you. You should visit the beehives every other day, and induce a single bee to sting you on the lower lip. Of course, it may be difficult to direct the creature to that particular place, and to limit the number of stings to one. That is a problem you must solve for yourself as best you can.'

Jamie's face, turned away from the Countess, was a mask of misery.

A footman came in with a large, square, flat object. I recognized it as an artist's block, a sort of book of heavy white drawing paper, for I had been taught to draw and paint, like every young lady talented and untalented, and had ruined many such blocks with my scrawls and daubs. The footman handed it to the Countess, who thanked him with one of her quick smiles.

Jules recognized it, too. He reached urgently towards it.

'Please!' he said.

'Stuff,' said the Countess. 'You cannot draw under my roof, or even under my sky, and withhold the results from me. I have some rights here. They include sending a servant to your bedroom to fetch whatever of yours I wish to inspect. Carmichael, where are my spectacles? There is a tortoiseshell pair through which I look at drawings. The effort is usually wasted. No, Jules, you may not grab it from my lap. I hope, when my spectacles are found by sapskull here, that I am not to be subjected to obscenity or modernity.'

'Oh yes,' said Jules, in despair, 'it is very obscene. Very modern. You would *not* like to look at it.'

I was by this time highly curious about Jules's drawing. He was so very anxious to keep it hidden. I did not think this was purely modesty, like his secret playing and singing. He had been drawing on the terrace, instead of going fishing. I could not imagine that the view from the terrace, even if he did not draw very well, could seriously anger the Countess. I thought probably he did draw well. He seemed to do everything well.

161

The others were curious, too. Aunt Marianne and Mrs Ramsay rose and went round behind the Bath-chair, while Miss Carmichael hunted for the Countess's spectacles. I joined them. Jamie alone sat like a dead man, and Jules danced about in an agony of self-consciousness.

The Countess would not uncover the drawing until she herself could see it.

The spectacles were found, on the Countess's lap, under the drawing-block. She put them on her nose, with maddening slowness. She folded back the cover of the block.

Jules ran out of the room.

There was a long, long silence while we all looked at the drawing.

'Good God,' said the Countess.

It was an elaborate drawing, done with great delicacy.

In the background were the towers of Strathgallant, perfectly recognizable although distorted so that they seemed illimitably gaunt and high.

In the foreground was a Bath-chair, also perfectly recognizable, also distorted so that it somehow resembled a perambulator in which a very rich baby might be wheeled about.

Pushing the Bath-chair was a rabbit. The rabbit wore a black bonnet and a black shawl and woolly mittens. It had long rabbit ears and rabbit whiskers, yet it was Miss Violet Carmichael. I did not understand how Miss Carmichael's little sharp nose could be a rabbit's nose, but it was so.

There was a drip at the end of the rabbit's nose. She had a drooping, defeated posture, and a browbeaten expression.

In the Bath-chair sat an eagle in a huge red wig. The red of the wig was the only colour Jules had used. It flamed out of the delicate grey pencilling. The eagle was unmistakably an eagle, and it was unmistakably the Countess. In one claw she held a lorgnette, through which she glared.

Looking closely, you could see moths flying in and out of the wig.

The rest of us looked at each, aghast, as the Countess stared at the drawing. Since I was behind her, I could not see her face. It was not difficult to imagine. I understood why Jules had run out of the room. I wondered how many days it would be, before he

162

dared come in again.

The Countess spoke at last. 'A fair likeness of Carmichael,' she said.

A spell was broken. The rest of us felt bold enough to comment.

'I have never admired caricature,' said Mrs Ramsay.

'The towers are out of drawing,' said Aunt Marianne, with her head on one side. 'Intentional, perhaps. El Greco, you know . . . A facile pencil . . .'

'I like Miss Carmichael's whiskers,' I said.

'What a clever boy that is,' said the Countess. 'I shall have this framed. He shall draw the rest of you. You as what, Marianne? Some kind of bird? A broody hen? Lucinda as a cow, with twin calves. Colin as an elephant. A star-crossed elephant, an elephant with a broken heart. Jules's self-portrait? An organ-grinder's monkey, himself playing the organ. And you, Perdita? A humming-bird, with a bee-stung lip, and a somewhat disordered crest. Harry he shall do from memory, as a verminous baboon of unclean habits. We shall have the set framed, by those bandits in Perth, and hang them with their faces to the wall.'

As we walked to the stables next morning, Jules said to me, 'Do I seem very young to you, Dita?'

'Sometimes,' I said. 'Sometimes not.'

'Do I seem younger than you are?'

'That is a complicated question, because sometimes I seem so young to myself. But sometimes not.'

'I understand. My mother, you know, always said that I was old for my age.'

'Oh yes. We have said the same, talking about you. Your grandmother says it is the effect of living in Paris.'

'Maybe that is right,' he said seriously. 'But in Scotland I have grown up suddenly. That is how it feels to me. I have grown up by five years in three days. I am old.'

'Not all the time, Jules.'

'Not all the time, and not in all ways. I know *that*. But in one very important way.'

'Oh,' I said, knowing what he was talking about.

'Is it ridiculous? Am I a little fool?'

'No.'

I do not know how that conversation would have developed because, as we reached that interesting point in it, we also reached the stable-yard, and Hamish Ogilvy was there in the archway waiting for us.

Alasdair Lawson was holding my Mameluke, who was already saddled and bridled. Some distance away across the yard stood a man holding Sycamore and the cob. I thought this an odd arrangement, if it was an arrangement. Hamish and Jules crossed the yard to their horses. Hamish was talking earnestly to Jules in a low voice.

It came to me, that the position of the horses *was* an arrangement. It allowed Hamish to say something to Jules which I was not to hear. I was puzzled by this. I did not think either had secrets from me. I did not like it. I did not like the idea of a conspiracy involving either of them, of which I was not part.

This jealousy of a little secret was, perhaps, more childish than any of Jules's childishnesses.

Hamish said that Jules should see the riverbank. He said that the ride to Achnacarron was the most beautiful, and would give me the chance of a gallop and Jules the chance of a long canter in a safe place. I had seen Harry Ramsay at Achnacarron. But he must be long gone. He would not stay at Duninveran for more than a few days. It was still amazing and offensive that he had gone there at all.

The shoulder between the arms of the river provided the gallop which Mameluke and I wanted. Benjie Craufurd flew ahead of us. I slowed before the ground descended again, and cantered down on a tight rein. A downhill gallop on a side-saddle is not very safe, if your horse has a way of dropping his head, and if Mameluke had a fault (which, to anyone else, I would not have admitted) it was that he dropped his head when galloping downhill. Benjie Craufurd did not slow his pace. He hurtled on down the slope to the river-bank, and to the Toll-house of Achnacarron. Far behind me, at a steady canter, came Jules and Hamish.

In the distance, before and below me, I saw Benjie run up to the Toll-house, and disappear. He had run in through the open door. I hoped the Erskines liked large, affectionate hounds. I

164

hoped they had left no puddings or joints of meat unattended on a table. I hurried Mameluke on, to avert any possible outrage.

A figure came out of the Toll-house, with Benjie. I was too far away to recognize him. I assumed it was Davie Erskine. He would give me a glass of barley-water, perhaps, or a mug of milk. Evidently he did like large, soft-hearted dogs, for I could see that he was crouching by Benjie Craufurd, petting him and playing with him.

He was still so, his back towards me, when I rode up to the house. Hearing Mameluke's shod feet on the riverside path, he rose and turned.

It was Harry Ramsay.

He was hatless, but otherwise dressed just as I had seen him before. He was certainly a handsome man, in the strong-featured Ramsay way, except that his face was so proud and ill-tempered.

He looked not at me, but beyond me: he looked up the hill to where Hamish and Jules had just appeared over the skyline.

'Have you been here all summer?' I asked suddenly.

'Of course not,' he said, still looking past me at the others. 'I came back yesterday. How do you find my substitute?'

'An improvement on the original,' I said. 'He has good manners.'

He leaned to pat Benjie, with his left hand. I saw the back of his ungloved hand. I saw on it still the mark of my whip. It must have been a far deeper cut than I had realised, to leave such a scar.

'Then my arrangement,' he said, 'should satisfy everyone.'

I expected him to renew his denunciation of what he called the slave auction: of what he called the brothel. My whip was ready, if he should do so. It was not a wooden stick, like the one he had broken. It was woven of thongs of leather, flexible from butt to tip.

But he did not mention the Countess's strategy, or my part in it. He asked after Colin.

'He is still at Strathgallant,' I said. 'But we only see him in the evening.'

'Ah. The passion for sport. His priorities stand so. How wise of him. And Jamie is still there, I suppose? And the Edinburgh Castle?'

165

'Jamie is there. As to the . . .'

I realised, just in time to avoid appearing stupid, that the 'Edinburgh Castle' meant Mrs Ramsay, Lucinda. Entirely against my own wishes, I giggled. I thought the name perfect. I hoped very much that I would not suddenly say it, at Strathgallant, without meaning to, as I had said so many unfortunate things.

I pulled my face together, into a proper sternness. I was not prepared to laugh at Harry's jokes. But I realised that it was not his joke. It could not be. He was too proud and ill-tempered to make jokes. The Countess had said his mother was a clever woman. Probably it was her joke. Well, I would not laugh at her jokes, either, after what Harry told me she had said about the Countess and me.

Jules and Hamish rode up. Jules pulled off his hat and waved it madly at Harry. I glanced at Harry, and saw what I had not seen before – his smile. A broad, warm, cheerful smile. He had no smile for me. That was well. I did not want his smile. But one would have said there was warm affection in his smile for Jules, if one could have supposed him capable of warm affection.

Jules jumped off Sycamore, as though he had been mounting and dismounting all his life, gave his reins to Hamish, and rushed at Harry. I thought they were going to embrace. I thought Jules thought so too, until he remembered that he was not in Paris but in Scotland, where gentlemen are less passionately demonstrative. They shook hands. But that was not quite enough for Jules, who gave Harry little buffets with his other hand, on his chest and shoulder, until Harry, laughing, ordered him to stop it.

His laugh was new to me, too, but it was not new to me. Normally that laugh made me want to laugh.

Harry extricated himself from Jules, and walked over to Hamish. Hamish had dismounted, and had the reins of the two horses over one arm. This left his other hand free to shake Harry's, which he did most heartily.

'I am astounded to see Monsieur Delibes riding so soon and so well,' Harry said.

'Ay! Waur it no' blaasphemous, ye'd ca' it a miracle.'

'The good teacher makes the good pupil, Hamish.'

'The guid scholar flatters the dominie, Muster Harry.'

Harry asked after Hamish's health and his family, and reported the state of his father's injury.

Hamish called over to me, as Harry returned to Jules, 'Wull ye no' dismount, Miss Dita?'

I had thought of doing so; but it would have conveyed that I was acknowledging, and even joining, this reunion by the river. I had no mind to do that. And my weight was not such that Mameluke suffered from my sitting him.

'We shall only be here a minute,' I told Hamish.

I was quite wrong.

Harry wanted to hear every detail of Jules's reception at Strathgallant, and his reaction to the castle and everybody in it. I did not hear all their conversation, as Mameluke was restless. From what I heard, Jules adored his grandmother, and was only terrified of her about one third of the time; his Aunt Marianne Kilmaha and his Cousin Lucinda Ramsay had been unfailingly kind to him; his Cousin Colin also, and with a single exception, his Cousin Jamie.

Harry asked a question I did not hear. Jules replied in a low voice, glancing at me. Harry had asked about me. Jules spoke for a long time, with a wealth of Parisian gestures which accorded oddly with his London riding-clothes.

I wondered what Jules was saying about me, and what Harry was replying. I tried to try not to listen. Unfortunately, I succeeded.

Harry listened to everything Jules said with the closest attention. He smiled often, laughed more than once, and, when he glanced at me, frowned. His heavy brows gave him a frown of great severity.

Was he warning Jules against me, as Mrs Ramsay had warned Jamie against me? It seemed terribly likely, as he was so fond of Jules, and so bitterly contemptuous of myself.

Hamish interrupted my efforts to eavesdrop, by telling me how blithe he was to see Mr Harry. For it seemed that Harry, alone of the boys who had come for those childhood summers, had kept in touch with Hamish and other grooms and keepers and servants, and written at Christmas, and sent gifts to the children.

I found this strange.

I remembered what I had discovered about myself – that my first judgements were wildly wrong. Jamie's gravity, Colin's honesty, Jules's frailty. Had I been equally wrong about Harry? To see his smiling, bantering, affectionate manner to Jules might have led me to suppose that I had: but I remembered also what he had said to me, and the insulting disdain with which he had said it.

I had not been wrong about those words, or that tone.

Jules talked of nothing but Harry all the way home.

I had heard of hero-worship. When the boys were small, during those summers, they had sometimes talked of older boys, great cricketers or athletes, defenders of the undersized against bullies, champions of decency and fair play. Colin had told me that this schoolboy veneration often survived into the army. I had guessed that he was the object of it, although he never said so. I supposed that what I felt for Rupert was a kind of hero-worship. Certainly what Jules felt for Harry smacked of idolatry. It was not silly, except that its object was ill-chosen. It did not seem silly to Hamish. He was too old and too wise to worship anybody except God, but he did not disagree with a word Jules said.

I could not, either. I could not tell Jules that Harry had not been kind to him. It seemed he had. It seemed that he was the most generous of friends, the most delightful of companions, the most amusing of raconteurs, the most expert of advisers.

Still, if he were all these things, he had been offensive to the Countess and cruel to me.

More and more loving Jules myself, I had to be grateful for Harry's kindness to him.

I had to admit to myself that his smile did strange things to his face, and that his laugh, from any other mouth, would have made me laugh. I had to admit that, in spite of myself, he had made me giggle.

I thought that, perhaps, the thing to be regretted was his parents' remarkable perceptiveness. Had Harry had no reason to guess why he was asked to Strathgallant, had he come with the others, knowing no more than the others ... Harry, to Jules, had shown qualities which, if they had been shown to me ... His smile, to Jules, transformed his face into one which, if turned to me ... I had scarred the back of his hand, for saying things which I myself had said ...

I rode home in great confusion of mind, with praises of Harry from Jules and Hamish pouring over my head like spring rain.

I wanted to ask Jules what he had said about me, and what Harry had said about me. It is horrid to know that one has been discussed, and not to know what was said. Of course I had a good idea what Jules might have said about me. The Countess had said that he adored me: and there were those interrupted remarks as we reached the stable yard. And, equally, I must have been very dense not to know what Harry thought about me. If he said it to my face, he would hardly scruple to say it behind my back.

I did not ask. But I would have liked to know if Harry thought me pretty.

I detected this thought inside my head, and examined it with disgust. Why should I care if Harry thought I was a fairy or a frump? (I was very sure I was *not* a frump, in my new green riding-habit.) Was it the purest and most infantile vanity? Did I demand that everybody thought I was pretty? Did I value Harry's opinion? Of course not – it was irrelevant to me. He had scratched himself from the contest which he thought was being held at Strathgallant – which the Countess thought was being held there.

Which Jamie and Jules thought was being held there, although they did not know the prize. Which Jamie was sure he had won. Which Colin had briefly entered, and from which he had been disqualified. What if Harry had joined the contest, from the beginning, all unprejudiced?

Confused speculations churned in my head, while praises of Harry rattled against my eardrums.

We came home to a joyful surprise. At least, I supposed it would be joyful: and it was a thoroughly predictable surprise.

Alexander Ramsay had arrived, coming by train to Glasgow, coach to Lochgrannomhead, and hackney-carriage to Strathgallant. He was reunited with his mother and his twin. They had gone off together, to have their reunion in private.

'Filial outpourings, I collect,' said the Countess. (Nobody

else I ever heard of used the word 'collect' like that. I think she retained those ancient usages quite deliberately.) 'Maternal outpourings. They are considerate to remove themselves. We should be quite sickened, I daresay. Lucinda will be enquiring solicitously about Alexander's bowels, and he will be faithfully reporting. He is a very handsome boy, Perdita, as you may possibly remember.'

'He was beautiful,' I said, remembering clearly. 'He was gentle.'

'He was and remains his mother's ewe-lamb to an unseemly and unhealthy extent.'

'More so than Jamie?'

'How the devil should I know? I am not privy, thank God, to the niceties of Lucinda's emotions. It is amazing that she has emotions, don't you think? She looks incapable of human weakness. I should not be talking to you like this, child, encouraging satirical disrespect for your elders. But I must speak my mind to somebody, or I should lose my sanity and be carried off to bedlam. You have the wit to interpret my remarks. Fancy being limited to Carmichael as a confidante. She has not the wit to interpret a laundry list, have you, booby?'

'No, ma'am,' said Miss Violet Carmichael humbly.

'All these years, I have missed coming here terribly,' said Alex. 'And you are the chief reason, Dita.'

I thought this an excellent beginning.

Yes, he was a very handsome boy. Yes, he was beautiful and gentle.

In height he was small-to-middle, between Jules and Jamie. The colour of his hair was ashy-golden, between Jamie and Colin. His eyes were flecked, hazel, brown and green, and so between Harry and the Countess. His face was bonier than Jamie's, gentler than Harry's, stronger than Jules's, more delicate than Colin's. He had the broad, sweet family smile.

In manner it seemed to me, at luncheon on the day of his arrival, that he had something of Jamie's gravity when he spoke to his mother or Aunt Marianne: something of Colin's happy buffoonery when he spoke to the Countess: something of Jules's shy sprightliness when he spoke to me: and something of Harry's pride when he was not speaking to anybody.

170

He had been offered a Fellowship at Magdalen College, in Oxford. He was the cleverest of them all, a scholar, an academic. His mother was full of it. Well, it was something to boast of. She boasted of it. He did not. He said that he wanted to go fishing again in the hill burns, and ride, and climb, and forget all about Medieval Europe (that was what he knew about). He said he needed a guide, an instructor, a companion. He said he had been living too long in the soft South, that he had forgotten the lore of the hills, that he had forgotten even how to tie a fly to a line, that he had been breathing lamp-oil instead of Highland air. He said the guide must be myself.

'Show it all to me again, Dita!' he said. 'Unless you're busy?'

It seemed to me that his eyes were beaming with admiration. It is very pleasant, when you are an ignorant seventeen-year-old, to be openly admired by a beautiful young gentleman, by the brilliant Fellow of an Oxford College.

'Where shall we start?' I said. 'Fishing?'

Fishing it was to be. I could do no less, could I?

Jules's face showed that he wanted to come too. I could not see Jamie's face. I thought Alex might want me to himself, this very first afternoon, and I thought that would be fair, after all that lamp-oil. But Alex glanced at Jules's face, and saw the little-boy longing to come fishing.

'You'll come too, old fellow?' said Alex to Jules, 'and wet a fly in the Ellarich water?'

'I may?' said Jules, his eagerness showing through his diffidence.

'Of course you may! How about you, Jamie? Can you take a break from the bogs and bohreens?'

I saw a struggle in Jamie's face. He said he would not come, that four was too many for a fishing party. He did not like killing fish. He decided to lend me to his brother and to Jules.

I supposed he would not fear rivalry from his own brother. He was not in a position, perhaps, to realise how attractive that brother was. He had not seen, perhaps, the look in that brother's eyes. Jules was a schoolboy. Colin was far away, not to return until evening. Nothing threatened Jamie, except his own roughness. And I had forgiven him for that, although he had not forgiven himself.

8

Yes, I was a flirt. I had only been one for a very short time. I excuse myself on many grounds, such as youth, and inexperience, and five years of solitude, which together made me greedy for excitement and admiration: and on the grounds that I could not tell what my feelings were, until I had felt them.

I sometimes had the notion that I was conducting a series of experiments. Some of them had blown up in my face. One had cut my lip.

Alex soaked up what he had once known, as Jules was soaking up what he had never known. As soon as he saw the pools high in the Ellarich Water, he remembered where the big trout lay. As soon as he had silkworm-gut in his hands, his fingers remembered the knots. There was nothing I could teach him. There was much that he could teach Jules. He seemed to take pleasure in doing so. I found this admirable, and endearing. It was what had gone some way to redeeming Harry. Alex needed no redeeming.

Jules bent his whole attention on fishing. Alex divided his attention between fishing and me.

'Dita, you are the most beautiful girl I have ever seen,' he said, when Jules was a little way off and out of earshot. 'I suppose Jamie and Colin and young Jules have said that. Harry too, I am told he has been hereabouts.'

'Harry has *not* said that,' I said.

'I wonder why not. Ha!'

The 'Ha!' was because he had hooked a fish. It ran madly about the pool, and the slim rod bent double in Alex's hand.

'Tomorrow,' said Alex, even as he played the trout, 'I shall ask you to marry me.'

172

'But that is ridiculous. You do not know me.'

'I have known you all your life, beautiful goose.'

'Oh. That is true.'

He began to draw the fish, now tiring, towards the bank. He beached it, grabbed it, and knocked it on the head with the little club called the 'priest'.

He looked up the bank to where I stood. Smiling, he said, 'I would ask you today, but I think that would be a mistake.'

There was such love in his smile and in his eyes, that I sat down suddenly on the bank. He looked adorable, crouched by the waterside, smiling up at me. He looked extraordinarily unlike a scholar, a Fellow of Oxford, a learned historian. It was extraordinary that he should be what he was and look as he looked and speak as he spoke.

'Why a mistake?' I blurted out.

'Because today you might feel obliged to say "no". Tomorrow you will say "yes".'

The certainty in his voice reminded me of Jamie. Well, they were twins. It made me uneasy. This was a dreadful situation. It was exciting and flattering, and Alex was beautiful and brilliant, but they were brothers. Twins.

Twins indeed. 'Tomorrow you will say "yes".' The rock showed: the steel girder that he had for a backbone.

Into my head, quite wildly, came a memory from the schoolroom. My governess told me that the ancient Greeks (or perhaps somebody else) posed the question: what happens when an irresistible force meets an immovable object? The point of the question was that it was unanswerable, because a world which contained a truly irresistible force could not also contain a truly immovable object, and the other way about. But it seemed to me that Strathgallant provided an exception. I was frightened.

I had brought this upon myself. I had been shockingly forward with Jamie, and I had certainly flirted with Alex. We were rushing upon a collision. I could see no end to it. I could not tell how I felt.

'I have been trained,' said Alex, 'to be wary of certainty. To check and double-check, to scrutinise, to take cross-bearings. I have been doing that, from the moment I saw you yesterday, and fell instantly and totally in love with you. I have watched you and listened to you, and heard about you, to find if there was any fault in you, body or soul. There is none. You are beautiful with the beauty of an angel of heaven and an imp of the pit. You are kind and brave and honest. I have examined my own feelings. I am very sure that I cannot live without you. Have you heard of the scientific method? You formulate an hypothesis, and then subject that hypothesis to all the evidence you can collect, and all the criticism you can devise. If the hypothesis stands fast, you can begin to trust its truth. I felt so elated, so transformed, when I saw you yesterday, that I concluded that I had fallen in love with you. I expected to, after all. I remembered you as a child, and adored the memory. Ever since that moment yesterday, I have subjected my conclusion to the most rigorous tests. My pedantic habit of mind wanted me to be sure, before I said anything to you. I am sure. My certainty has grown and strengthened. I can make you happy, darling Dita. We are two of a kind. The stones of Oxford will be a miraculous background for your beauty. You will shine there like a stained-glass window. You will meet people not unworthy of your attention, and they will fall down in rows to worship you. And the terms are short, you know. One is only there half the year. We shall travel. We shall come to Scotland, to the wild high places which suit you so well. Good God, I am lecturing you as though you were a hall full of undergraduates. My heart is so full that it overflows in this excess of words. At least you know I mean them. You can see that I mean them. This is not my proposal, darling girl. That comes tomorrow. Don't answer now. How strange you look. This cannot have come as a surprise. I am sure my feelings must have shown in my face. They always do, unfortunately. Look, Jules is into a fish. Shall I help him land it, or leave it to him?'

'Help him,' I said, in a funny squeaky voice.

'Yes, it would be a shame, if he lost his very first trout.'

The birds cried on the hillside. The water gurgled through the rocks at the tail of the pool. In the sky a buzzard hung like a crucifix.

I sat, feeling suffocated. There was no doubting the passionate sincerity of Alex's words. He had spoken lightly, gently. But he was talking about his life's happiness, and mine. Mine? I could not tell.

As though from another planet I heard Alex and Jules laughing excitedly: and as though at an illimitable distance I saw them beach the trout.

Another schoolroom memory jumped absurdly into my head. The ancient Romans (or perhaps somebody else) had punished certain criminals by tying ropes to their arms and legs, and the other ends of the ropes to the collars of horses, and then whipped the horses away in different directions, so that the victim was pulled apart.

I felt like one of those criminals.

I put on a merry face, and congratulated Jules on his fish. It was a beauty, not large, but deep, and brilliantly spotted. He had caught it on one of Jaikie McKechnie's flies.

I said, 'But it is sad, Jules, that you have already achieved one of your lifetime's ambitions, when you are still so young. You have that much less to live for. Still, there is the other.'

'I have lost the other,' said Jules, giving me a glance of curious brilliance.

'The rich wife?'

'Yes, I have lost that ambition. The wife I want is not rich.'

'That's a curious coincidence, old fellow,' said Alex. 'The wife I want is not rich either.'

They glanced at each other, expressionless. They understood each other perfectly.

I did not know how deep these feelings ran, how long they would last. I did not know how much the romances were to be believed.

I went away down the hill, calling for Benjie Craufurd.

When we reached home, Jules hurried in to change, because he had got uncomfortably wet. I put Benjie in his kennel, and Alex with me.

He said softly, 'During my interminable lecture, I said I was wary of uncertainty. But this has a consequence. When I am certain, I am doubly certain – an hundred-fold.'

'I do not think,' I said shakily, 'you can really be so sure so soon.'

'Oh yes, Dita. I can be sure so soon, although I should not have spoken so soon. But I came late to this race, you know, and I thought I had better make up for all the time I have lost. I have been wildly impatient to come here, but I could not, until the Fellows of Madgalen had made up their ancient, collective mind.'

'Race?'

'I have seen Jamie's face, and Colin's, and Jules's. I wish I did not like them all so much. I wish I did not feel so close to them. But I do, though I have not seen Colin for years, and only met Jules just before luncheon yesterday.'

Then he began to speak of Oxford – the snake's-head fritillaries by the river in the spring, the languid summer of boating and cricket matches, the misty autumn, with big yellow leaves from the plane trees flapping in front of ancient grey buildings . . . He spoke of it with love, and he spoke to me with love, and he said I should keep a hunter at livery, and follow the Bicester hounds . . .

There had been a sort of truce, between the Countess and the rest of the world, in the matter of the forthcoming ball. Suddenly the truce ended, and hostilities were declared again. This was the result of things beginning to arrive – cart-loads of champagne, hundreds of little gilt chairs on hire from Perth, crates of candles, bundles of dance-programmes – and my gown.

The dressmaker brought it. I was to try it on, and she was to take it away to finish it.

I was becoming used to the sight of myself in grown-up clothes. But not in such a dress. Not the sight of so much of myself. I would have gulped, but the bodice was so tight I thought I could not, and it was cut so low I thought I dared not.

The Countess insisted on seeing it. This was fair, as she was paying for it.

She inspected it, through the spectacles she deemed suitable.

'What a damned immodest confection,' she said at last. 'It will serve you right if you're ravished, brat, flaunting yourself like that. It leaves almost as little to the imagination as the dresses we wore when I was young. They *were* dashing. You bread-and-butter misses of today wouldn't dare to wear them. A wisp of muslin above, clinging silk below. Nobody wore corsets. What a woman had she showed. We were not prudes, I can tell you. It was disgusting, really. Not everyone could wear

176

those modes, though everyone had to try. It is a pity you were not young then, child. But of course, if you had been, you would not be young now, and that would be a pity too. Has Alexander proposed to you?'

'No, ma'am,' I said, relying on the letter of the truth.

'Whyever not? I told you they'd all fall in love with you. I wonder which one you'll take? I will not try to influence you, beyond saying that I wish you'd choose my old Colin. Lucinda Ramsay seems reconciled to the idea that one of her damned jewels may get you, or you him, as she'd put it. Of the two I'd pick Alex, I think. Less of a stick. Rides and shoots and goes fishing, like a gentleman. I don't know about Oxford. As full of sticks as a faggot-pile, no doubt. Unhealthy place, they tell me, full of creeping fogs. Everybody sneezes all the time. Of course Edinburgh's worse. You'll be sneezing too, you shameless little minx, unless you cover up that bosom you're displaying. Dear God, how I envy you. I would sell my soul, like Faust, to be young and beautiful again. But then I should fall in love, as I so often did, and men would fall in love with me, as they so often did, and it was all a great struggle and confusion ... There is something to be said for growing old. Not much, but something ...'

I came upon Alex looking as though he had been kicked in the stomach. His face was grey and his voice jerky.

'I have been talking to my brother,' he said.

'Oh,' I said, feeling suddenly a little sick. The collision had occurred.

Which was the irresistible force? Which was the immovable object?

'Am I to unsay what I said? Although every word was true. You know that every word was true, Dita.'

'Yes, I know.'

'Why did you not tell me? Why did you not silence me? Do you want a row of trophies on your wall?'

'I do not want anyone to be hurt, Alex!'

'No, I cannot believe you do. But this morning, when we climbed the hill, you were not like – someone already promised, someone already in love. I spoke as I spoke because you were –'

'Flirting,' I said, in shame.

'Responsive, let us say.'

'I do not know if I am promised. I do not know if I am in love.'

'Jamie says you are both.'

'This is all too new to me, Alex! I am a beginner!'

'And I. Oh Lord, Dita, you will have to choose not only between all of us, but amongst the whole of the rest of the world as well. Men of brilliant address and great fortune. I am an obscure little man, miserably paid, studying the fourteenth century. Am I to go away from here? If I stay, is it simply to have my heart broken?'

'I do not know,' I said wretchedly. 'Truly, I do not know.'

He gave a smile, which did not sit easy.

'As long as you do not know,' he said, 'I will stay. Will you promise me one thing?'

'If I can. Yes, of course, gladly.'

'If my case is hopeless, will you tell me?'

'Oh, Alex, yes, but I don't know when I shall know or whether I shall know.'

'I understand that. Don't send me away before you must. But don't keep me dangling on a false hope – a hope you know to be false.'

'No.'

'What am I to tell Jamie?'

'I don't know. I am frightened to tell Jamie that I – that everything was premature, that it came too suddenly at me, that I am not sure –'

'You are right to be frightened of Jamie. You are right to be careful what you say to him.'

'Are *you* frightened of him? Your own twin?'

'Yes, of course. I have always been a little frightened of him. He is sometimes frightened of things, you know, but never of people. I am not as a rule frightened of things like waves or heights or horses, but I am sometimes frightened of people. Of Jamie. He always gets what he wants. All during our childhood, and ever since, he has taken anything of mine he really wanted, anything of anybody's. He will be Prime Minister, you know.'

'Yes, I know.'

'He will be a very good one, one of the very greatest. But he will leave a lot of bodies behind, on his way to the top.'

'It is unheard of,' said the Countess. 'It is inconsiderate. It is distinctly embarrassing. People should know better. A number of arrangements will have to be reconsidered. The expense, already immoderate, will become crippling. It is lucky that I am very rich today. I shall not be rich next week.'

I looked at Miss Violet Carmichael, for an interpretation of this baffling outburst.

'Numbers,' said Miss Carmichael, in a frightened voice.

'Numbers,' repeated the Countess, with gloomy relish. 'We have been examining our lists. We have been comparing the list of those to whom invitations were sent, with the lists of those who have accepted or rejected. Practically every single person has accepted. We are entertaining far too many people. The castle will burst. Any person endeavouring to picture the collapse of the walls of Jericho, may learn next week exactly how that catastrophe appeared, from observation of Strathgallant. We have about a third as many available bed-chambers, as we have people desirous of inhabiting them. In my day one could calculate on a reasonable proportion of refusals, and make one's arrangements accordingly. People knew how to behave. Half the cards of invitation were intended simply for display, by the socially vainglorious, on some mantelpiece; they were not serious summonses. People have forgotten that rule, or chosen to ignore it. It is monstrous that there are so few refusals. Our neighbours will have to house more, many more, than they have so far undertaken to shelter. Carmichael! Have we heard from the Dracos and so forth? Are there replies to our shrieks for help? From Ravenburn? Strathlarrig? Carnmore?'

There were. All these great houses would be stuffed to the doors with our guests.

'We have brought this upon ourselves, of course,' said the Countess. 'They are all coming out of curiosity. The very few people who have seen me over the last few years have reported, no doubt widely and in the most scurrilous terms, that the chatelaine of this establishment is a grotesque, a freak, a comic monster, a sideshow at the circus worthy any man's sixpence. Reports have also doubtless circulated that this chit for whom

179

the whole extravaganza is arranged is the most beautiful girl in Scotland, albeit gnomish and of uncertain morals and behaviour.'

'How have they circulated, ma'am?' I asked, startled but distinctly pleased.

'Four young men are staying here,' she said, 'none either blind or illiterate. They have been writing letters. James alone has written a ridiculous number of letters, to prove if proof were needed what a diligent stick he is. Colin has written a good hatful to prove, I suppose, that he can write, which might otherwise be a matter of doubt. They would scarcely forbear to remark, when describing their circumstances here, that the place is frequented by a child of not displeasing aspect, as well as a gallery of freaks like Marianne and Carmichael here. Then again, no one under a certain age has ever set foot in this house. It is not without celebrity. It is famous in Scottish history, for the number of treacherous murders committed here, by guests of their hosts and by hosts of their guests. It is mentioned in fulsome terms in all the guide-books. We shall have not guests but tourists. Shall we charge them, for the privilege of making a conducted tour of the public rooms? Half-a-crown to view her Ladyship's spare wigs. A shilling to look at the Viscountess Kilmaha's water-colour paintings. A penny for the peep-show, Miss Sinclair half naked in her ball-gown. It will not pay for the champagne but it will help. Carmichael! What the devil did we decide about the furniture? To work, muttonhead! You had better keep out of our way, Perdita, or Carmichael will flatten you under our thundering wheels.'

The confusion of the next few days was frightful, not because there was any real difficulty, but because the Countess changed her mind so often.

Wives came in by the cart-load, from the villages and farms and crofts, to help with extemporising extra bedrooms, and scrubbing remote, unfrequented parts of the castle.

The cotillion of furniture recommenced, the Countess blaring commands in the midst of tidal-waves of chairs.

Hamish Ogilvy had to provide stabling for untold numbers of visiting horses, and Mrs McQueen for dozens of visiting ladies'-maids.

My dress came back complete from the dressmaker. I tried it on. I adored it. I thought that if I put on one ounce of weight, I would burst the bodice, and if I lost one ounce, it would fall off me.

The Countess's new dress arrived also. She would not let anyone see it. She had decided against ordering a new wig.

The weather remained fine. We prayed for a dry night.

A letter arrived for the Countess, totally unexpected, from Harry.

Mr Henry Ramsay thanked the Countess of Strathgallant for her gracious invitation to the ball celebrating the eighteenth birthday of Miss Perdita Sinclair, and had great pleasure in giving himself the honour of accepting it.

Mr Ramsay hoped that the Countess's earlier invitation to him, to stay at the castle, was still open. If so, he would have great pleasure in accepting that also. He quite understood, however, that his earlier oversight might have made it impossible for the Countess to continue to extend that invitation, the castle being already full, in which case he would contrive to lay his head somewhere nearby.

'There is a sort of apology there,' I said, 'especially if you read between the lines.'

'Fiddlesticks. Not so much as a damned whiff of apology,' said the Countess. '"Oversight" indeed! Not a mention of cursed verminous insolence. Showing his snivelling face practically in my garden. Sending a damned substitute.'

'But you like the damned substitute.'

'Perdita! How dare you use such language to my face? You shall wash your mouth out with soap and water. Carbolic soap. Salt water. You are disgustingly spoiled and pert. All this has gone to your head. It was probably a mistake to give you this party. It has given you delusions of grandeur which sicken me. I hope Harry does come. It will give me very great pleasure to have him removed bodily and with some violence. What a pity there is no water in the moat.'

I supposed Harry had decided to come to the ball to see how

Jules got on. Perhaps also to see his cousins, Colin and Jamie and Alex. Certainly he was not coming for the right reasons, to enjoy himself and to celebrate with me. It was cool of him to write so, and to brave the Countess's wrath. Perhaps he thought he could hide in the crowd, and evade the Countess's lorgnette. But I did not think he was a man who could easily hide in a crowd.

At any rate he had climbed down a little. Not much. Not enough. But a little.

Cool he might be, but he would get a very hot reception. It would be interesting to see him ejected from the castle. I wondered how many men would be required, and whether he would resist. I hoped the unpleasantness would not spoil my party: but I thought the Countess would make a sort of party of ejecting him, and her glee at having him thrown out would turn the battle into a kind of play.

Hard on the heels of his letter, Harry himself arrived.

He rode into the stable-yard, just as I had come back from a ride with Alex and Jules and Benjie Craufurd. He rode a tall bay horse. He looked very different from when I had seen him at Achnacarron. He wore a smart black coat, a tall hat, buff breeches and a bird's-eye neck-cloth. His boots were as shiny as Colin's.

One thing was the same, as I saw when he pulled off his gloves. There was still a livid mark on the back of his hand.

Another thing was the same – the warmth of his greeting to Jules, and the gladness of Jules's response. To Hamish Ogilvy also, and the other men. And to Alex, whom, however, he had quite recently seen in London. It seemed they had dined together, and talked far into the night. Alex had not mentioned this to me. I was not surprised that they should dine together – they were cousins, they had known one another all their lives – but I was surprised Alex had not mentioned it.

Harry took off his hat to me. I could not read his expression. I inclined my head slightly, in what was meant to be an inordinately dignified gesture. I am, perhaps, the wrong height for inordinate dignity.

Harry asked for Colin.

'Miles away, as usual,' said Alex, 'You never saw such a fellow for covering great distances. You'd think he'd have had

182

enough of forced marches in India. In his place I'd put my feet up while I had the chance.'

'You need things for comfort besides cushions,' said Harry. 'Colin may not have had them. Does anybody know where he went? I must talk to him privately and urgently.'

None of us three knew. Colin had said nothing of his plans at breakfast. None of the grooms knew. Colin had ridden away on Uffiz Khan, saying he expected to be back in the late afternoon.

'I have news for Colin which cannot wait,' said Harry. 'Hamish, is there somewhere I can write a letter?'

'There is a comfortable castle quite near,' said Jules.

'Yes, I'll adventure the dark tower in just a moment,' said Harry. 'But just in case I'm not admitted, I'll write the letter first.'

Of course Hamish had a sort of office where he kept the accounts of the stables – a desk and a stool in the corner of the tack-room.

'All very mysterious,' said Alex. 'Whatever can Harry have to say to Colin that is so secret and so urgent? If it were the War Office, they'd send a message straight here. They know where Colin is. They'd not use Harry as a messenger.'

'It is an intrigue,' said Jules. 'A matter of the heart.'

Alex laughed. 'That is the Parisian interpretation of every mystery.'

'I expect it's about a horse,' I said. 'Colin's trying to buy one. Or he wants to know the odds on an entry at York or Perth or Goodwood.'

'Why wouldn't Harry say so?' asked Alex.

'In case we spoiled the odds, by having a bet too.'

This was most obviously not the explanation. But I did not think that Jules was right, either.

Harry came out into the sunshine of the stable-yard, the sealed note in his hand. He gave it to Hamish, to give to Colin. Hamish, who was in his shirt-sleeves, had no pocket in which to stow the letter without it becoming crumpled. He put it on an up-turned bucket, where it would not be missed or forgotten, with a stone to hold it down.

'If you wait, you will see Colin yourself,' said Jules.

'I can't, unfortunately,' said Harry, 'unless he comes back

within the hour. I must get back to Eredine tonight, with the harvest starting. I shall try to see Great-Aunt Selina. Then I must be away.' He turned to me. 'But I shall be back for your birthday.'

'You will be thrown out,' I said.

He grinned. It was the first time he had smiled directly at me.

'I run that risk, I know,' he said. 'That is why I am going to poke my head into the dragon's cave now. I might take the old lady by surprise, and say what I have to say.'

'If you come with me,' said Jules, 'I think you can perhaps talk to my grandmother.'

'Yes, I expect that's true, but I don't want you to hear what I say.'

'More mysteries,' said Alex.

'Yes. I'm sorry. Not for long, I hope. Now listen for an explosion. If you watch the windows of the castle, you may well see me emerging in a graceful trajectory, before bouncing on the flagstones of the courtyard.'

They walked up to the castle, Jules accompanying Harry to help him, if he could, into the Countess's presence, and Alex out of simple curiosity. I did not blame Alex. I would have joined the audience, too, only I had to put Benjie Craufurd back into his kennel, and this had become a ritual involving prolonged caresses, jumpings, lickings, and whimpering attempts at blackmail, often successful.

It was twenty minutes later that I met Harry, walking alone towards the stables.

I was a little confused. I had not expected to see him alone. What increased my confusion, was that in his proud way he was the handsomest of all the beautiful Ramsays.

Suddenly there was no pride in his face when he said, 'Dita, I beg your forgiveness.'

I stopped dead, and goggled at him.

He was carrying his hat. He towered over me. His eyes were very green in the bright sunlight. His face was as gentle as Alex's, as strong as Jamie's, as weatherbeaten as Colin's, as sensitive as Jules's.

How I did compare them all. It was unavoidable.

He said, 'I did not see Great-Aunt Selina, for whom I specially

184

put on these unsuitable clothes. I was kept from her by a cordon of footmen. I was disappointed but not surprised. I did talk to poor Violet Carmichael. She came out to tell me to go away.'

'Oh,' I said.

I was not certain what terms Harry and I were on. He had been brutally rude to me. I had whipped him. We stood talking, he grave, I goggling.

'That old Carmichael has more intelligence than I ever realised,' said Harry. 'She guessed why I behaved as I did. She guessed that I thought – that I naturally thought – that you were a party to this degrading strategy. She told me about your refusal, and about the coughing fit. Was it a real coughing fit, Dita, or was it a way of forcing you to consent?'

'I wondered myself,' I said. 'I still do.'

'I see that you had to consent. Of course you did. And that you must continue to pretend to consent.'

'Oh – good.'

'Why did you not tell me this?'

'I lost my temper. Afterwards I wished I had told you.'

'You did?' There was sudden eagerness in his voice and in his face.

'Yes, of course. Instead I hit you.'

'I will buy you a new whip.'

'For a birthday present? I wish I could buy you a new hand.'

'No, the mark on this one is a good reminder to me.'

'Do you want to be reminded what a savage I am?'

'I want to be reminded not to judge too quickly, too harshly.'

'You were right,' I said, 'to think as you did, if you thought as you did. No, that is silly. You were right to speak as you did.'

'No, Dita. It was unforgivable. But I wish you would forgive me. The one person who has behaved absolutely rightly is you. You were right to refuse, right to consent, and right to hit me with your whip. I might have known you would do right, from my memory of you as a child. I ought to have known. There should have been no room for doubt in my mind. It was ridiculous – ludicrous – to suppose – what I supposed.'

'You were convinced by your parents.'

'Something of the sort. Yes, I had reason to be convinced. But not reason enough to be convinced of anything so grotesque.

185

Things are in a toil, aren't they? I failed in two of the things I came here to do – seeing Colin, and seeing Great-Aunt Selina. But I leave happier than I have felt for weeks.'

'Happier?' I croaked. For I thought I knew what he meant, and it had a strange effect on me.

He smiled and said, 'Save a dance for me, Dita. I hope we can fit in a waltz, before I am thrown off the top of the keep. Now I must go. I have been using the electric telegraph extensively, but it will not harvest my father's barley.'

As we assembled for dinner, Alex said to Colin, 'May we know what was in that letter?'

'What letter?' said Colin, (avoiding my eye as always). 'I have had a bundle of letters in the last few days. Do you want to know about the salmon fishing in Ireland last month, or the cholera figures in Central India this summer, or the racing results at Calcutta? Much other information, all freely available to the curious.'

'Harry's letter,' said Jules.

'Harry has not written to me. I would hardly expect him to, as I saw him just before I came here.'

'But yes! He wrote to you today!'

Colin looked blankly at Jules. Alex confirmed what Jules said, and mentioned Hamish Ogilvy and the stable bucket.

'Hamish was away to his supper when I got back,' said Colin. 'But yes, I remember an upturned bucket by the tack-room door. And yes, I think there was a stone on the bucket. Letter there was none. It must have blown away.'

'Oh no,' said Jules. 'It was a big stone, like a brick! The letter could not have blown away!'

'Then a horse or a man knocked into the bucket, shifted the stone, and the letter fluttered off.'

Alex nodded. 'Something like that,' he agreed.

'I am too tired and too hungry to worry about it now,' said Colin.

'But it is secret and urgent!' cried Jules. 'Maybe it can still be found. Maybe it has blown into a stable or through a window.'

'I'll have a look in the morning,' said Colin. 'I'll ask Hamish. I can't imagine it can really be so very important. You say Harry has gone back to Eredine? I could write to him, I suppose.'

'You will see him before you get his reply,' said Jules.

'True, young 'un. He can tell me his urgent secret then, if Great-Aunt Selina gives him the chance.'

'If I give whom the chance to do what?' asked the Countess, sailing in at this moment, propelled by Miss Violet Carmichael.

I gave Miss Carmichael a smile of the warmest gratitude, for saying what she did to Harry. I think she did not see my smile, since she was preoccupied with steering the Bath-chair. I could not thank her, then and there, out loud. It was not a matter to be mentioned in front of the Countess.

'Well?' said the Countess to Colin.

'We were wondering, ma'am, how soon you will eject Harry on the night of the ball.'

'Wait and see,' said the Countess rudely. 'What business is it of yours?'

'He is reported to have a message for me,' said Colin, 'and to have written a letter, now gone astray.'

'You are fortunate,' said the Countess. 'Harry's letters to me do not go astray. They are either unwritten, which is sufficiently infuriating, or they arrive, which is more infuriating still.'

I thought Colin would have sent down to the stables immediately after dinner, so that there should be a search for the letter immediately. He said he could not disturb Hamish and the grooms so much, at the end of a hard day. He said he would not go down to search himself. He was tired, and it was dark, and he did not think the contents of the letter could be vital.

There was no trace of the letter in the morning, after the most exhaustive search by a dozen men. Hamish Ogilvy was most upset. He said he should have put the letter in a safer place.

'But then I would not have seen it,' said Colin. 'You did right, Hamish, although it turned out wrong. Never mind. I shall see the writer in a few days.'

An atmosphere of hysteria invaded the castle. The Countess did not herself become hysterical, but she caused hysteria in others. The furniture was finally moved into its positions for the ball, so that hundreds more people than usual could sit down, and hundreds more take supper, and the orchestra could play and the pipers pipe without being kicked, and the dancers could dance without being squashed or maimed. Little gilt chairs invaded all the public rooms like a disease. Dozens of cubby-holes – musty though they had been aired, damp though they had been dried, dark though they were lit – were occupied by temporary beds.

Paddocks were emptied of our own horses, to make room for visiting horses, and the stables were almost cleared. A field was set aside for visiting carriages, and tons of gravel spread in its gateway, in case they were bogged.

Extra servants arrived, to all of whom the Countess took violent exception, on the grounds that they squinted, or walked pigeon-toed, or had damp palms, or suffered from adenoids. She dismissed the lot. Mrs McQueen quietly re-engaged them. She led them away and soothed them. She needed much soothing herself.

I did not see how Miss Carmichael would survive the miles of pushing she had to do, or the abuse that was heaped on her head.

Flowers arrived, in a train of carts half filled with ice – far, far more flowers than a dozen castle gardens could have provided. The Countess took a passionate interest in the disposition and arrangement of all these exotic blossoms. She was assisted by Aunt Marianne and Mrs Ramsay. I thought Aunt Marianne's ideas were unusual and pretty. But of course they may have been quite usual. I had never seen anything like any of this before.

The flowers made both Aunt Marianne and Miss Carmichael sneeze.

No guests, even those staying in the castle, were supposed to arrive before the day of the ball itself, because the castle was in such turmoil. A few did – Lord and Lady Kilchrennan and their son and daughter, Sir Charles and Lady Dalmally, the McHargue of McHargue and his gaunt family – and they regretted it. They were to be seen huddling disconsolately in corners of the terrace, while the Countess at the head of her armies burst to and fro, shouting, and Miss Carmichael panted at the handles of the Bath-chair.

It was then that I at last shed the illusion that the ball was for me. It was for the Countess. Even if there were no ball – even if it were suddenly to be cancelled – she would already have had the time of her life.

The incoming tide began to roll, in earnest, in the early afternoon. Carriages arrived in ones and twos and droves. The Countess saw no one. She was resting. At least, she had put it about that she was going to rest. Aunt Marianne, naturally, acted as hostess in her absence. She was assisted by Mrs Ramsay and, to look after the gentlemen, Colin, because he was the oldest of the great-nephews. Aunt Marianne, from nerves or perhaps from the flowers, came out in angry red blotches on her face. Her voice died, and she lost the piece of paper which allotted the guests to their bed-chambers. Colin skilfully got the men either into the billiard-room or out of doors, so that they were less in the way. Ladies'-maids began to scurry like mice up and down stairs, with ball-gowns, hot irons, curling tongs, needles and thread, and jugs of warm water.

Some lovely girls arrived, all taller than my midget self. Many knew each other, though I knew none. I tried to remember all their names. I tried to take them out onto the terrace, but they were frightened of getting freckles. Some were cheerful and friendly and some coolly on their dignity, and they all shot appraising glances at me. I shot appraising glances at them, too. It is as catching as measles, this shooting of glances.

It came time to dress.

Mary Cochran and I took infinite trouble with my hair, so that it looked, in the end, like *disciplined* seaweed in a soot-bath. I had new silk stockings and silk underthings and slippers. And my gown was my gown, the crinoline far too large to get even through Strathgallant doorways, except that the hoops were made of watch-spring steel. By way of jewellery I had only a set of small garnets, necklace and bracelets, chosen for me from her own store by the Countess.

She had jewels enough, in the personal strong-box in a dungeon, to begaud a female army. 'But a chit turning eighteen,' said she, 'should not be looped about with gems. The effect is vulgar. On me the effect will be vulgar, too. But pleasing, pleasing. You wait and see.'

Perhaps the effect was vulgar. Certainly it was stupefying.

The people who had come out of curiosity to see the Countess, had their money's worth.

She was the first thing I saw, when I came downstairs. She was the most startling thing anybody ever saw. She was being wheeled up and down the great hall by Miss Carmichael, in front of such guests as had arrived, as though on show, as though in a Roman triumph. She wore a new gown of gold brocade, and a shawl of fabulous lace; her best silver wig, and in it a tiara like the coronation crown of some Eastern despot; and a profusion of jewels of all sizes and styles and colours which hurt the eye with their brilliance – earrings, choker, bracelets, armlets, necklaces, pendants, brooches, a cestus of sapphires about her waist, and so many rings on her fingers that I thought her hands must be weighted down so that she could not remove them from her lap.

On her feet, which peeped from time to time beneath the hem of her gown on the footboard of the Bath-chair, were her old carpet-slippers. They looked like furry animals, shy but curious.

There were daubs of rouge upon her cheeks, which made her look like a painted doll in a nightmare; there was powder upon her neck, so thick that she might have been caught in a snow-storm, or been pelted by bags of flour. These things had been allowed when she was young. To her, they were still allowed. To her, anything was allowed.

Not the grotesque paint, not the huge antique wig, not even the carpet-slippers could detract from the strength and magnifi-cence of that old face. She looked like a hag and she looked like an empress.

I do not say that nobody had any eyes for me, or for the other young ladies (some of whom, dressed up, were indeed lovely): but people had to drag their eyes away from the Countess, to look at the rest of us. It was as well, I thought, that I had resigned myself to not being the centre of attention.

We dined in the banqueting hall, the first time it had been used for more than five years. The Countess was taken in by the Duke of Bodmin, one of the few Englishmen present, one of the few not in Highland evening dress. Taking her in, since she was in her Bath-chair, meant walking beside her with his arm awk-wardly in hers, so that he had to stoop. It also exposed his ankles to the wheels of the Bath-chair, wheeled erratically as always by

Miss Carmichael. I was sure that he stifled a yelp.

I sat at dinner between the middle-aged Earl of Clonculty and the very young Marquess of Mull. They were *excellent* company.

The Earl said, 'My wife and daughter took one look at you as you came downstairs, my dear, and both said they'd go into a convent. Different convents, to hide from each other their rage and chagrin. They said they should not have been invited here. They said that at least they should have been warned. They said it is intolerably unfair that they should be subjected to comparison to a creature as beautiful as you.'

The Earl's daughter, Lady Leonora, had been one of the friendlier arrivals. She and I had cast at one another the usual appraising glances. The difference between her and the others was, that it made us both giggle. I liked that family.

The Marquess was not nearly so glib. Also he seemed to be terribly hungry. He stared at me, with his mouth full, with a very satisfactory expression in his eyes.

But both of them turned, quite often, to glance the length of the enormous table at the Countess.

There was a buzz of conversation, and rumbles and squeaks and trills of laughter. Through this cheerful hubbub the Countess's voice blared continuously like a trumpet. Ever and anon she laughed, and the laughter her laughter aroused set the great chandeliers tinkling.

My programme was full.

I was to lead off the first dance with the Duke of Bodmin, then return to the great hall, where a bellowing major-domo would be getting the names of the latecomers wrong. Then: my Number Nine, a country-dance, was promised to Jamie. My Number Eleven, a waltz, to Jules. My Number Thirteen, an eightsome reel, to Alex. I kept Number Fifteen for Harry, because he had asked me to.

Colin had not asked me to dance. He looked magnificent and miserable.

The ball-room, when it filled, was an unbelievable pattern of colour and movement. I had never seen anything like it before. It was glorious! The young girls wore mostly white, with tartan sashes over their white shoulders. The men threw them utterly

191

into the shade, with their garish kilts, velvet doublets of blue and green and yellow and red, with great amber or cairngorm buttons, lace jabots at their necks, sporrans of fox or badger, and checked stockings with a dagger at the garter. The violins crooned and the pipes brayed, turn by turn. And I was in the midst of it all!

I danced an eightsome reel in a set which included Lord Mull, Lady Leonora, Colin, and four laughing and beautiful strangers. There was a moment when I set to Colin and he swung me: and he looked so grand and his smile was so forced that my heart would have gone out to him, if I had let it. The Marquess whooped and capered – he was right to have made a hearty dinner. Leonora was like a happy bird, almost flying. My gown held fast to my body. I was so excited and engrossed that I did not notice, until we finished with our bows and curtseys, that the whole huge floor had emptied, leaving only our set in the midst, with all the rest watching and applauding.

And then the other seven of the set were applauding, and calling messages of goodwill, and I *was* the centre of attention.

I curtseyed to the four points of the compass – to the whole company present. I made no effort to conceal the breadth of my smile, the depth of my gratification. From north and east and south and west came roars of greeting.

It was as though, in becoming eighteen, I had become a heroine – led an army, like Joan of Arc, or rescued a man from drowning. It was quite disproportionate. It was more than I deserved.

So thought the Countess, too.

'That's more than enough of that,' I heard her trumpet-blare. 'Play the reel again. Piper! I know it's your turn to rest and steal my whisky. Have a dram, and play the reel again. Carmichael! Form a set. No – don't stand gawping like ninnies, the rest of you. One exhibition is enough.'

So the sets reformed, and we all danced the eightsome again. But nobody was concentrating. Everybody, with more than half an eye, was watching the Countess.

Propelled by a whimpering Miss Carmichael, the Bath-chair, with the Countess inside it, was dancing an eightsome reel.

She was not prepared to let anyone else be the centre of attention for long.

9

Much of the night is a blur in my memory now. Much was a blur in my eyes then, because I was whirling round the ball-room, on the wings of violins, or borne by the shriek of the pipes.

But some of the night stands out clear and hard as a relief in bronze in slanting sunlight.

The first of these hard pictures is of Jamie. He suggested that we sit out the dance for which he had claimed me. I was half glad to agree, for I was panting with exertion after a foursome reel in which the McHargue of McHargue had thought it right to try to throw me through the ceiling of the ballroom: I felt my cheeks must be crimson, and my hair reverting to undisciplined seaweed. I was half sorry, for I had not imagined that I would so wildly enjoy the swirl and swing of a crowded ballroom. I was half frightened to agree, because I thought I knew what Jamie would say, and I did not know what to reply.

We found a chest of carven oak, in an angle of the hall, out of the thresh of the crowd. Jamie secured for me a glass of lemon-ade, and for himself a glass of champagne.

He did not say what I expected. But, in saying what he did, he made things more difficult for me, instead of easier.

He said, 'I shall not hold you to your promise, Dita. I cannot. I must not. I need you and I love you and I long for you, but I will not coerce you. The choice must be yours. The wish and the will must be yours. You have had a chance to compare us. You must have done so. You have a chance to compare me – us – with the flower of Scotland. It is here tonight. You have seen young Mull following you about wherever you go – not dancing, but watching you dance. You are an exquisite sight when you dance, like a sunbird, like a butterfly. Do you want a Marquess? You can

193

have that one. But I hope you will have me. You know that I adore you. I think you know that, in time, I shall be able to offer you a life of great excitement and importance. Yes, you shall be important, dearest girl, not simply as my wife but as a power for good in your own right. You are clever and lovable and beautiful, and you can have enormous influence. You can help the poor, the sick, the oppressed. God forgive me for being pompous, but I offer you a life of service as well as of gaiety and popularity and happiness. I think you will be the happier for that service. I think it will be a part of our happiness together. Does that mean anything to you, beloved Dita?'

'Yes,' I said, for I could not lie to him.

He was finding better words than he had used for a long time. 'I love you body and soul,' he said.

I was startled by an echo of words Alex had used. They were good words.

'Though I do not hold you bound by the promises you have made to me,' said Jamie, 'I give you notice that I shall never stop wanting you – that I shall never stop trying to win you – that I shall never rest in my – courtship of you.'

I thought he had been going to say 'pursuit'. 'Courtship' was better. He was still choosing well.

I was seeing him in full Highland dress for the first time. He was a startling and impressive figure. His buttercup hair was as smooth as glass, and his face a clear golden-brown.

'I think you have grown up very fast this summer, Dita,' he said unexpectedly. 'And I think you have suffered some growing pains.'

'Yes,' I said. 'There have been some – muddles in my life.'

'It may surprise you to hear that I have grown up, too,' he said.

'Will you never jump like a kangaroo again?'

He laughed, but in a moment he was serious. 'Oh yes,' he said, 'whenever you care for a kangaroo, you shall have my best efforts. Growing up does not exclude kangaroos, or wrestling-matches with your dog. It excludes the – complacent certainty with which I assumed that because I wanted something I should have it. You have taught me, my precious girl, not to take my success for granted. That is what I have grown out of.'

194

I stared at him, trying to read beneath that gravely beautiful golden face, trying to see through the clear grey windows of his eyes. He meant what he said. But I was not quite certain if it was true. If it was true, he had perhaps lost that in himself which was most formidable, most important to his future. He would be easier to live with, but he would not be Prime Minister. But I was not sure it was so. I did not think so much granite could dissolve so quickly.

'An answer, Dita,' he said softly.

He took my hand. Both of us wore white silk gloves, but through the silk I felt the gentle pressure of his fingers.

I looked at him helplessly.

From the ballroom the music stopped, and a hubbub of voices came towards the hall.

I thought my answer was 'no', but . . .

There had been magic between us, that had set my head swimming and my knees trembling. It was not dead. He had conjured it again, by those well chosen words, by the way he looked at me and by the pressure of his fingers on mine.

I opened my mouth to answer him. I did not know what I was going to say.

Jamie, seeing and understanding, said, 'Please God, help me now.'

And at that moment the Marquess of Mull ran up, and reminded me that the next dance was his.

Jamie rose. He could do no other. He looked at me with an expression of such longing, that I could believe that the granite had in truth melted.

He whispered, 'We will talk again, Dita.'

I nodded, still having no words for him, and went away on the irrelevant arm of young Lord Mull.

Followed another prolonged blur, with admiration mute (from the Marquess of Mull) or blurted out, with whirling and laughing, and with at the edge of my mind the picture of Jamie's face as I had last seen it, beseeching, heart-breaking.

I was promised to Jules for a waltz. He said that he could only waltz in the French style, which was quite different from ours, and he would make a horrid exhibition of himself, and so of me too, and I should not be served so on my birthday, and we had best sit the dance out.

So comes the second gem-sharp picture.

Jules was more exquisite even than ever before, in his beautifully-cut London evening dress, a coat that fitted him like a second skin, a starched shirt, a tall collar, blue-black hair that seemed iridescent in the candlelight. A stranger might have supposed him a fop, a milksop, a fragile exotic from a hot-house. It was delightful to know that he was active and adventurous. It was delightful to remember that this perfect little porcelain dandy had shouted with excitement when he caught his first trout: that he was already a bruising horseman: that he was the tree-climbing champion of Perthshire.

It was extraordinary to think that to this mixture, already itself extraordinary, was added an accomplished musician with, as we knew by now, an endless repertoire of charming French ballads.

He reminded me, when we were sitting apart from anybody, of another of his accomplishments. He drew from his breast pocket a piece of card, oblong, some six inches by four. He handed it to me. He half turned away, shyly, when I looked at it.

I gave a cry of pure amazement. It was another of his drawings. It was done in Indian ink, with a pen as fine as a needle. It showed a flower – no blossom found in nature, but a magic flower. The stem was not straight, but curved into the semblance of a woman's body, slender yet with a hint of voluptuousness. It was the stem of a flower, yet it was a very lovely woman's body. Leaves took somehow – while remaining leaves – the appearance of hands. The heart of the blossom itself was me – my face – or, to be more exact, an intensely flattering likeness of my face that made me angelically beautiful. The flower had a laughing angel's head no larger than a halfpenny. Bees hung, on blurred wings, above and about the flower: three bees: undoubted bees, with stings and stripes and feelers to their brows: and one had Colin's face, and one Jamie's, and one Alex's. And by the stem of the flower was a snail, peeping from its whorled and spirally shell, and the snail looked up with an expression of frightened worship of the flower, and the snail was Jules.

'People here say that the French are frogs or snails,' said Jules in a choking voice. 'I did not want to be a frog.'

'You are my favourite snail,' I said. 'I like all snails, but you are my favourite.'

'I like all flowers,' he said, 'but you are my favourite. You are not an orchid in the conservatory. Even now, looking so grand and beautiful that I want to shout, you are a wild flower of the hill, a harebell in the wind.'

'Oh Jules.'

'I am too young. I shall be older. Can you wait a little, Dita? You are not so *very* old. You can wait a little?'

He turned to look me full in the face, and stared at me with a burning intensity that would have been frightening in another man. But he was my playmate. It was not frightening, but moving.

'I know very well that I shall never love anybody else as I love you,' he said. 'I am passionately in love with Soctland, you know, and it is all you. The sky of early morning reflected in still water – that is your eyes. The evening wind tossing the trees by the river – that is your hair. That stag running on the hill – that is your speed, your grace. The sun going down and the moon coming up – that is your beauty . . .'

He paused, and grinned suddenly.

'All that is carefully prepared,' he said. 'There was more, just as good, but I have forgotten it.'

I smiled, but I did not laugh, because in breaking the spell of his words, he had not broken it.

I felt a wave of the warmest affection for this ridiculous, splendid boy. I was sure I should love him until I died. But I was not sure if this love was 'love'.

'They tell me I am a child,' he said, 'though I feel less and less like a child. You cannot make me an answer now, a promise. All I can beg is that you will not make a promise to anyone else, until you have given me time to – to have a right to talk like a man.'

He looked very like a man. His voice was that of a man. His drawing was that of a genius. There was nothing childish in his eye.

I had no difficulty in answering Jules. I thought I would have no difficulty ever, no hesitation ever, in saying anything to Jules, because I felt so comfortable and happy with him. I admired him and trusted him and loved him.

'Dearest Jules,' I said, 'I think you are a man, but a *very* young man, although a *very* clever one to make me look so pretty in your drawing, and although I did make a promise to somebody else, that promise seems to be cancelled, as far as I can tell, and I don't think I shall make it again to him, although it is difficult to be quite certain, and I don't think I shall make any other promises just for the moment, as they seem to lead to nothing but muddles and misery, but you will have to grow as quickly as you can, because although just at the moment I feel I could wait for ever, if it was left to me, I may not be allowed to, you know . . .'

I ran down, like a clockwork toy, but I had said enough for Jules. His face was radiant, and he kissed my hand.

And all the while the swooning music of the waltz was pouring through the castle from the ballroom.

I wondered, fleetingly, if the Bath-chair and the Countess and Miss Carmichael were taking part in the waltz.

My little Jules was so talented in so many directions that I was sure he could be a success in a dozen ways. He could be a musician or an artist or a steeplechase jockey. Anyone who married him would be lucky, not only for that reason, but also because he was loyal and affectionate and funny and enchanting company always. Marriage to him was an enjoyable prospect. Unhappiness would be impossible with him. He was a dear. He was remarkable, gifted, and a dear.

We were sitting close together, on a little sofa in a corner of the great saloon. It was a seat for one fat person, or two very slim people who were fond of each other. We were not quite touching. No one was near. We were unobserved. I had a sudden urge to touch him. But, before I could do so, he must have felt the identical urge, because he stretched out one ungloved hand to my cheek. I took his hand in mine, and pressed it to my cheek.

It was immodest: but not very: because he was so young and we were playmates. I had promised only to make no promises. As I felt then, I meant to keep that promise. It was all I could do. It was all that I needed to do. I was happy to do it. It postponed everything. Whether I should promise more, another time, I could not say, and did not have to say.

So it was harmless and not unmaidenly, to press my play-

198

mate's hand to my cheek.

It would not have looked so, however. It did not look so. It did not look so to the Countess, who chose this moment to sail into the saloon. She whipped out her lorgnette, like a pistol from a holster, and glared at us.

Jules snatched his hand away, and stood up guiltily. I felt myself blushing.

Still the music of the waltz throbbed through air which was heavy with the scent of all those expensive flowers.

'Guttersnipe and slut,' blared the Countess. 'Pantry-boy and scullery-maid. I have a good mind to send you both to bed.'

'Jules has done another drawing,' I said, hoping it might divert her.

'I shall not inspect the scrawl of a precocious alley-cat,' she trumpeted: but, at the same moment, she stretched out a hand for the drawing.

After a prolonged inspection of the card, she said, 'You have given Alexander the longest sting, Jules. Do you think you have that right? If I, Perdita, had had a drawing like this one done of me, I would have kissed the artist. Perhaps you were right to do only as you did. I was inclined, when young, to be impulsive. I was frequently misunderstood, as a result, and frequently understood only too well. Certainly you could do no less than you did. I congratulate you both . . . on this drawing. As for any further grounds for congratulation, I shall no doubt be the last to be told. Rejoin your guests, Perdita. You are missed, and asked for. Word flies about. There is scurrilous talk. At least, I hope there is. A party without scandal is like porridge without salt. This party is becoming like salt without porridge, creating in my throat an intolerable thirst. Forward, Carmichael! Take me to the nearest and most copious source of champagne.'

The Countess was quickly back from the bottle to the ball-room. Her Bath-chair was to be seen flying up and down between cheering rows of dancers, in the country-dance called 'Strip the Willow'. Even Miss Carmichael was laughing.

From that period of blur stands out also the memory of Aunt Marianne and Mrs Ramsay, deep in conversation. They did not dance. Mrs Ramsay was dressed with extraordinary richness.

199

She looked like a large chair, or sofa, upholstered in the most splendid brocade. Aunt Marianne, in the new gown the Countess had paid for, looked like a steamed pudding in oriental draperies.

Alex came to claim me, for the dance for which we had engaged one another.

He said, 'We have made an arrangement which I hope you will approve, Dita. I am changing over with Harry. I am to have his Number Fifteen, and he is to have this one. Is that all right? Do you mind being bartered?'

'Harry is *here*?'

'Yes. I've just seen him. He's just come, I think. He's keeping out of sight, he says, in case Great-Aunt Selina sees him and has him removed before he's done what he came to do.'

'What is that? Why did he come?'

'I don't know. But he wants urgently to see you, to talk to you.'

'I would rather dance than talk. Where is Harry?'

'He told me to ask you to go out onto the terrace. It is warm. There are people strolling. Shall I get you a wrap?'

'It is another waste of good music,' I said. 'But, as a matter of fact, going out onto the terrace is quite a good idea. I feel as though I had been boiled, like Aunt Marianne, I mean like a suet pudding.'

There was no moon. The terrace was lit by bands and splashes of light from the windows of the castle. I could see white shoulders, white jabots, blurred white faces of strolling couples, of groups. I could hear shreds of laughter in the darkness, and a buzz of voices. The pipes droned from the ballroom, before swinging into the lilt of my lost eightsome reel.

I walked out between the parterres, looking right and left, feeling the warm night air on my skin.

A voice called from the darkness, 'Dita.'

With Harry, to my surprise, was Colin. I could see them only dimly. Wayward beams of light from indoors danced on the jewelled buttons of their doublets, and on the hilts of their skean dhus.

Harry said, 'Thank you for consenting to the change, Dita, and thank you for coming out here.'

'You are wise,' I said, 'to stay hidden in the dark, I think.'

'I shall go in presently, and hope for the best. I have another errand, as well as this one. And I want to see you properly. You look sufficiently amazing, silhouetted against the windows. How can you contrive to have such a tiny waist, without snapping in half?'

'I hold my breath most of the time,' I said. 'Is that what you asked me out here to say?'

As we talked – friends now, after the last happy meeting – Colin stood a little behind Harry, looking like a bedizened giant, silent, motionless. I could not see the expression on his face. I could not imagine why he was there.

'Will you tell us, Dita,' said Harry, 'how you came by the name of Maudie Plimstock?'

'Good God,' I said, 'how are you mixed up in that?'

'Because Colin is my cousin and my friend.'

I digested this. It was, indeed, a sufficient reason.

I said, 'I was told the contents of a letter. And I was shown marriage lines.'

Colin groaned – the first sound he had made.

'By whom?' asked Harry.

'I don't know if I should tell you.'

'I beg you to tell us.'

'Well, by Violet Carmichael. She would not say where the letter came from. It was sent to her so that she could – warn me, or any other girl, if it was needful. It was needful, wasn't it? It was not sent to Great-Aunt Selina, because it would have hurt her so much.'

'I see. What did you hope for, Dita, when you faced Colin with the name of Maudie Plimstock?'

'The truth.'

'Colin did not know the truth. At least, not all the truth. Not one supremely important fact.'

'I knew the most important fact.'

'Important, but not the most important. Listen. I must be quick, and tell you this in a few words, before the end of the reel. Immediately after you had spoken to him, Colin sought me out. In misery. For help. For advice. He had been abroad for years. He did not know how things were managed.'

'What things? Divorce? Murder?'

201

'He told me he had been paying Maudie a sum of money twice a year, by way of a London bank. The payments were actually made to her brother Albert, and the receipts signed by him. There was a legal reason for this, so Colin was given to understand, and she did live with Albert and his wife. I found this strange.'

'She had to live somewhere, when Colin went to India.'

'I found it strange that Colin's money was going to her brother, rather than to herself. I could think of no legal reason for this. I am not as trusting as Colin, though I know no more about the law than he does. Accordingly I made contact, on Colin's behalf, with a lawyer I know in London.'

'Why could not Colin do that for himself?'

'He knew no lawyers in London. This kind of enquiry was Double-Dutch to him. Besides, as I say, he was trusting. My lawyer reported to me, only a few days ago, that Maudie was dead. He had inspected the parish register, and confirmed the fact of her burial. She died in childbirth, eighteen months after Colin's departure. God knows who the father of that child was. Her family had been fraudulently milking Colin ever since. They will not go to prison, unfortunately, because the trial would receive lurid publicity, destroy Colin's career, bring misery to Great-Aunt Selina and to this family. At any rate, Colin is spared that crippling outlay of money. And he is a widower. He is not married, Dita. He is free.'

'You came here to tell him so,' I said suddenly.

'Yes, of course. Since I was unable to see him, I left a letter for him. He never got the letter. We cannot quite make out why. Well, I knew he had not received the letter, or he would have been in touch with me at once, even if it meant riding from here to Eredine. I had ridden from Eredine here.'

'Why are you telling me this, Harry?'

'Good God, do you not think you ought to hear it?'

'Yes, of course, but why is Colin not telling me?'

'He asked me to tell you.'

'Why?'

'You had better answer that, Colin,' said Harry.

'I will. I will try,' said Colin, in a stifled voice. 'But not in your hearing, Harry.'

'All right,' said Harry. 'I will remove myself out of earshot. I hope to see you both later. You particularly, Dita.'

'Before you go,' said Colin, 'I must thank – try to thank – '

'You've done that. No need to labour the point.'

And Harry was gone.

Colin did not move, but loomed like a jewelled mountain in the darkness.

'I was ashamed,' he said. 'I was ashamed to talk about her – about that family – to you. Dita, the thing you must understand is that – only a certain kind of man becomes entangled in a situation like that – is weak enough – is enough frightened of the consequences of defiance ... And that same kind of man is frightened of telling the truth – frightened of the consequences of that ... The man trapped into marrying – that girl – is the man who would not face you with the truth that he had done it ... I thank God for Harry's friendship ...'

'Indeed you should do that,' I said.

'The army was – has been – a great necessity to me,' said Colin. 'It is necessary for a weak and silly man to have – a set of iron rules by which to live – a fixed appearance to take – a set task, a code of behaviour – all decisions, you know, taken for you, so that all you need do is what you are told – and you have no chance to show your weakness, indulge your folly ...'

'But you are a hero,' I said, startled. 'You are successful.'

I did not like the self-abasement of Colin's words.

'They gave me a medal for doing exactly what I was told,' said Colin. 'For conforming perfectly to the rules, like an obedient schoolboy ... They would have taken it away from me, I daresay, if they had heard me ... When you faced me with that name ... Can you understand that, when you came up to me, I was frightened to be truthful? Can you understand moral cowardice – you who have never felt one twinge of fright of any kind? I am not a physical coward, I think – I was not frightened of the carbines or the knives of the Pathans ... But I was frightened of what you would think and say, if I told you the truth ...'

'Why did you stay here?' I asked.

'I could not bear to go. I was hoping for a miracle in you, in myself, in circumstances. Harry was surprised that I stayed ... that I should subject myself to such torture ... But I had rather be tortured, in the same house as you, than . . . I have suffered the agonies of the damned, seeing you laughing with the others, knowing that they had a right to laugh with you . . . I have been punished, Dita . . . I think enough . . . I can come to you now openly and honestly . . . I am free to lay my – to lay my heart at your feet. I do so. I cannot go on without you. My shame is all behind me, my folly . . . No more lies, Dita . . . Never again, I swear before God, anything less than the fullest truth and trust . . . Oh God, once you said there was a chance for me, and I felt myself flying among the stars . . . Can you say it now? Can you give me any faintest glimmer of hope?'

The deep, unhappy, passionate voice came jerkily out of the darkness. He had not moved nearer.

I did not think I could offer hope to a man who had withheld the truth from me. But . . .

He said, 'No man with you at his side . . . With your strength and shining honesty at his side . . . could ever again be guilty of folly or weakness or lies . . . Your strength would be greater than that of the whole army, the whole Empire . . . to keep a man sane and honourable . . . To earn and keep your love and admiration, that would keep a man decent . . . I need you, Dita, not for my happiness only but for my manhood, my honour . . . Without you, I shall be no better than I ever was – but with you, oh God, I shall be a king, a lion, a leader, an archangel . . . It is alchemy, Dita. The magical turning of base metal into gold. You turn my base metal into gold. Made of your gold, I shall be a man of . . . some merit.'

His voice was suddenly husky. I could hardly hear him when he said, 'I cannot say more. I cannot speak.'

His voice was the voice of a man who was weeping. I could not see if there were tears on his face. It was intolerable to me that this hero and giant should weep. That he should break down into tears because of me. It seemed terribly wrong, immoral, dreadful, that he should be husky and speechless, because of me.

To right that wrong, I stepped closer to him, and put out a hand, and reached up towards his face, which hung like a moon above me. He took my hand and pressed it to his cheek. His cheek was wet.

He pressed my hand to his cheek, exactly as I had pressed

Jules's hand to my cheek.

The pipes whined to silence. A laughing crowd came out of the castle onto the terrace, some of the men carrying candelabra, so that they brought with them a pool of golden candlelight.

Colin turned, to hide his face from the light, and walked unsteadily away in the darkness.

The groups surrounded me, loud with goodwill and banter and pretty speeches. Sir Duncan Raden, among them, claimed me for the next dance. So I returned to the world; from some far point in space, I returned to the blur of the ballroom.

I thought it fortunate that, if my heart was to be battered at intervals throughout the night, there was distraction in between times. I was not altogether distracted. Those three conversations had been distressing and breathtaking and moving, too much so to be ever quite out of my mind, even when I whirled most dizzily with the most beautiful Duke. But people were saying it was the best and most brilliant ball Scotland had seen for a generation. That was gratifying, since it had been given (in theory) for me. And it was gratifying to be so much praised and petted. I could not be continuously tragic. It was my birthday, and it was my very first ball, and I had a duty to our guests.

I could not let myself think about Colin, or I should have hidden in the darkness of the terrace, like him, and wept, like him.

The time came for Alex's dance, that had been Harry's. I had a premonition that we would not dance. We did not.

We sat on cushions on a little marble bench, brought to Scotland from Italy by one of the eighteenth-century Earls after his Grand Tour. It was in one of the broad, dim-lit passages which connected parts of the castle with other parts. There was nothing furtive about where we sat. Anyone might have walked along the passage. No one did. The passage was on the way to nowhere. The whole world was somewhere else, busy or idle.

'I picked this niche for us, after deep thought and prolonged research,' said Alex.

'How come cushions to be here?'

'I brought them here.'

205

'Oh. Good gracious. That was thoughtful.'

'I admit that I was concerned for my own comfort, as well as yours.'

'Well, it is nice to be told the truth, even if it is not very gallant.'

Alex took my hand. I let it remain within his fingers. It felt comfortable there. I felt comfortable beside Alex. Candles from the six branches of a sconce at the end of the passage cast a glow which left half his face in shadow. His features seemed magnified and strengthened by the light and shade. The effect was dramatic. Alex looked like the etchings after Rembrandt which hung in the billiard-room. His eyes blazed in the dimness.

'You sat with Jamie in the hall, and Jules in the saloon, and you spoke to Harry and Colin on the terrace,' said Alex.

'Yes, but how do you know?'

'I watched you.'

'You should have been dancing with lovely girls.'

'I did that, whenever you were dancing with lovely boys. But when you were not dancing, I would not either. I have been prowling after you, like a Red Indian. You have looked so unimaginably beautiful tonight, Dita, that I have not wanted to take my eyes off you. And I have not done so.'

'Oh ... Then you saw ...'

'I saw Jamie holding your hand, and speaking with great earnestness. I could not forget that he is a pleader in the courts and an adroit politician. Then I saw Jules's hand on your cheek. I could not forget what a delightful and talented boy he is. I followed you out onto the terrace, after I had told you Harry was there.'

'You should not have done that.'

'Why not? I had been robbed of my dance. I deserved some recompense. I was not spying on anything secret or dreadful, was I? You were to speak to my cousin, and in the event spoke to my other cousin. I did not hear what passed. I am not an eavesdropper. I would *like* to be, but I don't know how to go about it. I am only slightly a *voyeur*. Not a good one, in the dark of the terrace. Well, what came of all these intimacies?'

'Nothing ... firm,' I said.

'Not with Jamie?'

'No.'

'In spite of the promises he believes you have exchanged?'

'He knows we were – too quick. He had – taken a step back, if you see what I mean.'

'But he loves you and is determined to marry you.'

'Well, yes. So he says.'

'Yes. What am I supposed to do, Dita? In loyalty to my twin brother? Bow out? Am I to do that? Am I treacherous to my own flesh and blood if I stay in the race?'

'Does that seriously trouble you, Alex?'

'It ought to, don't you think?'

'Yes, I suppose it ought . . . But does it?'

'No. I am in the race. The only reason I shall scratch is if you tell me too. I know you will be honest with me. I know I can trust you completely to treat me – gently. You will probably break my heart, but you will do so as mercifully as you can. The action will be quick and clean. Now, perhaps. You gave me a little hope. After tonight, have I still a little hope?'

He squeezed my hands. In returning the pressure, I answered him.

I was still frightened of Jamie, though he said the granite had melted. Jules loved me but he was not my grown-up love. About Colin I was confused, but I did not think pity was a good basis on which to start, and I did not think I could forget what he said he had left behind. About Alex I had – I need never have – any doubts or reservations at all. He had every quality that I most sincerely admired. He combined all that was best in the others – all that I could love, did love, in the others.

If I chose Alex, he would be the richest don there ever was in Oxford town. That was a nice thought. He would not love me more, perhaps, when he discovered, but he would hardly love me less.

'What do they think, all of them?' said Alex suddenly. 'Jamie and Jules and Colin. You smile. You smile at the world. How do they take that smile? What do they think is in your heart?'

'I do not know myself what is in my heart.'

He began to quote softly:

'"On one she smiled, and he was blest;
She smiles elsewhere – we make a din.

207

But 'twas not love which heaved her breast,
    Fair child! – it was the bliss within."'

'Bliss within,' I said. 'Well, yes, sometimes.'

'"Fair child",' he quoted, smiling.

'What are those lines?'

'Quite recent. The last stanza of a poem called "Euphrosine", by Matthew Arnold. An academic colleague of mine. Son of the great headmaster of Rugby. "On one she smiled, and he was blest". You smile at us all, Dita. "She smiles elsewhere – we make a din". I shall make a little peevish din. I expect Jamie's din will be louder. Jules will make a French din, of course, *un bruit épouvantable*. Colin's din does not bear thinking of.'

Colin's tears did not bear thinking of.

'"But 'twas not love which heaved her breast". Not love, Dita? Not love, yet? No certainty, no firm choice? I don't want to badger you, you know, but – I am quite anxious about the answer.' After a pause he said unexpectedly, 'The Marquess of Mull owns not only most the West Highlands, but most of London as well. I own a few suits of clothes and a great many books. Oh, I am not Uriah Heep. (Does Dickens come your way, in back numbers of *Household Words*?) I don't make a virtue of abject humility.'

'No,' I agreed, thinking of his dash and elegance on horseback. Least donnish of dons!

'I won't press my claims,' he said. 'I don't want to bore you, and I have none that you don't know about. I adore you and need you. That is my only claim on you, really. Just that I want you so much. Just,' he repeated slowly, 'that I want you so terribly.'

'That is a good claim,' I said shakily. 'I could not ask for a better claim than that.'

And then neither of us said anything, but sat and looked at each other with anxious faces, he holding both my hands in his, and our knees grazing, so that the watchspring hoops of my crinoline were thrust billowing out far beyond the end of the little bench . . .

In the renewed blur which followed, I looked out when I thought of it for Harry. I wondered how soon he would be detected, and what would happen when he was.

I saw him from time to time. No doubt he was keeping well away from the Countess. But he allowed himself to be seen by many of the guests. Of course he knew far more of them than did I or Colin or his Edinburgh cousins, because he was one of them. *They* did not know he was to be ejected. The story of his defiance was not one the Countess would have put about. The servants might have been given orders: but I knew from Hamish Ogilvy that the servants liked Harry. He wrote to them at Christmas, and sent presents to their children. They would say after that they had not seen him, had not recognized him after so many years.

Seeing Harry in the light, in Highland dress, I was struck by the splendour of his appearance. He was not as richly dressed as Sir Duncan Raden or the Marquess of Mull: but he was handsomer and more dignified. He held himself like a very active man only momentarily at rest. I was glad he knew the truth about me – one small truth about me. I was glad we were friends. It seemed from the affairs of Colin and Jules, that he was a good friend to have.

What I saw of Harry's doings puzzled me. He was up to something: but I did not know what it was.

I saw him beckon, from half behind a curtain, to Miss Violet Carmichael, who was for a moment detached from the Bath-chair. She gave one of her wails when she saw him, but he silenced her with an imploring gesture. He said something to her in a low voice, his face serious, his manner urgent. She nodded rapidly, so that the tip of her nose must have sprayed drops like a watering-can with a rose to its spout.

I saw him talking to Jules, and Jules nodding his head, wide-eyed.

I saw him draw aside one of the old footmen, whom he knew from years before.

When the Countess was eating her third supper, and the Bath-chair was for the moment immobile, I saw Miss Carmichael talking to Aunt Marianne and Mrs Ramsay. They seemed to be covering her with questions, as a high wind covers a rose-bed with fallen leaves. After she answered, she put a hand to her mouth, as though she had said more than she meant.

Then Harry approached me himself, as I came out of the ballroom on the arm of a happy young man called Torquil McLeod – one of my new friends, one of my new great friends.

Harry evidently knew Mr McLeod well. They greeted one another warmly. Harry congratulated me on my choice of partner, and Mr McLeod on his.

He said, 'Torquil, can you spare Miss Sinclair for twenty seconds, for an urgent private word?'

'If I may listen,' said Mr McLeod.

Smiling, Harry said that it was family business, a little domestic matter, quite dreary to an outsider.

'Then I don't even want to listen,' said Mr McLeod. He bowed to me comically, and withdrew a short distance.

'Can you come to the little blue drawing-room at three o'clock sharp, Dita?' said Harry abruptly.

'Is that what the others are doing?' I said. 'The ones you have been whispering to?'

He grinned. 'You're as sharp as you always were,' he said. 'Yes. I'm braving Great-Aunt Selina, and I shall want my hand held.'

'Oh well,' I said, 'that is a scene I don't want to miss. But I don't think I shall dare to hold your hand, in case I get scorched by the flames too.'

'Three o'clock. Promise.'

'Yes, of course. What is the plot, Harry? What are you up to?'

'You like Jules, don't you?'

'Yes, very much.'

'*Very* much?'

'Very much indeed.'

'So do I,' he said. 'So I am going to try to make his fortune.'

He was gone. I looked after him blankly.

The only way in the world that Harry could make Jules's fortune, was to arrange for Jules to marry me. That might happen one day, far in the future. I did not think it highly likely, but I did love Jules, and – it was a thing which was possible. It would be no doing of Harry's. I frowned, thinking of Harry trying to control my life, my choice. Perhaps after all he was not such a good friend to have, if he interfered and managed to such a point.

I prepared a cutting little speech, to be delivered at three o'clock in the small blue drawing-room.

'Your presumption is intolerable,' I said aloud, rehearsing: which greatly startled Mr Torquil McLeod, who had just rejoined me.

'This is an outrage,' said the Countess, not violently, but with dangerous calm. 'You have taken advantage of my helplessness in a cowardly and treacherous fashion. Carmichael, you are dismissed. I shall give you neither a character nor a penny of the wages to which you probably consider yourself entitled.'

'You can't do that!' I blurted out.

'Yes, insolent chit, I can. I not only can, I have. It appears, by the fact of your presence here, that you are an accessory to this banditry. That is exceedingly ill-advised. And you, Jules – you have, with certain aberrant exceptions, been sedulous to acquire my good opinion, since you imposed yourself on this household. Your presence on this occasion has undone whatever good you may have imagined you have done yourself. You two – Marianne, Lucinda – what the devil are you doing here?'

'Yes, what *are* you doing here?' said Harry. 'I didn't ask you.'

'I told them of this meeting, Mr Harry,' quavered Miss Carmichael.

'We saw you whispering to Violet,' said Mrs Ramsay solemnly. 'We thought it proper to enquire what conspiracy was afoot. We thought it proper, ma'am, to attend you here in case of need.'

'In other words, you were curious,' said the Countess. 'I don't know that I blame you.'

Harry, cause of the whole outrage, escaped the lash of the Countess's tongue, and the fire of her breath, because she simply ignored him. For her, he was not there. He did not exist. When he spoke, she affected not to hear. I saw him look at her with undisguised amusement and admiration. But also he looked determined.

'Your presumption is intolerable,' I murmured to myself, preparing to comment on what I knew must be his plan to make Jules's fortune.

'Jules is your grandson, ma'am,' said Harry firmly. She pretended not to hear him, but he was neither deceived nor deterred. He said, 'Whatever you may think, he was born legally in wedlock. Even if he had not been, he could hardly be blamed. He is your single descendant. He is intelligent, talented and honest. He has much to learn, and he is learning it. If a vestige of fair-mindedness holds up its head in the sea of your prejudice, you will recognize the truth of that. Jules is not only the rightful heir to Strathgallant and to your fortune, he is also a most suitable one. I entreat you to recognize the call of blood. Whatever other plans you may have made, I entreat you to forget them. Jules is your grandson, Great-Aunt Selina. Treat him as such.'

Silence fell. It occurred to me (as ridiculous thoughts had a way of doing, at the most serious moments) that had the drop on the end of Miss Carmichael's nose fallen just then onto the thick Turkey carpet, the splash would have sounded as loud as a gong.

The Countess looked thoroughly astonished. It was an expression I did not ever remember seeing on her beaky face before. It was her way to cause astonishment, not to feel it. It put her at a disadvantage. For a moment, she was speechless.

So was I.

So was Jules, who most evidently had had no idea of what Harry was going to say.

'Mercy,' said Miss Carmichael, breaking a silence that seemed to have lasted most of my life.

It sounded like a plea to the Countess, as much as an exclamation of surprise.

When the Countess did speak, her words were not at all what I had expected. She turned to Harry, acknowledging his presence for the first time.

'Was that speech the reason for this rendezvous?' she said.

'The whole reason, ma'am.'

'What prompted you to make it, at such a time?'

'I tried to make it on a previous and more suitable occasion,' said Harry mildly. 'I was not allowed near you.'

'You brought that on yourself.'

'I know I did. I apologise for my discourtesy in not writing to you. I had reasons that seemed to me good, but I cannot expect you to appreciate their merit.'

'Perspicacious of you. No doubt you had reasons that seemed to you good for flaunting yourself in this neighbourhood.'

212

'Yes.'

They put me in mind of duellists, gladiators, in the midst of an arena. The rest of us were just an audience, waiting for Harry to be slaughtered.

The Countess astonished me again (she was resuming her usual role). She said in a reasonable voice, as one sensible grown-up to another, 'In making your suggestion, you are driven by affection for Jules?'

'Yes.'

'By no other spur?'

'I have another and personal reason for wishing Jules to be your heir.'

'What can that be?'

'You must excuse me from answering.'

'Are you telling me to mind my own business? I might reasonably reply in the same terms.'

'No, ma'am. I repeat that I have most pressing and personal grounds for entreating you to adopt the course I suggest.'

'You must be mad.'

'Yes.'

'You admit to being a bedlamite?'

'In one important regard, yes.'

'There is,' said the Countess, 'merit in your suggestion. Obviously there is. The thought has occurred to me to do precisely as you say. Obviously it has. How could it not? I am not unnatural or unobservant, and that funny little Frenchman your protégé is all that you say. Incidentally,' she turned to Jules, 'I acquit you of complicity in this manoeuvre. You looked as surprised as I felt.'

Jules bowed. He was, indeed, still open-mouthed with surprise.

'Why is Perdita here?' the Countess asked suddenly.

'Harry asked me,' I said.

'Obviously. I was not directing my question at you.'

'She is concerned,' said Harry.

'Is she, indeed? And how do you react to Harry's plans for the future of this castle, Miss?'

How did I react to them? They were so different from what I had supposed were Harry's plans, that I had not had time to

213

react. I did so now, in the most predictable way. Much as I had been outraged at the Countess's stratagem, I had got used to the idea that I should be mistress of Strathgallant. At different times, I had pictured sharing it with Jamie, Colin, Jules and Alex. Now, if I did not choose Jules, and if the Countess agreed with Harry, I should be mistress of nothing. Though I deserved nothing, I had got used to the idea of having everything. It was impossible not to react selfishly. Only an angel could have failed to mind losing so much. I was not an angel.

I could not say any of this. I said, 'It is up to you, ma'am.'

'You are careful, child. You are adroit and discreet. How very unlike you. Are you growing up? What a pity, if so. I liked you better before. I should think you would wish to murder Harry. Perhaps Jules also. I have said too much, as you were always apt to do until this evening. Harry, your melodramatics were needless. I repeat that I have already considered the course of action you urge upon me.'

'And rejected it?'

'No.'

'I am thankful.'

'Nor accepted it. I am undecided. I am influenced, without assistance from you, by both the arguments you have deployed. The ties of blood pull me, I find, harder than I would have expected. I had flattered myself I was immune from such primitive and mawkish emotion. I am not. And the boy has shown himself an eager and apt pupil of everything relevant to his occupation of my place. It would be folly to be uninfluenced by so formidable an ingredient in the debate. Were I to consider one of my great-nephews as my possible heir, I would not find them flattered in all ways by comparison with my grandson. James can't even ride, for God's sake. Oh yes, I am some way to agreeing with you. I have many deplorable qualities, but I am not a fool.'

'That I well know,' said Harry. 'And that is why I feel a growing confidence that you will decide in favour of Jules. And that you will declare your decision, and make it binding.'

The Countess turned to Jules. She said, 'Would you like Strathgallant, boy?'

At this amazing question, Jules cleared his throat. He blinked at her. He looked very young. It was his hand that needed

214

holding, not Harry's.

He said, 'Yes.'

'It is a good thing I am here,' said Aunt Marianne suddenly. 'I suppose it was curiosity that brought me here, but it was a fortunate chance, quite providential, because . . . I must intervene. There is something you should know. Oh, this is dreadful. I am terribly distressed, but I must . . . My clear duty . . . Oh, but I wish somebody else . . . I am going to sadden you, shock you . . . Oh dear . . .'

'What is the woman gabbling about?' said the Countess impatiently.

But she must have had a premonition. We all must.

'I told you, ma'am, when Jules first came here, that I had known of him. That poor Isobel had written to me. That we had remained in touch, in spite of . . . So many letters I received from Isobel. I have them all, in a small chest, with lavender-bags . . . Fragrant . . . She wrote to me, naturally, of her – husband, and of his family, their way of life, of Jules's upbringing by his father and his relatives . . . Oh oh, I wish I was not obliged to repeat what Isobel wrote to me. I would not have done so, I would never have done so . . . I would never have been so cruel, brought you such pain . . . But now that you have this idea, you must know the truth . . . I have not the right to keep it from you . . .'

I began to feel a little sick, at the prospect of what was to come. Harry was frowning savagely. He wanted to hear ill of Jules no more than I did. The Countess likewise. She sat like a stone, in tiara and wig and daubs of rouge, waiting for Aunt Marianne.

Jules was staring at Aunt Marianne like a bird at a snake.

'Isobel's husband, and all his family,' said Aunt Marianne, 'were gamblers and thieves and cheats. It brought her such misery . . . And Jules was from his earliest youth brought up to be one of them . . . As a young child, to trick kindly people out of money . . . To bring them to his uncle's gaming-house . . . And, later, to be a – companion to old ladies . . . There is a French word, that Isobel used in her letters, that I cannot repeat . . .'

I could not look at Jules, whose glorious new world had crumbled like a dried toadstool at the end of summer.

215

10

'Not a word of this can be true,' said Harry. 'This is some cruel hoax. You have been deceived, Cousin Marianne.'

'No, dear,' said Aunt Marianne. 'I wish you were right, I so wish you were right, but . . . It is all in Isobel's letters. I have them in my bedroom, scented with lavender . . .'

The door of the little drawing-room opened and closed: and Jules had disappeared.

'You see that I *had* to speak,' said Aunt Marianne, looking very near to tears.

'Yes,' said the Countess, in a voice drained of all life.

'He has run away,' said Mrs Ramsay. 'That is tantamount to a confession of guilt.'

I had to agree that it was. I felt so ill with shock and misery that I felt I might faint. Miss Carmichael looked close to fainting.

'Not necessarily,' said Harry. 'I'm frightened for that boy. Excuse me.'

Harry hurried out. His face was taut with anxiety.

I had not seen Jules's face. I had not had the courage to look at him, to see what must be there, the guilt, the sick shock of being unmasked.

Aunt Marianne fell on her knees, awkward and ridiculous but pathetic, before the Bath-chair.

'Forgive me,' she said.

The Countess nodded, slowly, as though the effort of moving her head was almost beyond her. She looked immemorially old – suddenly older by far than she had looked a few short moments before.

It must all be true. Lady Isobel's letters could be neither forged nor false. Aunt Marianne knew her handwriting. She would not invent scandalous libels about her husband and son.

216

It must all be true.

It could not be true: it must be.

The Countess had become, with astonishing speed, devoted to Jules, indulgent and admiring. To the point that, as she had just said, she was contemplating changing her mind about me, and making him her heir. Of course. He was a professional at making old ladies fond of him.

I had become, with almost indecent speed, devoted to Jules. He was a professional in that line, too, and in acquiring the trust of a kindly man like Harry, and in gaining the affection of a clever man like Alex . . .

No doubt he had learned those gay French songs from *demi-mondaines* in his uncle's gaming-house.

He drew his caricatures there, to divert the gulls, so that they took their eyes off the cards.

He had learned to climb by going in through the upstairs windows of houses.

He had learned to learn in order to pretend, cozen, wheedle, deceive.

Everything that had seemed best about him, viewed in this new glare of truth, now looked worst.

'I think we should have guessed,' said Mrs Ramsay.

For once I agreed with her. We should all have guessed.

Our Highland nights are brief and transparent in the summer, and the sky was beginning to pale long before the music had stopped.

The Countess and her Bath-chair took no further part in the dancing. Her face showed nothing, to her capering guests, of the shock she had suffered. I tried to learn from her. She was like an old Roman, like the Spartan boy. Her heart must have been wrung. She had grown to love and she had been deluded. He was her grandson and he was no good. She was too old to suffer such a betrayal. She smiled, when a smile was required of her, and in repose her face was a mask of arrogance. I was astonished at her courage. I tried to copy it, but I think I did not quite succeed.

He had drawn me as a flower, and pressed my hand to his cheek. He was a thief and a cheat and an adventurer. He had come to Strathgallant as all these things, and run away abjectly when he was discovered.

Probably he never knew his mother had been writing to her sister-in-law. Certainly he could have had no glimmer of an idea *what* she was writing. I felt terribly sorry for Lady Isobel, and for the Countess, and for myself. I felt sorry for Aunt Marianne, having been obliged to hurt us all so much. Of course she was right. Perhaps she should have told the truth sooner, before the little Frenchman ensnared us all in his professional charm. I could see why she had not. It might have turned out unnecessary to hurt the old lady, to destroy her new happiness in her new grandson. In her place, I thought I would have done just as she did.

I pinned a birthday smile on my face, and dragged through the rest of the night. There was no sign of Jules or Harry. If Harry had gone after Jules, where would that chase lead him? To a Glasgow gaming house, or an Edinburgh brothel? To lonely old ladies, or rich inexperienced girls? To the pockets of drunkards, or the silver on their sideboards?

I thought Harry must feel more betrayed than any of us. But he had not said, 'I will kill that boy'. He had said, 'I am frightened for that boy'. Where stood Harry? What did he think?

I wondered if the Countess would want to see Lady Isobel's letters. I thought she would not. I did not. I did not want to read the word that Aunt Marianne had refused to speak.

I walked out onto the terrace with Alex. He was comforting. He knew what had happened – of course, his mother had told him – but he said only that he admired Jules's skill. I was thankful to lean upon his strength, and to be strengthened by the love I knew he bore me.

We strolled to the far end of the terrace. I had an idea that somebody was coming along behind us: but, when I turned, there was no one to be seen. It was still quite dark, and the shrubs and hedges could have hidden an army.

Alex did not talk of his love for me, or of my love for anybody, but of the success of the ball and the antics of the Countess. Yet I was not in the least surprised when, as we leaned on the balustrade, he put his arm about my shoulders, drew me towards him, and kissed me.

It was a gentle and comfortable kiss. I was not at all near to swooning with excitement, but I was comforted. Alex found the best of all cures for my misery. He was clever about other things than books.

We drew apart, friendly, unembarrassed. His arm was still about me, and my cheek on his shoulder. Below us was a commotion of men and horses, as carriages were manhandled and the right teams found for the right vehicles.

'If people are beginning to leave,' I said, 'I must go back on duty.'

'Yes. In a moment. Stay a moment. I don't want to share you with the rest of the world, just for a moment.'

He lifted my chin with his free hand, gently, and before I closed my eyes I saw his face swim down towards mine.

I was aware, somehow, of someone near. I struggled in Alex's arms, but he held me fast.

There was a loud and sudden thud, inches from my face. Alex's hold on me relaxed. He crumpled at my feet. Before I could cry out, or run, or do anything, I was enveloped in something black and coarse, blinded, deafened, muted, half suffocated. My arms were imprisoned to my sides by something that hurt them. I screamed, but I could not scream – I could hardly breathe. I struggled and I was powerless. I kicked out, and lost a slipper. I felt myself picked up and thrown like a sack over a man's shoulder. He threw me there, and held me there, as though I were no bigger than a rabbit.

My attacker was a man infinitely more powerful than I. Dizzily, sickened, I thought of the biggest and most powerful man I knew. Who loved me and had lost me.

Colin.

I was suddenly certain my attacker was Colin. Crazed. Perhaps drunk. Colin, who had the folly to be married to a backstreet drab, and the weakness to lie to me about it . . .

Then he was running. I bounced on his shoulder. He held me fast. The upper half of me was upside down, hanging helplessly from his shoulder, my head at his waist. I felt sick. I bounced on his shoulder as he ran, so that the breath was knocked out of my body. I was in extreme discomfort and I was very frightened.

The sack smelled of potatoes. I was as helpless as a sack of potatoes.

Though I could hear nothing, I realised we were running down steep steps. Down from the terrace. Away from the castle. Away towards the confusion of carriages and grooms and horses. It was still dark. I was being kidnapped, abducted. Should I be ransomed, murdered, robbed, raped? By Colin? Had he gone mad? He was a man of violent action, a warrior, a kind of savage. How savage would he be, insane with love and jealousy and whisky? I struggled desperately, and only hurt myself against the strength of his arms and whatever bound my arms. I was near to fainting and to utter panic.

We reached level ground. My captor stumbled, as though on rough grass. He did not loose his grip on me. He ran. Dimly I heard shouts, through the stifling potato sack which covered me. I thought they were not shouts of pursuit, but of grooms and stable-boys and coachmen.

I thought the vast crinoline of my gown must be waving like a sail. But of course the watch-spring hoops could be compressed, bent in any way, bundled by a pair of strong arms into something like a roll of washing.

Perhaps that was what I was taken for, by any groom who glimpsed us in the darkness – somebody's laundry, a bundle of dirty sheets.

My captor stopped. From the heaving of his shoulders I knew him to be panting. I felt myself lifted off his shoulder, and thrust onto a seat. I could not tell what kind of seat. I felt hardness beside me, a hard surface with projections, which thrust into my hip through the silk of my skirt, and into my elbow and shoulder through the sack. I thought they were the door-handle and window-catch on the inside of the door of a closed carriage. There was somebody beside me in the carriage, sharing the seat. I felt a hip against my hip, a knee against my knee, a hand on my shoulder through the sack. I was held into the corner of the seat, and I was held down. I could not move. I heard no voice. I felt a jolting. The carriage was moving.

My captor had friends, then. A carriage does not drive itself.

I would be missed, but not all at once. People leaving would imagine me dancing. People dancing would imagine me saying farewell to departing guests. A few people might picture me weeping in a corner about Jules. By the time I was missed, the carriage would long have disappeared into the darkness.

Darkness was fading into dawn. The carriage would presently be visible. But dozens of carriages were leaving Strathgallant, full of innocent and sleepy people. They would be blocking the narrow Highland roads, in all directions.

I could not tell what direction we took. We turned many corners, left and right, so that I was thrown against the side of the carriage, or against the shoulder of my captor. I was fighting for breath. The cord that held my arms was painful. When I tried to move, my shoulder was pressed back against the seat.

I wondered if Alex were dead. I had not known, at the moment it happened, what that thud meant. Now that I knew, the memory of it was sickening. Dizzily I pictured a shattered skull, blood and brains on the terrace.

Colin had killed. It was his trade. He was hardened to it, and honoured for it. He had a streak of desperate folly, that the army had taught him to hide.

The carriage felt small, light, ill-sprung, a cheap country brougham. The quality of my transport was not the greatest of my worries.

After a long, long time the carriage left the smooth macadam road, and began to bump at a walking pace along what I thought must be a rough track. This too went on for a long time, and there were more corners, and sometimes a rock or lump in the track that lifted a wheel, and set the carriage on a wild slant.

And then at last we stopped. I was pulled out. I was hoisted again over a shoulder, like a sack, like the potatoes whose earthy smell I had been breathing for so long. I was as helpless as ever – more helpless, because I was so stiff and cramped. I was terribly tired and in pain and frightened.

I was carried – somewhere. I thought we went up a step, and through a door. I could not be sure about this. My mind was scarce working, through fatigue and distress and suffocation. I could see nothing and hear very little, and my head was hanging down, to confuse my wits.

I was lifted down, and put on the ground. The ground felt moderately soft – not a stone floor, not grass or heather.

Suddenly the pressure on my arms relaxed. The cord was cut

or untied. I heard through the sack a bang – perhaps the slamming of a door. With hands so numb as to be almost powerless, I struggled to get out of the potato sack. I would have expected this to be easy. It was insanely difficult. I wept tears of pure rage at my impotence. Though the sack was loose over my head, it was very tight over my shoulders. It reached below my hips, beyond the tips of my fingers. It was tight over my hips. It had been pulled down over me, hard, to its fullest extent. It imprisoned my arms almost as effectively as the cord had done. Inch by painful inch I coaxed that hateful sack up my body, every movement an exhausting struggle, so that I sobbed for air. I lay down and tried to wriggle out of the sack: but it came with me. I tried to scrape it off on the floor, but only succeeded in scraping and hurting myself. At one moment I went berserk, and struggled and scrabbled and fought, sobbing, desperate. In this paroxysm I lost all that I had gained, and found when the fit subsided that I was just as I had been when I started.

I began again, keeping tight rein of my temper and on panic. As soon as my fingertips were free, I felt with them a rough wall. I was able to use the wall. As by pulling and wriggling I raised the hem of the sack an inch at a time, I could keep the slack I had won by pressing my back against the wall. Sack and wall were rough against my bare shoulders.

As soon as my arms were free of the sack to the elbows, everything became easy. Comparatively easy. I was able to tuck my head far enough down into my breast, so that my fingertips could reach the top of the sack. Then, slowly, painfully, but inevitably, I pulled it clear of my shoulders and head.

It was a very dirty sack, inside and out. Fresh earth clung to it. It came to me, ludicrously, that from it had come potatoes eaten that night at Strathgallant.

The huge dinner, the sequence of suppers, seemed very far away. In truth they were. The carriage had travelled for a long time.

I inspected my surroundings and, as far as I could, myself.

I was in a room, absolutely bare except for one dingy blanket on the floor. It was a little room, almost a cell, measuring perhaps eight feet by six. I did not recognize it. I was sure I had never seen it before. It did not belong to Strathgallant. Walls and floor were of rough stone. There was one narrow window, high, just below the ceiling. It was hardly larger than the arrow-slits in parts of the Strathgallant walls. Small as I was, I thought I could get no more than one arm through it: and small as I was, I could not reach it to do even so much. From inspecting the window, I saw that the walls were a full yard thick. I guessed I was in one of the little, ancient fortified farmhouses. There were not a few of these. Most were now unoccupied, because they were sited as fortresses rather than as farms, remote, inconvenient, and very uncomfortable. The room had a door, of massive oak. As a matter of form I tried the door. The lock rattled in its socket. That was all it did. It was one of the big old-fashioned locks, which take keys the size of saucers. The lock itself would be an oblong of iron the size of a playing-card, and half an inch thick. I guessed that this had been a store-room. No one who lived in such a place would have day-to-day possessions to justify such a lock. The room had held sacks of grain, salted meat, fish in brine, perhaps kegs of illicit whisky. The lock kept thieves out. It kept me in.

For myself, I could see my gown, my bosom, my arms and shoulders. They were all stained and smeared with ancient dirt and the fresh dirt of the potato-sack. My gown was torn at the breast. That must have been from the rough handling I had suffered. The watch-spring hoops in the crinoline were indomitable. Defiantly, saucily, they had sprung out into their proper circles, so that I was again enormously skirted. Nothing more incongruous could be imagined.

I felt my hair. Of course it was a wild mop. I did not think my face was cut or bruised. I thought I could feel the marks of dried tears in the grime on my cheeks.

They had been tears of rage and frustration. At least, I told myself they had.

It was full day, though I thought it was still very early in the morning.

I was missing one slipper. My left foot had a stocking only. I remembered that I had kicked it off, in the struggle when I was first seized. It must still be there, on the terrace, in full view. It would be seen. Gardeners would be busy on the terrace in the dawn, to make things tidy after the ball, to make things ready for a castle-full of guests. A gardener would run in with the slipper, and give it to a maid. It would go from hand to hand, until someone recognized it as mine. Mary Cochrane would know at once that it was mine. A lost slipper would surely speak of a struggle. No doubt a search had already begun. Probably they were dragging the Gallant. Now they would know, surely, that I had been seized. In that knowledge, they would search just such a place as this, though it might be a long time before they reached it . . .

Hope flared. I thought that missing slipper might be my salvation.

I sat; I lay down on the dirty, inadequate blanket; I hobbled about my cell, my slipperless foot uncomfortable on the rough stone floor. I tried to look out of the little high window. I listened intently for any sound.

At long intervals there were sounds. A horse; wheels; a murmur of distant voices; boots on stone. I heard the cry of plovers, and the twitter of little birds.

I tried to make out what had happened to me.

I was worth robbing only for the garnets the Countess had lent me. I still had them – necklace and bracelets. Robbery could be no part of the cause of this.

Was I to be held for ransom? It seemed an obvious possibility. I supposed the Countess would pay for my return. In that case, some note would already have gone to Strathgallant, or even been left behind when I was taken. There would be an immediate and enormous search. Or would there? Suppose the note said that, if there were any slightest sign of search, my fingers would be cut off one by one? Such things had happened, though not, I thought, in Perthshire.

I inspected my fingers, very small and dirty, and hoped I should be allowed to keep them.

Had anyone a violent grudge against me? I thought not.

Was it the opposite? Was this the work of somebody who wanted me so badly that he took this medieval way of getting me?

My mind went back to Colin, the man of violence, the man with a streak of folly.

The kidnapper had had help – had it still, as I knew from the voices I had heard. One other man at least, probably two, perhaps more. Colin had tough military friends all over Scotland, with servants tough and discreet and loyal. More easily than anybody else, he could recruit a gang for an exploit such as this.

The thing must have been planned exactly, like a military operation – Alex struck down by a weapon that was to hand, the sack ready, the route to the carriage planned to be quick and invisible, the carriage itself waiting in the right place, the road explored, this place chosen and prepared. More than anybody else I knew, Colin had the training and experience to manage such an affair.

The attacker had picked me up like a rag-doll. That was Colin's way, and suggested his massive strength.

It was easier to imagine Colin's hand striking down Alex, than any other hand.

He had wept. A man who could weep for love, was half insane with love. It all made horrible sense to me.

Colin had gone off alone, day after day, for whole days at a time, seen by no one from when he set off until he returned, able to cover great distances on his great horse. He said he was exploring the hills against the season of deer-stalking. He was exploring the hills, and finding this house; and arranging for the carriage and the men; and making all his precise arrangements.

He had begun to plan, then, at the moment when I mentioned Maudie Plimstock. He knew, at that moment, that he would not have me willing. He wanted me willing or unwilling.

Whoever did it knew me, even in the dark. Whoever did it was at the ball, able to watch me and follow my movements and choose his moment. It could not be an outsider, a stranger, a criminal. It must be one of us. Of us, who but Colin?

So, what now? What could he gain from hurting and frightening me, but my anger?

If he loved me, surely he would not injure me. But suppose all this were not love only, but also jealousy. It was the other side of the same coin. Alex was struck down not only because he was there, because he was in the way, but also because he was kissing me. I thought of Othello. Another soldier. He was maddened to murder by jealousy. It was his wife he killed, the woman he loved, because he loved her. If Colin could not have me, would he kill me so that no one else should have me? Could a man who wept act so? Could a man who did *not* weep act so?

225

I thought about it, hour after dreary hour, trying to explain the past, trying to guess at the future. I knew that I was jumping to conclusions, but the more I thought about it, the more likely my guesses seemed.

Heavy footsteps approached the door. I stood up. I put a hand to my breast, to hold up the front of my dress where it was torn. There was a grinding noise, as the key turned in the massive old lock. I held my breath. The door opened a little. A man stood in the half-open door. He completely filled the space, blocking it against my escape. He looked at me curiously. He was a big, fat, heavy man with long greasy black hair and a long greasy coat. He did not look like a countryman. He did not look like anyone I had ever seen. He looked debauched, evil, merciless. He was unshaven. His face was black with dirty stubble. Across the room, I could smell the reek of whisky and cheap tobacco.

He put down on the floor a tin plate, on which there was half a loaf of bread and a lump of yellow cheese. He put down beside it a small metal jug of water. He reached into the pocket of his greasy coat, and drew out something small and white. He tossed this object into the middle of the floor.

It was my slipper.

Now there was no clue, anywhere in or about Strathlarrig, as to what had become of me.

Except that, I supposed, Colin would be missing too. Would they think that was another abduction? Was it possible to imagine that Colin had been abducted? Would they suppose that Colin and I had eloped together? Would they guess at the truth? What was the truth?

From the look of the little slice of sky I could see, I thought it was noon. It was many hours since I had eaten, and then I had only a dish of raspberries. I had not thought I would be hungry. I had not thought of food at all, having much else on my mind. But I fell upon that bread and cheese, as Benjie Craufurd used to fall upon his meat and oatmeal. On the bread and on the pale surface of the cheese, my filthy fingers left marks in the shape of fingers. When I wiped my fingers on the silk of my skirt, they became dirtier rather than cleaner. Well, the dirt was mostly earth from a potato field, wholesome enough. Had it been soot or

226

sewage I would have ignored it.

I tried to eat slowly, but I gobbled like a nestling.

I was thankful for the water, too. It was clean and clear, but stained a pale brown colour. It was burn water, peaty. I had been used to drinking such water, on the hill, all my life. It did very well, unless a dead sheep lay across the spring.

It was only after I had drunk all the water, that I thought of using some of it to wash. But I should have needed the whole River Gallant to get clean, and fresh clothes to feel clean, and a comb of double strength to look tidy.

I inspected the tin plate which I had licked clean, and the tin jug which I had emptied. They were cheap things, made by some factory in Lanarkshire, of the sort used in the slums of cities, and in crofts all over the Highlands. Could they be weapons? I grasped the plate by the rim. I thought a backhand blow, with the edge, to the face, might do some damage – a blow to the eyes or the mouth. I could not imagine getting in such a blow to the fat greasy man who had brought me the plate. I could not imagine getting in such a blow to Colin.

The jug was too light to use as a club. My dancing slippers were soft, and weighed a few ounces. My necklace, used as a whip, would do no more than tickle.

I sat down, my great skirt billowing.

Hoops of watch-spring steel. One of those might make a whip to damage even the fat man, even Colin. They would not be disabled, but they might be distracted . . .

At one point, the tin plate had a roughened edge, as though someone had tried to take a bite out of it. This was the nearest I had to knife or scissors.

The hoops were not in the silk overskirt of my gown, but in the stiffened petticoat below. I knew that the hoops were continuous strips of steel, all the way round, except where the ends of each joined at the back. I thought the two ends were not welded or riveted, but held together by special stitching in the petticoat. By contriving to drag the back of the petticoat as far as I could round to the front, and by contorting myself so that I almost faced backwards, I was able to attack the place of the join with my roughened plate-rim.

Of course, it would have been far better to have taken the petticoat off. I could not do so without taking the whole gown off, for the petticoat was part of the gown. I was not sure that I could reach the little buttons at the back of my bodice. I was very sure I did not want to strip in this place, among men like the greasy fat man.

I do not know how long I was labouring at the destruction of that petticoat, in most awkward positions, with a most inadequate tool. By scratching and scraping and picking at the stitches with my fingernails, I did at last uncover a little of the narrow band of steel. I found the end, and freed it. I tried to pull it out, and succeeded only in cutting my fingers. I had to tear away much, much more of the petticoat. It took what seemed hours – what was certainly an hour. Each time I had scraped and picked away a bit of the stitching, I tried to pull the hoop out of the stuff, and each time I had to attack the next stitches.

I had it clear at last, a dull snake of steel, a veritable whip, a vicious weapon, very long, springy, sharp-edged. I could not grip it without cutting myself. I contrived a grip, using one of my slippers. I tried it. The watchspring steel whistled about in the confined space, and I thought it would slice a man in half. I hid my whip under the blanket on the floor, with just a few inches clear, almost invisible against the stone. I practised pulling it out quickly, so that I could seize any chance that came.

I did not truly think that any of this would be of any use to me. But it was the best I could do. It was all I could do.

The sun began to go down. In doing so, it shone directly for the first time through the window of my cell. One bright, dusty beam slanted in, and made a radiant badge on the stones of the floor.

I was more and more puzzled, and no less frightened.

If Colin wanted me, why did he not come to me? What good was I to him or to anyone, locked away on my own?

The sunbeam swung so that it was almost horizontal, as the sun sank. The bright splash of sunlight was no longer on the floor but on the wall. At this time, twenty-four hours before, I had been dressing for my ball, happy and excited, and a little alarmed, and in raptures about my gown and about myself.

I heard hoof-beats, wheels, voices. It was an arrival, not a departure.

My heart began to thud. My breath rasped in my throat. I stood up, certain that I was now at last about to face my captor. I made sure that the end of my watchspring whip was where I could grab it and, in one continuous movement, swing it. I held up the front of my torn dress, to cover as much of my bosom as it would.

Footsteps, and the turning key. The creaking of the door, and a man in the doorway.

I was speechlesss with astonishment. I could only stand and stare.

The horizontal sunbeam flared on a head of thick, smooth, buttercup-yellow hair, and on a handsome face golden after weeks of sunshine.

Yes, it was Jamie.

He said pleasantly, 'I am afraid you have been bored and lonely, dearest, but they assure me you have been fed. One more night here, and then we shall be married in the morning. Why do you look so surprised? I told you that our marriage was a thing which would happen. We are promised to one another. Nothing has changed, except the methods you have obliged me to use. I cannot really apologise for them, because if you had not looked like changing your mind, I would not have had to employ them.'

'You released me from my promise!' I blurted out.

It was not what I had intended to say, but it was what came out of my mouth.

'Ah,' he said, 'I released you from your promise, but not myself from mine. Remember that I am a lawyer and a politician. Language is the tool of both those trades. I use it to serve me. I am, of course, trained to do so. In offering you your choice, I was making a large and quite meaningless gesture, as politicians habitually do. Because your choice is no longer relevant. Choose what or whom you like, dearest girl, and it will not make the slightest difference. I am in the position of offering a blind man a free tour of a picture gallery, or allowing a man without hands the use of my knife and fork. You can see that I shall be Prime Minister? I hate to extol myself, but you can see that to verbal adroitness I add the capacity for meticulous organization, and to both a total dedication to success. That, at least, you knew about.'

'You said you had outgrown it,' I said numbly.

'Oh no. I misled you a little, perhaps, without lying. I said I had outgrown the assumption that because I wanted things I should inevitably get them. I did not say, though you may have imagined me to say, that I had outgrown determination. From the moment of poor Colin's arrival at Strathgallant, it was clear that I should not inevitably get you, unless I took the necessary steps. The probability of my winning you by, er, conventional means was further reduced by the successive arrivals of Jules and of my brother Alex. I took the necessary steps. You may remember that, when you were riding with Colin and fishing with Jules, I went off on prolonged, solitary expeditions. Quite in the manner of Colin. I found this place. I learned the road to it so that I could find it in the dark. You know also that I wrote many letters, and that I am among other things a criminal lawyer. I assisted in the defence on one occasion of a particularly vicious Glasgow criminal, leader of a kind of private army of bullies and cut-throats. We secured his acquittal, by organizing the lies of himself and his friends into a credible pattern. He is grateful to me. He also knows that I have documentary evidence that could send him most of the way, perhaps all the way, to the gallows. I have treasured that evidence. I thought it might one day be useful. It has been useful. I wrote not to him, because he is not good at reading, but to an intermediary. Thus my recruitment of the three fellows who have been helping me, one of whom, I think, you briefly met this morning. You probably thought he looked like something out of the worst of the Glasgow slums. You were quite right. He is. No one within fifty miles of these parts has ever clapped eyes on any of my three helpers, except in the darkness, and nobody will clap eyes on them. They will be gone tonight. You and I will be alone. As a consequence of the way we shall spend the night, our marriage in the morning will become quite necessary. Great-Aunt Selina will be a little shocked at your conduct, but she will the more appreciate the necessity of our marriage. So will all who wish you well. Else, I am afraid you will be spoiled goods, branded, hopelessly compromised.'

He paused, and sighed, and smiled.

I suddenly felt bottomlessly tired and weak. It was a long, long time since I had slept. I subsided onto the blanket on the floor.

He said, 'Other letters, of course, secured the hired carriage, which nobody saw in the dark. Others a short lease of this house, of which my occupation is, of course, entirely legal. Yet others alerted the Minister in Crask to our forthcoming nuptials. He believes us both to have a great dislike of pomp in private matters, and he applauds our decision to make no extravagant display. It was quite wearisome writing all those letters, when I would rather have been walking on the hill with Benjie Craufurd and you. But I am rewarded.'

'By raping a woman who hates you.'

'Strong words, Dita. I hope both will turn out to be gross exaggerations. Be that as it may, you know as well as I do that my reward goes far beyond my possession of yourself, intensely desirable as you are and passionately as I continue to desire you.'

I began to see a great light. I began to understand why he had gone, and was continuing to go, to such barbaric lengths.

'Great-Aunt Selina,' he said, 'may not altogether applaud your choice, but she will surely honour her promise. She might not have done so, I apprehend, if Jules had remained in her favour. But as things are, she will adhere to her plan out of obstinacy, if nothing else. I shall have Strathgallant, and I shall have a great fortune. I shall put it to better use than any other possible recipient – poor blustering Colin, or my pedantic collegiate brother, or, certainly, that little French criminal you seemed to like so much. Ah God, what I have suffered from poverty! How it has held me back! How wildly I have envied richer men! What torture and humiliation it has been to ask my mother for the wherewithal to buy a coat, or to take a train!'

The sun had gone down behind the Western hills. The horizontal sunbeam was snuffed out. But that head of smooth buttercup hair seemed to illuminate the room like a torch.

'Harry told me about that ingenious plan of Great-Aunt Selina's,' said Jamie. 'It was cousinly in him, don't you think? He was shocked by it, most disapproving. I found his attitude grotesque. Of course he is not poor. Not as rich as I shall be, but not poor. I am not sure how Harry knew. Simply guessed, I think, or the Eredines did. Do you know the law concerning a married woman's property? I do, naturally. To all intents and

231

purposes, she has none. At the moment of her marriage, total control of all that she has passes to her husband. And all that she acquires in the future. Her property becomes his property, as she does. It is an extremely satisfactory arrangement. I warmly approve of the state of the law, and pledge myself, as you may bear witness, to resist any change in it.'

Jamie was terribly pleased with himself. He was hugging himself for his cleverness, and for the great fortune he would have.

Of course he would not have it.

'The Countess will give you nothing,' I said, 'when she hears what you have done. Do you think she will think you have earned the right to Strathgallant?'

'Certainly. She will press it on me. She will be the more ready to give me everything, when she learns how I rescued you, and you married me out of hand in love and gratitude.'

'*Rescued* me?'

'Of course. Where do you suppose I have been all day? Making myself obviously guilty by hiding here? No no, I have been at Strathgallant, of course, most vigorously leading the search for you. I was in the midst of them all, in the dawn, before anyone realised I had been away. We have been dragging the river, combing the woods, exploring the attics of the castle, sending messages everywhere. The atmosphere was quite restless. Great-Aunt Selina has been beside herself. I think the shock may shorten her life, resilient as she undoubtedly is. I shall be sincerely sorry, you know. There is much in her to admire, though much to deplore. But it would be idle, as well as hypocritical, to ignore the silver lining.'

'You are a cynical monster.'

'Not altogether, dearest. I shall put that fortune to good use. I remain quite serious about all that. Well, to return to the turmoil at Strathgallant, the burden upon me was the more onerous, because I was the only one of us there. Jules, as you know, ran guiltily away when he was unmasked by Cousin Marianne, and Harry ran after him, for reasons we do not fully understand. Neither Colin or Alex has been seen since the small hours of the morning – since the moment, more or less, when you also disappeared. This has given rise to the wildest speculation. Colin in particular has been darkly suspected of the kind of impetuous audacity one associates with his profession. As to Alex's where-abouts, no one can make the wildest guess.'

'Did you kill him?'

'I think not.'

'You could not care if you had.'

'I would be glad if I had. I have always detested being a twin, and the twin of such a paragon, combining scholarly dedication with physical courage and skill on horseback. I could kill him for riding well. But I don't think I did. To revert once more – a note came to me by the hand of a stranger, whom only I saw, of course, during the late afternoon. I gave myself no time to explain anything – simply sped off in a pony-trap, crying that I had been given a clue as to your whereabouts. We shall return together in triumph, coming by way of the Manse in Crask.'

'But I shall tell them all that you have told me.'

'There are several answers to that. The first is that I shall be your husband, your lord, and I shall not be indulgent to wild and slanderous romancings. To other things, yes – to prodigal expenditure on dress, for example. But not to the unbridled use of your tongue. The second answer is that nothing, but nothing, connects me to those men outside, to the carriage, to this house. The men do not know my name. The owner of the carriage believes me to be called Campbell, and my temporary landlord believes me to be a Mr George Murray. Neither has seen me personally. Both have been paid in cash. I had great difficulty, incidentally, in extracting that cash from my mother, who believes it to be intended for my forthcoming journey to London on political business. A third answer to your threat is that it is blankly impossible for me to have abducted you. I never left Strathgallant. There I was, in the dawn, among the last of the exhausted revellers, beginning to ask, like everybody else, "Where is Dita? Where are Colin and Alex?"'

I wondered numbly where Colin and Alex were, indeed. But there is selfishness in terror. I was more worried about myself.

'If you are so ill-advised as to make the sort of speech you suggest,' said Jamie, 'your story, being seen to be impossible, will be ascribed to the hysterical fancy of a young female who has been maltreated and terrified. It will be seen as an excellent thing that you have a steady, adult, professional man to look after you.'

I was silenced. He had thought it all out. The legal brain was as good as the military brain, for planning and executing an abduction.

In suspecting Colin, I had thought of action, violence, a streak of folly, and great physical strength. What Jamie had fitted him far better for the act. What he had was a willingness to stop at nothing. What he had was a sane, rational overwhelming greed.

And of course he had strength and to spare, for picking up and carrying a very small person like me.

The disaster was that Harry should have told him that, with me, went so much. I supposed Harry had thought that a man like Jamie – a man like the person he thought Jamie to be – would react as he had reacted. Harry thought Jamie would refuse with disgust to dangle after a fortune. Harry had been deceived as badly as I. It was no comfort, that I was not the only fool.

It was sickening to think that all that gentle passion, that delightful impulsive love-making, had been a fraud.

Oh yes, Jamie would be Prime Minister, since he could act so brilliantly and lie so consummately. If he wooed the electorate with one tenth of the cynical skill with which he had wooed me, why then, they would depose the Queen and vote him a crown.

I would be his consort. I would kill myself first.

It was getting dark. Soon I would be left alone with this disgusting man.

I was still sitting, drained of all strength, where I had collapsed on the blanket. My fingers found the exposed inches of the whip of watch-spring steel. It was not time to use it. By the metal lay the slipper which was to be my grip. If Jamie thought it strange that I had taken off one slipper, he did not remark on the fact.

With my other hand, I continued to hold up the torn flap of my bodice. I saw Jamie staring at what he could see of my breast. I did not know what was in his eyes or behind his eyes.

'I should reassure you on one point,' he said, speaking with a quiet reasonableness which, at that time, in that place, was more awful than any bellowing. 'In taking possession of yourself as well as of Strathgallant, I am not making any large sacrifice in

234

the cause of my finances and my future. Quite the reverse. You are a very desirable little thing. What your clothes reveal of your body makes me quite avid to see more.'

There was that in his voice that made me think he would indulge his curiosity at once. That he would make me strip. That he would tear my clothes off me if I refused.

I groped for my slipper and, with the slipper in my hand, for the end of the whip.

Footsteps approached the door, and someone knocked.

'Right,' called Jamie. To me he said softly, 'I shall not hurt you with my tooth again. I hope I shall not hurt you at all. That is, of course, very largely up to you. In a moment we can be more comfortable. Just now I must pay my fellows off.'

He went out, locking the door behind him.

I heard voïces, interminably, as though they were haggling about their wage.

There were still pale streaks low in the western sky, visible through my narrow window. They purpled. It was full dark. The sky had the incomplete, transparent darkness of the northern summer, but my room was pitch.

I prayed.

I heard laughter – Jamie's once-loved laugh, and the guffaws of his hirelings. Well might they be bosom cronies, he and those back-street cut-throats. I heard wheels, hoofs, the clink of harness. I supposed the men would be taking the hired carriage, so that it would still have no traceable connection to Jamie. In the morning I would ride to the Manse in the pony-trap. For such a journey, a dungcart would have been no better, and no worse, than a royal state coach.

Footsteps, the lock, Jamie again, now carrying a lantern.

Leaving the door open, he crossed the room to where I sat. He shone the lantern over me.

He said, 'Move your hand.'

I thought he had seen or guessed at the whip. I moved my right hand, innocently as possible, leaving the slipper by the whip on the floor.

'The other hand,' he said.

With my right hand, stealthily, I took again the slipper, my grip, and with it took hold of the whip. I moved my left hand

235

from my breast. The torn flap of my bodice fell forward. It revealed my breast almost to the nipple – to the very edge of the nipple.

'How beautiful,' he said softly. 'A beautiful little alabaster mountain. And the peak still hidden. Coy peak. Shy peak. I imagine the pink of a sunset, of almond blossom, against that perfect white.'

He put the lantern on the floor. He bent, and reached a hand towards my breast. I nerved myself not to recoil – because, if I had done so, I would have put my weight onto the hidden whip under the blanket.

He put his hand on the bare skin of my breast, where no hand had ever been before. My skin crawled with loathing at his touch. He began to pull the torn bodice down, so that my nipple was uncovered.

'Pink rosebud in the snow,' he murmured.

Perhaps he was trying to convince me that it was my body he loved, as well as my money. Perhaps he was trying to convince himself. Perhaps it was even true.

All his attention was on my breast.

My hand protected by the slipper, I pulled the whip from behind me, from beneath the blanket, and with all my strength hit him on the side of the face. He was not as quick as Harry. The whip hit not his hand but his ear and cheek. It half wrapped itself about his head, before springing away. The whiplash of sharp-edged watch-spring left a bright line of blood across his face. His ear was slit and his cheek laid open. Blood gushed. He screamed like a wounded hare. He clapped a hand to his face, and screamed again when he saw the blood on it. I swung the whip. He caught it, in the other hand. He screamed a third time, as the metal cut his hand. He dropped the whip. Both his hands were now daubed with blood. He grabbed my wrist. He made me drop the whip. He took a handful of my hair. By my hair, he pulled me to my feet. He towered over me. The lower part of his face was masked with blood. Still holding my hair with one hand, he tore my bodice away from my body with the other. I was naked to the waist, the torn threads of my bodice flapping about my hips. In tearing my bodice, he smeared my breasts with blood.

236

Never once relaxing his agonising grip of my hair, he bent to pick up the lantern. He pushed me in front of him to the door and out of the room. We were in another room, a little larger, with a small but normal window. There was no glass in the window. It was curtained, but with curtains as tattered and inadequate as my bodice. The room held a table, two rickety chairs, and an iron bed with a bare, dirty mattress.

He was hurting me. I thought he would pull the hair out of my scalp. There was blood everywhere, from his face and from his hands. He threw me down on the bed, letting go of my hair. He was sobbing. I could hardly see his face for blood. He put down the lantern on the table. He stood over me, dropping blood onto my skin. He began to tear with both hands at what remained of my dress.

There was a sharp crack, an explosion, outside the house, near the window. It was an unmistakable noise. It was a gun. Jamie seemed to be hit in the back by an invisible hand. He toppled forward, and collapsed on top of me. His face, still pouring blood, was on my waist. He lay still. I screamed. I think that was my first scream. I struggled out from underneath his weight. His body was utterly flaccid. He lay face down across the bed. In the back of his velvet doublet, clearly visible in the lantern-light, was a small hole.

The room had another door. I ran to it. I remembered that I was half naked. Fighting down my revulsion, I took the lantern and ran back to my prison. I picked up the blanket from the floor. It was dabbled with blood from Jamie's face and hands. I put the blanket over my shoulders. I felt the wetness of the blood on my bare shoulders. I was not sobbing or hysterical. I was desperate to get out of that hateful place. I could not think what had happened. I did not try to think. I ran back past Jamie's body. The other door of the larger room was locked. The key was in the lock. I turned it with difficulty. It was old and stiff.

The door was the outside door. I gasped the air of freedom. I ran out of the house, and into the arms of a man. An enormous man, who clutched at me. I screamed. I think it was only my second scream.

'Dita, Dita, you're safe.'

It was Colin.

11

Then I did burst into tears – my first since those tears of rage at the potato-sack. Colin held me, soothing me.

Soon I was mistress of myself. I was safe. I was unharmed. There was nothing to cry about.

Colin went into the house, with the lantern. I waited for him outside. There was nothing in that place I ever wanted to see again. I was not frightened, standing outside in the darkness. Colin was near.

Colin swore at the sight of so much blood. I told him what had happened.

'Good God, what a soldier you would make,' he said.

'But without a gun. I'm so glad you had one.'

'But I didn't,' he said, in a startled voice. 'All day I have been itching for one, but I didn't have time to get mine from the room, when I saw you taken.'

'You saw?'

'Dimly. How else could I be here, if I had not seen and followed? I saw you in the distance. I didn't see who hit Alex and carried you off. I just had time to catch a horse – God knows what horse, somebody's unfortunate carriage horse, waiting to be harnessed. So I've been helpless.'

'Tell me everything, Colin. All that you have done and seen.'

'I've seen little and done nothing. Tell me your story first, Dita. Tell me as we go. It was obliging of Jamie to leave us a pony and trap. I had to let my borrowed horse go, some distance off, and creep the rest of the way on foot. By the way, is this your shoe? I found it in the further room.'

'It's my whip-handle,' I said.

He knelt in the heather, and shod me, by the light of the faithful lantern.

Slowly, because the pony was sleepy, we trundled the long way back to Strathgallant. I told Colin all my story. All that I did not mention, was the fortune that Jamie was after. As I told it, all that he did was for love of me. I could not help it that the story magnified my attraction. Colin was not to know the truth about the Countess's new will.

Colin interrupted me with questions, because I was a little rambling in my narrative. I was tired. He wanted to understand exactly what had happened, at each point.

When I had finished, he said again, after a pause, 'My God, what a soldier you would have made.'

'No. I was a crybaby. I cried twice.'

'Once with rage and once with relief. I cry too, you know.'

'Yes, I know.'

'Would you have let Jamie force you into marriage tomorrow?'

'I don't know. Yes, I think I would have had to marry him, after I had been – deflowered.'

'Yes,' he said heavily, 'you would have had to. It is a barbaric rule, isn't it? And many people would not believe you had been forced, utterly against your will. Jamie was a handsome fellow, after all, and making a name for himself.'

'But,' I said, outraged, 'nobody would believe that I set off willingly, in the middle of my ball, to a horrid deserted farm-house, for an illicit night . . .'

'Not my Aunt Lucinda? The man's adoring Mamma?'

'Oh. Well, yes, she would probably tell herself . . .'

'And not stop short at telling only herself. People are terribly eager to believe the worst, you know. They love smacking their lips. Especially in a place like Edinburgh, a boring provincial town pretending to be a capital city. Especially aging women contemplating a beautiful young girl. Yes, Jamie was quite right. Unless you had married him at once you would have been ostracised.'

'Perhaps I shall be in any case.'

'Not with what I shall have to say. After all, I saw the abduction.'

'That is a comfort. You are a comfort. Tell me your story.'

239

'It is brief and devoid of incident. I saw you go out onto the terrace with Alex. I went out after you. I was feeling . . . That is not part of the story. I had an impression someone was prowling along behind you, just as you say you had yourself. Well, we now know that we were both right. I imagined Jamie must have muffled his head in something dark, or one of us would have seen his hair. I saw you and Alex together at the far end of the terrace.'

'Oh,' I said, embarrassed, remembering what Alex and I had been doing.

'I was a long way away,' said Colin, 'and it was dark. So I could not make out what happened next – suddenly three people instead of two, and suddenly two again, and then only one, a curious shape. That was you over Jamie's shoulder, with your head in a sack. This oddly-shaped figure in turn disappeared. I hurried up. I found Alex lying groaning, just recovering consciousness.'

'Badly hurt?'

'Quite a headache, I imagine. And fairly angry, I should think. Well, it was supremely obvious what had happened, and the only thing was to give chase immediately. Otherwise nobody in the world would know what had become of you. I had no time to get help, no time to arm myself, no time to do anything but pelt down those steps to the park and hope I followed the right carriage. Luckily I was in time to see a bundle being pushed into a carriage which was quite separate from all the other carriages, and ready to move off at once. I found a sleepy horse hitched to a rail, in a halter, so I borrowed it and gave chase. I had to keep far enough behind to escape detection, but not so far that I risked losing you. That on a most awkward carriage horse without a saddle or a bit. Not a comfortable journey.'

'Poor Colin.'

'Not as uncomfortable as yours, and hear me making far more fuss. When the carriage turned off the road onto this track, I got off my steed and sent him packing. I hoped he would find his way home. Then I followed your carriage on foot. It was not difficult, you were going so slow. But it was coming on daylight by then, and I knew I was a bit conspicuous.'

Indeed he must have been – a giant in Highland evening dress, going along a remote cart-track to a deserted cottage.

240

'I got as near the house as I dared,' Colin went on, 'but it wasn't very near. I had to lie hidden until I saw what I could do, and the ground all round that house is like a billiard-table. I saw two men go into the house with a bundle that was obviously you. The other two unharnessed one of the carriage horses, and put it between the shafts of a broken-down little gig. Almost at once, one man came out of the house and got into the gig. He was wearing the kilt, but that was all I could see. He was muffled up in a scarf, and he had a bonnet pulled down over his ears. I know now that it was Jamie. I couldn't follow the gig on foot, and I couldn't leave the house where I knew you were. Still I must just wait and see. A man came out of the house, and sat in a chair by the door with a shotgun in his lap. Every so often he was relieved. One or other of the three was there all day. I couldn't get nearer than fifty yards from the house without being seen. I would be no good to you with a charge of buckshot in my chest, and I could not forget that you were a hostage as well as a prisoner. The men were obvious sweepings of the slums, even at that distance. That was another reason for being careful, for your sake as well as my own. The plan I made was to wait until dark, then try to collar the sentry and get his gun. I could do nothing in the meantime, unless the situation changed. So I did nothing. That was my day.

'Back came a different vehicle, towards evening. It was Jamie, in a pony trap. For a moment I thought he had come to rescue you. I was just about to whistle to him, so that we could join forces. Then I saw him greeted like an old friend by the sentry, and the whole thing became obvious. Obvious, but utterly amazing.'

'That Jamie should be so violent?'

'That the Jamie we know today – knew yesterday, rather – should do anything so brutal, yes. But I still had hours to sit and think, while the sun went down, and I remembered things about him as a boy.'

'He was solemn.'

'He was a very, very bad loser.'

'Oh.'

'So was Alex, actually. I am afraid I blame their mother, for bringing them up to believe they had a divine right to win. Alex

241

has changed. Jamie hasn't. I mean, didn't. Well, as it began to get dark, I began to feel that somebody else was doing what I was doing.'

'Watching? Hiding?'

'Yes. I just got a hint of a movement, a tiny noise. It was someone being very, very careful. I hoped it was an ally. In the full dark, I might have tried stalking him, but I didn't know exactly where he was, and I couldn't move from where I was without being seen. From the house, as well as by my hidden friend. I was distracted by a fox, too – I thought he was another spy.

'The next episode was that the bully-boys went off in the carriage, with just one horse. That might mean that Jamie was alone in the house with you. But there might be another or others, who had been there when the party arrived and had stayed indoors. It didn't seem to me likely, but it was obviously possible. The thing to do was to get right up to the house, and look and listen, as soon as it was full dark. I had to know how many people there were before I burst in there. Of course, I couldn't tell what my lurking friend was planning, or whether what he did would affect my plans. I wasn't completely sure he even existed.

'Well, I crawled up to the house as soon as I thought I was safe from being shot out of a window. The front, where the door and the bigger window are, was dark and silent, so I went round to the back. I could see there was a light in the back room, but I couldn't see in. I heard a voice, a man's voice, Jamie's. No words. Then those screams. His screams. Extraordinary. I've heard the same from a wounded wild hog, in India. Very soon afterwards, the shot. I ran round to the front of the house. Whoever had fired the shot had legged it away in the dark. I could hear running footsteps. The track is baked hard by the sun. I thought of giving chase, but I thought you were more important. I'd just arrived at that decision, when you came out of the house and bumped into me.'

'And burst into tears.'

'Yes, isn't it odd how we have that effect on one another?'

Colin's story was convincing at all points, and I was sure it was untrue. I thought he had brought a gun – his own revolver,

242

which I knew he had with him. I thought he had gone round to the front of the house when the light disappeared from the back, and shot Jamie through the window by the light of the lantern. I thought he had hidden the gun somewhere about his huge person, or thrown it far away into the heather. I thought he had entirely invented the other watcher.

I had been wrong in thinking Colin was an abductor – wrong, probably, in thinking he was capable of treating me so. I was certainly right that he had fired a gun in order to kill a man – he could not be in one battle without doing that, and he had been in many. It was no great matter to him. He would lose no sleep over it.

A sense of what had happened to me came over me like – like a potato-sack, stifling and frightening. A man shot in front of my eyes; a dead man falling across my body; my own skin puddled with his blood.

But I did not mind Jamie being dead.

Colin said suddenly, 'I have been wondering what I would have done, if I had been armed.'

'Shot Jamie, I hope.'

'Perhaps. But not like that. Not out of hand, in cold blood, from the dark, in the back. I don't think my finger would have obeyed my order to pull the trigger. I have pulled many triggers, and certainly tried to kill, but in the heat of battle, and when it is kill or be killed. I cannot be sorry that Jamie is dead, after what he had done and was planning to do to you. But I am glad that it was another hand than mine.'

If this was the story that Colin had decided to tell, then he was perhaps right to be consistent in telling it. But I would have preferred the truth. The blood I was sure was on his hands did not make him repellent to me. There were things about him still I was not at all sure of, but I did not mind him being a murderer.

After all, I had done my very worst to Jamie myself.

'An aspect of the situation I can't quite like,' said Colin presently, 'is that immediately we return we must make a full report to the County Police and the Procurator Fiscal. And I think they may find it tempting to name me as the man outside the window.'

'I can say . . .' I began.

'That you found me by the house, by the door, close to that window. That is all you can say. That is all you know, about my movements.'

'Nobody should suffer, for firing that shot,' I said. 'Whoever did it earns my undying gratitude. I wish he had fallen somewhere else, but otherwise I can find no fault.'

I hoped that, when I spoke like this, Colin would be frank with me. I wanted no more lies from him.

But he said, 'Aunt Lucinda Ramsay knows all the best lawyers in Edinburgh. Someone of her choice will assist the Prosecution, I suppose. An expert at cross-examination, who will extract from myself and from others what I visibly felt about you. How is jealousy, for a motive? You are lying in disarrayed clothing on a bed, your seducer is leaning over the bed . . . I can imagine the Prosecutor citing the case of Othello.'

I was startled that he should mention what had been in my mind.

I said, 'How do you know how I was lying and he was leaning, unless you saw?'

'You told me,' he replied.

It was true. I had. He had the answers. Still I did not believe him. Who could have believed him? Who could doubt that jealousy was one of the things in his mind? I thought he would indeed have a hard time in court, if they put him there for Jamie's murder. I could not help him. I had found him on the spot from which the shot was fired, and – I thought he had fired it.

Exhausted as I was, I could not sleep in the bouncing little trap. When I closed my eyes, what I saw was the sobbing, bloody mask leaning over me, and then the body falling on my body.

Greed for great wealth. Love for me too? I would never know.

Harry had told him. Why? From goodwill? From family feeling, ancient friendship? But, though they were cousins, I did not think Harry and Jamie had been close. They were not congenial. But Harry would go to great lengths to do what he thought was his duty. That was clear from the histories of Colin and Jules.

To Colin, Harry was much closer than to Jamie. They *were* congenial.

Surely, surely, Harry must have told Colin about the Countess's plan.

That this supremely obvious thought had not occurred to me before, shows how tired and shocked I was.

The gallant bareback ride, following the carriage – the day in hiding – the stalk up to the house – the shot – the rescue. It was not me he was saving, it was his chance of a castle and a fortune.

Colin had deceived me about his wife, and in that had shown weakness and moral cowardice. I thought he was deceiving me about Jamie's death, out of another sort of cowardice. Was he deceiving me about his love? He had wept. I had felt the tears on his cheek. They were real tears. Could a man weep with desire for a castle and a fortune? Why not? They were full as much worth weeping for, as an undersized girl on her eighteenth birthday.

My thoughts bounced erratically about inside my skull, as they will when you are strung as tight as a fiddlestring by horror and disgust, and at the same time physically exhausted. It was as though the bouncing of the trap bounced my brains.

I thought that if Jamie knew about my future, Alex knew. This was certain. Suddenly it was not certain. Harry might have trusted Jamie to tell Alex. Anyone would trust one twin to tell another, not knowing that Jamie was a monster, not knowing that he would strike down his twin, with a club, from behind, in the dark.

If Alex made love to me again, what was I to believe?

Jules knew, beyond doubt. Jules had fooled Harry to the top of his bent, as he had fooled all of us.

I was the poor little rich girl, which was strange for a penniless waif. Everyone wanted me for my money. They wept for my money, drew charming pictures for my money, danced like kangaroos, kissed me, murdered and were murdered, all for my money. In myself it seemed I was nothing – a small ordinary girl, with regular features and a narrow waist. Not repellent, perhaps, but if without money then without importance.

'I hoped you might sleep,' said Colin after a long silence.

'I would be frightened of my dreams.'

'I do not think you are frightened of anything mortal.'

But I was frightened of my own future. With money, I should

245

be courted for the wrong reasons, and never believe a word of love I heard. Without it, I should not be courted at all. It was a lowering thought.

So I was a little dismal, when we came back at last to Strathgallant.

To my amazement, the stable clock struck eleven, as we passed the arch. I had supposed that it was almost dawn. It was hard to believe that so much had happened so quickly.

There was uproar in the castle. Everyone, servants and family and guests, looked haggard with exhaustion. A few had snatched a few hours' sleep in the dawn, before my disappearance, or Colin's, or Alex's, was noticed. Most had been on their feet for forty hours.

Colin and I were surrounded by a most heart-warming joy. I was surprised to see so many people in tears. I remembered, numbly, to keep my disgusting blanket wrapped firmly about me, while I was embraced and my hand was shaken, as I had nothing underneath it, except dried patches of Jamie's blood.

I desperately wanted a bath and my bed, but I could not have them at once.

Of course Colin was the hero. It was no surprise to anyone that it was he who had rescued me. It was exactly what was expected of Colin. I heard tear-wet murmurs on all sides, that we would make a lovely couple. I realised, dazed as I was, that the night's work had in the eyes of all these loving people almost made a bridegroom of Colin and a bride of me. The story must end so – the knight-errant, and the maiden he rescued from the dragon.

I was almost too tired to stand, in the midst of the crowd in the hall, so I clung to Colin, who had had as hard a time as any of them, and for as long, and looked as though he had just got out of bed. My clutching his arm lent colour, no doubt, to the romantic ending everyone was writing to the story.

I was in a mood then – naturally I was – to write that ending myself. Wave upon wave of gratitude to Colin filled me, as I clung to his arm.

I said I was too tired to tell my story. I said I would tell it in the morning. Word was sent by a groom to the County Police and the Procurator Fiscal in Lochgrannomhead.

Mrs Ramsay looked almost unhinged with sleeplessness and worry. There were dark lines under her eyes, her hair was disordered and her dress untidy. I did not blame her.

She looked at us blankly. 'Where is Alexander? Where is James? Why have you not brought them? James went to find you. Why have you left him? Where is Alexander?'

In rescuing me, Colin had rescued the wrong person.

Miss Violet Carmichael, tears running down her face, said that the Countess had gone to bed, in utter exhaustion, but of course could not sleep for worry. I should go to see her at once.

I did so. I was shocked at the change in her. Leaning against her pillows in the great bed in her great room, she looked too frail to last the night. She stretched out her arms to me. They trembled. I saw tears in her eyes, which I had never seen there before in all my life, like little stars in the steady golden glow of the night-light.

'I have prayed,' she whispered, 'until the good Lord must have grown bored to death with the sound of my voice.'

And so, my tousled and dirty head on her breast as I knelt beside her bed, I wept for the third time.

And when I raised my head to look at her, she was transformed. Though there were tears on her lashes, there was a smile (that wide warm smile) on her lips, and her old face had recovered its strength and its spirit.

I marvelled that my disappearance had so aged her, and my return so revived her. I could not understand how I was so important. I did not seem to myself to merit such love from so great a lady.

Still I wore the ruins of my glorious gown, and the disgusting blanket like a plaid over my nakedness.

The Countess, holding my hand in both of hers, said, 'Colin found you and brought you back? Of course he did. Who else but my brave Colin?'

She, too, was writing the predictable romantic happy ending.

One more thing had to be done that night, dreadful as it was to do, late as was the hour, tired as we were. Mrs Ramsay had to be told that her elder son was dead.

We told her together, Colin and I, in the same small blue

247

drawing-room where Jules had been unmasked a lifetime before. Aunt Marianne was there, to comfort her friend.

We told our story briefly, leaving much out, as mercifully as we could.

Mrs Ramsay's reaction was strange. She simply refused to believe one word that either of us said. It was impossible that Jamie should have struck his brother down. We had not seen in the dark. We had made a mistake. If Jamie and I had been together in some remote house, it was I that had seduced him there. If I had been roughly handled, it was not by any son of hers. Jamie had been here, at the castle, leading the search for me, all night, all day, until he went off to rescue me. It was my fault that he was now missing – perhaps Colin's also. It was our fault that Alex was missing.

Jamie could not be dead. Someone else, perhaps. We had been mistaken in the darkness.

Of course Aunt Marianne believed us, because a son of hers had not just been murdered. She tried to make Mrs Ramsay accept the truth. She was wonderfully patient.

'So great the love for little Perdita that Jamie had,' she said. 'Who shall wonder if... From outside, some poacher, perhaps...'

'I do not know why you are telling me this impossible nonsense,' said Mrs Ramsay impatiently. 'I do not know why you have not brought my sons back.'

Colin, Aunt Marianne and I looked at one another helplessly.

And Aunt Marianne looked a little oddly at Colin. What was going through her mind was as obvious as though she had set it to music and sung it.

And then Alex appeared. He staggered across the drawbridge at midnight. He was brought to his mother, to us in that small blue room. He was like a drunkard with fatigue, and as tattered and grimy as myself.

Mrs Ramsay looked as though she wanted to take him on her lap. I thought we should not have been there, to see this reunion. But we were agog to hear what had happened to him.

He did not really know what had happened to him. He

remembered being with me on the terrace. (If he remembered more, he did not mention it in company.) He remembered an explosion in his head, and darkness. His next memory might for all he knew have been hours later – in fact, it was a few seconds later – Colin leaning over him, saying something, running off. He sat up, feeling groggy, with a very sore head. He was in time to see Colin running away down the stone steps from the terrace. He managed to follow. He lost sight of Colin, but saw an inert figure being bundled into a carriage. Without thinking, dizzy from the blow on his head, he staggered over to the carriage just as it began to move. The carriage stopped. Someone jumped down from the box, and grappled with him. There was another explosion in his head. Someone else had jumped down, on the other side, and run round behind, and knocked him out again.

Mrs Ramsay gave a sort of bellow of rage and grief, at this point in the story.

Alex grinned ruefully, and felt the back of his head.

'Only one lump,' he said, 'but that the size of a duck's egg. They must have hit me in exactly the same place.'

He did not recognise the one man he saw. He saw no other face.

He recovered consciousness to find himself in a confined space, like a coffin. After a moment's panic he realised he had not been buried alive: his world was jolting. It was violently uncomfortable for his headache, but at least it proved he was alive. Thinking as clearly as he could, he realised he was in the boot of the carriage, where luggage would normally be stowed.

After a time the carriage was stopped. The boot was opened and he was lifted out. He was dropped on the ground. His ankles were tied together, and his wrists were tied behind his back. He showed us the marks on his wrists. He was dragged into a ditch which was covered with rough grass, and hidden. He heard the carriage rolling away.

He thought that he then fainted, and spent a long time in a sort of swoon, unconscious or half unconscious. By the time he was recovered, it was already evening. He dragged himself out of the ditch, and set to work on his bonds. He could not reach the knot that bound his wrists with his fingers: he had to cut the cord. He could not reach the skean dhu in his stocking. He had to find a sharp stone. He could not find one. He dragged himself along the edge of the road for hundreds of yards, before he found a rock with a sharp edge. Then he was so long cutting the cord, that it was full dark before he was free.

And then he did not know which way to go, because he did not know in what direction he had been taken. He steered downhill, thinking that thus he must eventually come to a river. He fell often, from fatigue and dizziness. He came to a small river and then to a big one. He was sure it must be the Gallant, although he did not know the place in the dark. He was utterly undecided whether he should go upstream or down. He chose to go upstream, for no logical reason, and it was the right choice.

'When they took Alex,' I said to Colin, 'was when you were catching your horse.'

Colin nodded. 'One should have eyes in the back of one's head, for that sort of work.'

'If I'd had those,' said Alex, 'I'd know who hit me.'

'We'll talk about that in a minute,' said Colin. 'No need to distress your mother further.'

He was right, of course. Alex must be told about Jamie, but not in front of his mother.

For her part, she seemed to have lost her glee at recovering Alex, and was muttering about Jamie. Why had we not brought him back? Why had Alex not brought him back?

I found that I could take no more, though I was angry with myself for my weakness. Colin would say what had to be said to Alex. Aunt Marianne would look after Mrs Ramsay.

Mary Cochrane bathed me like a baby. I fell asleep repeatedly in the bath. She cried out when she saw all the blood. But, when she scrubbed me, she began to believe me that none of it was mine. I was not so much as scratched. It seemed amazing, but I had suffered no hurt whatsoever.

Even my scalp was no longer sore, where Jamie had pulled my hair.

I slept round the clock, and came to the surface to find my bedroom full of the noonday sun. I felt a little stiff, but otherwise as good as new.

After such a day and night, I thought I would see a changed

face in the glass. But it was the same face. A little tired, and with hair needing attention even more than usual, but otherwise familiar.

I went downstairs, to find that all the guests had departed during the morning. Some had expected to stay longer, and been expected to, but tact took them away. The habit of good manners was even stronger than curiosity. I thought it did them all great credit. I liked them all, but I was relieved they were gone.

There was general surprise in the household that, after such an ordeal, I was not in a state of hysterical collapse. I was a little surprised myself. But I was perfectly well. I wondered if I were unnaturally hard-hearted. But I thought not.

The Countess had kept to her bed. Dr McPhee had been to see her. He wanted to examine me, too, but I told him there was no need. He saw that there was no need.

'I believe you're made of India-rubber, Miss Perdita,' he said. 'You'll bend and bounce before you break. I hope, though, that horror doesn't catch up with you.'

Mrs Ramsay also kept to her room.

'I think I have persuaded poor Lucinda,' said Aunt Marianne, 'to face the truth, which, however repugnant... So wrapped up in her sons... Do not fear for her reason, so strong-minded and intelligent as she is, but such misery... Dr McPhee, laudanum, a merciful dulling to the edges of the mind... De Quincey recommends, though with qualifications, of course... Opium perhaps dangerously habit-forming...'

Colin had told Alex the whole truth after I had gone to bed. He had not wished to keep the exhausted Alex up for so long, but Alex had demanded the truth before he put his head on a pillow.

'He said he would not sleep until he knew exactly what happened,' Colin told me.

'I can understand that. The next one to tell, I suppose, is Great-Aunt Selina.'

'We'll have to get permission from the doctor first.'

'Yes, but it will be worse to send her mad with curiosity than to exhaust her by talking... How did Alex take the – the story about Jamie?'

'He'll tell you. Here he is.'

Alex still looked a little the worse for wear, and he said the crown of his head was infernally tender. But he looked again like a scholar of sporting tastes. Though damaged, he was himself again. He had slept almost as long as I.

Of course, like the rest of us, he wore black. I felt a fraud in my black. I supposed Colin felt still more of a fraud.

'This is a shock so violent,' said Alex, 'that it takes a fair time to get used to. I am nowhere near used to it yet. Perhaps in a sense I never shall be. I can perfectly well understand my mother simply failing to absorb what you told her – simply rejecting it as inconceivable, as the ravings of the delirious. But I am shocked rather than surprised.'

'What?' said Colin, very surprised himself.

'Dita knows what I mean. Jamie was Juggernaut, the Indian god's chariot that crushes all opposition like beetles under a boot.'

'He must have been like that,' said Colin slowly, 'Evidently he must have been. But I never saw that side of him until yesterday. A determination to win, yes, a very great dislike of losing, but I never saw him as Juggernaut.'

'Some of his colleagues did. I did. Dita did.'

The Inspector of Police, a Constable, the Procurator Fiscal and a doctor had been taken to the place of the murder. They came on to Strathgallant, to take depositions from Colin, Alex and myself.

I went first.

The Procurator Fiscal was a Lochgrannomhead solicitor called Mr Craigie, a thin man in black with the face and the voice of a hoodie-crow. I took the oath. I began to tell him my story, exact in all details. Mr Craigie wrote at my dictation, his pen scratching like a hoodie-crow's claw, covering sheet after sheet of expensive-looking paper.

I could see Mr Craigie looking more and more shocked, as I described the sack being put over my head and my being taken off in the carriage.

I discovered the reason for his outrage. 'Ye're an ower *wee* lassie for siccan ploys, Miss Sinclair,' he said, his legal English

252

relapsing into the Doric in his emotion.

'Well, it is easier to kidnap a small female than a large one,' I said. 'I expect that is why I was chosen.'

He did not approve of my levity. Indeed, I was not really in any mood to joke, reliving the things I was describing.

I concealed one thing only, in all my story – Jamie's true reason, the fortune he was snatching.

It was strange to watch my account of Jamie's stripping me half naked being taken primly down by the pen of a lawyer.

I was careful to include in my deposition Colin's story that he was not alone watching the house.

'Yon's hearsay,' said Mr Cragie. 'Inadmeesible.'

'Well, Captain Ramsay will tell you himself.'

'Ay, that he wull.'

I did not quite like the tone of Mr Craigie's voice. The worst of it was, that I fully shared his doubts.

Colin went next. He came out after a long time, looking solemn.

'I don't think they quite believe I saw another man watching,' he said.

'Oh dear. Oh Colin.'

'And the police searched round the house this morning. They found a gun. It had been fired. The barrel was fouled, it had been fired recently. They could still smell the powder. The gun takes the same size of round as the one the doctor dug out of Jamie. They can't quite prove that that gun fired the shot that killed Jamie, but they can come damned close to it.'

'But whose gun? What gun?'

'Mine.'

Alex went next. His deposition was much shorter, because though his evidence was relevant, he had not been anywhere near the actual scene of the crime. He told me after that he was asked, as I had been, for an exact and detailed description of the one man he had seen. He thought Mr Craigie was quite cross with him, for not giving a wholly satisfactory account of a man he had grappled with for two seconds in the darkness.

'The old boy congratulated me for my courage in rushing up

253

to the carriage,' said Alex. 'But it was no such thing.'

'Of course it was,' I said.

'No, I was like a drunkard after that bang on the head. I wasn't thinking or acting rationally at all. I was charging about like a baby.'

I thought this was not quite true. If he had acted out of pure instinct, then his instinct could hardly have been better.

The Procurator Fiscal wanted depositions from some others, too – surprising witnesses, who had seen nothing and seemed to me irrelevant to the case.

They were horribly relevant.

One of them was Aunt Marianne.

'A dreadful thing,' she gabbled afterwards. 'I feel like Judas! Colin so gallant, and I had to say . . . It did seem strange to me, when he was telling poor Lucinda . . . I was asked, you know, if I could shed any light on Colin's feelings for *you*, dear . . .'

'Oh dear.'

'If he were – as we all know quite well he was . . . Motive, so often the subject of drama, tragedy . . . The green-eyed monster . . . I said I could *not* answer for another person's inmost feelings, but I'm afraid I could not help conveying . . . I hope I may not have done irreparable . . . But any of us, asked the same questions, and replying on oath . . . The truth will out.'

'Yes,' I said miserably, 'I'm afraid it will.'

So it was horrible but not surprising when the Procurator Fiscal made out a warrant for the Inspector of Police, and the Inspector arrested Captain Colin Ramsay on a charge of the wilful murder of his cousin.

'There's meetigatin' circumstances,' said the Police Constable. 'Mebbe.'

An atmosphere of numbed horror settled over Strathgallant like a fog.

The Countess kept to her room and to her bed, seeming to have shrunk, to have withered to a wisp of dry straw. Miss Violet Carmichael looked ill with fatigue and worry. I sat with the old lady many hours of each day, partly to relieve Miss Carmichael, partly as a way of paying back a tiny part of the debt I owed. The Countess did not want to talk or read or listen, but my being there seemed to comfort her.

Mrs Ramsay also kept to her room. Aunt Marianne was much with her, and also Alex.

Jamie's funeral service was in the castle chapel. Mrs Ramsay attended, supported by her surviving son. The Countess was not strong enough. Only the family and some of the servants were in the chapel. The Episcopalian parson from Lochgrannomhead conducted the service, in a booming portentous manner, as the Countess had not had a private chaplain since she became a recluse. Alex read a lesson from *The Pilgrim's Progress*.

'My sword I give to him that shall succeed me in my pilgrimage . . .'

I thought there was a terrible irony in those words, considering who had died, and how, and why.

Jamie was buried in the castle's own graveyard, which had been consecrated ground for more than a thousand years.

So he took possession of one little piece of the estate he had wanted so very badly.

The keepers and foresters and herds were on constant alert to drive away gawping tourists and men from the newspapers. From what we heard, from Dr McPhee and from the tradesmen, the whole of Britain was smacking its lips over the affair. It was still the season when Scotland was full of travellers from England, who had all read the romances of Sir Walter Scott, and thought the murder had come straight out of them. The newspapers wanted drawings of the castle and the farmhouse, of Jamie and of Colin and me. Apparently they printed pictures of me, 'artists' impressions' based on descriptions by people who knew what I looked like. Or perhaps they hired Jules to draw me. I was, unfortunately, the person they most wanted to see. I became a prisoner in my own home.

I took to walking and riding very early in the morning, before the world was awake. Alex was my usual companion. We spoke very little. It seemed somehow to be crass to be calling and chattering in those lovely silent dawns, when we whispered through grass sweet with the heavy dew of late summer, and through the millions of cobwebs woven overnight, of all of which each strand was like a diamond necklace when the sun first kindled the dewdrops.

Alex did not try to make love to me, from tact, from kindness, from a sense of what was proper at such a time. But he knew that I knew that he was there, comforting, gentle, strong, waiting for the moment that would surely come, when he could kiss me again without being hit on the head.

A curious and worrying thing happened.

Aunt Marianne's room was ransacked, while she was out tending her 'secret garden'. No jewels were taken – indeed she had very few – nor anything of value to an ordinary thief, but only the bundle of letters written to her from Paris by Lady Isobel.

'Jules,' I said.

'Oh but . . . My dear . . . Impossible!'

'Nobody else in the world could have the slightest interest in taking them. I suppose Harry might, if he is still on Jules's side. But that is impossible.'

'But neither Jules nor Harry has been near here, since the night of . . .'

'One of them must have got a servant to do it.'

'But, Perdita! The idea is . . . One has grown to trust . . . Loyalty and faith, you know . . .'

'Yes, it is a horrid thought,' I said. 'But what else can possibly have happened?'

With Mrs McQueen's help, we asked all the indoor servants, and all the outdoor servants who had been within range of the castle, to account for their movements all that morning. Of course many of them could not. They could not remember. Or they had been alone, dusting or polishing, or making beds or scrubbing floors, so that their stories could not be confirmed or denied by anybody else. In the end, we found that several housemaids and footmen could have seen that Aunt Marianne was safely away in her garden, and could have gone unseen to her room. I knew and liked and trusted them all. So, which was more to the point, did Mrs McQueen. It was impossible to suspect one more than another. It was impossible to suspect any of them.

But it was impossible not to suspect all of them.

I noticed them looking at one another, warily, asking the same questions in their minds that we were asking. It made for a miserable atmosphere.

I remembered that there was particular loyalty and affection for Harry, among the servants. He had used it to trick me into going to the Toll-house at Achnacarron. Had he used it again, to destroy the evidence against Jules?

We kept the whole affair from the Countess. She had miseries enough.

I told Miss Violet Carmichael, what I should have told her long before, that her message to me about Colin was in one important respect incomplete.

'It is another irony,' I said drably, 'that now I know Colin is free, he is in prison awaiting trial for murder.'

And it was still true that he had made love to me, believing that he was still married.

Colin came back to Strathgallant, escorted by the Inspector of Police, in a closed carriage to evade the eyes of the gawpers.

He was free.

The Procurator Fiscal had taken a further deposition, from a witness who had come forward.

It was Dougal McKechnie, who had given himself up to the Police in Lochgrannomhead, saying he could not keep silent when an innocent man was accused.

Of course the whole countryside had known immediately that Captain Ramsay was arrested, and why. Word got to Dougal wherever he lay hidden, from the people who were feeding and protecting him. But he knew the real truth of what had happened.

He had seen – because such a man, always a-prowl, sees everything – that there were strange doings and strange people at the deserted farmhouse. He could not understand why a gentleman was consorting with such cut-throats. He thought they were thieves or rum-runners. He watched the house, because he thought there might be profit in it for himself. So it was no coincidence that he was there. Watching that night, he had seen the carriage, and a bundle he thought was a person carried indoors. He had seen Colin. Colin had seen him, too, without realising it – like me, he had mistaken Dougal's red hair for a fox. Dougal had seen another man, who came later and very furtively. He could not describe this other man, because he saw him only at a distance and in the dark of the night. He saw that the other man had fired the shot through the window, and run off. He could be perfectly sure that it was not Colin, because even in the dark Colin's great size made him unmistakable. Colin ran round to the front of the house after the shot, after the disappearance of the murderer.

Still in hiding, still watching, Dougal saw Colin take me away in the trap. It was light enough by then for him to see us clearly. He knew me, of course. He thought about the matter for several days. He did not want to go back to prison. But he thought he owed me a debt, for trying to warn him that the police were coming. He thought he would be paying part of his debt, by saving my rescuer from the gallows.

'Bread upon the waters,' said Colin.

There could not be jubilation, not at Strathgallant, not then: but there was a gigantic relief.

We hurried to tell the Countess, and she seemed to put on youth and strength in front of our eyes, when she understood what had happened.

She rang for wine, and drank to Colin's deliverance. Our combined efforts could not keep the glass from her lips, nor the bottle from refilling the glass.

She said, 'I suffered some months ago, as I now realise, from a damned careless loss of memory. It has resulted in a serious miscarriage of justice. Is the jackanapes from the police still here?'

'He is having tea in the Housekeepers's Room,' I said.

'What an extraordinary thing to be doing. Fetch him here.'

And to a staring Inspector, who was amazed to find himself in a Countess's bedchamber, she announced that she had given Dougal McKechnie permission to take what fish he liked, by what methods he liked, out of her water. She had forgotten to inform her own keepers. At the time of Dougal's trial, she had forgotten the whole affair. This lapse was to be ascribed to great

258

age, to illness, and perhaps to the drugs which Dr McPhee was at the time prescribing for her. Her memory had fortunately returned. Dougal must be released at once, since he had been falsely charged and falsely convicted.

The Inspector knew perfectly well that this was a pack of lies. The Countess was once again obeying her own rule – that persons of quality lie when necessary. He had to accept what she said. He was most evidently glad to do so. I have never seen a man come nearer to winking. He liked Dougal, and he admired him for what he had done.

'Hae he stull your pairmishun tae tak' your fush, m'leddy?'

'Yes. Tell him so. He may fish as my guest, provided he uses rod and line.'

'An' the flee?'

'I would prefer him to use a fly, of course. But everybody else uses worms and crayfish. They shouldn't, but they do. I do not see that I can make rules stricter for him than my other guests observe.'

'Thank God for Dougal,' said Colin. 'A bevy of glittering lawyers came to see me in my cell, but they looked very dubious when they heard my story. It was your evidence that was going to hang me, you know.'

'Yes, I know,' I said. 'How did you get hold of those lawyers?'

'I didn't. I don't know any lawyers. Harry took charge of that.'

'Where is Harry?'

'I had a message in prison that he was in London. I don't know if he's back.'

'Good gracious. Why London?'

'I can't tell you, Dita.'

'Following Jules?'

'I can't tell you that either. I've been incommunicado, as they say.'

'Well, now that you're communicado, if there is such a word, you can take me for a ride in the morning.'

Mrs Ramsay would not see Colin or talk to him.

'Poor Lucinda,' said Aunt Marianne, 'trusts her own instinct, you know, more than the word of that scallywag . . .'

'She cannot still think Colin killed Jamie!'

'It is feeling rather than thought, you know, dear . . . which leads to the *greater* inner conviction! The German philosophers have profoundly examined this point, in relation to religious belief, patriotic fervour, and so forth . . . So illuminating as they are! Logic influences the mind, but leaves the heart untouched . . .'

'But that is unjust!'

'Even if her mind accepted that, dear, which it is far from doing – even so, her heart would not. A mother's instinct, you know . . . I myself have never thought the same of any Indian, since my Rupert . . . And that was so many years ago . . .'

If the Countess was transformed by Colin's deliverance, so equally was Miss Violet Carmichael.

'It was always perfectly obvious to me that Captain Colin could not have fired the shot,' she said, in the Countess's bedroom.

'It was not obvious to me,' I said. 'And I was there.'

'But you have not *thought*, Perdita dear!'

'Have you thought, muttonwits?' said the Countess, whose voice was recovering its full and awesome strength. 'It is not an operation of which I believed you capable.'

'He followed the man who struck down Mr Alexander,' said Miss Carmichael, 'the man who carried off dear Perdita. The man we now know to have been poor Mr James. He was in time to see the carriage they used, and to catch a horse and follow the carriage. How could he possibly have gone all the way to his room to fetch his pistol?'

'I had assumed that he was carrying it in his sporran,' said the Countess.

'Why would he do such a thing, ma'am? At a ball? So awkward, the weight, and so dangerous, the possibility of an accidental discharge of the weapon!'

'He was carrying it in order to shoot somebody,' said the Countess. 'At least, that is what I supposed. There can be no other purpose in carrying a pistol. There can be no other purpose in the very existence of a pistol. I assumed that Colin

260

was, in the tradition of his ancestors, proposing to shoot whatever rival for Perdita's hand seemed most to threaten his own pretensions. But I grant a certain force in your point. Not much. A little. It appears that Colin did not have his firearm. Some other had it. Someone who knew that it existed, and where it was to be found. It is a pity, as a matter of fact, that Colin was not carrying his pistol. If he had shot James at once, Perdita would have been spared a certain discomfort.'

'But he would still be in prison ma'am,' I said.

'Pooh! We'd get Dougal McKechnie to get him out. It's a thing he seems to be good at.'

Someone who knew the pistol existed, and where it was to be found. Someone who knew about the inheritance. For both these reasons, an intimate – one of the family. Not Colin, as we now knew beyond doubt. Not Alex, who had been knocked out and tied up. Jules had disappeared much earlier in the evening, and no one knew where he had been or where he was. Harry likewise.

Unlike Mrs Ramsay, I could not be impervious to logic. The murderer was either Jules or Harry.

Which?

And then I had a dreadful idea, which my mind, I think, had been flirting with half-consciously, for days.

Jules and Harry were in league. All of us had known all along that they were friends. They were more than friends. They were colleagues. They were companions in crime.

The heir to an embarrassed estate had made contact with the little French fugitive, and had recognised in him an accomplished criminal, a smiling villain. He had introduced the boy into Strathgallant. Jules's task was to wrap his tentacles of charm and talent round the Countess's heart and round mine, so that, whether he became the Countess's heir or whether he married me, he would become master of an enormous inheritance.

Which he would share with Harry.

I guessed Harry had something in writing from Jules. Something utterly, legally binding. If I were Harry, knowing Jules, I would want something in writing.

Between them, meeting somewhere and somehow secretly,

261

Jules and Harry decided that Jamie, or Alex, or Colin, was ahead of Jules in the race for me – for Strathgallant. Hence Harry's dramatic appeal to the Countess, in the small blue drawing-room, to make Jules her heir.

Why would he do that, if he were not to profit massively himself?

Aunt Marianne's revelations turned all their cake to dough.

They did not run away, to London or anywhere else, after the revelations. They went no further than the terrace. Why had we assumed they had gone far and far? They meant us to do so. We had done so. They went no further than the cover of the rose-bushes and the box-hedges. One or other had by this time stolen Colin's pistol from his room. A safe thing to do, in the middle of a ball. Both knew that it existed, and where it was. Then, armed, they saw, they followed, one or other, one or both.

I did not mind that one or other had killed Jamie. But I was sick with disgust that they had let Colin accept the blame. The noose.

If they were to profit from this treachery – one or both – then they must come back to Strathgallant – one or both. It was hard to guess what they would say, what they would do. Alex and Colin were still in the field against them. But, from what they said and what they did, they would give themselves away, to me, somehow, at some point.

I thought they would try to murder Alex. What is one more death? I would warn Alex. Between us, we would have the furious alertness of the very angry.

I had reached this point in my thoughts, when Harry's return was announced.

12

Harry looked tired, having, he said, travelled far and fast. He stood in the hall, chatting to Colin and congratulating him on his release. His pleasure, his goodwill, *seemed* to be genuine. Everything about Jules had seemed to be genuine. One of them had killed Jamie, and been content that Colin should be killed too.

I stared at Harry, trying not to seem to do so.

He did not look like a murderer. Jules did not look like a gambler and thief, Jamie like a greed-crazed abductor, Colin like a liar contemplating bigamy.

With Harry had come a companion, a slender gentleman of extraordinary elegance, elderly, with a pointed silver beard. Harry presented him to Aunt Marianne and myself as the Vicomte de Brey.

The Vicomte kissed Aunt Marianne's hand, but not mine. I was puzzled by this snub, until I remembered that, among very correct old-fashioned people, it was considered improper to kiss the hands of unmarried females. His English was at least as fluent as mine, although he spoke with an accent.

I could not imagine why Harry had brought this elegant old nobleman to Strathgallant, nor why the latter had subjected himself to an exhausting overnight journey from London to visit a house of mourning and misery.

Well, he had come to see the Countess, and was immediately led to her chamber. I came too, and Aunt Marianne, and Harry, and Colin. We were all to hear what the Vicomte had to say. Miss Carmichael, of course, was already with the Countess. Mrs Ramsay was in her room, and Alex with her.

We stood round the great bed, as I imagined the courtiers of Louis XIV round his. I suspected the same thought might have

263

passed through the Countess's mind, because she became imperious even by her standards.

'I seem to be the centrepiece,' she said, 'of some fustian melo-drama. I am reminded of the Haymarket Theatre fifty years ago. What means this invasion? You resemble an army. You should be carrying trees. Who is the gentleman who resembles an over-dressed goat?'

'Please tell my great-aunt what you told me, Vicomte,' said Harry.

The Vicomte bowed to Harry and then to the Countess. He put one hand, carrying an eyeglass on a ribbon, into the front of his waistcoat. He put his other hand behind his back, and with it lightly from time to time flipped up his coat-tails. He was posed to make an oration: and he made it.

'I was, Madame, for some years Minister for External Affairs in my country's government. I had previously been con-nected in a semi-official capacity with the Quai d'Orsay, and was so connected after the term of my official tenure of high office. I knew intimately a number of the more senior servants of the Ministry. I knew none better than the lamented Pierre Delibes.'

'I wonder,' said the Countess, 'if I want to hear this.'

'Pierre Delibes,' said the Vicomte, 'was a man of the highest honour and integrity, diligent to a fault, certain to occupy the most distinguished positions had not his career been tragically terminated. There are scores of people in Paris, politicians, of-ficials, *gens du monde*, who can and would willingly testify to his unimpeachable character and reputation. I have been told by my young friend Ramsay here that you have received a report in a different sense. Gambling, women, drink, I do not know. I am baffled to imagine where such a report could have originated or what its purpose could have been. Pierre Delibes was no gambler. He was thrifty and provident. He was a devoted husband. As an intimate friend I can state positively that his marriage was exceptionally happy and close. Its unconvention-al beginning surprised many of his friends, but his wife was wel-comed into Parisian society when it became evident that she was devoted to him and to his interests.'

'His brother kept a gaming-house,' said the Countess.

264

'Pierre Delibes had no brother. He was the only son of a family whom I also knew well. His father was a Major General of *Chasseurs* under the restored Monarchy. His brother, uncle of Pierre, was Bishop of Fermaincourt. That is not quite relevant to the history of Pierre himself, but it perhaps illuminates the standing and reputation of the family of which he was not the least admired and respected member.'

'What of his son?' said the Countess. 'What of Jules?'

'I have known Jules almost all his life,' said the Vicomte. 'I knew him well before Pierre's death, and better, perhaps, after it, because I was able to assist his mother, Miladi Isobel, in regard to the boy's education. Again, I have heard from Harry Ramsay that some *canard* has been put before you. I can understand neither the source nor the reason. Jules has not always been a paragon. He is not what you call a prig. He has been mischievous and sometimes wilful. Occasionally he worried his mother by his pranks so that she was driven to consult myself or other friends. He was never evil. Until his mother's death, he was a devoted and dutiful son. He was as diligent at his books and as honest in all his dealings as his – father. He is a son of whom any man or woman would be proud.'

The Countess had been listening with the closest attention, never taking her bright, amber-coloured eyes off the Frenchman's face. I had never before seen her give to another person such attention for so long.

Now she raised her eyes to Aunt Marianne. I think we all followed her eyes, and turned to look at Aunt Marianne.

She looked completely puzzled, bemused. Her hands fluttered.

'But Isobel's letters!' she cried. 'I could not be mistaken! Her hand! Her knowledge of things here, all the people, the family . . . They were her letters!'

And they had been stolen. And we were still no nearer knowing why, or by whom. And our guesses to both questions were still the same.

'Believe me, Madame,' said the Vicomte. 'I knew Pierre Delibes all his life. I have known Jules almost all his life. The one was, the other is, honourable, diligent, thrifty, respected. You might suspect me to be influenced by partiality, to speak well of these people because they were my friends. But it is by pure chance that I am here, and not some other who would have said the same things.'

The Countess turned to Harry, a question in her eyes.

'That is true,' said Harry. 'I was quite unable to believe what Cousin Marianne said, not only because I had come to know Jules well, but also because I had met people at the French Embassy who had known Pierre. I know that Cousin Marianne was quoting from the letters. I do not know why the letters were written. Believing as I did, I went to London and to the French Embassy, hoping to get from my friends there more detailed information and, if possible, an explanation of those extraordinary letters. The latter I did not get. The former I did. At least a dozen gentlemen were able to tell me far more about Pierre than I had previously known. Any one of them would, for the sake of Pierre and of Jules, have been willing to make the journey the Vicomte has been kind enough to make, and to tell you what he has told you.'

'It was I who came because I knew Jules as well as Pierre,' said the Vicomte. 'Because, in addition, I am not a professional diplomat but a retired politician. I am attached to the Embassy in an honorary capacity, for a short time, to assist with certain negotiations, because of my personal intimacy with two members of your country's government. I have more time at my disposal than have my professional colleagues. I was in any case glad of a reason to revisit Scotland, where in my youth I had many friends.'

'The letters,' said Aunt Marianne in a stifled voice. 'Isobel's letters . . .'

'Could they have been a joke?' I said suddenly. 'A sort of long-drawn-out tease?'

'That,' said the Countess, 'is a suggestion at once ridiculous and deeply insulting. It had occurred to me. Isobel had a sense of humour which caused her sometimes to commit what the censorious considered outrages. I am surprised that she should take the trouble to deceive Marianne. But I can think of no other explanation.' To the Vicomte she said sharply, 'This is all true, is it?'

'On my word of honour as a nobleman, as a gentleman, and as

a Frenchman.'

'That ought to be good enough. Where is the boy?'

'He came with us, of course,' said Harry. 'But not quite as far as the castle.'

'Frightened?'

'Yes.'

'Hiding in the park until you tell him it's safe to come in?'

'Yes, ma'am. Wouldn't you, in his place?'

'I don't think so, with you to hold my hand. Fetch him, Harry.'

'Yes, gladly, but before I do there is another surprise. I am not sure how you will take this. Are you feeling strong, Great-Aunt Selina?'

'Dear God,' said the Countess. 'I shall feel quite strong enough to hit you with a heavy object if you keep me in suspense.'

Harry grinned. Serious again at once, he said, 'Jules knew that he had been born to Pierre and Isobel Delibes after their marriage in Paris. The birth is of course recorded. He is accordingly now seventeen years old. A year younger than Dita. I found this quite incredible. Even granted the superficial polish of Parisian manners compared to the loutishness of our own schoolboys, is it really easy to believe that he is only seventeen? He himself had always been puzzled by his precocious maturity. But he accepted that that was what it was – simply precocious maturity.'

'What caused it?' said the Countess. 'Calf's-foot-jelly in infancy?'

Harry asked a totally surprising question. He said, 'Can you remember your son-in-law's appearance, Great-Aunt Selina?'

'Of course I can. A fool, but a good-looking man.'

'His hair?'

'Black. Jet black. Celtic survival, or the seed of some damned Spanish vagabond washed ashore from the Great Armada.'

'Ah. Extensive search has revealed no record of the death of Julian McLarty, your grandson, ma'am, whom your daughter took with her to Paris. There is record, though it took some finding, of the death in infancy, at the age of a few weeks, of a child baptised François Delibes. We are indebted to friends of Monsieur de Brey, in Paris, for that information. Pierre Delibes

267

adopted his step-son, who was brought up as his own younger half-brother. I assume that Lady Isobel agreed to this course because she was making her life in France: that her son, though brought up to speak both languages, should be altogether a Frenchman. Jules is Julian. He is nineteen years old. He is Sir Julian McLarty.'

'Do you know,' said the Countess after a pause, 'I always suspected that.'

This was a lie as barefaced as the one about Dougal McKechnie having permission to fish.

Jules was reunited with his grandmother and with the rest of us. It was impossible to remember to call him Julian. It was difficult to get used to the idea that he was a Scottish baronet, since his whole life had formed him into something so different.

He took my hands when no one was looking, and said, 'I am so happy that I am older than you, Dita. It changes everything.'

I nodded. But I pulled my hands away

There were things it did not change.

The night of the ball, he had not known who he was, or how old he was. He wanted Strathgallant, with or without me.

Once again Harry had been to enormous trouble on Jules's behalf. It seemed to me practically certain that they were confederates. The one was to get Strathgallant, with or without me, and the other was to get his reward. That Jules did not, it appeared, steal or prey on women – that he had not previously been a cynical adventurer – did not alter the horrid logic.

Who else could have shot Jamie? Who else had a reason for doing so?

Aunt Marianne went to tell Mrs Ramsay the news.

Miss Carmichael said to her, 'A surprise as overwhelming and as welcome as that about Captain Colin! His freedom!'

'From prison?' said Aunt Marianne, who still seemed as bemused as a sleepwalker.

'From *any* restraint,' said Miss Carmichael. 'Free to come and go, and free to speak!'

Obviously Aunt Marianne had no idea what Miss Carmichael was talking about, as she had no idea that Colin had ever not been free. She looked completely bewildered. She carried her bewilderment into Mrs Ramsay's room.

Alex emerged from the room, having been relieved, visibly bursting with curiosity. I told him everything that the Vicomte and Harry had said. He listened as attentively as the Countess had listened to the Vicomte.

'I can understand my Cousin Isobel bringing up the boy as French,' he said at last. 'He was going to be French, after all. She must have supposed he'd be in France all his life.'

'And I daresay she was disgusted with Scotland,' I said, 'being so bored with Sir Robert McLarty. She adored Pierre. She wanted to make a complete break. It wasn't just convenience or commonsense – she *wanted* Jules to be French instead of Scottish.'

'Yes, and after the other baby died, Pierre probably wanted a son he could think of as his own, a Delibes. They may have made the decision only after the baby's death. That all makes sense.'

Colin, joining us at that moment, said, 'There's one thing that makes no sense to me at all. One absolutely crazy element. Those letters. Why were they written? What in God's name possessed Isobel to write them? I can't accept your notion, Dita, that it was all an elaborate joke on poor Cousin Marianne. Nobody would do anything so laborious and so pointless. So cruel, too.'

'I don't accept it either, now that I think about it,' I said. 'Then why *were* they written?'

'And why stolen?' said Alex.

'Jules or Harry or both must have wanted to look at them,' I said. 'There's no other explanation.'

'Then why not just look at them?' said Colin. 'Why take them?'

'Because they weren't here,' I said. 'They were in London. A servant took them and sent them to London.'

'I don't like that, Dita,' said Alex. 'I don't like your finger being pointed at Jules or Harry or any servant. It's utterly speculative.'

'Yes, I know it is, but who else had any interest in seeing those letters? And who else could have . . .'

I stopped. I was not sure about voicing my next thought aloud.

'Shot Jamie?' said Alex. 'Is that what you were going to say?'

'Well, yes. I'm sorry. It must be painful for you to think about it. I should not have started that remark.'

'It is painful for me to think about it, but it is also unavoidable. I am bound to think about it. Who could have shot Jamie? Who wanted him dead?'

'What did you think at first, Alex?' said Colin.

Alex looked embarrassed. 'As a matter of fact, old fellow, I thought it must be you. Feeling as I fancied you did about Dita . . .'

'As I did and still do. I don't blame you at all. Thank God for Dougal McKechnie. But where does his evidence leave us?'

It was supremely obvious where it left us – as obvious to both of them as it was to me. Colin looked thoughtful, Alex actively miserable. Neither could avoid the unavoidable logic of opportunity and of motive.

'Is it possible you were followed?' said Alex to Colin.

'Yes,' said Colin heavily. 'I had a bumpy ride, and I was looking ahead, not behind.'

'How did – whoever it was – have time to go to get your pistol?' I asked.

'Yes, how?'

'It must have been taken earlier,' said Alex.

'Not much earlier,' said Colin. 'It was there when I was dressing, before dinner. I remember seeing it under my shirts.'

'Then it was taken between the time you left your room, and the time I was knocked on the head.'

'Then the murder was planned,' said Colin, 'in that space of time, or earlier.'

'Yes,' said Alex thoughtfully. 'I had pictured something sudden, unpremeditated – pictured a man driven for the moment mad by jealousy or rage. But of course you're right. The thing must have been planned. Wait – how can that be? Whoever did it could not have known in advance – '

'Unless whoever did it was in Jamie's confidence,' said Colin. 'Is that possible?'

'No,' said Alex positively. 'Jamie would hardly have admit-

270

ted anyone into his confidence, except the henchmen you saw. Certainly not anyone immediately involved, any member of the family.'

'Something was planned,' I said. 'Something else may be planned, too.'

Harry knew that, with me, went Strathgallant. Jules doubtless knew it. Something else might indeed be planned.

'Please be careful!' I said to them.

They nodded. Colin looked grim. Alex looked distinctly nervous. I did not blame him.

Alex returned to his mother, who did not like him to be long out of her sight. I saw her point. If she had recovered the full use of her intelligence, after the shock she had suffered, then she was more than intelligent enough to have done all the calculations we had done. I did not think Alex would confide our suspicions to her: I did not think he would need to.

The Vicomte was pressed to stay, but could not. Harry and Jules saw him off, making all kinds of arrangements for future meetings. Harry then returned to the Countess's room, while Jules joined Colin and myself.

Jules wanted to ride. He had not realised that we were still ringed by gawpers. He said he would ride with us in the dawn.

Colin and I were a little constrained with Jules, though we tried to be natural, because of what we had been discussing. I thought he noticed it, and was hurt.

Miss Carmichael told me, before tea, that Harry had repeated his plea to the Countess, most urgently: Jules – Sir Julian – was her grandson, and should be heir to everything.

'Of course, his argument is the stronger now!' said Miss Carmichael. 'No question of, er, any irregularity in his birth! One of the first families in the East of Scotland! Not a drop of French blood! His foreign appearance to be ascribed to Celtic ancestry, as her Ladyship said, or to some Spanish castaway! And such an account of his diligence and thrift and so forth, from that distinguished gentleman!'

Oh yes, I thought, there is an arrangement between them. Jules will inherit, and Harry be rewarded. The thing was

271

screamingly obvious.

'But her Ladyship refused!' said Miss Carmichael. 'I was quite downcast with disappointment!'

So was Harry, I supposed. So would Jules be.

'She said that she had given her word to *you*, dear!'

Having conveniently forgotten, no doubt, that she had forced me by her coughing fit into accepting her detestable plan.

'She said that there might be *fragments* or *vestiges* left of the McLarty estates, and until lawyers had been consulted, and trustees told of Sir Julian's identity, no decision could be reached! Mr Harry argued that *nothing* was left of the McLarty lands or fortune, and she could not wish to have a pauper baronet grandson – but she was adamant! I daresay you know that mood of hers, dear! The harder Mr Harry pressed his case, the more adamant her Ladyship became! I am not sure if that is a permissible usage. "More adamant"? Can there be degrees of adamant? I used, you know, to teach such things to dear Lady Isobel, but I have had less need, latterly, to bother about correctness at all! Her Ladyship's use of language is always so untrammelled! I always pretend to be shocked, you know, because it amuses her to shock me.'

'Does she *not* shock you, Miss Carmichael?' I asked, startled.

'Good gracious no. After living in this castle for over thirty years, I am long past being shocked by anything. Have you puzzled out the mystery, dear? Do you know who shot poor Mr James?'

'Yes, I think so.'

'I also. That *is* shocking. Even I am shocked that kindness and affection should have been returned so. I am a little concerned, though, as to how we are to *prove* what we know.'

'When you say "know", Miss Carmichael –'

'I mean "know", dear,' said Miss Carmichael, with a firmness I did not remember ever having heard in her voice. 'If I am to be *brutally* frank,' she went on, 'We must surmise that the desperate competition for your hand had not been entirely . . .'

'Not entirely,' I agreed. 'If my face were my fortune I should have to marry the Marquess of Mull.'

'Such a clumsy young man! But not ill-natured! Meanwhile we know, dear, that while your face is *much* admired, it is *not* the whole of your fortune. Unfortunately this knowledge is shared, is not it? Mr Harry . . .'

'Told Jamie.'

'And not him only, we are to suppose. What I suggest, dear, is this. We know that whoever it was that killed Mr James, the one person it was *not* was Captain Colin.'

'That is quite true.'

'If you were to choose him, dear – which indeed has been my fondest . . . But that is none of my affair! – if you were to choose him, he would as we know benefit prodigiously.'

'Yes.'

'And by the same token, others would *not* benefit. The one who murdered Mr James would not benefit.'

'No,' I said, wondering what on earth the strange lady was about to propose.

'Having murdered once, will he scruple to murder again, for the same reason?'

'No. We have discussed that. They must be very careful.'

'We can rely on Captain Colin to be careful, dear, and to look after himself. He has come unscathed through battles! He will not easily allow himself to be led like a lamb to the slaughter! But if an attempt is made on his life! And we are watching, and see who makes the attempt!'

'He is to set himself up as a decoy,' I said slowly, 'like a painted wooden duck on a lochan?'

'Exactly so, dear!'

I stared at her, my mouth probably hanging open in astonishment.

'Of course,' said Miss Carmichael, 'You will have to give the murderer a reason to make the attempt.'

'The only reason would be,' I said with difficulty, 'if it looked as though I were going to marry Colin.'

'Just so, dear! I knew you would understand! I think you will not find the Captain backward, if you give him a sign of your preference!'

'I am to pretend to choose him . . .'

'It would be a great joy to her Ladyship if your choice were genuine, dear! So relieved as she was when it turned out he had not murdered Mr James! So glad that it was he who rescued you!

So hopeful that the *romantic* circumstance might sway your mind and heart!'

'Well, it might have,' I said, 'but there was a difficulty with Maudie Plimstock.'

'My fault! My interference! You need never have known that she existed!'

'That would not have been very satisfactory, either ... Miss Carmichael, am I to tell Colin that I am – choosing him, or show him, or something – am I to delude him? Trick him? Lead him on? Am I really to be as – cruel as that, to the man who saved me?'

'It would be best, dear! He will be more convincing in his response, if he believes in the authenticity of your feelings! I think that among his *very* many virtues is not to be found a great talent for play-acting! But if you have scruples – and of course, dear, they do you credit! – then perhaps you should let the Captain into our little secret. But it is *not* what I would advise. And after that, you know, you must make sure that you are seen! It will be no help to us, if you encourage his advances in secret!'

'I must be shameless, on top of everything.'

'Not precisely shameless, dear. Merely a little indiscreet!'

'I cannot believe,' I said, 'that it is you speaking.'

'Funnily enough, dear, nor can I! But a crisis brings out unexpected qualities in us all!'

I saw the force of all that Miss Carmichael said, but I could not follow her all the way. I could *not* let Colin make love to me, as though I were choosing him from all others, without his being aware that it was a play we were acting. I could not let him launch himself as a painted decoy-duck on the water, unless he knew he was doing it.

The atmosphere that evening would have been edgy, and full of troubled suspicious glances, had not the Countess decided that she was was strong enough to come down to dinner.

She did not mourn Jamie, I was sure, as much as she would have mourned her other great-nephews. She was overjoyed at Colin's innocence: and transported with joy that Jules was – had been – the honest stepson of an honest stepfather, and the legitimate son of her daughter's first marriage. This knowledge so filled her mind that the shock of Jamie's death was almost forgotten. So was the threat hanging over the household that another great-nephew, or a grandson, would be arrested and hanged for murder.

Mr Craigie the Procurator Fiscal had fully informed himself about us all, and about our movements on the night of the ball, and the day after, and the night of the murder. This being so, there was no reason to be surprised when he came again to Strathgallant the following morning. He had heard from the County Police who were guarding our policies against gawpers, that Harry and Jules had returned. He knew that they had disappeared shortly before the abduction. He doubtless knew that Jules had protested love to me – everybody in the castle knew it, and many would have told him. Both must be, automatically, high on anybody's list of people suspected of the murder.

He spent a long time with each of them, preventing any contact between them until he had finished.

He went away looking dissatisfied. Alex and I watched him go.

'My hunch is,' said Alex, 'that the evidence of each clears the other. Jules swears that he was with Harry, and they were already setting off for London. Harry swears that he was with Jules. As long as they have rehearsed, they make each other safe. If you believe one of them, you must believe the other. But if you believe neither . . .'

'What do you believe, Alex?'

'I am sick at heart to believe what it is less and less possible to disbelieve.'

I nodded.

Alex showed signs of wishing to give me more positive comfort than words could give. I wanted comfort, and perhaps his – but not then.

Other people had to be made to believe that I was choosing otherwise.

I thought there might be all kinds of difficulties in staging the scene. There were none. It did not need preparation – it simply happened. The west terrace – scene of so many recent dramas –

275

was our stage. The whole west front of the castle formed the stalls of our theatre.

Colin joined Alex and myself. He said that Alex was called for by his mother. Alex left at once, as always. He grinned ruefully at Colin before he went, and gave him my arm that he had been holding.

Colin at his most serious, his most emotional, spoke jerkily, with difficulty. He did so now.

He said, 'I have not abandoned hope, Dita. Perhaps should. Incapable. Unrealistic, perhaps, but... I cannot bear to approach you with a lie still between us. You deserve the truth, more than anybody else in the world.'

'But I know the truth, Colin.'

'No thanks to me. One thing you don't know. I'm probably killing my last chance by telling you. My last chance of you, of happiness, of honour and manhood. But I must speak. You must know. I should have told you weeks ago. I should have told you when I first came here. This, as well as that other.'

I looked at him, frowning. We were arm in arm, standing by the parapet, looking down over the broad glen of the Gallant. I knew what he was going to say.

He told me that he knew about the Countess's plan. That whoever married me would own all that we could see from where we stood, as well as untold other wealth.

I thought he was telling me because one day I would find out.

'Harry told me,' said Colin. 'I think he expected me to refuse to come. I think that is why he told me – to get me to refuse to come. He thought that if none of us came, Great-Aunt Selina would make a more – a different arrangement. I decided I could come without dishonour. I was wrong, but that is what I thought. I was curious. I had no home of my own in Scotland, and I wanted somewhere to stay. I decided I would come. But I vowed to myself not to ... Until I saw you, that day on the hill. Sooty seaweed in the wind. Your adorable little face. Your pleasure at seeing me. Honour, good resolutions out of the window. I forgot everything except how much I wanted you.'

'Forgot everything, Colin? Wanted only me?'

'Good God, d'you think I'd need a bribe to take you? D'you think any man would? This place is glorious, but... If I came

276

by it that way, I'd give it away.'

He went on most earnestly in this vein. We were side by side, arm in arm, motionless by the parapet, among the roses.

He went on in this vein, and I did not believe a word of it.

I did not know what to do. I was afflicted by conscience, and other things. I was sure we were observed – it was inevitable, on a terrace commanded by hundreds of windows. Colin's long, disjointed, passionate speech would seem, to someone far off and behind us, to be the declaration of a lover. Well, so it was. If I broke away from him and walked off, I would seem to be rejecting him. If I told him I disbelieved him, he would walk miserably away, and I would seem to have rejected him. That was no part of Miss Carmichael's plan.

The longer he talked, and I did not go away or send him away, the more he must think that I believed him – even that he was melting my heart. That was part of Miss Carmichael's plan, but not of mine.

I thought I must tell him the truth, even though he was lying to me. But I must find some way to do it, so that it would not have a visible effect. Knowing Colin, I knew that my words would have an instantly visible, unmistakable effect.

I decided that I must explain about the decoy, and the need for play-acting, and then to say the rest of what I had to say. I waited until Colin should come to a pause.

He did pause, faltering to a halt in the midst of telling me that the light in my eyes was more valuable to him than every jewel in the Countess's coffers.

I looked up at him, surprised. He was staring down across the park at the river, which was there just visible between trees. A man was fishing with rod and line. He took off his hat, and fanned his brow with it. He had a thatch of foxy hair, glaringly visible even at a distance.

'Dougal McKechnie,' said Colin.

'Fishing by permission,' I said.

'Do you know, I haven't properly thanked him for saving my neck?'

'You should do that.'

'Yes. Of course I must. Dita – dearest child – I have said much of what I wanted to say... Leave me hope... Oh – Dougal's moving away downstream – I must run to catch him –'

'Colin, before you go, I –'

'Forgive me. Later.'

On the tip of my tongue was the explanation of Miss Carmichael's plan – my redoubled warning to him – the importance to the plan of my seeming to have chosen him – my inability to choose him because he had lied to me. All this had to be said, and at once, if I were not to deceive him as he deceived me – and it was not said, because before I could find the right words, Colin had kissed my hand and was away like a stag down the stone steps to the park, and bounding away among the startled fallow-deer towards the river.

The manner of his departure would have given no hint to any watcher that I was other than delighted at his advances. It gave no hint to him, either.

Presently I saw Colin's gigantic figure beside the smaller, slighter form of Dougal McKechnie. I saw them sit down side by side under a tree.

I wondered idly what they were saying – what words of thanks Colin would find. The Highlanders hated being thanked, and responded with a stammering air of ungraciousness: I wondered how Dougal would reply.

It was then that the truth suddenly came to me, there among the roses, looking down over the glorious valley, idly watching those two distant and contrasting figures.

Dougal was not on the river-bank, just then, by chance. Colin was not on the terrace by chance. They had arranged to meet, as though by chance. They had business.

Miss Carmichael was completely wrong. I had been completely wrong. We had all been easily, instantly convinced by a well-thought-out story from a surprising source, because we wanted to be.

I examined my new-found truth carefully, from all angles, trying it for gaps or weak points. I remembered Alex telling me about the methods of scholars and scientists. You devised an idea (but I thought he had used a grander word) and tried to disprove it. If it stood, you could believe it.

Mine stood. There was no disbelieving it.

Colin's story was probably true, in its early part. He had fol-

278

lowed the carriage, and then stayed in hiding until it was safe to move nearer the farmhouse. There was another watcher – he did imagine he had seen the fox – and the fox was the other watcher. There was no third man there – never any third man there. Colin and Dougal had met, talked, made a plan together. Colin shot Jamie, and invented the man who ran away.

Dougal's story was no doubt partly true, too. He had watched the house and its strange tenants, hoping for pickings. He had seen the carriage, and Colin. He was probably being paid by Colin to say what he did. It was possible that he saved Colin out of gratitude to me. What was certain was that he had seen no other man.

And now the conspirators were met by arrangement. They were revising and rehearsing their stories, perhaps, or discussing Dougal's payment. And no one would think it odd that they talked long and earnestly and privately, because the one had saved the other's neck.

But I had been there. I had been completely sure that Colin had shot Jamie. It was supremely obvious to me, to everyone. And then we all believed Dougal McKechnie, the poacher, the gaolbird on the run, because we all wanted to do so.

The letters, the stolen letters, – how came they into it? Colin had everything to *gain* from their existence, because they removed one rival without further effort. The theft of the letters must have been the work of Jules, or his confederate, by way of a servant...

Yes, and the theft was done before the Vicomte de Brey was enlisted.

Colin and Jules were the confederates, not Harry and Jules. Colin stole the letters. No – he was in prison when it was done. Still, the servant... No, Harry could not be let out of it. Harry had produced Jules, and had saved Jules. It was Harry who knew the servants so well, and could beguile them into doing curious things...

Colin, Jules and Harry were all three confederates.

God knew, Strathgallant was big enough to carve up three ways.

Colin had come, to try his luck with me on behalf of the confederates. Jules had come, as a second string to their bow. Harry

279

had stayed outside, where he could be a free agent.

Probably Colin *was* still married. I only knew from Harry's mouth that Maudie Plimstock was dead.

Probably Jules *was* a cheat and a thief. We only knew from the mouth a man produced by Harry that he was respectable. Lady Isobel's letters were more to be trusted. That was why they were stolen. They were stolen because they were to be trusted – because what they said could be proved the truth.

Probably he was Jules Delibes, not Sir Julian McCarty at all.

We had believed a great many things because we wanted to believe them.

My head spun with the truth.

Jamie had been killed, because he was on the point of winning me. How if Alex looked like winning me? It was of the utmost importance that Alex be warned.

I hurried in and upstairs. Alex was with his mother, who was suffering from a crisis of nerves. They were not to be disturbed. Well, he was safe there.

Nobody knew where Harry and Jules were. They were out somewhere. They had business of some sort together. No doubt they had, indeed.

I came out onto the terrace again, blinking in the brilliant sunshine. I went to the parapet, and looked down towards the river.

There was no sign of Colin or Dougal McKechnie. Perhaps, by arrangement, they were meeting Harry and Jules.

It was almost time for luncheon. I thought the Countess would come down, with Miss Carmichael. I thought Alex would come down. He would be reappearing into frightful risk, if the others thought I was choosing him.

They might think so. He had been my only comfort, in the dreadful days after Jamie's death. They might be right. Would they wait to kill him until they were sure I was choosing him? Would they kill him *in case* I chose him?

Evil and the threat of violence seemed to hang over the sunlit terrace like greasy smoke from some gigantic fire.

I heard the shot.

It came from near the river-bank, far away across the park. Deer stampeded away among the trees and bracken. Birds flew up in panic from a copse of elms and beeches.

Without thought, I ran down the steps into the park, and across the park towards the clump of trees.

Alex was dead. It must be so. He had left his mother to go for a solitary walk, using some small side entrance. He had been watched and followed. It must be so. I sobbed as I ran.

I thought: they will not shoot me. I am the goose that is to lay their golden egg. But I will die first, or kill them all.

I saw that someone else was running towards the copse, from far upstream, over open ground. I saw a mop of foxy hair. This was a murder that Dougal had not seen, then – he could not have.

We reached the copse together, panting, scarlet, speechless. We went in under the deep dappled shade of the trees.

We saw it at the same moment, crumpled by a tangle of brambles. A gigantic body, unmistakable in any light, in any position, dead or alive.

I heard a scream. It was my scream.

It had no face. The face had been blown off. On his shoulders was a lump of bloody porridge.

Dougal saw the face as I did.

He muttered, 'Ma Goad.' He took my arm, and turned me away from the shattered horror. He led me to the edge of the copse.

My head swam. I sat down quickly on a drift of beech-leaves; and presently he helped me back across the park to the castle. He was gentle and considerate.

They found a gun, a few feet away from the body, in the brambles. The keepers thought it came from the castle gun-room, that it was one of Lord Kilmaha's guns. One of the guns was missing. Its matched pair was there. Nobody could remember seeing the empty space in the rack, behind the glass door of the guncase.

They said the gun had been loaded with buckshot. The cartridge in the other barrel, unfired, was buckshot.

They said the shot was fired at point-blank range. They said that it followed that whoever fired the shot was known to Colin. It was someone Colin trusted.

Dougal McKechnie had been, as I thought, too far away to see

281

anything. He had seen no one running away through the wood. He could not have done so, coming from the opposite direction.

I had seen nothing except the flight of frightened birds and the stampede of frightened deer.

It would have been easy for the murderer to disappear into the big woods further downstream, or to double back and slip unseen into the castle.

Alex had been with his mother, every minute of the time. Aunt Marianne had been there also, helping Mrs Ramsay in her misery.

Harry and Jules had been once again together, somewhere out in the park. Once again, the deposition of each made the other safe – if both were to be believed.

We ate no luncheon that day. The Countess did not come down.

'This must stop,' said Miss Violet Carmichael, with that new energy which had astonished me.

'A good resolve,' said the Countess, whose voice was weak but whose eye was bright. She was propped on her pillows. She was once again haggard with shock and grief, for she had loved Colin well; but her mind was not confused nor her spirit broken.

I felt a sick fury. My mind *was* confused.

Either the great truth I had perceived in the morning, amongst the roses, was wildly false – or the wolves were turning on each other.

Who was next?

'They are killing for greed,' said Miss Carmichael vehemently to the Countess. 'They are killing for Strathgallant. This is your doing. You made Perdita too great a prize. You cannot bring those two young men back, but you can prevent further violence. It is your duty to do so.'

The Countess looked at her with amazement and a flash of anger.

'How dare you blame me?' she said.

'You must forget that distasteful arrangement, that Perdita must choose among them, that if she does so she is your heiress. It was evil folly, and has bred only violence and misery.'

'You are dismissed,' said the Countess. 'Go.'

'Stuff,' said Miss Carmichael.

I gasped. The Countess blinked.

'You need me to wheel you about, ma'am,' said Miss Carmichael more midly, 'and I need you to keep me occupied. But the time has come for me to speak my mind. I used to be stern with Lady Isobel when she was wicked or destructive. I have not forgotten how it is managed.'

'What creature is this?' said the Countess wonderingly.

'I have been the companion you wanted, ma'am – a slave you could tyrannise and shock – '

'Play-acting, Carmichael?'

'Oh no indeed! Only to a small extent. I have been providing the service and the companionship of which you stood in need. But now you require a different kind! And I shall provide that.'

'Enlighten us further.'

'Like dear Lady Isobel, ma'am, you are in danger of becoming – spoiled.'

'Dear God,' said the Countess.

'And, what is more to the immediate point, some others are in danger of being murdered. The former danger I shall endeavour to forestall. The latter, you must. There must be no more of this dangerous nonsense, which will leave in the end one claimant only for Perdita's hand and your fortune. You must take away the reason for these deaths. You must immediately, now, today, declare Sir Julian your sole heir. As Mr Harry proposed!'

The Countess looked at her, with a sharpness that belied the haggard lines on her face.

'And if I do, then what?' she said at last.

'I wonder, indeed! That is what will be so interesting!'

'Pigswill,' said the Countess, showing that her spirit was indeed unbroken. 'Someone will murder Jules.'

'Not if,' said Miss Carmichael, 'you make a further provision. That if Sir Julian does *not* survive to succeed you, all goes to some charitable cause! Deaf and dumb children, for example! Poor little things!'

The Countess pondered this. So did I.

Miss Carmichael's idea answered the Countess's objection. But it left Jules and Harry dividing the fortune, as they had planned all along. Sin was rewarded. Unless they were somehow convicted of killing Colin, they were both safe, and both immensely rich.

The only merit of the plan was that Alex would not be murdered. Perhaps I would marry him – two paupers together. Perhaps that was the best that could be salvaged out of the whole business, the whole carnage.

The Countess raised a number of objections to Miss Carmichael's scheme. Her greatest objection she did not mention – that it was not her idea, but somebody else's. As they squabbled, I found the brief, frozen picture of Colin's smashed face leering at me, and I was filled with anger that the people who had done such a thing should profit.

I said suddenly, breaking in on the bickering ladies, 'We must not only stop more murders. We must find out who did the murders.'

'But I know who did the murders, dear,' said Miss Carmichael. 'We have already discussed that.'

'You knew before, yes. But you were quite wrong. At least. . . Oh. I wonder if you were? Everything in my mind is muddled, now that Colin has been killed.'

'How odd!' said Miss Carmichael. 'Everything in my mind is even clearer!'

'Well?' said the Countess, staring at her transformed companion with renewed amazement.

'Oh, I cannot tell you, ma'am, until we have proof! That would be most wrong!'

'There will be another murder, immediately, in this room, Carmichael,' said the Countess, 'unless you tell me who murdered my great-nephews.'

'I should not advise violence, dear ma'am. Dr McPhee would not approve of sudden exertion. For my part, I cannot take the responsibility of telling you!'

'In case you're wrong, muttonhead?'

'There is *no* chance of that! In case the shock is injurious to your health!'

'Presumably I must know some time.'

'But not from *my* lips, ma'am! *I* should not have caused a relapse, or incurred Dr McPhee's displeasure!'

'You mean you don't mind if I die of shock, as long as you haven't administered it.'

'You will not die of shock, ma'am. Of brandy, perhaps, but not of shock. You are, if I may say so, made of sterner stuff!'

'I think that's probably true, Carmichael. So – Perdita's point is taken, is it? Besides having no more family butchery, we identify the butcher and prove his guilt. This at whatever cost to our feelings.'

I glanced at Miss Carmichael, worried. Jules was deeply and horribly implicated. The shock of learning that he was, at the very least, accomplice to two bloody murders would – not kill the Countess, perhaps, but strike her hard indeed.

Oh yes, I was muddled in mind. For had I not just cried out that I wanted the guilty punished?

'The announcement of my altered testamentary dispositions,' said the Countess, ' – longer words than, I daresay, either of you expected anyone as old and frail as I to use – my new will is to help us catch the villain?'

'Yes,' said Miss Carmichael flatly.

I did not understand what she was about. But she did.

They all answered the summons.

Jules came first, because he was the first the footman found. His eyes were full of apparent misery. Behind the misery must lurk, I knew, suspicion, some alarm, and boundless glee. I looked at him with a loathing which I tried to hide. I did not want him forewarned by guessing what we knew.

Harry came next. His face was grim. Grimness was all that could be read into it. There was something frightening in his face. Well might there be.

Aunt Marianne came next. She had been weeping. Her face was puffy, like that of an ageing baby. She had been very fond of Colin.

Mrs Ramsay came, supported by Alex. She looked a little grey and shrunken, but she managed an impressive dignity. I had not seen her – few of us had seen her – since Jamie's death. I was surprised not by how much change there was in her, but how little.

Alex looked as though he would never smile again. He and Colin had been particular friends. Great as the shock of Jamie's death had been, I thought Colin's moved him more.

'You had better all sit down,' said the Countess. 'One or more of you are in for a shock.'

She looked appallingly old, but her voice had recovered its strength.

We sat ourselves in chairs about her bed, very demure and attentive.

'Early this summer I made a decision about the future of this castle and estate, and of the fortune which provides the income for its maintenance. I have now changed my mind, which is the privilege of senility. I have accepted your advice, Harry, a circumstance which is as humiliating as it is, no doubt, salutary.'

Something blazed in Harry's eyes. He turned from his great-aunt's face to Jules's. They exchanged a long look.

They had won.

I thought Miss Carmichael was right. We were seeing proof before our eyes.

Harry turned from Jules to me. He stared at me with an expression I could not read. I tried to meet his gaze squarely. I stared back. I did not consent to be outfaced by a treacherous murderer.

'Sir Julian McLarty – my dear little Jules – I have decided to leave the whole mess of pottage to you.'

I looked round at them all, to see how they were taking it.

Aunt Marianne said despairingly, 'Those letters... Isobel's letters...'

Those letters, indeed. The truth they contained, indeed.

Mrs Ramsay said, with all her old importance, 'My Reaction to your Decision, ma'am, is one of surprise only that you took so long to arrive at it. Every sentiment of Familial Affection and Loyalty must Applaud.'

Alex looked distinctly rueful.

The Countess looked at him, her amber-coloured eyes as bright as lamps. '*Every* sentiment, Alexander?'

'I had entertained a fleeting, presumptuous hope, Great-Aunt Selina, that in winning Dita, as I shall continue to try to do – '

'You would win a little extra on the side. I don't blame you. How did you know about it?'

'From Jamie. Who else?'

'How did he know?'

'He did not tell me.'

'At least you're honest. A credit to Oxford, and the study of medieval history. Take the chit, if she'll have you, but don't expect Strathgallant for a wedding present.'

Alex glanced at me. He said, 'What I want is more important than castles.'

'A noble sentiment,' said the Countess, 'if a little puerile. Jules's reaction can be anticipated. We know he wants Strathgallant, so we needn't embarrass him by making him say so. What about you, Harry? This was always your idea, but why? Were you going to be rewarded by half Jules's kingdom?'

I jumped. I had not thought the Countess could see so far.

'Jules has already offered me half his kingdom,' said Harry. 'Naturally. Being Jules, he was anxious to repay, grossly to over-repay, what he thought was his debt to me.'

'Don't tell me you refused. Nobody is that noble.'

'Of course I refused,' said Harry, with a touch of impatience. 'It would be monstrous to break up an estate like this. It would be a betrayal of the past and of the future, of your ancestors and the grandchildren of your tenants. Besides, it would not be, I take it, what you intend. If you leave all to Jules, then you intend Jules to have all.'

'Your arguments have the logic of the insane,' said the Countess.

'Yes, I admit a certain force in that,' said Harry. 'I admit a degree of insanity. My position is like Alex's. What I want is more important than castles. I am overjoyed at your decision, Great-Aunt Selina, because it enables me at last to lay siege to the woman I have adored all my life. Woman! An undersized and uncontrollable brat. A wielder,' he touched the scar on the back of his hand, 'of a shrewd whip. Thank God you're not burdened with a fortune, Dita. You may not welcome my advances, but, by God, you're going to be subjected to them.'

287

13

I looked at him stupidly. His words were sinking in only slowly.

'Bravo!' said Miss Carmichael unexpectedly. 'What a *noble* attitude, Mr Harry!'

'What mutton-headed fustian,' said the Countess. 'How could any man not half way to bedlam *prefer* a penniless wife?'

I thought: if he doesn't want Strathgallant, why does he want me? If he doesn't want a fortune, why has he done two murders?

Alex was murmuring to his mother. He turned to the Countess and said, 'Will you excuse us both, Great-Aunt Selina? My mother should rest again, I think.'

'You'll give up your seats at Mr Harry Ramsay's epic farce-melodrama? Well, as you wish. But I want to hear more.'

'I'll say no more in front of an audience,' said Harry. 'At the risk of seeming disobliging.'

Jules immediately rose. He looked a little stunned. He gazed long at Harry's face again. Aunt Marianne followed him out. They went away together.

There was no suggestion that Miss Carmichael should leave. I thought a mule would not have dragged her from the room.

I stared at Harry in fascinated horror. I felt stifled. I felt hatred and contempt and intense curiosity.

'Now, sir, explain this irrational vomit if you can,' said the Countess.

'Of course I can,' said Harry mildly. 'But declarations like the one I am planning to make are not usually –'

'The circumstances are not usual,' said the Countess. 'After your verminous incivility, you are clearly obliged to make some restitution. You can do so, in small part, by explaining yourself.'

'Very well. The whole thing is simple in the last degree. I adored Dita as a child, and I was horribly jealous of Rupert. After I grew up I met many women, but none of them effaced my memory of Dita. I was consumed with curiosity to see her again. But you had become a recluse, and she with you. I had to wait until she too grew up – until she left the schoolroom and entered the world. I thought that would be this summer, because I knew it was the summer of her eighteenth birthday.'

'Did your parents know about this lifelong and barely credible devotion?'

'Yes, of course. They teased me about it. But they loved Dita too, you know.'

'Yes, I know. Everyone did. Everyone still does. It is very bad for her.'

'I was agog to see Dita again,' said Harry, 'to see if she had grown up as beautiful as we thought she must, to see if she was still as gallant and honest and glorious as she had been.'

'Strong words, boy.'

'Strong feelings, ma'am. And then I heard about your plan. All of us to come here. Strathgallant's future and Dita's future to be looked after in one distasteful transaction.'

'You heard. How did you hear?'

'You only guessed,' I said. 'Or your parents did.'

'No,' said Harry. 'I misled you there, Dita. I think you might have realised that. How could I have been so certain, simply on the basis of my parents' guesswork?'

'How did you know, then?'

'Alex told me.'

'Good God,' said the Countess.

'You remember,' Harry said to me, 'that when Alex and I met, we had seen each other recently.'

'You had dinner together in London. It was a long evening.'

'It was a long and a wet evening. Alex drank a great deal of port.'

'How shocked his mother would be,' said the Countess.

'His academic colleagues too, I should think,' said Harry. 'I thought a don would be good at holding his port. Alex is very bad at it.'

'He got drunk and blabbed?' said the Countess inelegantly.

'How unlike him. As a matter of fact, it rather enhances my opinion of him. He's not a stick, like poor James, but he is rather a prig.'

'Why didn't you tell me?' I said to Harry.

'Tell you that Alex drank too much and babbled your secret?' said Harry. 'Of course I couldn't tell you that.'

'Oh,' I said. 'No, you couldn't . . .'

It struck me that, for a butcher, Harry had a nice sense of honour.

'Alex says Jamie told him,' I said. 'But Jamie said that *you* told *him.*'

He looked surprised. 'No,' he said. 'I told Colin, because I was shocked and I thought he'd be shocked too. I told Jules, because he was your grandson, ma'am. I didn't tell Jamie. I had no need to. He knew.'

'How did he know?' said the Countess. 'That is the question we have not answered. Never mind. The question has become academic. What interests me is your being so shocked by a supremely rational solution to a number of difficult problems. This is what I find mysterious and vexing. Elaborate, boy. Elucidate.'

'I can elucidate without elaboration,' said Harry. 'Picture me. There was I, agog to see Dita again, in love with my memory of her, half resolved to make her my wife even though I had not seen her since she was twelve years old – and then this.'

'It made you *less* inclined to love her? I find that bizarre.'

'*I* do not,' said Miss Carmichael. '*She* would never have known whether you truly loved her, and –'

'And *I* would never have known if I truly loved her,' said Harry. 'Quite right, ma'am. The world, seeing me installed here, would have assumed I wanted Dita for her fortune. The world might have been right. I would never have been quite sure. I can imagine nothing so certain to breed misery, suspicion, abrasion. Every tenderness I showed or felt might have been for Dita's millions, not for herself. Every passing irritation she felt might have arisen from contempt for a man who had married a fortune. Any sort of wilfulness, of spirit, might have said, louder than any words, "Remember all this is mine, not yours". Our life would have been poisoned at its source. Unhappiness would have been almost guaranteed. I could not do that to Dita. I could not do it to myself. I could not come here.'

'But you did come here!' I blurted out.

'I came, I saw, I was conquered. I could not enter the race, but I was consumed with curiosity about the prize. I terribly wanted to see you.'

'You saw me.'

'I saw you, I adored you, and I could not have you for the reasons I have explained –'

'The vapourings of a bedlamite,' said the Countess.

'Not at all!' cried Miss Carmichael.

'And I was so furious that things had worked out so, that you had joined in the building of a fence about yourself . . . that I expressed myself a little strongly.'

'And I whipped you,' I said.

'And I deserved to be whipped. And your anger and your whip, and your beauty when you were angry . . . And your apology to Alasdair Lawson, after you had accused him of lying to you . . . Oh God, Dita, I knew you were the only woman I could ever love. So I tried to persuade my great-aunt to disburden you of a fortune, as she has just done.'

'And very properly,' said Miss Carmichael. 'But what you did *not* do, ma'am, as I suggested, was to add that if Sir Julian . . .'

'The deaf-and-dumb children,' said the Countess. 'No, I forgot about them, in the excitement of seeing the result of my words . . . Lucinda's reception of my decision did her credit, don't you think?'

'So devoted as Mrs Ramsay is to her sons,' said Miss Carmichael, 'one would indeed expect her to wish that one of them might inherit Strathgallant. Surely she must have wished so, if she knew –'

'She didn't know,' I said. 'She kept warning Jamie against me, because she thought I was a penniless orphan '

'On whose authority have you *that* information, dear?'

'Jamie's . . . Oh. He was pretending. She knew all along. She was determined that one of them would marry me . . . Is that possible? Why would Jamie pretend his mother was against it, if she was for it?'

'That is obvious, dear,' said Miss Carmichael. 'Mrs Ramsay has little money, Mr James none of his own. She was bound to oppose a union with you, unless she knew what she should not have known. The pretence was necessary to them, to the credibility of Mr James's courtship of you.'

'And stolen kisses are sweeter,' said the Countess.

I remembered them with dismay. Yes, perhaps they had been.

'What a lot of lies I have been told,' I said.

'Your explanation is convincing, Carmichael,' said the Countess. 'Tedious and badly expressed, but convincing. Lucinda knew if the twins knew. The twins knew if Lucinda knew. God knows how any of them knew, but so it must be. What a greedy woman. Mother-love can be carried too far. Or not far enough, as in my case with my poor Isobel ... Lucinda came here with James, before any of the rest of you appeared. So James had the first run, as they say on the race-course. Then Colin came. Did Colin cut James out, Perdita?'

'Not exactly,' I said slowly. 'Jamie was completely confident – appallingly confident ... He never believed that Colin and I ... That is strange, you know. I was in the way of despising Jamie, because he was frightened of horses. And Colin was so huge and so modest and so brave and so sweet. I liked him. It must have been obvious that I liked him.'

'It was,' said the Countess. 'Embarrassingly so.'

'Yes, well, it was all a new experience for me, you know ... But Jamie was never worried by Colin. I wonder why?'

'Because he knew that Colin was married,' said Miss Carmichael.

'How did he know?' I gasped.

'Because his mother told him.'

'*She* knew?'

'Of course she knew. It was she who told me.'

I looked at her in stupefaction.

'Then why didn't she tell me herself?' I said. 'Why make you do it? And why didn't you tell me that it came from her?'

'What foolish questions you do ask, dear. Surely the answers are obvious. If *she* told you, it would have seemed the stratagem of a devoted mother to eliminate the rival of her son. You would have doubted her motive, and probably her information. You did not doubt my motive, or the truth of what I said. I did not tell you the knowledge came from her, because I promised her not to. She extracted that promise for the same reasons. I thought at the time that she behaved sensibly and mercifully, and was saving you, I thought, from a broken heart or a bigamous marriage.'

I nodded dumbly. All this was unanswerable.

'How did Lucinda know about Colin's marriage?' asked the Countess suddenly.

'From her late sister-in-law,' said Miss Carmichael, 'from Captain Colin's mother. At the time of the calamitous marriage, Lady Ramsay had to confide in someone. It was natural, though unfortunate, that she should have chosen Mrs Ramsay. And then, when Mrs Ramsay learned of your Ladyship's dispositions, and imagined the threat posed to her own hopes by the Captain –'

'She got a copy of the Marriage Lines, to put Colin out of the race,' said the Countess. 'How, I wonder? Can you do a thing like that by way of the penny post?'

'You do it by way of a son,' said Harry. 'That's why Alex was in London.'

'I can't believe that of Alex,' I said after a pause.

'Can't you, Dita? I admit it's only a guess, and you probably now know Alex better than any of us . . . But I'll tell you another thing. The letter I wrote at Hamish Ogilvy's desk. The one that told Colin he was a widower. The one we left on the bucket. It didn't blow away. It was taken. By someone who knew it was there, and who didn't want Colin to get it.'

'Not Alex,' I said.

'Who else?'

Well, who else? I was silent.

'Captain Colin would have found out, from you, eventually, Mr Harry,' said Miss Carmichael.

'Yes, but by that time Dita might have been betrothed to either twin.'

'Or abducted,' I said. 'Alex may have been a little – devious. But nothing he did was so very terrible. And at least we know he is not a murderer.'

I stared at Harry. And the murderer, whose motive I could not understand, and who said he loved me, stared back.

'I see the hand of Lucinda in all this,' said the Countess. '*What* a greedy woman.'

'For her sons, rather than for herself,' suggested Miss Carmichael.

'Offal. If one of her sons was lord of Strathgallant, do you think she'd stay humbly in Edinburgh? And now all her cake is dough, because everything goes to Jules.'

'If he survives,' said Miss Carmichael. 'Where is Sir Julian now, do you suppose?'

'My God,' said Harry, 'with Jules out of the way . . .'

He jumped to his feet.

'Mercy,' said Miss Carmichael.

'Jules is in no danger at this moment,' I said, looking at Harry.

Harry looked back at me, as though he did not understand.

'Oh yes he is, dear,' said Miss Carmichael. 'You will excuse us, ma'am.'

She hurried out of the room, followed by Harry. I trotted behind them, with the single idea of watching Harry. I did not know what he was going to do, but I thought it would be something horrible.

It was such a pity.

I heard a footman, in the hall, telling Miss Carmichael that Sir Julian had gone out of doors with Lady Kilmaha.

'Then the boy's quite safe for the moment,' said Harry. 'Nobody would try in front of my Cousin Marianne.'

'Her leddyship waur carryin' two muckle keys,' said the footman.

'To her private garden, no doubt,' said Miss Carmichael. 'She often enlists help there. Many a shrub I have planted myself, under her directions! Very few, I am afraid, have managed to thrive . . . Sir Julian with her? I cannot picture him grubbing amongst dear Lady Kilmaha's pansies, but perhaps it is another subject he feels he should master!'

'I wonder where Alex is,' said Harry.

'Always with his mother. So dutiful a son. Shall we step out, Mr Harry? Will you join us, Perdita?'

'No, thank you,' I said.

'I desperately want to talk to you alone, Dita,' said Harry, 'but this is not the moment.'

'No.'

I wanted to go out, too. But I wanted to be alone. I wanted to think. I saw them go out onto the terrace. I went in the other direction, behind the castle.

I wondered how many lies Harry had been telling. Perhaps none. Was that possible? I thought not.

I thought Colin had killed Jamie, which was a good thing to have done. I thought Harry had killed Colin, which was a dreadful thing to have done. Why? For me? For me only? Was that possible? But he had helped Colin – put him in position to marry me, if I would take him.

He did not want Strathgallant. Was that possible? He wanted me, but only without Strathgallant. Was that possible?

I had known them all so well, and now I did not know them at all. Not Harry, not Jules, not Alex. I was floundering. Having felt old and experienced, I felt young and ignorant.

I heard a shout from somewhere. I could not tell where it came from, nor whose voice it was. A keeper calling to a boy, a shepherd to his dog, one forester to another . . .

I was near Aunt Marianne's 'secret garden'. The high stone wall faced me, one of the four which enclosed it. In the wall was the green-painted door, which Aunt Marianne kept locked. She never allowed anyone to go in there without her. She kept the key in her room. I thought it was indulgent of the Countess, to give Aunt Marianne sole use of the old walled garden.

I wondered idly if she had indeed enlisted Jules's help, with some absurd gardening task she had set herself. I tried the heavy old latch of the door. The latch moved, the door did not. It was locked. No one was there. The place was silent and deserted. They had come and gone, or they had not come.

From beyond the door, from inside the garden, came a faint scraping noise. I thought it was the sound of metal on stone.

Well, sometimes Aunt Marianne made war upon the moss which grew thick on the paved paths of her garden. She scraped it away with a spade. I thought it a pity. I thought the moss prettier than the stone . . .

Why should she lock the door of the garden, to scrape moss

from paving-stones?

Where was Jules?

Two keys. The footman had said she carried two big keys.

There was another key of use in the garden. It fitted the padlock, which secured the cast-iron cover of the well. This arrangement was made after I went down the well, when I was small. Aunt Marianne kept that key, too. She had brought it out to the garden. She wanted water, then. That was reasonable. The weather had been fine and hot. Her flowers would die, unless she watered them.

But that cast-iron well-cover was terribly heavy. Aunt Marianne always got a man to help her move it. I had tried to move it alone, and I could only manage a painful inch at a time, with great effort, dragging the iron over the granite lip of the well.

That was the noise I was hearing – that I heard again now. The well-cover, bit by bit, coming off or going on.

She had gone out with Jules. She wanted Jules's help in moving the well-cover. Between them it would be no great labour.

Where was Jules now? Why was the door locked?

Who had cried out?

The most awful thought came into my head. For a moment I had the ridiculous idea that Aunt Marianne had pushed Jules down the well, and was now pulling the cover over it. Then I realised that Jules had pushed Aunt Marianne down the well, and was pulling the cover over it. Of course he was killing her. She knew the truth about him. She could swear to the letters, though she no longer had them. Only she had seen them. Only she threatened him. But as long as she lived, she threatened him with disgrace and ruin

Harry knew.

'The boy's safe as long as he's with Marianne,' Harry had said.

Indeed the boy was safe. But she was not. Harry said what he did, to stop any search for them, to give Jules time for his deed.

Harry was getting half Jules's kingdom. Everything he said was lies. No doubt he lied when he said he loved me.

I did not linger, to think thus. It flashed into my head all together, in one awful piece.

I could not climb this wall where the door was. It was fifteen feet high, and smooth granite. But at the back, the side of the garden furthest from the castle, trees grew near the wall. The branches were lopped off, so they should not overhang the garden, but as a child I had climbed in by one of these trees. What I had done I could do.

I raced round to the far wall, going as fast as I could in clothes ill-adapted for running. They were still less adapted for climbing trees. I had to kilt my skirt and petticoats up to my hips, in order to grip with my legs. I felt my stockings and my petticoats shred, as I struggled up the tree. I heard the tearing of silk, and felt my hands and arms and legs being scratched and cut. I got to a branch which almost reached the top of the wall. It was a young and slender branch. I hoped very hard that it would bear my weight. I crawled along it, astride, my skirt about my waist. The branch bent dangerously under my weight. In the split second before I must have fallen to the ground, I reached out and grasped the coping on the top of the wall.

Thank God no broken glass had been set into the coping.

I struggled up onto the top of the wall, and managed to lie along it. And then at last I was able to see what was happening at the well, twenty yards away. I was in a position to see Jules murdering his aunt.

I saw Aunt Marianne struggling with the cover of the well. She had only got it a short distance from the opening. I saw her move it a little more. I realised at once that she was capable of moving it faster, but she was desperate to make as little noise as possible.

I thought I heard a sound of splashing, from far down where the water was.

After a long, hot summer, the level would be far down, indeed.

My plan was made in two seconds. I must overpower Aunt Marianne. I must get from her the key of the door. I must open the door, get help, get a rope. I could do nothing on my own to save Jules.

So be it.

I wriggled so that I lay across the wall. I lowered myself until I gripped the coping with my hands, so that I should have the least distance to fall. I knew that I was in full view of Aunt Marianne, but I thought with luck she would be too preoccupied to look in my direction. She would hear me when I dropped, but then I would be ready to fight her.

I was wrong on all counts. Even as I landed in a flower-bed, I felt a shocking blow on my head, from behind. I was knocked dizzy, though not unconscious. I found myself being dragged. I struggled. I was powerless. She was strong. She looked plump and flabby but she was strong. She dragged me across the garden very fast, hurting me as I bumped over flagstones and through rose bushes.

I screamed.

I was bundled, helpless, struggling, to the well-head. I was hit again on the side of the head, so that for a moment I was dizzy and incapable of movement. In that moment I found myself over the yawning mouth of the well, and then suddenly the world tipped – there was nothing below me – I was falling. I fell for what seemed hours, down and down in the darkness. I smashed into the water. The water felt solid, so great was the impact, so awkward my position. Still I went downwards, under the water, deep. My lungs were empty, the breath knocked out of them when I hit the water. I was desperate for air. Terrified, I struggled to the surface. My head came clear just before I must have burst for lack of air. I breathed in a huge shuddering breath. The shock of the cold water cleared my head. I looked up. There was the disc of sky far, far above. A lip of blackness bit into the disc. It was like a picture of the eclipse of the sun. It was the cast-iron cover going over the well.

I groped for Jules, and found him. He was conscious, but only just, struggling feebly to stay afloat. He moaned. I could see nothing at all of him, or of the walls of the well. It was pitch dark, though there was a disc of sky above.

A disc already, as I watched, smaller in size.

Jules would not long stay afloat, unless I supported him. I wondered how long I could stay afloat myself. It was terribly cold. Already, after a few seconds, I could feel the cold seeping into me, to take away my strength.

I felt about for a crevice, a nail, any handhold in the stone of the walls on which I could support some of my weight. There

298

was nothing. The walls were of smooth masonry, slimy, impossible to grip. Jules weighed heavy on me. I struggled to keep his head clear of the water, and my own.

The disc of sky was smaller still. She was still moving the cover slowly, for the sake of quietness. Soon it would be closed. It would be padlocked. The key would be thrown away. We would have disappeared, completely, inexplicably, for ever.

Jules's terrible dead-weight was dragging me down. I was weakened by the blows to my head. The awful killing cold was entering my bones. Some instinct kept me struggling, although a part of my mind told me to surrender to the weight and the water and the cold, and end our suffering sooner.

For it could end only in one way.

The disc of sky had shrunk to a narrow crescent, like a day-old moon. One more heave, and the sky would disappear from us for ever.

I prayed, not for rescue, but for God's mercy on my soul. I had a minute to live, hardly more. When I went down, so would go Jules.

Into my head, interrupting my prayer, came the sudden huge question: *Why?*

I looked up, for my last sight of the sky of the dear world – and all of a sudden the disc was a disc again. The full bright circle. Something bit into it. Oval. A head. Head and shoulders.

A voice boomed down, hoarse with anxiety, 'Jules?'

'He is here!' I screeched.

'*Dita!*'

'Yes. Please be qui –'

I could not finish 'quick', because I swallowed a mouthful of water.

'Keep afloat! Stay alive!' boomed the voice from above, echoing and crashing down the tube of the well. 'One minute!'

The voice was so distorted by the echoes that I could not tell whose it was.

The disc of sky, the imminence of rescue, gave me new strength. I splashed, and stayed afloat, and kept Jules afloat. I could not do it for long, but I thought I could do it for a minute. The cold was my greatest enemy. Without the strength given to me by hope, I was like to be killed by that cold.

That last minute was long – dear God, it was long. Though there was hope, and help at hand, I was terribly near to despair. I was nearer and nearer to the knowledge that, though there were friends above, I could not endure the weight and the effort and the cold.

I prayed again. I knew that we were lost. I prayed not for our bodies but for our souls.

The voice boomed down again, and shapes filled the disc of the sky. Something like a snake whistled down at me.

'Two ropes,' boomed the voice. 'Dita! Can you hear me? Can you understand?'

'Yes,' I screamed.

'Loops at the ends. Get yourself into one, under the arms. Call if you need it higher or lower. With that support, get Jules into the other. Do you hear and understand?'

'Yes!'

I felt the blessed, rough, reassuring rope, though I could not see it. Keeping Jules's head above water with one hand – a desperate business – I wriggled my shoulders into the loop. I pushed one arm through, so that the rope was under my armpit. I transferred Jules, now limp, to that hand. I pulled my other arm through. I found the other loop of rope. Somehow I got it about Jules's shoulders and under his arms. I could not have done it without the support of my rope.

Then Jules began to rise out of the water. He revolved slowly as he went. I could see this against the light above, though the disc was mostly blocked by the dark silhouettes of our rescuers. They kept Jules clear of the walls of the well. Water streamed from his clothes onto my head.

I relaxed against the blessed noose of rope, fearful only that the cold would kill me before they pulled me up.

I saw Jules being swung over the lip of the well. Immediately I felt the rope tighten across my back and under my arms. I grasped it with fingers too numb to grasp. I began to rise up out of the water. I heard the torrent of water falling from my clothes to the surface below. I heard the laboured breathing of the men who were pulling me up. The blessed sky, the top of the well, came nearer and nearer. Suddenly I was clutched by hands and hauled out onto the flagstones about the well.

I saw Harry's face. I saw that he was weeping. I felt delirious with joy at my deliverance. I was shivering with cold.

I said, idiotically, 'Don't cry. It is I who am wet . . .'

I felt the glorious sun striking warm on my face. But I thought I would never be warm again.

As well as Harry, there were other men, two keepers and a groom.

One of the keepers was weeping, unashamed.

I said, 'Thank you.'

I saw that two more men were carrying Jules away on a hurdle. He was covered in blankets. He was as pale as chalk, and blood was seeping into his wet black hair.

'How is Jules?' I asked, stammering because I was shivering so hard.

'Cold, and cut, and half-conscious, but alive, thanks to you, my darling love,' said Harry.

I saw that Aunt Marianne was on the ground, lying on her face. Miss Carmichael was sitting on her shoulders, holding a spade and ready to hit her if she moved. This seemed to me, in my disordered state, a just and rational state of affairs.

Two more men raced into the garden, with another hurdle. They laid it on the ground beside me, where I sat damply on the flagstones. It was covered in blankets.

'No,' I said. 'Thank you, but I will walk.'

'You can't!' said Harry.

'I shall b-be warmer if I walk. I m-must move. I want to move.'

'On my arm, then.'

'N-no, I'll make you all wet.'

Harry looked at me with an expression that made the world spin – more than Aunt Marianne's blows to my head had done.

Well, I did walk, but two of them supported me, Harry and the weeping keeper. I was draped like an Indian in a blanket. With each step I felt strength return. I decided I would *not* die of cold, or of anything else. Certainly not until my burning curiosity was satisfied.

'What . . . ?' I stammered, as I stumbled between the two of them towards the castle. 'Why . . . ?'

'Stories later, darling girl,' said Harry.

And so I was helped to my room, and Mary Cochrane peeled off my sodden and ruined clothes, and bathed me as she had when I came back from the shambles with Colin, and gave me hot drinks, and produced a flannel night-dress.

And that I did not want. I would not put it on. I would not go to bed. I was warm and dry and safe, and perfectly strong and well.

And violently curious. If curiosity was, as they always said, one of my besetting sins, I was never more sinful. I think I may be forgiven.

'I have simply had a cold bath and then a hot one, Mary,' I said. 'Why do you think I am an invalid?'

She wailed and beseeched, and I put on an afternoon gown of watered silk (I thought it an apt choice) and she did her best with my hair (at its wildest, after its wetting) and I walked cheerfully downstairs, feeling as well as ever I had in my life.

The first person I saw was Dr McPhee. He had tended the cut on Jules's head, given him a draught, and commanded him to stay flat on his back for a day and a night. He was on his way to do all the same things to me.

'Dear Heaven,' he said, 'to be young and resilient.'

'And curious,' I said.

'You might have stepped out of a bandbox, Miss Perdita, instead of the Valley of the Shadow of Death. I'm told you both slipped and fell into the well.'

'Oh. Is that what happened?'

'Mr Harry Ramsay and Miss Carmichael seem to agree that is what must have happened.'

'Ah. Well, if *they* agree, I think we should accept it.'

'Who are you all protecting, Miss Perdita? Why has no word been sent to the Fiscal?'

'Poor Mr Craigie,' I said, 'must be so bored with coming all the way up here . . . Where are Harry and Miss Carmichael?'

'In the morning room yonder. The whole clan's gathered. There's a grand conference in progress. I'd dearly love to attend it myself, but I doubt I'd no' be welcome.'

There was indeed a grand conference – the Countess, in her best red wig; Miss Carmichael, looking a little dishevelled, after her experience of sitting on Aunt Marianne; Mrs Ramsay, with

Alex in dutiful attendance; Harry, who had changed his clothes because I had made him all wet; and, to my very great surprise, Aunt Marianne, who sat with a vacant expression in the middle of a small sofa. She had not changed. There was a good deal of earth about her.

They all seemed absurdly surprised to see me, as though a little cold water should have kept me in bed for a month.

There was again a look in Harry's eyes which made me want to sit down quickly.

'You are weak, dear?' cried Miss Carmichael. 'You should not have come down!'

Well, my knees did wobble, but it was nothing to do with cold water.

I told them all that had happened to me, which was fair, because there were more of them, and they were just as curious as I was. Even the Countess sat silent, listening.

Aunt Marianne sat without a sound and without expression. She did not look at me.

When I had finished I turned to Harry. 'But why did you come? and *how* did you come?'

'We heard a scream.'

'Oh yes. I think I screamed.'

'We did not know it was you, or where, or why. We found the door of the garden locked, as you did, and came to some of the same conclusions as you did.'

'That Aunt Marianne was killing Jules? Or that Jules was killing Aunt Marianne?'

'Neither, dear,' said Miss Carmichael.

'I broke the door down with a piece of rock,' said Harry. 'The rest you know.'

'I haven't properly thanked you,' I said.

'Don't. I'm thanked by seeing you.'

'What has happened? Why? I don't understand anything. Why is Aunt Marianne here?'

'We thought she could contribute to our discussion,' said Harry. 'And we wanted her where we could see her.'

'We understand some things, dear,' said Miss Carmichael. 'We are trying to discover the rest.'

'And when we do,' said Harry, 'we will have to decide whether to send another message to the Procurator Fiscal.'

'What have you understood?' I asked Miss Carmichael.

'We were asking ourselves, were we not, dear, how dear Mrs Ramsay and her sons knew all about her Ladyship's plans. Of course, today's odd events provided the answer.'

I looked at Aunt Marianne. She had been in the room, when the Countess announced her plan and had her coughing fit. We all assumed she had not been paying attention.

'Marianne,' said the Countess, 'must have assumed that she would be my heiress, since I had, as far as I knew, no living descendant. She knew that I had. When Jules appeared, she already knew of his existence. That knowledge she kept from me. Very sensible of her. So, when we made our plan together –'

I caught Miss Carmichael's eye. I saw her shrug, and smile slightly.

'Marianne at once wrote to Lucinda,' the Countess went on. 'I imagine the arrangement was, that in return for Marianne's information and for her help, she would be suitably rewarded when Lucinda became queen of Strathgallant. It was a perfectly feasible notion. It nearly worked. Was that how it was, Lucinda?'

'It was an Act of Friendship on Marianne's part,' said Mrs Ramsay defiantly. 'Why should not one of my Jewels be the Beneficiary? Why should not I? All our lives we have lived meagrely. You, ma'am, accustomed to gigantic wealth, can have no Conception of the Miseries and Humiliations of Poverty. Someone was to be enriched. Why not us? Who worthier?'

'We won't attempt to answer that question at this present,' said the Countess. 'How much were you going to give Marianne?'

'We had not descended to the Vulgarity of Figures. We were not Apprised of the extent of the Fortune. We were not used to thinking in such Large Terms. We had lived in Narrow Circumstances.'

'So had Aunt Marianne,' I said.

'Pigswill,' said the Countess. 'She had everything she wanted.'

'She has had nothing that she wanted, ma'am,' said Miss Car-

304

michael. 'Travel. Her own home. Her own money. You have given her things when she has asked, but always she has had to come to you to ask. But all the time she knew that, one day, when, er –'

'When I started to feed those excellent worms in the burial-ground, yes. She knew that she could become the bore of Paris and Vienna – and suddenly she knew, from us, that she could *not* be. I do see that the shock must have been quite dreadful. So she took that action about which, so far, Lucinda has shown no trace of embarrassment. James laid siege to you, Perdita. Colin they were not worried about, as we know. Jules must have bothered them a bit. Alex –'

'I am not proud of my part in this,' said Alex. 'But I am not so very ashamed of it. I grant that I knew what I should not have known. Having been told, I could not shed the knowledge like a coat. I grant that I kept it from you, Dita, that I knew. But I did and do love you. I want you. Is it a crime to have wanted Strath-gallant too?'

'I think that's fair,' said the Countess, after a pause.

I thought it was too.

'Then Mr Harry popped up,' said Miss Carmichael, 'into the very middle of dear Perdita's ball, like the Demon King in a pan-tomine! I remember, when I was quite a girl, in Perth . . . And Mr Harry said that Sir Julian – Mr Jules, as we knew him then – must be her ladyship's heir!'

'Undoing all their plans, if I agreed,' said the Countess. 'Which, if I remember, I may have shown some signs of doing. Accordingly it was at that point, and at no previous point, that Marianne quoted Isobel's letters at us.'

'Those baffling letters,' said Harry.

'Which never existed,' I said suddenly.

They all stared at me. Aunt Marianne stared at me.

'But of course they existed!' cried Miss Carmichael. 'They were packed away with lavender bags! They were stolen!'

'The chit's right, muttonhead,' said the Countess, marvel-ling. 'The letters were a complete invention. Nobody else saw them. Of course not. They never existed.'

'But the theft . . .' said Miss Carmichael.

'Marianne turned a few things upside-down in her room,

went off to that damned garden of hers, and came back and said the letters were stolen. What could be easier?'

'Lavender bags and all,' I said.

'A *most* ingenious touch,' said Miss Carmichael, looking almost admiringly at Aunt Marianne. 'It convinced us *completely* that the letters existed! Who could ever imagine *imaginary* letters scented with lavender? A curious philosophical concept, is not it?'

'No,' said the Countess. 'It's the most impudent and the most successful lie I ever heard of. What dupes we all were.'

'Of this I knew Nothing,' said Mrs Ramsay. 'I would not have Permitted the utterance of Slanderous Falsehood.'

'Please believe that,' said Alex, looking round at the rest of us.

'By that time,' said the Countess, 'James realised that his hopes of coming by Strathgallant were dwindling, owing to the manifest charm of other suitors. I do not know how he came by that farmhouse –'

'I do,' said Alex unexpectedly.

We all looked at him.

'Cousin Marianne told him about it.' He turned to me, and said, 'Of course Great-Aunt Selina is right. He knew that Colin or Jules or even I were getting – closer to you than he was. He needed something like that farmhouse. He needed local knowledge. Remember he didn't ride. He needed help from someone on whom he could depend utterly not to betray him, consciously or unconsciously. I imagine Cousin Marianne approved his plan. It might even have been her plan, but it is so much in character for Jamie...'

'Is this true, Marianne?' trumpeted Mrs Ramsay. 'Did you send my Jewel to his Death?'

For the first time Aunt Marianne spoke. Her voice was tired and expressionless. She said, 'The idiot you call your jewel gave himself away... Everything would have worked out... For me, for all of us... He let himself be followed... Not on the night that he was killed, but days before... So that somebody else knew what was planned, and where... Jealousy, greed... Bad losers, both of them, as poor Colin used to say...'

Mrs Ramsay looked at her in stunned horror.

Bad losers, both of them. As Colin had indeed said. But Alex had grown out of it.

'I must say,' said Harry after a long silence, 'I thought Colin had killed Jamie. What are we to think now?'

'I thought Colin killed Jamie,' said the Countess, 'and a damned good deed it was. I thought Dougal McKechnie was lying. I was doubly pleased with him.'

'No,' said Aunt Marianne, always in that tired expressionless voice. 'Colin was a gallant gentleman. He would not have shot down his enemy, in the back ... Never. He would have rushed in, grappled ... He did not know where to go. He had not been spying on James. Therefore, he must have followed the carriage, as he said ... Therefore, he could not have had time to get his pistol, as he said ... The murderer knew where to go. He had been there already, following the stupid James ... He had leisure to get the pistol, and ride to the farm ...'

'Who?' said the Countess.

Aunt Marianne looked at her vaguely. She shook her head. Either she did not know, or she would not say.

'Mr Alexander,' said Miss Carmichael suddenly, 'were you not in your brother's confidence at all?'

'No,' said Alex, 'of course not.'

'You had no *inkling* of what he planned?'

'Of course he had not!' said Mrs Ramsay furiously.

'The scene,' said Miss Carmichael, 'that *dreadful* scene – dear Perdita quite in tatters! One can picture it so vividly!'

'Does one want to?' asked the Countess.

'We must try, ma'am! I am sorry if it is painful, Mr Alexander, dear Mrs Ramsay, but we must try! You must assist me!'

Alex looked puzzled. But he nodded.

'The window with only *shreds* of curtains, I believe,' said Miss Carmichael.

I could not imagine what she was at. We were all looking at her. Even Aunt Marianne raised listless eyes and stared at her.

'The bedstead with a bare mattress only! Is not that right, Perdita dear?'

I nodded.

'The lantern on a hook '

'On the table,' I said.

'No dear, on a hook in the wall. Is that not right, Mr Alex?'

'No, it was on the table,' he said.

'Ah yes. Silly, silly me. On the table, to be sure. *How did you know*?'

'It was in Dita's deposition, which I was allowed to read.'

'It was not. I also read the deposition. The lantern was mentioned, but not its position.'

He shrugged. 'Then Dita must have told me.'

I looked at him. I knew I had not told him.

Bad losers, both of them. Alex had grown out of it. Had he?

Alex suddenly rose to his feet. He gave a funny little stiff bow, and hurried out. No one made any move to stop him.

'Where's he off to?' said the Countess. 'A curious time for an urgent call of nature.'

'Twins understand one another, you know,' said Miss Carmichael. 'They read one another's minds! It has often been remarked upon, in literature and by the medical faculties!'

'We are to understand,' said Harry slowly, 'that Alex guessed what was in his brother's mind, followed him days before the ball, identified the house, saw Jamie there with his bruisers, knew when Dita was carried off where she was being taken, had plenty of time to take Colin's pistol, did take it, went to the house, used it . . . Is that it?'

'No,' I said. 'That is silly. Alex was unconscious in a ditch. He was tied up.'

'Who says so?' said Harry.

Alex had said so. Alex's whole account, of his whole night and day and night, was his only. We had all believed him.

'He had rope-burns on his wrists,' I said suddenly.

'I could put rope-burns on my wrists in thirty seconds,' said Harry, 'with a few inches of rough string.'

'Did Alex know about Colin's pistol?' asked the Countess.

'Dear ma'am,' said Miss Carmichael, 'even I knew about the Captain's pistol!'

'Alex couldn't shoot his own brother!' I said.

'For Strathgallant?' said Harry. 'For millions? For you? To save you from what Jamie was doing?'

'A bad loser,' said Aunt Marianne, almost inaudibly.

I glanced at Mrs Ramsay. She seemed to have turned to stone, as grey and silent as a stone.

308

'This is very far from proof,' said the Countess.

'No, ma'am, it is very near it,' said Miss Carmichael. 'The lantern.'

'Ah. That lantern. I thought you were showing questionable taste, evoking that scene to the mother and brother of the victim. But I see that you were less of a sapskull than usual. That lantern won't hang him, you know.'

'Nobody will hang him,' said Harry. 'I should think when he left this room he went straight to the stables. He is miles away by now, and travelling fast.'

'Where?'

'I don't know. Or want to know. I don't want punishment for the man who shot Jamie that night. I thought no worse of Colin, when I thought he'd done it.'

'Where were *you* when it happened?' I asked him suddenly.

'In the Station Hotel at Crianlarich,' he said, surprised. 'I understand the shot was actually fired in the early evening. Jules and I were then in the bar-parlour, drinking whisky-and-water.'

'Oh,' I said.

Mrs Ramsay rose to her feet. Her face was like a mask. She swayed. Harry darted to her, and supported her. He helped her from the room.

'At least Alex didn't kill Colin,' I said.

'He was with his mother and Lady Kilmaha,' said Miss Carmichael. 'So they have said.'

'Oh my God.'

'Was he with you when Colin was killed, Marianne?' asked the Countess sharply.

Aunt Marianne looked at her without any intelligence in her face. She said nothing.

I said, thinking as I spoke, 'They were not afraid of Colin because they thought he was married. Then – then Alex took the letter Harry had left for Colin. He read it. So they knew Colin was free.'

'They knew perhaps, dear,' said Miss Carmichael, 'that since he had lied to you, he still represented no risk to them!'

'That is not very convincing,' I said. 'They were – are – all such awful liars, they would not think it something repellent.'

Harry came back.

'It's as though she'd been hit with a club,' he said.

'Harry,' I said, 'that note you wrote to Colin –'

'That we think Alex took. Yes?'

'If he read it – and though it's a horrid thing to say, I suppose any of them are quite capable of reading other people's letters – he knew Colin's wife was dead.'

'No. I wasn't explicit, just in case the letter did fall into the wrong hands. I used a sort of code Colin and I had worked out as schoolboys. We invented it here, years ago. Nobody else would have made head or tail of it.'

'Alex was here too, in those days. He knew your code.'

'No. It was private between Colin and me.'

'Then,' I said, 'they still thought he was married. They didn't kill him. They had no need to. You . . .'

'Mercy,' said Miss Carmichael, 'they did know! It was just after the French gentleman had said those *heart-warming* things about Sir Julian. I was overjoyed, and in my excitement babbled something to Lady Kilmaha about –'

'I remember,' I said. 'You said it was news as welcome as Colin being free. Not just free from prison, but free to speak. I thought Aunt Marianne did not know what you were talking about.'

'But of course she knew very well! Oh, how dreadfully responsible I feel! Lady Kilmaha went straight back to Mrs Ramsay and Mr Alexander, and of course told them *at once* that Captain Colin was free!'

'And then Colin and I had a long, intimate conversation on the west terrace,' I said. 'According to your plan. We were overlooked by Mrs Ramsay's window.'

'But Alex was with his mother and Cousin Marianne –' Harry began. Then he stopped.

'We saw them,' said Aunt Marianne suddenly from her sofa. 'We sent Alexander out.'

'Lucinda knew that Alex . . .' began the Countess incredulously.

'She was glad . . . She thought Colin had killed James . . . He had been released only by the lies of that man . . .'

'Good God. A mother's vengeance.'

'I did not want Colin hurt . . .' said Aunt Marianne. 'But all our plans . . .'

I glanced involuntarily at Harry.

He said, 'I was in the park also, to answer your unspoken question. I was completely alone, and I think unseen. I was not with Jules. I was thinking. I can't imagine any reason why I should want to kill Colin – he had faults, God knows, but I was very fond of him – but I would have had the devil's own job proving I didn't do it.'

'What were you thinking about?' I asked.

'You.'

'And so, to avert sentimental irrelevances,' said the Countess, 'we come to today. You were perfectly right, Carmichael, that my announcement that Jules was my heir would have interesting consequences.'

'I did advise you, ma'am, to add the further announcement –'

'If you mention those deaf-and-dumb children again, addlepate, I shall throttle you.'

'All their cake was dough all over again,' I said.

'So Marianne put it back in the oven,' said the Countess, 'by putting Jules in the well.'

'Why me too?' I asked.

'Because you saw her, you ninnyhammer.'

'Oh yes. As simple as that. How very badly Aunt Marianne did want all that money.'

'The thing that surprises me,' said the Countess, 'is why she didn't kill me years ago. That would have made all this uncomfortable business unnecessary.'

'I would have prevented her, ma'am,' said Miss Carmichael.

'Would you, indeed? I think you would have helped her.'

'There were moments, ma'am, when I would have been *delighted* to do so!'

'What are we going to do?' I said.

'Well, what? What do you think, Harry? I don't know why I bother to ask you – you seem to have the sense of a snail.'

'I think we should do nothing,' said Harry. 'I suppose none of us will ever hear of Alex again. His life is ruined. I should think he'd bury himself in some big town in the south of England, or in Canada or Australia. If we testify to all we know, Aunt Lucinda

311

is convicted as an accessory before and after a murder, Cousin Marianne as that and as guilty of attempted murder. Is that helpful to us? To Colin?'

'I can't very well continue to entertain Marianne here,' said the Countess. 'That is to say, I can, but I am unwilling to.'

'Oh no,' said Harry. 'She surely belongs in a discreet, kindly institution. Dr McPhee is the man to consult.'

'Do you hear that, Marianne? Discreet and kindly. You will be happier there, I expect.'

Aunt Marianne did not seem to have heard.

'Mrs Ramsay is punished enough,' I said, 'even for having Colin killed.'

'Yes,' said the Countess. 'I do not envy Lucinda the rest of her days. Perhaps Alex will write to her from Tasmania.'

'Really, it is *all* Mrs Ramsay's fault,' said Miss Carmichael. 'The characters of those boys! So very determined! Quite warped, by her excessive pride in them!'

'Not quite all her fault,' said the Countess, looking at Aunt Marianne. 'I suppose I am to a very small extent to blame, for my scheme, about the excellence of which I have still not changed my mind. Perdita is partly to blame, for being loved so much.'

'I don't think she can help that,' said Harry.

'No, boy, I don't think she can.'

I went to see Jules, as soon as they told me I could.

He was still shaken, to the point that he actually wanted to stay in bed for the rest of the day. His head was bandaged so that he looked like a Rajah in a turban. He did not know what Aunt Marianne had hit him with. She had asked him into her garden – to help her off with the well-cover! And he had moved it!

He made too much of my keeping his head above water.

I was thankful that he was only a little damaged, and would soon be perfectly well. But I was more thankful that all my silly suspicions had been so utterly unfounded. He was decent, loyal and affectionate.

He was lovable.

We had been through an experience together which neither would ever forget. We had been companions in the Valley of the

Shadow of Death. I sat by his bed and we held hands, and looked at one another with silly, joyful smiles.

I felt a wave of love for him – the brilliantly talented boy, the champion tree-climber, the friend for life, the Scottish baronet ... who was sufficiently older than I.

They took me away, in case I tired him. I kissed his cheek before I left.

Harry was quite right. Alex had gone straight to the stables, had a horse saddled and bridled in a hurry, and ridden off. Nobody noticed which way he went.

After dinner I said to Miss Carmichael, 'You set a trap for Alex, and he walked into it. But what made you set it? Why did you think he'd shot Jamie?'

'I did not think so, dear, until that very moment! But I was watching him with his mother, you know, and I felt *very* strongly that the relationship was quite unhealthy! She is *not* an endearing personality, yet he seemed to cling to her! That gave me the idea that he was wrong in the head!'

'And that was all it was?' said the Countess. 'That was all that put it into your funny old head, that the boy had shot down his brother?'

'Of course I was not sure, ma'am! If Mr Alexander had said that he did not know where the lantern was, because he had not been there, then we should have been none the wiser!'

'But,' I said, 'all along you have been saying that you *knew* who killed Jamie. And then you said you knew who killed Colin. Were you quite wrong?'

'*Quite* wrong, dear. But of course, in spite of a certain natural disappointment, relieved to find myself so!'

'Whom did you pick, Miss Carmichael?' asked Harry, smiling. 'Me?'

'Oh *no*, Mr Harry. I did not think for a second that a gentleman of your *nobility* of character could kill!'

'Jules, then?'

'Good gracious, no! How could one suspect Sir Julian of violent crime, so prettily as he plays the pianoforte and so elegantly as he draws!'

'The process of elimination is eliminating everybody,' I said.

'What damned long words,' said the Countess. 'Who *have* you got left, fluff-brain?'

'But, of course, I was convinced that it was Perdita who had murdered Mr James!'

I goggled at her.

'It seemed to me supremely obvious! In planning your abduction, dear, Mr James, so I reasoned, naturally armed himself with Captain Colin's pistol! The pistol was not taken to the farmhouse – it was already there! Mr James turned his back for a moment, quite unwisely, and Perdita shot him! It was quite the correct thing to do! Any girl of spirit would have done the same! I applaud you for it, dear!'

'But I didn't do it.'

'I know that now, dear, but you must admit that it was a *very* convincing theory!'

'Good God,' said the Countess. 'You've almost convinced me that it did happen like that.'

'Then, of course, I supposed,' said Miss Carmichael, 'that Dougal McKechnie was lying not to save Captain Colin, but to save you, dear! Which was also quite proper, and did him credit! And Captain Colin likewise! They *both* invented the man who ran away in the dark, in order to protect you from embarrassment! So gentlemanly of them both!'

'Still convincing,' said the Countess.

'As a matter of fact, I tried to kill Jamie,' I said, 'with the hoop from my dress. But I just made a horrid mess ... Why should I murder Colin, Miss Carmichael?'

'Because he was compelling you into marriage, dear! So obvious again! He knew you had killed Mr James, and he threatened to expose you, unless you consented to become his bride!'

'Would I have murdered him rather than marry him?' I asked dubiously.

'Oh yes, dear! So upset you were, that he deceived you about his wife! You could *not* have been happy, or *thought* you could not, with the Captain! To be *shackled* to a man you despised – to a young lady of strong views like yourself, dear, that would be quite enough motive for murder! You could easily have slipped indoors from the terrace –'

'I did slip indoors,' I said. 'Come to think of it, I went indoors, to warn Alex.'

'That's ironic,' said Harry.

'You could have *sped* to the gun-room, taken dear Lord Kilmaha's shotgun, slipped out of the castle by a side door, *sped* through the trees –'

'But Dougal McKechnie saw me running across the park, towards Colin, after the shot.'

'We were all prepared to disbelieve *anything* Dougal said, dear, if by lying he could repay you for your kindness to that family! It was not until Lady Kilmaha tried to murder you and Sir Julian this morning, that it occurred to me I might have mis-judged you!'

Even the Countess was silenced.

Mrs Ramsay left early in the morning, without farewells. She was helped into a closed carriage by a footman and a senior house-maid, both in their Sunday best. They were to take her home to Edinburgh. After that, her life would be what it would be.

Dr McPhee came to see Aunt Marianne. Harry spoke to him before and after he saw her. I did not hear what they said to each other. Another doctor was to come, and an institution be found. Meanwhile she was to be kept to her room, with a man outside the door.

I glimpsed her. She seemed to be sleep-walking. I did not envy her dreams.

We had a message that the horse Alex had taken was found tied up at the Crianlarich railway station. No one had seen or recognized its rider, or had any idea what train he had taken.

Jules was well enough to get up in time for luncheon. He still wore his turban of bandages, but he was steady on his feet and quite cheerful. He joined us on the terrace in the sunshine – the Countess, Miss Carmichael, Harry and me.

'I was bored with being in bed, and bored with being in a dif-ferent room from you,' he said, taking my hand.

And then and there, in front of the others, he said, 'Dita, I adore you. I shall love you until I die.'

I knew it was true. And I adored him. He was adorable. I knew that I would love him until I died.

I burst into tears, and flung my arms round his neck. I forget his bandages, I forgot shame, I forgot everything. And then, over Jules's shoulder, I saw through my tears the twisted smile on Harry's face.

I took my arms from Jules's dear neck, and stepped back, and stared at him dumbly. Tears were still streaming down my cheeks.

'I wish,' said Harry, in an odd, strained voice, 'I wish you both . . .'

And Jules understood. And he stepped back, so that I faced Harry. And the smile left Harry's face, and he stared at me solemnly. And he opened his arms, and I went into them, and it was a good place to be.

I kissed the scar on the back of his hand.

'What a way to behave,' said the Countess.

'A very good way, ma'am,' said Miss Carmichael.

'Yes, muttonhead, that's what I mean.'